MARLOW INTRIGUES – BOOK 1

Illicit Love

JANE LARK

Sapphire Star Publishing
www.sapphirestarpublishing.com
First Sapphire Star Publishing trade paperback edition, May 2013

The characters and events in this book are fictitious. Names, characters, places, and plots are a product of the author's imagination. Any similarity to real persons, living or dead, is coincidental and not intended by the author.

ISBN-13: 978-1-938404-55-9

Cover Design by Carrie Butler

Cover Images by Subbotina Anna, Elena Itsenko, and Kiselev Andrey Valerevich

www.sapphirestarpublishing.com/janelark

Dedication

I am dedicating Illicit Love to my family and readers.

To my husband, who has become a widower, and my daughter, who has been left motherless by my addiction to writing over the last ten years—thank you for all your support and patience, guys. I really love you. Dreams do come true.

Then to my parents who have endured me throwing things their direction to proofread for a decade, for all the hours you have invested in me, thank you.

I also wish to remember my brother-in-law Steve Bown who passed away in December 2012, far too young. His vibrancy and sense of humor is sorely missed. For his family who will treasure their time with him.

Then lastly to my readers, I hope you enjoy Illicit Love, it's wonderful for me to know my characters now have life in these pages, and they wouldn't have this without the power of your imagination.

To discuss Illicit Love once you have read the story go to my blog http://janelark.wordpress.com

Acknowledgements

I wish to acknowledge and thank by name all my friends and work colleagues who have taken the time to read my work through the years and then given me feedback and encouragement—Julie Alldritt, Deborah Belcher, Paula Boshier, Lin Sharland, Kirsty Prescott, Annmarie Prosser, and Rachael Taylor.

I would also like to thank a very special group of people, my fellow Romance authors who are members of the United Kingdom's Romance Novelists Association (RNA), the Bath and Wiltshire Chapter. This group of wonderful people have given me encouragement, guidance, and the information which has helped me become a published author. Thank you for investing some of your precious time in me. Also thank you to the RNA for continuing to run the New Writers Scheme which allowed me access to this network of authors.

Finally, I would like to say thank you to Sapphire Star Publishing and my fellow authors here. You are a wonderful publisher and a great team to work with. Thank you all for your belief in me, and your support through the whole process. It's wonderful to work with such a fabulous team of people and authors.

Chapter One

Perfectly positioned to view one of the ton's fairest sons, Ellen's eyes were drawn from Lord Gainsborough's playing cards to the man seated across the table—Lord Edward Marlow, the second born son of the tenth Earl of Barrington. He was newly in town and therefore a novelty, an enigma. Every mistress and courtesan in the room had been watching him all evening and she was no exception.

Lord Edward's long, manicured fingers moved, poising above his cards. Ellen openly stared, the low light in the room and its stale hazy air, thick with tobacco smoke, hiding her scrutiny from the watching crowd.

His hair was dark brown and gentle curls tumbled from his crown, licking his forehead and the high collar of his black, tailed evening coat, Brutus style. In the candlelight, thrown by the chandelier above, his hair glistened with a variety of rich, roasted coffee bean shades.

His head lifted and she indulged her eyes with his severe yet perfect, profile. He exuded authority. The man was sleek strength and sophistication. The muscle of his jaw tight, his lips rose as if to smile, but hesitated as though some thought stopped him, and she saw doubt or indecision pass across his expression. Then his eyelids lifted and his dark, intense gaze clashed with hers, a deep blue, more like slate-gray.

Embarrassed and a little flustered, Ellen's appraisal fell to his hands.

His fingers teased out a card and threw it to the table while she felt his gaze burn into her.

Desire stirring, she pictured the pleasure those fingers could give a woman and the air in the room was suddenly hot and thick, despite the cool winter night outside.

Ellen lifted her open fan and fluttered it gently to cool her skin as her gaze drifted back to his face. He was watching her still. One dark eyebrow rose and his broad lips smiled. Her gaze hovering on his, she mirrored his smile, her heart pounding as though she was already coupling with him. She imagined his mouth on hers and a hot blush touched her skin. The sweeps of her fan increasing, her imagination drifted on towards indecency—impossibility—picturing tangled limbs and warm flesh.

Light caught the jet-black pools in his eyes, as though he saw the pictures she was forming in her thoughts and his captivating smile twisted with implied agreement. It turned his features from handsome to utterly devastating.

A hot flush spread like a caress down her throat to her breasts and lower, racing across her skin.

"I shall raise you a hundred, Marlow. Will you match me?" Lord Gainsborough's brusque challenge sliced through the silent communication she shared with Lord Edward.

His gaze tore away, his blank expression cutting her, apparently dismissing their flirtation. Instead it focused on Lord Gainsborough.

Ellen stood behind Lord Gainsborough and slightly to his side, in her protector's shadow, oppressed. Oppression was Lord Gainsborough's pleasure and Lord Gainsborough's pleasure was her life. Her gaze fell to the seam at the center of the back of his black evening coat. The pressure of his bloated body strained it. Excess was another of his passions.

Revulsion stirred. She despised the man—her protector. Yet preference was irrelevant. She was tied to him, trapped by him. He had blackmailed her into obedience five years ago and now here she stood, her soul and conscience dead while her body lived on, fulfilling his dissolute desires. She was empty, a vessel, deaf to the voice of morality and blind to shame.

Laughter hovered behind her closed lips, ringing in her thoughts, a sound of silent madness.

Lord Gainsborough liked flaunting his pretty vessel—his precious trophy. Sometimes he let others touch, taunting them with what they couldn't have. Wickedly she wondered how he would react if she let someone of Lord Edward's ilk touch her. He'd be furious.

Hiding her self-deprecating smile behind her fan, Ellen glanced over its top at the gorgeous man across the table. Was it very wrong for her sinful body to want a man like that? How would it feel? How would it feel to be free from her so-called protector for an hour or two and play his games with a man of her choice? Choice was a holy grail; a cup fallen woman longed to drink from. And she'd love defying Lord Gainsborough.

As though pulled by an invisible cord winding between them, Lord Edward's gaze lifted to her while he contemplated Lord Gainsborough's call. His eyes widened, darkening, perhaps reading hers, and what appeared to be amusement twitched his lips before he looked back at his cards.

Ellen snapped shut her fan and lowered it to her waist, turning her attention to the game. Only Lord Gainsborough and the younger Lord Edward were left in play. The others sitting about the table simply watched, and behind them stood a crowd three deep. The dense ring of silent observers, were men in the formal black evening dress Brummell had made popular, with the occasional female, mistress or courtesan, draped from their arms. They were men enjoying the hedonistic lifestyle of the sleazy gentlemen's club, or gaming-hell as it was more commonly known. Gaming-hells, like this one, provided the thrill these men craved from high stakes games, with women and wine to ease the rush.

For Gainsborough, she knew this place fuelled something else—his desire to be envied. He brought her here to show her off. Lord Gainsborough wore her as women wore their jewels. She was an adornment—his precious, beautiful, trophy. He'd not even dislike Lord Edward's attention—he'd relish it. Yet if Gainsborough knew she was enticing Lord Edward, she would pay a price.

"I will meet your hundred, Gainsborough, and raise you ten."

"Are you sure you have it, boy?" Lord Gainsborough's tone rang with condescension, ridiculing Lord Edward. It fell flat. Lord Edward was younger, but he was in his prime. She would place him at his peak, mid-twenties at the least.

Receiving no answer, shifting in his seat, her protector pulled at the cuffs of his evening coat, while the eyes of their crowd turned to Lord Edward.

"Now your brother is back, Marlow, surely you have lost your portion. Should I request security for your funds?"

That barb seemed to hit a mark. Suddenly leaning back in his chair, Lord Edward's eyes narrowed, his nonchalant air shattering as anger flashed in their blue-black depths. For all his beauty and youth he lacked nothing in masculine strength. Ellen sensed ruthlessness in the look he threw back at Lord Gainsborough.

"Play the game, Gainsborough. I've no desire for conversation."

"But you are able to honour your debts? I need not wait for you to tug your brother's purse strings for payment?"

Ellen watched Lord Edward's grip tighten on his cards while his other hand reached for his glass. A slowly indrawn breath and he appeared back in control.

Everyone had heard the talk. He'd been running his brother's estates since the age of eighteen, while his brother, the eleventh Earl, wasted both time and money abroad. Now his brother was back. Potentially to bleed dry the estates which were prospering under Lord Edward's careful hand.

Lord Edward had arrived in London a week ago, angry and bitter, from the reports of the gossipmongers in the ton, and his behaviour this evening certainly concurred with the tale. His mask of serenity had slipped, revealing the man beneath the façade. He appeared out of sorts with the world, playing hard and deep, drinking heavily — and this from a man known for his dislike of vice.

His gaze lifted, meeting hers, anger and mockery in the look, as once more he caught her contemplating him. The determination in his eyes seemed to challenge her to speak. To what, agree with Gainsborough? Does he think I would condemn him? I am in no place to cast judgement.

Again his gaze ripped away from hers. "I have enough of my own blunt, Gainsborough," he said, looking at his cards. "I have no need to beg from my brother."

The nuance in his voice made her feel as though the words were said for her.

"I'm glad to hear it. Then I will raise you another two hundred, guineas."

Lord Edward's narrowed eyes lifted suddenly to look at her protector.

He didn't have it, she was certain of that. He could not afford the stakes but would stupidly bury himself in debt because of some bizarre falling out with his brother, or stubborn male pride.

Unwilling to play audience to his downfall, she lowered her gaze and saw Lord Gainsborough's cards had changed. The ten had become an ace, and the eight exchanged with a king. Disgust twisted Ellen's stomach. Gainsborough would win by deceit and Lord Edward would be neatly leashed with the debt a whip in Lord Gainsborough's hand. Her protector had no decent, honest bones in his body. He manipulated people. That was Gainsborough's art; he used, broke and discarded people like puppets. She prayed daily he would cut her strings and cast her off — set her free — even though she had nowhere else to go. But he never seemed to tire of the power she gave him. Yet she need not watch him secure another victim in his sadistic sway.

Her heart pumping hard, looking up, she found Lord Edward's eyes on her again. An odd feeling assailed her, a sense that he saw into her thoughts. His assessment was no longer admiring, nor mocking or angry, instead his gaze intently studied hers, searching for something.

She darted her gaze down and up, trying to direct his attention to Lord Gainsborough's cards with her eyes while simultaneously flicking open her fan and then fluttering it beneath her chin to distract attention from their silent communication.

Lord Edward's brow furrowed. She could see he didn't understand.

Widening her eyes, she once again looked to Lord Gainsborough's cards, then snapped her fan shut and tapped the tip against the long sleeve of her satin glove.

Smiling, or rather smirking, Lord Edward looked down at his cards.

Ellen glanced about their audience but she saw no one watching her.

"I will meet your stake, Gainsborough, and double it to see your hand. Show me your cards." With that Lord Edward tossed two jacks and two eights onto the green felt and then Lord Gainsborough laid a royal flush down in opposition to the pairs. Lord Gainsborough's hand won. An exclamation rang from the gathered crowd, voicing congratulations for Gainsborough. Then comments of consolation followed, as Lord Edward's shoulder was slapped.

Ellen held her breath, her gaze fixed on the table, her heart pounding. She was too afraid to look up in case Lord Gainsborough identified her collusion when, if, the accusation came.

It did. "You are a damned cheat, Gainsborough! Take off your coat!" From Lord Edward's voice she could tell he was standing, facing them across the table.

Ellen stepped back as Lord Gainsborough rose, his bulk lifting from the chair. He was old enough to be her father and looked older still after years of debauchery, broken veins marring his fallen cheeks and bulbous nose. But despite his age and weight he could still move quickly when he wished. Tonight he did not wish, he stood slowly, making no effort to do Lord Edward's bidding.

"Don't be ridiculous, boy. I am a Viscount. I have no need to cheat." Gainsborough's voice welled with ridicule. He knew this game. Act the aggrieved. Turn the accusation back upon the accuser. Be above reproach, and you are. She had watched him play it numerous times.

"Yet still, I ask you to remove your coat, my Lord, and prove your innocence, if it is so." Lord Edward's eyes searched their audience then and settled on a man similar to him in age. "Find Madam, have her bring her brutes and we will sort this out." The other man instantly disappeared obeying the request.

"You are talking nonsense, Marlow. I refuse to be challenged like some damned guttersnipe! Come, my dear, we're leaving." Painfully gripping Ellen's arm Lord Gainsborough turned her away. "My man of business will contact you, Marlow. Then you will settle your debt." As Gainsborough thrust the words sideward over his shoulder, his grip steered her into the parting crowd.

"You played me false, Gainsborough! You'll wait until it's proven!" Lord Edward's voice resonated throughout the room, a barked order carrying no deference for Lord Gainsborough's seniority in age and status.

Irate voices rose, supporting Lord Edward, "Yes, Gainsborough!"

"Take off your coat!"

"Prove it!"

The crowd grew, closing the avenue before Ellen. Lord Gainsborough's hand fell from her arm as he turned back. She knew he was starting to realize he was not going to win so easily this time.

A swell of satisfaction stirred in Ellen's chest. Revenge would be another sin to add to her list of many, but it tasted sweet, even if the victory was minor and he'd no knowledge of her part.

The crowd about them parted again for the gaming-hell's tall, sylph like, aged and highly painted female proprietor to forge a path towards them. Ellen was aware of two of Madam's burly doormen moving behind her.

"Lord Gainsborough? What is this accusation? My house is honest. Please, if you have done nothing wrong, you shall not mind removing your coat."

Gainsborough took a breath and then snorted, scoffing at the crowd, apparently casting them all fools. But he was cornered, he could do nothing but concede.

Slipping the buttons of his double-breasted evening coat free, he looked at Ellen, growling, "Woman, help me!" before turning his back to her and holding out one arm. "Tug the sleeve loose." He threw her a warning look over his shoulder as he spoke. She understood it exactly. He expected her to hide the cards.

Afraid. Her heart thumping. Gripping his cuff in fingers and thumb, Ellen felt the cards hidden within his sleeve, but she refused to help him. She loosened his cuff from his hand then let go and lifted hers to ease the coat from his shoulders. The cards fell to the floor and she gasped to make it appear accidental, but the sound was lost amidst the outburst of the watching crowd. They shouted in shock and disgust, a burst of masculine irritation.

This would cost her. Their battlefield had revised and her involvement was too visible, but she was not letting Lord Gainsborough crush her first assault.

Gainsborough's anger and accusation struck her as he looked back, and she stepped back, afraid he would strike her physically, her heart pulsing as panic turned her stomach to ice.

"As I told you," The statement of vindication turned Gainsborough's attention to Lord Edward, "the winnings are mine, Gainsborough. The question is what should I request in compensation for not handing you to a magistrate?" Lord Edward's steel like gaze passed from Lord Gainsborough to her and a wicked smile played on his lips. Her heart missed a beat. What was he doing?

His gaze passed back to Lord Gainsborough. "Give me the woman in consolation."

"For an hour, no more," Lord Gainsborough barked.

Ellen blushed. They were bartering over her as they would over horseflesh. Another piece of her died. Men had taken her self-respect as well as her body. They were arguing over the vessel, not her, not the living, breathing, feeling woman within it.

"Two hours and you may keep your stake beyond what is on the table."

Ellen opened her mouth to protest and closed it again. What good would it do? They did not care for her. Her eyelids falling over the moisture in her eyes, she drew a breath. She'd helped Lord Edward—he was hurting her. The cost of her involvement had just tripled.

"You agree?" Lord Edward prompted.

"I agree," Lord Gainsborough snarled.

Because there was no other choice, Ellen thought, not willingly. Her manipulator had met his match, and she'd given Lord Edward the means to make this manoeuvre. Even her satisfaction in seeing Lord Gainsborough beaten at his own game was hollow. It was earned at her expense. She was a fool.

"Madam, we need a room," Lord Edward ordered, soiling the images Ellen had appreciated earlier. This is hell not heaven. I want choice not coercion.

The air escaped her lungs and Ellen opened her eyes.

He stood barely a foot away, facing her, watching her intently.

He was taller than he'd seemed when seated, a good seven to ten inches taller than her. He towered over her. His appearance was no longer impressive but imposing.

She'd thought him authoritative before, now she knew him to be overwhelmingly commanding. Fear grasped her more tightly.

"Please follow me, Lord Edward." Madam Marietta beckoned with her fingers.

Without speaking, he lifted his arm, a look of steel daring her to refuse to accept it. Compelled by his will alone, Ellen laid her fingers on his coat sleeve. The gentle weight of his other hand covered them, as though fearing she would run he urged her to stay. The impression it conjured up in her head was a knight in shining armour, like the heroes in the fairy tales she'd read as a girl.

But this was no act of chivalry.

He was no saviour of a lady's virtue.

He had just bartered with another man for the use of her body! He was no rescuer come to release her from Gainsborough's evil grip. I should not long to lean on his strength.

Yet, the strength beneath her fingers and the assurance implied in the hand resting on her own sent warmth running into her blood. It suggested security—constancy. Like the scent of fresh bread stirring hunger, his touch set alive silly speculating notions in her head—dreams—desires for a happy-ever-after that could never be.

Silent, Ellen found herself guided in Madam's wake. She knew instinctively all eyes were on her back and she felt Lord Gainsborough's burn between her shoulder-blades, imagining them narrow with anger and calculating revenge. Her courage failing her, Lord Edward's aura of undaunted power kept her walking as they crossed two rooms in which Madam's customers played at tables. The attention they drew apparently did not disturb him. But when they reached the hall as if sensing her fear, his arm fell away from beneath her hand and instead his fingers gently but firmly gripped hers.

"I would rather not go upstairs, Madam. Have you a private parlour we could use down here?" While he spoke his fingers squeezed Ellen's, as though offering the comfort and reassurance her spirit craved.

The temperate strength gripping her hand unsettled her, setting speculation whispering through her head again. He is not my rescuer.

Marietta hesitated, looked aloft, and then clearly thinking quickly held forth a hand encouraging them to follow her about the foot of the stairs and along a narrow hallway. There she opened a door. "This is my own sitting-room. No one will disturb you here, my Lord. Is there anything I may bring you?"

When they entered the room Lord Edward let Ellen's fingers go and she took the opportunity to move away.

Crossing the room, she trailed her satin clad fingers over the chair-backs as she passed them until she reached the far side.

"A decanter of port and two glasses, Madam, nothing else…" Ellen looked back, answering his pause and met his gaze. "Unless you are hungry or have another preference?"

She shook her head before finding her voice. "No, my Lord, thank you, I am in need of nothing." *What a lie, I am in need of everything.*

She turned away and ran her fingers over a polished mahogany writing desk which stood against the wall. The room was different to the public areas. It was decorated in tasteful greens not the gaudy gold and reds which adorned the gambling rooms, and she also knew dressed the bedchambers above. There were two winged armchairs and a chaise-lounge, all upholstered in moss green velvet which matched the closed curtains. In the grate at the center of the hearth, a low fire burned and on the floor before it a Persian rug covered the boards. The walls were dressed with painted patterns of green ivy.

The door clicked shut. Ellen turned back swiftly and her fingers gripped the rim of the desk behind her as her gaze reached across the room to meet Lord Edward's again. Madam had gone and he stood watching Ellen, assessing her as he'd done in the card room while she'd watched him. Then he held out his hand reminding her of a man approaching a nervous colt. Did he not realize she was used to being payment in kind? He need hardly fear she wouldn't give him what he wanted, she was no debutante. *I am a thrice damned courtesan.* There was no need for courtship or kind words. She knew what he wanted. He didn't even have to ask.

His mouth suddenly lifted to a smile, tilting at one side. "Why did you tell me?"

It took her a moment to register that he spoke of Gainsborough's little trick. Why did she? Because she'd seen something in his eyes she'd warmed to, or just because he was handsome and she was drawn by his looks, or possibly only because it gave her opportunity to rebel? It could be any of those things, but she knew herself too well. The person she'd once been, the stranger surviving deep inside her heart of ice, couldn't see another human-being brought as low as her. He hadn't had the money. She couldn't see him trapped, even if he was a man.

Her misguided generosity had led her here. She was trapped. Caught in the hands of another man who'd sate his lust for her body — the woman within it was irrelevant really. He wanted to use it but he'd use her too.

Her eyes caught her reflection in the mirror hanging above the fireplace at his back. Her beauty was incomparable. She was not blind to it. She'd been told it dozens of times. It lay in the starkly pale blue of her eyes, the dark sweep of ebony hair across porcelain colored skin. God had made her perfect in face and figure. The look of a Goddess, her husband, Paul, had once said. Then compliments had pleased her. Now beauty cursed her.

A sound escaped his throat, drawing her attention back to him. She didn't know if it was a prompt, but she responded anyway. "It was obvious you could not afford the stake, my Lord. I am surprised you took the bet."

He dismissed her words with a wave of his hand as a tap sounded on the door. "Enter!" His voice carried considerable confidence for a man she'd classified no greater in age than his mid-twenties, but then he'd probably lived his whole life with the proverbial silver spoon in his mouth.

"Put it there." He pointed to a small table as a footman brought in a tray baring the decanter and glasses he'd ordered.

"Thank you."

The words of gratitude surprised her as the servant left and closed the door.

Lord Edward's gaze crossed to her again. "You will take a drink?"

She nodded. She'd need the fortitude strong liquor brought to see this through.

Turning away, he answered her earlier statement, "I'm not in such dire straits as rumour would have it. I care not if I win or lose, as proven by my letting your friend keep his money." His shoulders lifted in a shrug as he spoke, before pouring the port from the decanter.

When he faced her again he had a glass in each hand and walking towards her, he held one out.

She took it, looking at the ruby colored liquid. "Then why play, my Lord?"

"Because I find myself at a loose end. I need diversion. Please, sit, Miss… What is your name?"

He asked as though he'd only just realized he didn't know it.

"Ellen, Lord Edward." Her voice sounded cold even to her, and formal.

"Sit then, Ellen. Let us get to know one another."

Perching on the edge of an armchair she felt like a mouse before a cat, waiting for the moment he would pounce.

He sat in the chair facing her and leaned back, his legs splaying slightly, drawing her attention to the physical strength in his muscular thighs.

The instinctive awareness which had ailed her earlier returned. She was attracted to him, despite all else. The room suddenly felt hot, and blushing, she looked up and met his gaze. The light in his eyes implied he saw her susceptibility, but he did not speak of it. "Your age, Ellen?"

"Women do not speak of their age, my Lord," she snapped, angered by his ability to move her and apparently remain unmoved.

He smiled, a heart stopping expression. It set hers skipping against her ribs.

Am I really so shallow I will simply succumb to his looks?

"I am four and twenty, if it makes you feel better to know my own," he answered, his tone relaxed. "There, it's not so hard to say one's age."

"I cannot see why you care to know it." She could remove a year, two, even claim to be younger than him, she could pass for three and twenty, but she was unwilling to lie. Her life had been so full of sin, adding another lie, no matter how small, felt suddenly intolerable.

He said nothing, waiting on her reply.

"I am eight and twenty, my Lord. Older than yourself, and now you have embarrassed me."

"It matters not. We are adults, Ellen, age makes little difference."

"Then why ask?" she bit back annoyed by his languorous tone. He disturbed her, she felt hot and uncomfortable, afraid — and not afraid. Her heart thumped; a hammer ringing on an anvil in her ears.

"Because I cannot understand what you are doing with a man like Gainsborough. He must be twice your age. You cannot persuade me it is his looks or character which draw you."

Spurred, anger flashed through her. Who was he to judge her? He'd bartered over her body. How could he accuse her of poor choice? Surely it was obvious why she was with Lord Gainsborough, she had no choice. But she would not admit it. Not to him or anyone. She would not face that humiliation. Instead she played the part of a woman who chose to be a man's chattel.

"Because he was the highest bidder, my Lord, what other reason would you think?" Deliberately she edged her voice with a sultry cutting pitch. The role of harlot was now instinctive. She would act it for Gainsborough too once this was done, to placate his damaged pride.

"Are you telling me I cannot afford you, Ellen?" He was amused by her; she heard it in his voice. She imagined him laughing at her, inwardly.

Lord, the self-confidence of the man was infuriating.

"Your words, my Lord." She took a sip of port from the glass in her hand.

"Yes, my words." he repeated, his pitch sobering. He drained his glass, set it aside and stood. "But I do not need to pay, do I, Ellen?"

A dart of longing pain stretched through her core, confirming his words. No man had stirred this reaction in her since Paul. He was right. Her body craved his.

"Come." He stepped towards her and leaned down. Mesmerised by him, she watched his movement, while uncertainty and fear warred with attraction.

His long, beautiful fingers wrapped about the bowl of her glass and lifted it from her hand.

Unwilling to look up, unable to meet his gaze, she heard the click of the base as it was placed on the table.

His fingers then closed about hers and encouraged her to her feet.

She was silent as he lifted the string of her fan from her wrist, stripped off her gloves and put them down beside her half empty glass of port. Then he moved closer and one hand pressed against the small of her back while the other curved beneath her chin, lifting her face.

"Ellen?"

She met his gaze, hearing a question and a statement in that single utterance of her name and somehow knew he wouldn't force her, as others had done before. He was asking permission and offering admiration, she saw it in his eyes.

"You have such beauty. I swear I've never seen the like." His gaze holding hers, his curled fingers trailed upwards, the tender, gentle touch following the line of her jaw and sweeping up across her brow, before brushing down her nose. Then his thumb rested on her mouth, running over her lips.

"Do you wish for this too?" he whispered.

There was no need to ask what he meant, her body sang with longing for his, her skin was already hot and sensitised by the flush of desire. The pressure of his palm at her back pulled her lower body hip to hip with his, making the level of his arousal blatant as the outline of his erection pressed against her stomach.

He'd said he wanted diversion.

She needed him for release. If only for an hour or two, she could escape.

Her lips brushing the pad of his thumb, she formed the single word of agreement, surrender, her arms lifting to his shoulders. "Yes." No, for the first time since Paul, this was not surrender, this was choice.

The rhythm of her heartbeat lurching to an even greater pace, her gaze locked with his, captured by the invisible link she felt woven taut between them.

His hands fell, resting on her hips in a gentle brace, just for a moment.

His touch was like an expression of awe, not domination. His hands skimmed upwards across her ribs and then reaching the soft flesh of her breasts, his palms and fingers clenched her through the thin material of her gown. Time stopped, suddenly suspending as his gaze dropped to her lips and he lowered his head.

When their lips met, the rush of desire in her veins was overwhelming. Instinctively her fingers slipped upwards delving into his soft hair, clasping it. His tongue slid into her mouth and he tasted delicious. He drugged her senses, taking her away somewhere else, somewhere outside of her sordid, soiled self. His crooked thumb dipped into the low neck of her gown and brushed across her breast, stroking her casually as his mouth ravished hers. A pleasant spasm ran from her breast, spiralling down through her body to her stomach and into her womb. Her body already ached for fulfilment.

Feeling brazen to the core and every bit the wanton whore life had made her, her tongue passed across his lips, into the warmth of his mouth and her fingers fell to his shoulders, splaying and running downwards. They slid over the taut muscle beneath his evening clothes, revelling in his athletic physique and descended to his breeches.

An erotic, pain filled sound resonated from his chest and reached her mouth as heat. But abruptly his fingers left her breast, grasped her hand and removed it as he broke their kiss. Yet his eyes were dark with longing as they met hers. She knew her look mirrored his.

The timbre of his voice thick with desire, he said, "I would like that, Ellen, but it is not what I want tonight, not yet. Let me lead. I want to see you gain your pleasure first."

He wished to give her pleasure? The ice about her heart cracked and warmth seeped into her blood. This was more than lust, much more, it was longing beyond a physical need. She'd given herself to men for years, she knew what pleased them. None of them had cared for what pleased her. Pleasure during sex—was it still possible? If it had been like that with Paul, she'd forgotten.

His head bowed and his lips brushed her neck while his gentle fingers slipped the straps of her gown from her shoulders then followed the neckline of her dress, slackening the material and drawing it down. With his head lowered his hair caressed her skin as his fingers lifted her breasts free, then one taut peak was absorbed in the warmth of his mouth. It sent a tremor across her skin and pain and pleasure reaching inside her.

He did not just want her body, he wanted her soul. It had only ever been Paul's. But with Edward Marlow she wasn't sure she could keep it safe. When Gainsborough touched her — when she touched him — she detached her mind. He took her body, but only her body. This man would claim everything.

He lifted away from her again and began plucking pins from her hair, watching the dark curls fall to her naked shoulders and over her breasts.

"If someone comes in?" Ellen heard her breathless words.

"No one will." His voice was deep. He sounded as lost in lust as her. His hands rested on her shoulders and turned her to reach the back fastenings of her dress. The small ivory buttons slipped free one by one, and he kissed her exposed skin.

"You're so beautiful." The whisper brushed her neck as her dress fell in to a pool at her feet. Then his fingers swept her hair across her shoulders before tugging at the lacing of her light corset.

When her corset fell away too, he began stripping off her chemise, lifting it over her head and baring her breasts before throwing it aside. Then his hands reached about her and gripped them, drawing her back against him as he kissed her neck.

"You are nature's finest art."

Her head tilted back savouring his caresses and his hand slid down over her stomach and then slipped under her cotton underwear. No one had ever caressed her with such tenderness. She ached for him — he made her feel — every nerve in her body was humming for his touch — it was a rising floodtide inside her. It was torment, unbearable. It stole her awareness of everything but him. She wanted to cry out, to protest and scream. She did not. He did not stop. Oh, she was afraid of it, of this unfamiliar feeling.

There was an explosion of pleasure. It rushed through her blood, a flood, racing, ripping her apart, an unearthed power she hadn't known existed tearing into her limbs and leaving them weak. She felt him take her weight as she nearly fell and her fingers gripped his forearms. His lips brushed the skin behind her ear and he did not cease.

"Not again, please." Her words were breathless. She was afraid of the torrent that might flow now the dam was breached, afraid of losing control. He was still a stranger. It was too hard to trust.

His answer was to turn her and kiss her. She willingly returned it, her hands gripping fists full of his hair, as the tide of his passion swept her away again and he leaned her back a little so the chair's seat pressed against her calves until she fell back. She knew it was by design when he knelt before her and smiled and then his gaze dropped and he began loosening the ribbon securing her drawers. He slid them off leaving her naked — exposed — while he was still fully clothed.

His warm breath brushed her breast. His eyes were glazed and his pupils wide dark onyx pools as his gaze swept over her body.

Awareness of the room, of him, refilled her. "This is not fair." She hesitated, unfamiliar with desire. "I want to touch you."

Amusement and compliance shining in his eyes, he released the knot of his cravat while she pushed his coat from his shoulders.

Once he was stripped of neckcloth, coat and waistcoat, she tugged his shirt from his waistband and lifted it off over his head before throwing it aside. Then she reached for the buttons of his breeches but his hands stopped her.

"Not yet."

Why? What else could come?

Lean muscular contours rippled across his torso, shadowed by a dusting of dark hair across his chest which narrowed to a line delving into his waistband. Instinctively she licked her lips, only to be disturbed from her admiration by a sound of humor in the back of his throat.

"Careful, you'll make me think you've not known pleasure like this." His voice was low and husky, laden with lust and unexpected humor.

His hands gripped her hips and drew them forward, tumbling her backwards, and his head bent to kiss her stomach. Her muscle tightened, caught by surprise, but she was equally overwhelmed by a feeling of tenderness—care. It pierced her disordered thoughts. It was in his touch. She knew if she asked him to stop, even now, he would.

Moisture rushed into her eyes. This man is kind and gentle. Longing swelled inside her, body and soul. Desire and hope.

But he is not my rescuer. She had to push the thought away and shield herself behind denial. Her heart could not be involved in this. It was a physical hunger. He knows the art of sex better than other men I've known, that is all.

His fingers slid down her thighs and up again. "Relax, Ellen," he whispered, looking up and smiling.

She closed her eyes, took a breath and tried to, but she felt so nervous and uncertain. When his lips touched her, her fingernails dug into his flesh.

She'd thought herself incapable of embarrassment after a lifetime of humiliation, yet this intimate caress made her blush. No one else, not even Paul, had kissed her there.

She clung to him, hanging on as he urged her back into the pool of sensual delight. He knew more than Paul had done, Paul had made her happy, but never like this.

This time when the flood swelled, smashing aside her sanity, Edward did not let her escape but pushed her over another wave. It was then he freed the buttons of his breeches and filled her.

An exclamation of satisfaction left her lips.

His slate-blue-eyes looked into hers and his closed lips smiled as he pressed into her again. He smiled more and she gripped the arms of the chair.

Well, she had wanted escape. He was certainly giving her that.

The sweet sensations transported her beyond the room, body and soul, and she clung to him, watching him through a haze of lust.

He was so beautiful, hard, masculine, and gentle.

She loved this man, she had known him only moments but still she knew she loved him. He'd possessed her body and her heart.

He released her hips and held her hands, weaving their fingers together.

How could this? How could anyone stand such..? Light exploded within her.

The man was a God, an athlete, his strength, his stamina, his gallantry all spoke of it. There was no doubt.

"You are…" She stopped, hardly knowing what she said, and then her fingernails digging into his flesh she fell over the edge of reality into an abyss of sensation far below.

A virile cry escaped his throat, erupting from deep in his chest and he hastily withdrew.

When she felt the warmth on her stomach, she was plummeted back to reality and felt cheated, insulted. She was still a whore whom he would not want to bear his child. He was no hero, just another man. For a moment she hated him, even though he'd only really shown forethought and kindness. He'd reduced the possibility of a child. What good would a bastard child bring? No good, except a memory of this one night of release and him.

Ellen felt cold, thrown from a warm hearth in to snow, soiled again, naïve and foolish. She'd given herself completely, crying out. Anyone in the hall outside might have heard her. She hadn't just let him use her, she'd let him pluck and strum her sensual strings. He had played her like an instrument for his amusement. She'd spent years under the influence of men and still she had not learnt this lesson. Men took. He simply had a greater skill and different tastes.

Yet the delicious feelings he'd stirred up inside her still ran through her blood, overwhelming her tangled senses. Without looking at him, she accepted the handkerchief he pulled from his coat and held towards her. Then she wiped her stomach, expecting him to reach for his clothes and make himself ready to leave. Instead he did something which surprised her. He handed her, her glass.

"Drink, it will steady your nerves."

She sipped the ruby liquid and as its warmth slid down her throat, she dared herself, lifted her gaze and looked at him.

His fingers slotted the buttons of his breeches into place and then he bent over and picked up her undergarments. Seeing her watching, he smiled. There was no hint in it that he intended to simply walk away, no rake's art, nor aversion. He looked embarrassed too. She could see his pulse flickering at the base of his throat.

Drinking down the remainder of the port in one swallow, she waited. She wanted a word from him, an acknowledgement, something. Something to confirm his life had been changed by this, by their private interlude. She wanted it to not be her imagination.

But what could change?

Nothing.

He did not have the money to free her from Gainsborough.

She could not escape.

Just because he was beautiful and gentle and she'd engaged her heart in this, it did not mean he returned her feelings. The man was in his physical prime, he could have any woman he wanted. *It doesn't make him my hero.*

She had to stop this ridiculous hope from rising to lessen the pain when he walked away.

Her stubborn heart clenched in her chest. He'd been kind. He was being kind now.

How pathetic she'd become, craving so much for kindness she would love a man after little more than an hour, simply because he'd thrown her crumbs of it.

She accepted her undergarments from his hand and rose, pulling them on while he donned his shirt and tucked it in.

"My corset?" She couldn't tie it alone with the lacing at her back. "Would you send for Madam?"

"I'll lace it." He smiled, a masculine blush darkening the skin across the bones of his cheeks and took the garment from her hand. She turned.

Her fingers pressing it to her ribs, his threaded the laces at her back.

The gentle tug as he worked each lace, the pressure of her corset as he pulled it tight, the brush of his fingers as he tied it off—sent warmth racing through the heightened senses of her skin.

Daft, foolish woman to make so much of this. His skill with the lacing of a corset was testament to the level of his past experience.

He bent and picked up her dress. "Lift your arms, Ellen." And so, she was dressed.

While his fingers worked the tiny buttons at her back into place, her senses reeled and her head told her heart over and over again, this was no more than sex.

When he returned to the task of his own attire he faced the mirror to retie his neckcloth.

Ellen blushed, remembering those fingers, now adeptly crafting a fashionable knot, playing master to her body's whim moments before.

He smiled at her in the mirror.

She caught sight of her disordered hair and her heart kicked in fear.

Panic locking the air in her lungs, she knelt and began picking up her scattered hairpins. She couldn't leave the room looking like this.

In a moment he was on one knee beside her, helping her. He must have sensed her concern for he caught one of her hands and held it still. "There's no need to worry, Ellen."

For you perhaps, but not for me, for me there is every need. She pulled her hand free and continued the task, but tried to make light of her fear. "Not if you can dress a woman's hair."

"I can make a fair go of it." His voice was jovial in response.

All pins recovered they rose, her eyes meeting his. She took a breath. "Then do your best, my Lord, please."

His hand cupped hers and looking down he tipped the pins she held into his other palm. She shivered, remembering his touch; the things he'd done. In answer his eyes lifted, and she saw an unspoken question visible, pondering her skittish start.

"Edward, at least, Ellen," he admonished while one hand pressed her shoulder, turning her to the mirror. She looked at his reflection as he took a single lock of ebony hair in his fingers. Then, their sixth sense speaking, his gaze met hers in the glass. He smiled before looking away and concentrating on the task.

His touch was soothing, light and tender. Her body bathed in it, like rain on dry ground, her heart soaking it up.

When the job was finished their gazes collided in the mirror once more, desire burning clearly, like fire, in his. But the echo of it was in hers as she looked at her reflection too. "When can we meet, Ellen?" The question was whispered.

She shook her head in denial then tore her gaze from his, turning to retrieve her discarded fan and gloves. There could be no repetition. Gainsborough would not allow it.

Lord Edward will not help me. He cannot.

His grip caught her elbow and turned her back. "Do not deny me."

Stiffening her spine, Ellen lifted her chin. *I have to.*

As though he sensed the change in her, his hand slipped away before she spoke.

"My Lord, there can be nothing more, I thought that was clear."

Such cold, unemotional words. She set her face and eyes to match them, locking him out of her heart.

Did she imagine the sudden look of pain in his eyes? This was just sex for him, surely. He felt nothing. He would walk away unchanged. *My heart is wounded. Not his.* She couldn't escape Gainsborough. Dreams were not reality. Succumbing to Edward tonight had been enough risk. She did not dare repeat it. But she did not want him to know fear held her back. Nor did she wish him to pity her. "Your agreement was with Lord Gainsborough. I am his, not yours, my Lord, Edward."

The look in his eyes hardening, it was not pity she saw but disgust.

"I must go."

He moved, forming a wall between her and the door.

She met his gaze and waited, without answering the accusations lying there. This was who she was. He'd known that. He could not change it, and he could hardly judge her.

His lips a tight line, he bowed his head and stepped aside. But before she had time to reach for the door-handle his fingers caught hers.

"Tell me your full name? At least tell me that." His deep pitch was so full of emotion the ice she'd begun re-laying about her heart cracked, flooding her body with warmth. Warmth she longed to hold on to.

"Ellen Harding." Her married name, but even that she did not normally reveal.

Withdrawing her fingers from his, she made a final plea. "Please, do not acknowledge me again if I see you, my Lord. There can be no communication beyond tonight." But something dreadful pierced her chest as she spoke, and perhaps it showed in her eyes because his lips fell to hers, the kiss deep and fulfilling, belittling her denial. And she knew he knew it, but she could not unsay those words, she had no choice but to walk away. *He cannot save me, no one can. I'm already lost.*

Setting her palms on his chest she pushed him away, turned from his grip and grasped the door-handle, refusing to look back.

Masculine conversation spilled from the adjoining rooms and filled the high ceilinged space as she crossed the hall, broken by the occasional trill of a woman's laughter rising above the lower tones. She kept walking, ignoring the sound of a door slamming behind her, and the heavy tread of quick masculine strides hitting the floorboards.

Crossing into the first room she saw Lord Gainsborough seated at another card table by the far wall. He was waiting, watching. He rose. The men about him turned to follow his look, rising too. Her heart racing she took the few steps to where he stood.

Ribald jests and jeers greeted her from the male audience who were oblivious to the reality of his little welcome scene.

Refusing to cower she met Lord Gainsborough's glare of accusation.

She'd angered him, yes, but she could see he was equally enthralled to think another man had taken her but yards from where he sat. She knew his sadistic lusts must have thrilled at it, while his need for control revolted.

A round of laughter rang from another room. The men about them turned back to their game. Gainsborough's hand lifted.

As she heard the front door slam shut she felt the first strike across her face. The world about her tilted, time shifting to a slower pace as her vision hazed.

"Good God, Gainsborough, no need for that!"

"My God, man!"

A dozen calls of outrage echoed in her head. Reaching out blindly to stop her fall, she felt Lord Gainsborough's painful grip catch her and haul her back, holding firm.

"Mind your own damn business!" his bellow rang. "Out of my way!"

Chapter Two

Maintaining his vigil on Gainsborough's townhouse, Edward leaned his back against the iron railings of the park at the center of Grosvenor Square. The cold air of the harsh frost seeped through his loose fitting heavy wool greatcoat and leather gloves.

Clapping his hands together briefly, he ignored the misty vapour of his breath rising on the cold winter air. Then he tilted the rim of his hat forward and folded his arms over his chest.

The property was a grand, lavish statement of the man's wealth.

Well, Ellen had told Edward bluntly she was with the man for his money. In comparison to it, Edward was a pauper.

Even if he'd been heir to his father's estates not second born, he could not have matched Gainsborough's wealth.

But why then had Gainsborough cheated?

Edward watched the man descend the steps from his front door, his wife fixed on his arm, his eldest daughter and grandchild in their wake.

For God's sake, his daughter was a similar age to Ellen. It made Edward sick, the whole sordid bloody affair, including the part he'd played in it. When he'd woken the morning after, with a thundering head, he'd thought it a dream, and then images and senses had merged into memories he couldn't refute.

He was not his brother. He had no appetite for vice or excess. He did not drink, gamble, or idle away his time with women. He'd never paid for sex, nor ever would. He did not condone the immorality of it. Sex simply shouldn't be for sale. Women threw themselves at him anyway. But none of those women had responded like her. *Skill*, he told himself in explanation. It was her living after all. But it was more than the sex. The woman had touched his insides — somehow — changed him — drugged him.

He was obsessed — addicted.

Lust, his brain delivered the single word to justify his feelings.

Lust? Yes, but... He thought for a moment but reached no conclusion. *God. Who knew?* He'd never felt like this before. He couldn't think, couldn't sleep, and couldn't even bloody breathe without want of her. It was not him. His reputation leaned towards dull and staid.

He blamed his brother. Since Robert's return life had become boring and Edward had been restless. It seemed the outcome was he *had* turned to *all* of his brother's vices.

What am I doing here? She'd made it plain she was with Gainsborough by choice. She wouldn't meet *him*. She'd given herself because Gainsborough had willed it.

But Gainsborough hadn't willed her to say the man had swapped his cards. Protecting *him* was *her choice*. And every expression of her body as Edward had made love to her had told him she was lying. She wanted him. Her responses had been absolute truth.

That was the conundrum disturbing his sleep. She haunted him. He could not forget her.

Pushing away from the railings, his gloved hands curling to fists, he gave up his vigil as Gainsborough's coachman called to the horses in the straps and flicked his whip, stirring the thoroughbred blacks into a trot. The strike of the horses' hooves rang on the cobble, as did the iron rim of carriage wheels rolling into motion and the rattle of harness caught the frigid air.

Edward turned away. How easily he'd been tumbled from a confident man to an infatuated youth. But God help him, he could not just leave this, he wanted more of Ellen Harding. Three nights he'd played at Madam's. Three nights there had been no sign of her. He'd hoped if he waited here, Gainsborough would lead him to where he kept his mistress.

And then what will I do?

His hands plunged into the pockets of his greatcoat, his legs slashing its skirt with long impatient strides. His eyes oblivious to the blue sky and people passing him in the street, his mind sifted through his spiralling thoughts.

He could not entice her away from Gainsborough with wealth. Edward did not even want to if he could. She'd said she wasn't interested in anything else. Yet a wedge inside him refused to believe it. What had been between them had not been trade. *Had it?* God, the woman had gotten into his veins like a damn dose of opium. This infatuation was a curse.

It had felt right to hold her and touch her. And there was something seriously wrong about her relationship with Gainsborough.

Why did she help me if she's happy with him? It couldn't just be about money.

I shouldn't have touched her. I should have asked her while I could.

He thought of his brother. He loathed lustful men. Yet he'd just proved he was no better. Twitching up the collar of his caped greatcoat to keep the chilled air from his neck, he walked on, walked away.

He'd find his cousin and some physical activity to consume his restlessness, boxing or fencing, or both. After tonight if he did not see her, he'd go home. Home? It wasn't that anymore. Though, at least there his frustrated energy could be put to decent use, and he could forget about Ellen Harding. Robert wouldn't turn him away no matter that they were at odds. It had been Edward's decision to leave.

A pain lodged in his chest, beneath his ribs, as sharp as a stitch. His fingers pressed to it over his coat as he halted at the edge of the curb and a street-sweep shifted before him with a tip of his cap to brush the filth from the street for Edward to cross.

Edward withdrew a coin from his pocket and tossed it idly to the boy, who caught it in his grubby hand with a grin, kissed it, then slipped it into his pocket before lifting off his hat and nodding his thanks.

Edward turned away, a strong inexplicable sense of unease resting over him.

∽ ∾

My dearest John, I think of you always, know that I love you and miss you, sweetheart.

Ellen signed the letter to her son, *Mama*, blotted the ink with sand, folded it and sealed it with a little melted wax, while her maid watched. Then she addressed it and kissed the seal. Her heart aching as she did. She longed to see him. But that was not a possibility. She could not even consider it, if she stopped to think about him her heart would break, and so she tried not to. He was safe and that was all that mattered.

"Millie," Ellen whispered, holding it out to her maid, "here, put it in your dress, not your pocket. If anyone asks, say you are going for threads and ribbons and bring some back in case they check."

Millie accepted the letter, bobbed a curtsy and answered in a similarly soft voice, "I wouldn't tell, Ma'am."

With a sigh Ellen reached to grasp and squeeze Millie's hand in silent thanks. "I know, Millie. I do not mistrust you." Ellen let Millie's hand go as a knock rang on the drawing-room door.

Millie slid the letter into her bodice.

"Come in, Wentworth!" Ellen called to Lord Gainsborough's butler—her jailer. None of the servants were her choice. She was no guest here, she was a prisoner, and therefore she was fortunate in Millie's compassion. She did indeed trust her maid, but no one else.

"A letter."

Ellen's heart raced as she heard Wentworth's statement as a question.

Millie bobbed another curtsy and Ellen realized Wentworth held a tray. It bore a letter.

Relief flooded Ellen.

Millie quickly disappeared, sweeping past the butler and then escaping out the door.

"Thank you." Ellen took the letter from the tray, knowing immediately what it meant. Gainsborough would call later.

Rising from her seat, Ellen's eyes met the butler's insolent, disparaging gaze, it spoke of revulsion not respect. He condemned her status and yet not the man who kept her. Her chin lifting she dismissed him bluntly, "You may go, Wentworth."

When the door shut she turned and faced her reflection in the mirror above the hearth. The black and yellow stains across her cheek and about her eye had faded marginally, she could cover them, but the cut over her eyebrow would need to be hidden beneath her fringe. Millie would have to find a new style for her hair. The sigh of vexed frustration which tugged into her lungs, tweaked the bruising at her ribs.

Her fingers pressing to her side she took a more cautious breath and turned away from her image, looking past the swathe of the blue chintz curtain into the street beyond.

She often watched life pass by, like a canary in a cage. She could go out if she wished, none of them were afraid she'd run, but where was there to go.

Turning away, her gaze skimmed across the pale blue hues of the room, stopping to rest on the small vase of snowdrops which she'd picked in the garden that morning as she moved to sit in the armchair. Her mind reached back to the woods where she'd played as a child. Snowdrops carpeted the ground there, just like snow. She'd picked them then, once, when she was sixteen. But that innocent girl in the memory was alien to her. She had forgotten family, safety and home.

Returning her attention to the letter in her hand, her thumb slipped beneath the seal. The summons was for tonight at nine.

She left the letter on the low table beside her chair and picked up her book. But her eyes did not lower to the page instead they drifted upwards to the plaster cornice bordering the ceiling across the room. She leaned back and her memory slipped back too, to Edward, as it often did, longing for something that could never be. Closing her eyes she shut out the folly of her thoughts, but she could not stop the hope from filling her heart. For the umpteenth time in days she wondered where he was, what he was doing now, *if* he'd thought of her?

⊰⊱

As the doorman took her cloak Ellen felt a shiver race across her skin. She had never felt so concerned about being abroad in Lord Gainsborough's company. It was silly. She'd been his mistress for years. Her presence was expected and generally ignored.

The smoke of gentlemen's cigars filled her lungs. The scent of brandy and musky male cologne mingled in the cloudy overheated air. She lifted her fan, hiding behind it, her eyes focusing on the floor, as she took Gainsborough's arm and he began to walk across the room.

If Edward was here, it was better she ignore him.

She sensed a difference in Gainsborough tonight. She was being displayed, his trophy, but that was always so. Parading all about the room he took an age to pick a table. Then he made much of sweeping back the tails of his evening coat when he sat, and once seated, he looked up at her before calling for his cards to be dealt. He was keeping his eye on her more than normal too.

Ellen looked at the dealer's hands, fighting the instinct to glance about the room, and watched Gainsborough's cards thrown across the table facedown.

Gainsborough's fingers caught hers and set them on his shoulder, in what Ellen could only read as an unspoken warning.

So that was his message — ownership. Edward was here.

A deep bark of laughter rang from across the room. Her muscles jarred in a sharp spasm, making her jump.

He was.

Gainsborough's fingers pressed over her hand in another warning. He'd chosen the table for the best proximity to make a statement to Edward. She could virtually hear Lord Gainsborough's body yelling, *'she belongs to me'*.

Edward laughed again.

Stealing a single glance over her fan, Ellen saw him. He was leaning back in his chair, smiling. She had tried to carve every detail of his features in her memory four nights ago, but Edward in the flesh was more magnificent than the image she remembered. His reality captured her breath.

He looked up, his gaze meeting hers across the room. She looked away.

She could hear his voice above the general hum of male conversation, but she could not make out the words. He laughed again, a deep ringing, reckless and carefree sound.

God, I am a fool. In the hours since they'd parted she'd analysed every touch, every word, a thousand times, over and over, building a house of cards from her hope — a house on sand — it had no foundation. *This was the truth.*

He doesn't give a damn, and nor should I!

She sold herself to men. He'd bought her. Perhaps not with money, but none the less his deal with Gainsborough had been a purchase of sorts. The only difference was skill. A skill which spoke of the number of women he'd already bedded.

I was just one more.

She tried not to listen to Edward anymore and concentrate on Gainsborough's game, unsuccessfully. She felt sick. Was he laughing at her? About her? Had he spoken of the things she'd let him do?

A footman offered her a flute of champagne from a silver tray.

Lord Gainsborough must have ordered her a drink and she'd not even heard.

She lifted her hand from Gainsborough's shoulder and accepted it, nodding to dismiss the footman. Her fingers gripped the narrow stem and she brought the rim of the glass to her lips, looking at Edward.

He'd leaned to say something to his friend, his hand on the other man's shoulder, but that sixth sense which seemed to stretch between them must have whispered. His gaze turned to her.

She looked at Gainsborough's game, drinking the champagne. The bubbles caught in her throat, making her cough.

Lord Gainsborough looked up.

She offered him a taut smile, setting the glass down on the table at his elbow.

He caught her fingers and pressed them firmly back on his shoulder.

Her other hand lifted her fan and fluttered it beneath her chin.

Unable to resist, her eyes darted back to where Edward sat.

He was leaning over his hand of cards, light dancing in his dark eyes, as the man beside him, she now recognised as the one he'd spoken to the other night, smiled and made some comment. When Edward looked at his friend he saw her watching.

She looked away.

"You have me, I'm done." Edward's words carried over the other voices easily, louder than before.

Glancing towards him, Ellen observed him throwing his hand of cards onto the table.

He rose, his eyes turning to her as he moved in her direction.

She looked away and prayed he would not approach. Surely he would not be so stupid. She'd asked him not to speak to her again.

Her heartbeat pounding, she pretended to fix her gaze on Gainsborough's cards while in the periphery of her vision she followed Edward's movement.

He walked past her, barely a foot away and said nothing, not a word.

Tears stinging her eyes, she increased the motion of her fan.

He couldn't speak to her, she'd told him so herself. But he had not even acknowledged her presence, and it hurt.

She lifted her hand from Gainsborough's shoulder, leaned forward and whispered, "I am in need of the retiring room, my Lord."

His gaze spun to her and his hand caught her wrist. The grip was painful

"Do not take over long, Ellen, I will send one of the women to look for you, if I must." The threat in his eyes mirrored his words. He did not trust her.

She was not going to find Edward. She just needed solitude to master her emotions.

"Yes, my Lord."

He let her go.

She walked away, snapping shut her fan and then holding it to her chest. Her heart thumping, she weaved a path through the tables, twisting and turning, making her way through the crush of drunk and over eager men who watched the games, ignoring the hands that stroked her bottom or grazed her breast.

For a respectable woman they would part like the red sea for Moses. For a harlot, like her, they deliberately blocked her way, and often only a sharp elbow in their ribs or a shove would move them.

Normally she ignored their uncouth leers. She knew what she was, what to expect but tonight she felt vulnerable and violated.

Forcing her way through the last of the crowd she reached the hall and found the corridor leading to the women's retiring room, the same corridor she'd been led through four nights ago.

She passed the door to the room where she'd given her body and soul to a stranger and fought the potent memories it stirred. She did not wish to remember it any more.

The retiring room was empty and leaning back against the door she struggled to control her emotions.

What is wrong with me?

"For goodness sake get a grip, Ellen."

Her heart racing and her soul aching, she took her weight from the door and turned to the small cheval mirror on a table. A stool stood before it but she didn't sit. Instead she leaned forward, rested her palms on the tabletop and faced her reflection. The painted woman who looked back was like a china doll, fragile and hollow. She felt inhuman.

God, help me. There is nothing left of me anymore. Where are all your high and mighty, airs and graces, now? I am no better than a White Chapel whore, panting after a man for his looks and prowess. Disgusted with her image she stood and turned away. She'd come to terms with the poor hand fate had dealt years ago—her body belonged to men, they exploited it. But Edward hadn't used her — she'd been his yearning accomplice. She couldn't hide behind the myth she'd spun for sanity's sake anymore. She couldn't pretend circumstance had prostituted her. She could no longer claim to have been forced. She'd prostituted herself for Edward Marlow.

Tears in her eyes, she wished he had not come to the club or played cards four nights ago. He'd made her life so much harder. Too hard.

She slowed her breath, fighting tears. Crying would only stain her make-up. This was her life. She'd learned to live it before, she could learn again. She had no choice.

When she left the room, feeling defiant, she walked briskly, her posture rigid and her chin high.

In a moment, hands gripped her arm and covered her mouth, muffling her scream as she was pulled sharply back into the shadow beneath the stairs.

"Hush," Edward's deep tenor rumbled in her ear.

Relief and recognition ripped through her — memories.

He pulled her across the narrow hall into a room, shut the door, pressed her back against it and kissed her. It was a searing and possessive kiss. Her fingers sank into his hair greedily holding his mouth to hers, oblivious to anything but him as his hands gripped her waist.

Edward broke the kiss, pulling an inch away. She met his gaze and saw desire. It matched hers. She did not deny it. She wanted him. For a moment they simply stared at each other as she breathed in the air he breathed out. His breath smelt of brandy, sweet and sharp.

A brace of candles lit the room behind him, their flickering gold light playing on his hair and skin.

They were in Madam's private parlour, the room where they'd made love. *Sex.* This thing between them was purely physical.

His thumb brushed her cheek. "Why the powder, Ellen, you had no makeup the other night?"

Unable to hold his gaze her vision focused on his neckcloth and she tried to move away afraid he would see her bruises, shifting sideward and seeking to distract him. "You should not be here, Edward."

But his hand gripped her shoulder and his eyes traced across her face as she looked back. She knew he could see the marks and her fingers clasped the door-handle behind her.

"*He hit you.*" It was an incredulous statement, etched in disbelief; spoken in the voice of a man who would never hit a woman. Aggression burning in his eyes, she saw his pupils flare as the cause of it clearly dawned. "Because of me! I'll kill him!" His words were as vicious as a physical blow and reaching around her he grasped the door-handle, his fingers closing over hers.

She pressed back against the door, refusing to move and braced one hand against his chest. "No!" The justifiable ire in his eyes, made the restriction about her heart tighten a notch. Righteous anger only made him more handsome. "He'll kill you before you could touch him. He has too much power, Edward. There is no winning against him. Leave it. Please. It is not your affair. I don't ask it of you."

He knew nothing about her. He could not wish to fight for her. She could not let him. She could not bear it if he failed. She did not want him dying for her.

Defiance shone in his eyes, but then, as her words visibly sank in, she saw another understanding dawn. He let go of the door-handle and his hand braced her cheek, his thumb resting against the barely hidden bruise by her lip as his gaze reached into her. "That is why you are with him isn't it? Because you have no choice? I can give you choice, Ellen."

Her eyelids dropped. She couldn't bear the promise in his eyes. *I wish you could—but you are not my saviour. I cannot endanger you on a selfish whim.* Shaking her head, she opened her eyes. "Edward, you scarcely know me, whether I am with him by choice or not, I am still his. You will only make it worse. Please, just go, before he finds out we have spoken. There can be nothing more between us."

His expression hardened in denial and his gaze bored through her eyes into her soul. "Give me your address and tell me how I may see you. Then I will go. I shan't take, no, for an answer, Ellen."

Footsteps rang beyond the door and Ellen's heart skipped into a sharp allegro. Without thinking, she answered, "Wood Street, near St James, number four. But you cannot call upon me. My servants are Lord Gainsborough's. I only trust my maid. Please, speak to no one of this."

"Send me word then, through your maid, and tell me when I may see you. Contact me at White's so your communication will not be traced to me."

He leaned forward and kissed her after he'd spoken and she could not deny him; she could not deny what she felt. Her fingers gripped his nape and then slipped into his hair, pulling him closer. She wanted him. She wanted him for more than just sex. She wanted him because he cared.

He drew away slightly, his lips caressing hers one last time, before he whispered, "I shall go. He'll be waiting for you. I do not want him to harm you again because of me."

She moved aside and his hand rested on the door-handle again, but he didn't turn it, he was motionless for a moment, as though distracted by thought. She touched his arm. "Edward?"

His eyes focusing on her, he smiled. "I will get you away from him, Ellen."

The statement rang in her head with the note of a vow as he opened the door and left.

Breathless she turned to the mirror over the mantle, the one in which she had watched him re-dress her hair four nights before. *He isn't my rescuer. He cannot help me. Can he?*

Chapter Three

Ellen watched Millie brush her hair in the mirror on her vanity chest, the maid's long rhythmic strokes running from her crown to her waist. These nightly caresses were the only constant in her life. Usually they calmed her, but tonight she was wound tight like hemp rope. It was agony to sit still, her thoughts writhed and her fingers twisted in her lap.

Edward had promised to help her. *Lord Edward Marlow,* she savoured his name. Life would be so different with a kind protector.

Gainsborough had taken her tonight but she'd shut him out and clung to an alternative—Edward. Edward had created hope and on it she was building an illusion, she imagined tenderness and devotion, love, not sex.

And she was not risking those dreams. She would not contact Edward until she was certain it was safe. This opportunity was too precious.

It was days later when the chance finally came and Ellen's fingers shook as she penned the short note, blotted and folded it, her eyes darting to and from the door where Millie stood ensuring no one could enter unexpectedly.

Ellen had lived on edge for three weeks while she waited for this moment. Gainsborough had returned to his estates today. She knew for certain he would not be back for days. It was safe, but would Edward come?

They'd not spoken at all in the intervening weeks. He'd taken no more risks. She'd seen him less than half a dozen times at Madam's, and when he was there she'd not even dared to meet his gaze.

Holding the short note to her breast she willed him to feel the same—*to come*. He was life and breath to her now. She'd written nothing other than that she could meet him, where and how, and signed herself *E*, afraid someone else may see it.

She prayed he would come.

"Please take it to White's, the Gentlemen's club in St James Square, Millie. Hand it to a footman there. Say nothing to him other than that it must be placed into Lord Edward's hand. Here." She drew two shillings from her reticule and gave them to the maid. "Give one to the footman to ensure he does as you ask and there is one for you." Ellen had begun stealing shillings from Gainsborough's purse as he slept for just this cause. Millie knew she had no money. Now Millie knew her mistress was both a whore and a thief.

"Yes, Ma'am." The maid bobbed. Millie was aware of the risk Ellen was taking too. "Thank you, Ma'am."

"Thank *you*, *Millie*. Go, hurry. Do not speak to anyone."

"Yes, Ma'am," Millie confirmed, curtsying again before leaving the room.

Leaning back in the chair, Ellen looked to the moulded plaster frieze edging the ceiling, uncertain how to pass the time until tomorrow. What if Edward was no longer in town? It had been days since she'd seen him. What if he'd lost interest in her? What if he had thought better of becoming embroiled in her life? She could hardly blame him if he chose not to come. He owed her nothing.

And yet she hoped. It was a living, breathing, deep-seated sensation inside her. She had tried so hard to quell it, but she simply could not. Hope had been unleashed and it would not go back into its cage. It was a constant turmoil of emotion roiling inside her, waiting desperately for its chance to run free. She'd barely slept and hardly eaten, her thoughts reeling.

Now she must wait again and try to tame it.

❧❧

Leaning back in the armchair Edward shifted the ankle of one booted foot to the knee of the other, watching his cousin, Rupert, read the Times. Edward's stomach rumbled. He had been living on nervous, restless energy for days, with no appetite for food, or anything in fact. His fingers commenced a rhythmic drum, flowing from one to the other in a line on the leather-clad arm of the chair.

A letter had arrived from his brother, Robert, yesterday, requesting both Edward's advice and return. He'd been thinking all night over whether he should go. After all he'd heard nothing from Ellen. She wouldn't even meet his gaze in Madam's, so rather than torture himself he'd stopped frequenting the place, refusing to sit there and keep watching Gainsborough paw her. And Edward wasn't stupid, he knew Gainsborough was staking his former claim, flaunting Ellen and telling Edward she was beyond his reach. But Edward rejected the notion. He was not accepting it.

Damn it. He'd done what she'd asked. He'd stayed away until she deemed it safe, but if she did not contact him soon…

I will what? Kick her door down? Steal her away? Call Gainsborough out? There must be something I can do other than just sit and wait? The tedium of it was excruciating.

"You are not attending, Ed!" His cousin's sharp tone cut through Edward's thoughts, abruptly interrupting them. "I've been speaking to you for an age. I said, what are your plans for today? I'm going to Manton's in Dover Street this afternoon, to the shooting gallery, I wondered if you wished to come?"

It was a haunt Gainsborough favoured.

Edward shook his head. "I will probably go to Jackson's." The pugilist master's studio in Bond Street was a good place in which to vent his recent frustration.

"And I shall leave you to it, after yesterday." Rupert rubbed at his jaw in reminder of the blow he'd taken.

"I apologised, Rupert. I told you, I lost my concentration."

"Believe me it did not feel as though you were not attending, it felt as though you intended to kill."

It was true enough. Edward laughed. Gainsborough's son-in-law had walked through the door and caused a distraction. The blow had been for Gainsborough.

A month ago Edward had prided himself in being level headed. But since Ellen Harding had possessed him, he was someone else, someone he wasn't comfortable with. He was no longer certain of who he was at all.

He lifted his ankle from his knee, set his foot back on the floor and lifted the other leg, his fingers continuing their rhythm on the arm of the chair.

"For God sake, what is wrong with you, Ed?" his cousin challenged, peering over his paper. "You're fidgeting. I asked you if you wished to meet afterwards."

"I don't know. I'm not sure what I'll do later."

With a suddenly intent gaze, Rupert folded the paper and threw it aside, leaning forward in his seat. "Ed, *is* something wrong? You act odder by the day."

Yes, Edward laughed again, inwardly. He did feel very odd, as though there was a hole in the region of his chest and if he told his cousin he'd fallen head-over-heels-in-love with Gainsborough's courtesan, Rupert would think him touched in the head. He was mad to love her. He knew that himself. But love her he did. He could not help it, nor deny it any longer. The obsession he had for Ellen Harding had to be love and not just lust. He'd certainly never encountered such all-consuming emotions before.

"Ed! You are wandering off again."

Edward smiled at his cousin's expression of genuine concern, "I'm tired, Rupert, that's all," lifted his ankle from his knee and set both feet on the floor, then pushed on the arms of the chair to stand. "In fact, I think I'll go. A drive will clear the cobwebs from my head. I'll bid you good-day." He bowed. "Rupert."

"Ed, for God sake, take care, don't drive your damned phaeton off the road, you've no concentration lately." Nodding vaguely, Edward walked away and Rupert leaned back in his chair looking exasperated and lifting a hand in parting.

"My Lord." A young footman stopped Edward in his path to the exit with a bow. Then he held out a piece of folded paper. "I was given this for you."

Edward felt his heart slam against the wall of his chest and took the note, then discreetly slid it into the breast-pocket of his morning coat, before exchanging it for a coin. "Thank you for your discretion."

Within minutes, Edward was steering through the streets in his curricle, his mind not at all on the task; the paper burning a hole in his pocket.

He flicked the ribbons and sprung his bays, but the capital's streets in the afternoon were irritatingly busy with heaving humanity, of all classes. Turning a corner he marginally missed a small boy who'd run across the road, as well as very nearly dislodging the groomsman balancing on the phaeton at the rear. Admitting defeat Edward reined in the horses and set a more even pace, utterly at odds to the pulsing need for an outright gallop coursing in his blood.

When he finally pulled into Bloomsbury Square, where his brother's townhouse stood, Edward called back to his groom to take the reins and wait in the street. Then he leapt down, ran up the steps to the door and wrapped the knocker impatiently until Jenkins drew it open. Already drawing the letter from his pocket Edward irritably thrust his brother's butler aside and crossed the chequered marble floor to the drawing-room.

His attention on the paper in his hand he was deaf to the butler's request for his hat and coat and blindly ignored the footman's bow as he passed. Instead he read, his strides pacing across the room, his heart thumping in his chest.

She proposed a meeting, at one tomorrow, at the gates of Green Park. He looked at the clock. The note had been written yesterday. It was now already nearly twelve.

Thank God I went to White's this morning.

He squatted down at the hearth, the hem of his coat dragging on the floor, touched the edge of the letter to the flames and watched it begin to burn. He let it fall into the hearth and waited until he knew it was just ash, then walked away.

She had asked him to come alone, not to trust his servants, not even to ride in his own carriage but to take a hackney. He suddenly felt incredibly cold. *Perhaps I am insane to get involved in this — involved with her.* He knew if he met her again there would be no turning back.

Hell, there was no turning back now. The woman was already too embedded in his blood. Whether he willed it or not, Ellen Harding was a part of his life now — a part of him. He had no choice but to go to her.

᪽᪽

He'd been waiting ten minutes when he saw her. She was simply and elegantly dressed, her appearance nothing like that of a courtesan. The long dark navy pelisse she wore was to keep her warm in the chill, early March winds. Spring was still as yet unbroken.

The demure garment hung to her ankles, with double breasted buttons across her chest, and an upturned fox fur collar framed her beautiful neck and face. Her hands were within a matching fox fur muff at her waist. The dark navy hat, sitting high on her ebony hair, was decorated with jay's feathers that swept up from the brim above her left ear. And a narrow, navy veil, woven in a fine net, was drawn down over her eyes and nose.

His hands curled into fists inside the pockets of his thick, many-caped greatcoat as he watched her, waiting for her to notice him.

She had thought to hide herself, he guessed, but he would know the curve of her jaw, that mouth, the column of her neck, anywhere, even within a crowd. He had committed it to memory half a dozen times in recent weeks and lain awake night after night recalling every detail.

She looked over her shoulder, glancing back up the street, as if she half expected to be followed. Then she looked to the traffic in the road, waiting until it was clear before she crossed to the park gates. She'd still not seen him.

Within her muff he imagined her hands clasped together, her thumbs circling one another. He'd seen her tendency to fiddle when she stood at Gainsborough's back. She was forever twisting and turning her fan; never comfortable, nor secure. The other courtesans he'd seen in London were women of excessive confidence, bold, never meek and maidenly in their manner as Ellen always seemed. With Ellen he could not even lay her lack of confidence at the door of her age. She was older than him, and yet her nervous behaviour made her seem half a dozen years younger.

She was on the path some distance before him now, her short, quick strides slicing at the skirt of her pelisse. Her gaze was on the pavement ahead of her, oblivious to the men who passed her and looked back, as nearly every man did, even with her beauty covered by a veil.

She looked up.

The moment she saw him, he could tell she'd not thought he would come. It was in the sudden drop of tenseness in her shoulders and the smile opening her mouth as if she would speak and acknowledge him from afar. But such an outburst would be folly, even though he had come as asked without acquaintance or equipage, someone may know him. Her mouth closed on the exclamation as she increased her pace, weaving through people walking the other way.

He silently cursed every man who looked at her twice. But then she was clearly a woman of standing, walking alone, the conclusion was obvious. A protective wave of masculine hormones ran through his blood, an instinctive need to defend his territory.

Angry at himself he turned to walk through the gates of the park, sensing her follow him. *Fool, she isn't yours.* She was Gainsborough's, and when he spoke to her he must not forget it.

He'd walked nearly two hundred yards before she drew alongside, and when she spoke her voice was breathless but full of joy he'd not heard in it before. "You came. I didn't think you would."

A vice like grip contracted tightly about his heart as his senses were filled with the scent of her, the sound of her. God, he had this bad. "You had no need to be in any doubt. My feelings are unchanged, Ellen." His voice was harsher than he intended in response to the need and longing ripping through his chest.

"You are angry though?"

He'd chased away the pleasure from her voice. "No," he answered, smiling, looking sideways at her, "just desperate to be alone with you."

He ached to reach for her hand but made no move to touch her, following her lead. It was hardly the fashionable hour and a less frequented park so they would be unlikely to meet anyone he knew, but even so he was aware of her concern for caution.

She held slightly aside from him while they walked along a path on the edge of the open grass. To their left was a dense shrubbery of evergreens. Ahead of them other couples laughed in flirtatious conversation.

"I thought because you have stopped coming to Madam's..." Her words trailed off.

"Because I cannot bear to watch you with *him*, that's why. I was beginning to wonder if *you* had changed your mind."

Stopping suddenly, she turned and met his gaze for a moment before looking away to watch a couple further on, as though unable to accept his observation. "This has been the first opportunity. He's gone for several days."

She started walking again, a little ahead of him, her eyes fixed on the distance where the white winter sky met the horizon of the city's park.

He felt the meaning of her statement hanging in the air between them. He began walking too. She was so uncertain of herself, he realized, she didn't even dare presume he would wish to see her more than once, despite the fact he had only a moment ago declared his feelings were unchanged.

He followed her, a step behind, his open hand hovering at her back, not touching, as if to protect her from what the world had thrust upon such slim and unsubstantial shoulders.

That living this life was not her choice, couldn't be in doubt.

"How long do we have?"

"I must be back before dark, if I am not the servants may tell tales."

"But then we have a couple of hours."

He caught her elbow and gently drew her aside into the privacy of the less dense branches of a large rhododendron bush. Inside the cavity, surrounded by its evergreen leaves, they were at least afforded some privacy. He lifted her veil, tipping it upwards over the rim of her hat. No make-up. No bruises. Only beauty. More than beauty, magnificent perfection.

His head bent and he kissed her, a kiss she freely gave. His hands settling on the curves of her hips, he drew her body closer. Already his groin was aching, heavy with the weight of his need for her.

"Ellen." His voice was breathless as he rested his forehead against hers. "God, I've missed you. I can think of nothing else but where you are, what you are doing. I think I'm going mad."

She smiled, a hesitant look, suggesting she was as much affected by him as he was by her. One hand left her muff and her fingers traced the line of his jaw then settled on his lips. She was thinking something, but she did not speak. Her hand fell.

"We could go to an inn, find a room?" For all his confidence and authority he felt like a child begging for a treat.

She nodded. He bestowed another brief kiss on her lips, took her hand in his and squeezed, then let go. "You go first." He held out his hand. "I will follow and meet you at the gate. But you will have to take my arm from there. I will not leave you walking through the streets alone."

An overwhelming rush of warmth raced through Ellen. He was everything her imagination had hoped, concerned and considerate. She walked from the cover of the branches before him and made a path directly to the gate. But when she crossed the road she felt his fingers touch her elbow. On the opposite path she slipped her fingers from the muff and laid her gloved hand on his arm. It felt good, normal, like any other couple in the street.

They walked at least a dozen streets before he finally turned into the doorway of an inn.

Inside she stood watching, her hands clasped within her muff, while Edward leaned to the landlord's ear and money exchanged hands. Then she caught the landlord's sideways glance at her. It was swift, narrow-eyed and presumptuous, obviously judging her a harlot, and implying indecent thoughts.

She longed to slap him. He made what she'd seen as beautiful seem suddenly sordid. She was not normal. She wasn't a lady with her beau. What she was, was a whore about to be bedded. There was nothing romantic in this. Whether it was Gainsborough or Edward, the outcome and the position were the same. She'd been stupid imaging it as anything else—painting this affair as a picture of love and devotion. It was not that, no matter what Edward said or what she thought, he could not rescue her from this life and nor could he take back the intervening years of pain. She had better learn to accept this for what it was, a brief opportunity for escape, an interlude, not an affair.

Edward took her elbow, his fingers as gentle as ever, unaware of her change of heart. "I ordered food, I didn't know if you'd already eaten. I thought just bread and cheese, and ale. I'm sorry the place is humble, but it seems clean. I didn't think you would wish to risk looking for anywhere more luxurious. We are certain to meet no one who would recognize us here."

She nodded.

His fingers at her elbow, he guided her into a dingy hall and led her upstairs. The paint was tarnished and chipped in places, but he was right, it was clean.

Edward stopped at the second door and bent to set a key in the lock. The door creaked as he pushed it open and then he stood back and held out his hand, encouraging her to pass.

Her breath caught in her lungs as she stepped inside, remembering what they had done before.

A single tall, thin, window in the far wall let in light and the muted sounds of the street. The room was still gray though, as the day was cloudy. It wreaked a little of stale tobacco and was simply furnished, but she had hardly expected a palace. The narrow double bed stood against the back wall. In the opposite corner a single wooden chair faced a small square table, which from the ingrained ink stains, had often served as a desk. A flat topped wooden chest stood at the end of the bed. She crossed the room pulling her hands from the fur muff, discarded it on the desk and walked to look from the window, down onto the busy pavement and street below.

She felt Edward's hand rest on her waist, his fingers urging her to turn to him. She did, her hands lifting to his shoulders as his head lowered and his lips found hers.

His hand slipped from her waist and splayed at the small of her back, while his other settled on her side, the heel of his palm resting at the edge of her breast, his fingers curving about her ribs.

All self-pitying thoughts over the inadequacy of their surroundings, or the opinion of the landlord, vanished, absorbed and diminished by his kiss. As long as she was with Edward, in whatever capacity, she found she didn't care. Her lips parted for his tongue and her fingers gripped his hair as his hand slid between them searching for the buttons of her pelisse. His leather clad fingers were cold as they skimmed the curve of her breast which swelled above the square neck of her gown. He broke the kiss, smiled and looked down at the front fastening of her dress. Then he bit one finger of his glove, tugged it off and tossed it onto the desk.

She laughed at the roughish smile he cast her before returning his concentration to the buttons of her bodice. Once they were free he recommenced their kiss and slipped his fingers into her bodice. A rush of desire slid through her stomach.

A hard knock struck the bedroom door, then without bidding she heard the sharp, sudden creak as it opened.

Edward broke the kiss abruptly and turned, setting his body between her and the door.

Her fingers touched her lips and looking down she saw the milk white skin of her breast as a stark contrast to the dark navy of her pelisse and day dress, she felt like a whore again — *I don't care.*

"Set it down and go!"

"Sir, as you wish," the gruff landlord answered in a mocking tone.

Undoubtedly the man had deliberately entered to see more. When the door shut Edward crossed the room and turned the key in the lock, then he collected the tray and set it down on the chest.

Ellen's shaking fingers withdrew her hatpin and removed her hat. She set it down by her muff, then pulled off her gloves and set them down too. Next she slid off her pelisse while he poured two mugs of ale and moved to light a fire in the hearth.

This situation was dream like. She did not feel like herself at all. Laying her folded pelisse over the back of the single chair, Ellen watched the flames catch the wood in the hearth. She was reminded for a moment of nights beneath the stars with Paul, about an open campfire. Life had seemed so simple then, despite their poverty and the hardship they'd endured daily. She had felt like a queen because Paul loved her, all else, all other worries, had paled into insignificance. *And now?*

Edward's task complete, she watched him rise from his haunches and shrug off his heavy wool greatcoat. It was the height of male fashion. On Gainsborough it looked gregarious, on Edward it extolled his muscular physique.

Discarding his other glove with hers, he then laid his coat over her pelisse before rubbing his hands together, warming his fingers.

"Had you been waiting for me long at the park?"

"No." He smiled, clearly offering reassurance. "Have I been waiting for you for long before the park? Yes, all my life." He let the statement fall as though it meant nothing, as though it was a joke at his own expense, but his tone implied it was more than that. Then, as if regretting his revealing jest, he immediately crossed to the tray, offering to cut her a slice of the sweet scented fresh bread. She accepted and watched him cut some bread and cheese and set it on a plate with a spoonful of plum chutney.

Could she really believe he had stronger feelings for her too?

"Thank you." She took the plate from his hands and moved to sit on the edge of the bed, hitching up her dress a little so she could rest one knee on the mattress and face him, while her other foot dangled to the floor.

He filled a plate for himself, came around the other side of the bed and lay down on his side. His booted feet hanging over the edge of the bed, he bent his elbow and rested his head in the palm of one hand.

The pose was boyish.

A sharp pain struck her chest, running into her breast as she thought of John. Her secret. But blinking away tears she continued eating, hiding her reaction.

"How did you end up with Gainsborough?" His question was nonchalantly put, but she could see the tension in his jaw suggesting it was something he'd applied considerable thought to. It was a question she had dreaded from his lips. She could not answer it, not yet, perhaps not ever. She would have to be certain of his loyalty first.

"I'd rather not speak of it." She closed that conversation down and in return, picked the only thing she knew about him to change the subject. "Is your brother glad to be home?".

"And there you choose my sensitive subject." He sat up, finishing off his slice of bread, and brushed the crumbs from his morning coat. "I believe Robert is not thrilled with the prospect of knuckling down to life as an Earl, but he hardly has a choice.

As for his skill? That is my issue. Or rather Robert's lack of skill. But then he has the knowledge of his steward so he does not need mine. Although I admit he did write to call me back to Farnborough this week, but I believe it was more to sooth my vanity than from any real need. And no, Ellen, I do not intend to go." His fingers covered hers on the bed as he answered the unspoken question he must have seen in her eyes. ˙

"Would you go if not for me?"

He smiled, swallowed, and for the first time she saw a vulnerable look in his eyes. "Yes."

It was the truth, nothing more, she knew that, and she refused to risk reading anything more into it. But mentally she clung to the hope which the single word insinuated — this *was* more than sex. Yet she was too afraid to ask if she was right, she couldn't bear hearing him deny it. It had hardly been a statement of undying love.

Picking up their plates, he set them back on the chest at the end of the bed. Then he moved to lie back down, opening his arms to her. "Ellen?"

She went to him, kissing him as he embraced her. She wanted to give him back the attention he'd given her at the club. Her fingers searched for his coat buttons as his slid her dress from a shoulder and he took control of the kiss she'd begun, pressing her back onto the bed.

Breathless, she refused to concede, fighting to undress him first. It was different today. There was more urgency.

Suddenly untangling their limbs, he pulled away, smiling, dark intensity glowing in his eyes as he stood and held out his hand.

"Perhaps it would be easier if we stand."

Her stomach full of butterflies, she accepted his hand. She felt foolish and nervous. She wanted this to be perfect.

"Let me lead today," she urged, reaching for his coat buttons again.

Laughter, interest and expectation all glinted in his eyes. "If you wish."

"I wish, Edward," she answered, slipping his buttons loose. Her fingers shaking, she did not look at his eyes.

When his buttons were loose he took off his coat and she stripped off her dress, feeling more uncertain.

She knew how to be a whore. She was unsure of how to be herself. But she wanted to please him. She wanted this to be right, as she'd imagined it could be.

"Ellen?" His hand on her arm and at her nape, he kissed her and her body turned to jelly but again she grasped for control. Leading would be novel. She wished this to be different.

She broke their kiss and urged, "Let me, Edward," pushing him back onto the bed.

A short sound of humor left his throat.

Ignoring his mockery she turned and bent over to pull off his boot.

"That's a beautiful view, Ellen," he jested laying his palms on her bottom.

Smacking his hands away, she said, "Instead of mocking me you could remove your cravat."

"I wasn't mocking," he responded, but complied.

It felt so strange being with him, extraordinary and unexpected.

His boot fell to the floor along with his stocking as his cravat sailed over her shoulder. She pulled at his other boot while she felt his fingers tugging the laces of her light corset.

The other boot fell and her corset dropped to the floor.

She turned.

He was lifting his shirt off over his head revealing his glorious chest.

She smiled as their eyes met and he stood. She knew he'd seen her admiration and she felt cold and uncomfortable suddenly as he tossed his shirt onto the pile of clothing on the floor.

Her fingers spread over the ridges and hollows of his stomach.

He gripped her chemise and lifted it.

Naked to the waist, Ellen blushed, and smiled when he did, her gaze clinging to his as her shaking fingers freed his buttons and his tugged loose the ribbon of her drawers.

His eyes were full of longing—the same longing she'd seen there that night in the club. The air left her lungs. His desire frightened her today because it meant so much more to her now. He had promised things to her. She wished to give in return. She wanted this to be right. Forcing her courage, she stepped forward and slid her arms about his neck, pressing her breasts against his chest and her lips to his. *I love you.* Foolish, foolish words.

Need clutched his groin as her slim, soft body pressed flush against him. His fingers slid up the slender column of her neck and into the roots of her hair as he plundered her mouth, cradling her scalp. God, he loved her.

Her hair fell, cascading about her shoulders and pins dropped to the floor. A mewling sound suggesting satisfaction leaked from her mouth.

He gripped her hips ready to lift her to the bed but she pushed his hands away and broke the kiss.

"Let me," she said again, her pale gaze clashing with his.

Compliant, he stood still, breathing deeply while her eyes followed her gentle touch as it explored the contours of his chest. He was entranced by her, watching her as she watched her fingertips skim over his skin.

Her dark eyelashes contrasted starkly with her pale blue eyes and her black hair lay across the alabaster of her shoulders. There was not a single blemish on her skin.

Her gentle fingers brushed over his biceps and arms before they gripped his hands and then her thumbs pressing into his palms she dropped to kneel on the rough floorboards. The air froze in his lungs.

Oh God.

He should not let her do this. He did not wish her to work her craft. But the pleasure was excruciating. She knew how to drive a man mad.

A shiver raked his skin as he watched her. He was lost.

When she let go of his hands, his fingers instinctively threaded into her hair, cupping her scalp and following her rhythm.

After a while, burning with an unbearable hunger, his thumb pressed into her mouth and urged her to stand, his heart pulsing.

"Ellen," his hand held her scalp as he kissed her. She did things to his insides he could not explain, made him feel weak. He leaned her back until she tumbled onto the bed. But then her palms pressed against the pectoral muscles of his chest and stopped him again.

"Ah." He conceded with a frustrated humorous grunt, rolling to his back and giving her the lead once more.

She was blushing when she straddled his waist, her eyes watching him and her cold palms on his chest.

He recalled the sensation of entering her. It had been in his dreams ever since that first night. But when she descended it was not at all the same, it felt forced, unbearably abrasive and painful.

Clarity hit him like a bucket of iced water. *Hell.* She was watching him clearly looking for response, busy giving him what she thought he wanted—Cyprian style. This was solicitation. She was not in the least aroused.

His body mentally and physically revolted, angry and shaking, he gripped her waist and set her aside. Then leaving her there he climbed from the bed, escaping his disgust.

Lord.

Damn.

He reached for the mug of ale and drank; his eyes focusing on anything but her. *You heartless fucking bastard, Edward!* He'd let her ply her trade because it suited him. It wasn't like that. What they'd done at the club had not been like that! *Had it?* Not like Gainsborough and any others she'd bedded.

Bile rose in his throat. He was sickened to think she'd felt forced into this—by him. What on earth did she hope to gain by it? Or did she simply not know better?

He looked back at her. "That is not what I want, Ellen." His voice shook as badly as his nerves.

She looked stricken, bewildered, kneeling on the bed and watching him with an expression of confused pain, her fingers clutching the covers. "I don't want to have sex with you if you do not desire it. You owe me no debt. If all you want is help I will help you without this." The anger in him dissipated suddenly as in a cracked tone he gave her the option honour demanded; even though his desire was a living entity inside him, belying every word. "If you would rather go, or just talk, tell me?"

The distress in her wide eyes was tragic, a scene drawn directly from a Greek play, Diana cast out by Zeus. His gaze swept her body in an instant, from the crown of her head, over her pert breasts, to the curve of her waist and her slightly parted thighs. Heaven only knew how he would walk away but he would if she denied him. His eyes lifted back to her face and he met her gaze.

He wanted to go to her, to soothe away the tears he could see there, but he wouldn't do it, not until he was certain this was her choice as much as his. If he comforted her, coerced her with arousal, he would never know the truth.

"I want to give you what you gave me." She answered quietly. He'd drained the last of her confidence.

A lump lodging in his throat, he took a swig of the ale to clear it and then set down the pewter mug.

"Ellen…" He went to her, sitting on the bed but not close. Not knowing what to say.

Her hands covered her face, hiding a blush which ran down her neck and a mortified sob escaped the barrier of her hands.

He could not leave her suffering. "Ellen." He gripped her hands, pulled them down, then braced her chin and held her gaze to his. "What gives me pleasure is you wanting me." He threw a disgusted glance at the bed, where they'd lain. "Not, that damned performance of it." Then looking at her again, he said, "Whatever you do with me, you do because you want to, Ellen, not because you feel you should. If you don't want anything physical between us, neither do I."

"I want to." Her lips clamped shut on the childlike denial. It was a boon, at least she'd meant to please him and not felt pressured.

"I'll put it another way, Ellen, do nothing for me unless it gives *you* pleasure too." Sucking in a shuddering breath, his fingers fell from her chin as he finally released the knot of anger and revulsion inside him. "I am not an imbecile, Ellen, you aren't even aroused. Gainsborough may not care, but I do. God, it revolts me to think you would equate me with him." He shrugged off his anger. "Do you want something to drink?"

She shook her head, then slid her slender arms about his neck and pressed her lips to his, her weight knocking him back to the bed.

This time he was more cautious, keeping his head and letting her lead the kiss, his fingers tracing across her back and buttocks. Even those gentle curves were perfection. He curled his fingers and ran them up her side, brushing the swelling curve of her breast which pressed against his chest. He felt rather than heard her reactive sigh, it was the pressure of soft flesh against his chest and warm air in his mouth.

Her leg slid across his thigh. He bent his knee.

Clenching her buttock, blood beat in his veins and hunger burned in his stomach but he was not letting his reins go, not yet.

With her cold fingers gripping him he returned her kiss waiting until he was sure she understood this was for them both. And when she pressed down and he was certain he let his primal beast roar and rip free, his hands clasping her as his thigh pressed back.

"Ellen." He breathed her name as though in pain. Then she was battling against him for control as before. It was intoxicating, the way he caressed her, distracting. She could not think and he took control his hands all over her.

Ellen clung to him, falling into ecstasy. It spun delicious pain into her nerves, and left her limbs limp and shaking.

"Edward!" she screamed as he tumbled her onto her back and leaned over her, his muscles taut with intent.

She was not conceding. She was not giving him control. She wanted to lead. She wanted the novelty, the feeling of power, to know she could, to know he'd let her, to feel equal.

What he'd said was true, she'd been too nervous to be aroused before, thinking too much, but her motives were unchanged. She wanted this to be different. Her breathing heavy she held him back. "Let me, I want to lead."

His dark eyes shone like glass. He clearly did not understand. She saw the question in his eyes that said, *why*. But again he did not deny her and rolled back. "As you wish, Ellen. Have your way."

She was going to. She was determined to do this as she wished. 'Whatever you do with me, you do because you want to.' There was so much promise in those words. This was much more than sex.

She straddled his magnificent body and splayed her fingers on his sculpted chest.

He was silent and unmoving bar the lift of his chest as he breathed.

She sank down.

He did not push her away, his fingers clasped her thighs and his jaw clenched.

She bit her lip, watching him. He appeared drunk, his gaze holding hers. This was how she'd imagined it. Just like this. Adoration shone in his eyes.

Her fingers slipped to the muscle of his abdomen. The sensation inside her swept all else away. Being with him was beautiful. Her spirit soared. Her personal litany of his possession ringing in her thoughts—release—escape—this is not just fulfilment of the flesh—this is more.

It is more!

And he was so unknown to her, nothing more than a stranger really, yet she felt so close to him emotionally as though she'd known this would happen between them all her life. It felt right.

He reached up and pulled her down.

As she returned his kiss she knew this was no longer her working a craft she'd learnt with other men or him displaying skill, this was them, bound together.

Weeks ago, in the gambling-hell, she'd been afraid of letting go—now she raced towards it with obsession. The only noise she could hear was their breaths. She was transfixed by the way he could make her feel, intoxicated. Her fingernails bit into the muscle across his ribs as the brink came in a rush, chasing through her body, a flame dancing and flaring across her already heightened senses as her fingernails dug deeper.

His strong hands took control, holding her fiercely. His movement was urgent as she clung to him, her mouth against his, unable to return his kiss.

A primal cry escaped from deep in his chest and filled her open mouth. Then he was hastily lifting her from him.

She felt a shiver rake his muscle and heat on her stomach as she hugged him.

For a moment he didn't move just lay still with his eyes closed. But when they opened he smiled and tumbled her backwards onto the bed, humor shining in his gaze before he pressed a kiss on her lips. There was gratitude in it and his hand lay lightly on her hip.

When he rolled onto his back, she pillowed her head on his shoulder and slid her leg over his, letting her hand rest on his midriff.

He drew the sheet across her and wiped her stomach. Then his hand fell on her hair and his fingers sifted through it while his other hand trailed circles on her upper arm. She fell asleep.

Chapter Four

Fully clothed Edward lifted his weight from where it had rested on the windowsill. He could see her fingers shaking as she secured the buttons at the chest of her pelisse. He moved forward, caught her hands, set them aside and took over the task. She looked up studying his face as he did. He did not meet her gaze.

He hadn't left her long to dress. He couldn't bring himself to wake her any earlier. She'd looked so peaceful in sleep, young. Again he wondered at the fact that she was the older of the two of them. Age had not touched her beauty. She could pass for a debutante in her first season.

Season? A sound of humor escaped his throat bringing a question to her gaze.

He shook his head.

She was no debutante. What she was, was a courtesan who'd bluntly refused to speak of her origin. Yet his brain could not equate her with a woman of anything less than reasonable birth. It was in the tone of her voice, her posture. His mind turned to the one thing he knew — her trade was not her choice — then wondered at the cause. An over eager lover who had taken her virtue and not offered marriage?

Who was the family who'd turned their backs? Or did she have none? No father, no brothers to protect her. No wonder her beauty had brought her to this.

He couldn't think on it.

His gloved fingers skimming her cheek, her pale blue eyes met his, so starkly different to the luxurious fall of her ebony hair. He was so moved by her beauty.

She looked saddened by their need to part, but there was no other option. He'd seen what Gainsborough could do to her. He couldn't let her take risks until he'd worked out what to do. If she'd told him how she'd met Gainsborough it may have helped, but she clearly wasn't going to make helping her easy. He needed to think.

She turned away from his touch, picked up her hat and re-secured it, then pulled the veil across her face.

"Are you ready?" she asked, turning back.

He nodded, taking a breath, almost afraid to ask the question he longed to in case she refused. "May we meet tomorrow?"

Her expression was uncertain but she nodded none the less, blushing and turning away from him again to collect her gloves.

"Not here though, somewhere else." She spoke with her back to him, pulling on her gloves and then picked up the muff.

Edward stepped forward, clasping her waist and then pulling her against him so that he could kiss the delicate skin behind her ear. "I could pick you up in a hackney if you wished, if you tell me where to meet you?"

She turned in his arms and pressed one gloved palm to his cheek, a shallow smile touching her lips and happiness warming her eyes again. "I can wait for you on the corner of Jermyn Street at eleven, but you must not be late."

"I shan't be."

Her lips brushed his.

The door-handle rattled and Ellen jerked back and stepped away.

It was undoubtedly another ploy of the landlord's to play voyeur. "Y'u done yet? Yu'r time's up!"

Ellen's chin lifted and he recognised her distaste for clandestine assignations. He didn't like them either but until he decided how to free her from Gainsborough they could not meet openly.

"We're leaving!" Edward barked back at the door, taking her elbow as she slid both hands into her muff.

When they left the room the landlord was standing outside, a smirk on his ugly face.

Edward's fist balled, but Ellen's fingers closed over it, briefly, before she walked on ahead. He assumed her silent implication said it would do no good. She was right of course.

She must have experienced years of such disparaging looks and cruel comments. In response, he saw the shell she'd developed to shield her through those years draw into place. Her shoulders stiffening, her chin lifted higher and her eyes focused ahead.

He was not sure he could be as strong. Perhaps her greater age did show after all, but never-the-less he was determined to strip her of her armour. The woman he'd fallen for was the one living beneath it.

◆◆◆

Accepting Edward's offered hand Ellen stepped up into the carriage. The driver shut the door and Edward immediately reached past her to draw the curtain across the glass and protect them from the visibility of passers-by. Private, obscured from interested eyes on the street, he pulled her close and kissed her. Hunger and longing instantly lit a fire inside her. This was how it had been each day for nearly a week.

Edward's embrace pressed her back against the squabs and she slid her legs across his lap.

She'd learnt in the days since Gainsborough had left London that her appetite for Edward was insatiable, as was his for her. Laughing, after a few moments, she pushed him away. "You will have me in disarray before we even reach the inn and then what will people think."

His voice escaped in a guttural tone. "You know damn well they think it anyway so I hardly give it credence." Her fingers tenderly straightening the knot of his cravat, she then hugged his shoulders and settled her cheek against the capes of his greatcoat, while his arm lay across her back, his hand resting at her waist.

"Millie thinks I have run mad, she found me singing while I bathed this morning." His forefinger brushed along her nose, then slipped a stray strand of hair from her face and tucked it behind her ear. "I told her, in Wentworth's hearing, I have made a friend. I said we met in Gunter's, in Berkeley Square. He knows I trust Millie. He thinks I wouldn't lie to her. He thinks my days are spent gossiping." She laughed again, light hearted and carefree.

His finger tilting up her chin, her eyes met his. They were almost black in the shadow of the hackney, the slate blue-gray a narrow rim around his pupils. She could not really tell what expression was on his face until he smiled. "She's right. You are completely different than you were but five days ago. You have lost your shell, Ellen. There is no weight on your shoulders anymore."

She smiled too. "Why need I worry about anything when I have you to worry for me?"

A kiss fell on her forehead in response, another touched her nose and then his lips covered hers. Once again she was engrossed in him, her fingers in his hair and slipping up and down his back, while his grasped her breast over her pelisse.

True to form, when the hackney carriage stopped they were jolted from the seat. Gripping his hand, exiting the carriage, she felt her lips stinging from his kisses and saw creases in her skirt. When he let go her hand, he buttoned his greatcoat, hiding his swollen groin, before combing his fingers through his hair and then straightening the knot of his cravat.

"You look a sight, my Lord," Ellen whispered in a teasing voice.

Laughter sounding in his throat, he gripped her arm and leaned to her ear, steering her forward. "As do you, you wicked woman. You're a wanton." He led her in through the inn's public bar, "You deliberately entice me."

She looked up as he guided her on and through another door to the stairs, and whispered back, "But I believe today, my Lord, the fault is all yours. I took control of myself but you must kiss me again."

"So I am impatient," he growled, but there was humor still beneath it. "Can you blame me with a beautiful woman beside me in the confines of an enclosed carriage? After all I am a man and not a saint. Madam, thy name is temptation."

She laughed.

This was how it was between them now, she could barely remember that first day when they'd hardly known what to say. Now their conversation was a continuous play of words, as much as their love making was a mutual game of touch.

He reached about her, opened a door, stood back and gave her a shallow bow. "For today, Madam, I offer you the luxury of only the finest of feather beds." The room smelt of lavender and clean linen, and a tray stood on a chest at the foot of the bed, bearing plum cake, a steaming pot of chocolate and an un-opened bottle of champagne. It was a lovely room, sunshine streamed in through a wide window shining back from the white plaster walls.

She smiled more broadly and turned to face him, her fingers moving to free the buttons of his greatcoat. "Now I know you are a liar, my Lord, you are definitely a saint and not a man at all. It's beautiful."

"Ellen, I am very much a man."

He shrugged off his coat, threw it aside, then hauled her close and kissed her firmly as her fingers pulled the knot of his neckcloth loose. In a moment she broke free, twisting from his grip and tossing his cravat aside, laughing as he chased her. He tried to catch her, but she dodged from his path, placing the bed between them.

Watching her, visibly waiting for her next move, his fingers undid the buttons of his morning coat. Laughing again, Ellen kicked off her slippers one by one and thrust them across the bed in his direction. Then she set one foot onto the bed and, smiling, swept aside her pelisse and started seductively inching up her skirt.

He licked his lips, his smile twisting as he shook his head at her.

Her skirt slid over her knee and then she gripped her stocking, slipped it from her thigh and down her calf before throwing it at him too.

Edward caught it and held it to his nose, his face showing the same appreciation one would for a fine wine.

"You are intolerable, Edward Marlow." She made a run for the tray of refreshments, but screamed in play as she found herself firmly caught about the waist and thrown gently to the bed. Then his fingers undid the buttons of her pelisse.

"And you Ellen Harding are a tease, and irresistible." Her pelisse loose, his hand reached into the bodice of her plain yellow, low cut, day dress and freed one breast. Warmth absorbed it.

Ellen pushed him off, still laughing as she climbed from the bed, tucking her breast back within her bodice. "I would like my chocolate first, my Lord, if you please, while it is hot." She walked away from him and pulled loose the sleeves of her pelisse, then let it slide off behind her, provocatively, as she crossed to the table. A sound of masculine amusement echoed about the room as she reached for a cup, a moment before she felt his fingers undoing several of the highest buttons of her dress. Then he eased it lower and kissed her back.

Glancing at him across her shoulder, lifting the pot of chocolate, she asked, "Do you wish for this, champagne, or plum cake?"

He smiled warmly, but left her and bent to pick up her pelisse, then laid it over the back of a chair. "The only thing I am hungry or thirsty for, my dear, *is you*."

"While I, my Lord, am more discerning."

He approached her again and his arms slipped forward about her waist, holding her close as he kissed her neck. "So am I, Ellen, so am I, and I shall try to make sure *you* can be for as long as I live, if you will give me the chance."

For a moment she heard a deep sincerity in his voice, but dismissed the thought as foolish and his words as banter. She wanted nothing to mar the pleasure she'd found with him, not even childish imaginings, their connection had out stripped that. She wanted it now for what it was—an island sanctuary—a private world existing just for them. When she was with him there was nothing else, even her memories of Paul were fading, and her fears for both the present and the future receded. With Edward there was only ever love and security, she felt cherished.

Her arms rested over his at her waist as she leaned her head back to enjoy his embrace for a moment. Then he squeezed her tightly and let go.

"Go on, Ellen, I will leave you be for a moment so you may drink your chocolate and eat cake."

"There, and now you are a saint and Marie Antoinette."

Laughing, he sat on the chest and lifted his boot to his knee to work the damn thing from his foot. This was always when he missed his valet. But then what Cooper would think of this affair he dare not even consider. He doubted anyone would understand, yet he didn't care what they thought.

"Are you sure you don't want anything?"

"Yes, honestly I ate well enough at breakfast. I truly *am* only hungry for you."

"You are a flirt, Edward Marlow." Her voice rang with the happiness visible in her smile. God, he could not believe the difference in her in just five days. She was no longer hesitant, nor self-conscious. She was a different woman with him and he couldn't stand to see her ever change back to what she'd been before. And today he had a proposal for her that would mean she never had to.

His lips tilting into a smile, he felt the expression in his heart. "And you, Ellen Harding, are everything a man desires, so how can you blame me for being in need of you." Her smile broadening with a coquettish air, she sidled close to him as he set one stocking clad foot to the floor beside the other booted one, then she slotted herself between his legs. His hands resting on her hips, he looked up as she looked down, not daring to pull her to his lap as she gripped her cup of chocolate in one hand and a slice of cake in the other. Her pale blue eyes, her dark hair and the whiteness of her skin awed him. It did each time he saw her. He wondered if they lived together until they were a hundred if her beauty would smite him like this even then. He could never imagine becoming accustomed to it. He thought he would always revere it as a precious thing.

A smile still toying with her lips, she swallowed down a mouthful of cake and chocolate. "So why are we celebrating today, my Lord?"

"Edward, if you please, enough of your teasing, Miss. And I have cause to celebrate every day I am with you, Ellen. Why should I not splash out and find you a decent bed and an inn with some standing and good food? We didn't even receive an odd look as we entered, did you notice?"

She drained her cup and licked the chocolate from her lips, looking gloriously happy and dishevelled. His heart lurched. He took her empty cup from her hand and set it down, then kissed each of her fingertips, before pressing a last gentle kiss into her palm. He curled her fingers about it. "To save for later, Ellen, when you are alone."

"I am never alone now I have you," she declared, affection shining in her eyes, saying more than she knew probably, admitting she'd been lonely before he'd filled the void.

Another smile from his heart touched his lips. She was special this woman, he would dare any man in his position to deny it. But then he thought of Gainsborough, again. *God, I wish I could keep that man out of my head.*

"But I did think we'd agreed to be cautious, this inn is a little—obvious—Edward, what if someone knew one of us?" If she challenged his choice of inn clearly that damn man was in her head too, like a bloody canker which wouldn't go away.

"It's only for a day, Ellen. I wanted to give you more than a dirty room in some seedy inn, just for once I did not wish to have to be circumspect. I've booked the room under Mr and Mrs Brownlow and for a whole night. No one will ask questions. No one will think it odd."

Her fingers uncurling, they slid across his cheek, and he rested his head against her delicate embrace.

Her touch felt cool despite the fire already burning in the hearth.

Was it madness to love her so much? To place her happiness above his no matter what?

She fed him her last mouthful of cake, her pale eyes dancing with frivolity and something else as she turned his head up to hers. "I love you, Edward," she whispered.

Edward felt his heart soar and burst like a fire cracker. While Ellen continued her declaration ignorant of the jubilation she'd engendered.

"I think I am insane to say so. I hardly know you. We have known each other barely a month, and here I am, head over heels in love with you." Her last words were uttered on a nervous laugh as she bent to cover his lips with hers.

Words forgotten, cupping her nape Edward tumbled back
to the bed, pulling her with him, his heart singing with joy.

⋦⋩⋩

"Ellen." Edward whispered to her over an hour later, as
they reclined naked beneath the covers on the comfortable
feather bed.

"Yes," she sighed contentedly, snuggling against the
warmth and comfort of his body, one leg draped across his, one
hand splayed on his chest. Glancing up she saw his eyes fix on
the white plaster ceiling.

"I don't know how to explain what I feel for you, but I
think I should try. I feel..." He paused, apparently searching for
words.

She rose a little, rolled to lay her palm on his chest and
rest her chin on top of her hand, while he pulled a second pillow
beneath him, and then set his hands behind his head. His gaze
met hers. "It is akin to insanity, isn't it?" He laughed. "That first
night," One hand slid from beneath his head and fell atop her
hair, then played with a single lock, twisting it through his
fingers. It was a wonderfully tender caress, "ever since it, you've
been like a drug in my veins. I can't bare thinking of you with
him, Ellen. I don't want to let you go." He took a breath. She felt
it pull into his lungs, beneath her palm. "I know you are afraid to
leave him..."

"Edward," Instantly she pulled back, shifting to kneel
beside him and pressed her fingers over his lips, "stop. I did not
tell you I loved you because I wished you to make false promises
to me." Leaning back on her heels, her fingers slipping to rest
gently at his hip she added. "Nor do I want Lord Gainsborough
discussed in our bed. Forget him." She held his gaze. "Besides I

have known you barely a month, it is probably just an obsession. I was being silly."

"Whatever it is, it's a feeling we share, I..." Leaning forward she covered his mouth again.

"Edward." It was time for blunt words. "I know you can offer me nothing other than this. I don't expect it. Honestly. I cannot leave Gainsborough anyway." It was not a lie, she was trapped, but it hurt to say it. She had hoped for more, but that was a dream, she didn't expect him to make it reality. He couldn't.

She turned away, getting up before he could see the tears she felt in her eyes.

Rolling over he followed her across the bed and then his fingers clasped her wrist, but his grip wasn't over-tight, it just asked her to stay. "Stop running."

She slipped her hand free, slid off the bed and bent to pick up her undergarments then turned to face him, her clothes in her hand and held to her chest. His eyes absorbed her naked body with his usual reverence. That dark awed look of his always sent a coiling spiral of heated desire through her tummy. His gaze lifted and met hers, intent and asking why.

"What are you afraid of?" he challenged, his tone accusing.

She didn't answer, just watched his nude, nubile body shift into motion as he cast aside the cotton sheet and followed her off the bed to stand before her. Then his forefinger lifted and tipped up her chin and her gaze. "Stop running from me. I am trying to say I love you too, and I *can* offer you something. I can offer you marriage. I want you to be my wife and not go back to him, Ellen. Marry me."

A sharp pain struck her heart and her eyes glanced up to the ceiling, unable to look at him as she caught a breath into her lungs and stepped back. She prayed for strength, fighting tears as her anger flared. She shook her head. Offering the impossible was no help. She could not accept him. It hurt.

Was the man wearing blinders? Surely he could see it was no answer?

Her fingers, clutching her underclothes more tightly, she looked at him again. "Is this what you intended celebrating? Shall we break open the champagne, Edward? Or should I remind you what I am? I am not a woman men marry! And I cannot leave him!"

Furious, she turned and collected her dress from the floor. He moved to touch her, but she knocked his hand away. "Don't, Edward!"

She couldn't marry him. *In the fiction of dreams—yes. In reality—no!*

Perplexed Edward dropped back to sit on the bed, his fingers running through his hair. She slid on her drawers and tied them, then pulled on her chemise, ignoring him, her lips fixed in a stiff line, anger oozing from her.

For some inexplicable reason his offer of marriage had made her seethe. He could only assume she thought he wasn't serious. He was. He'd thought long and hard enough about it to be sure. He'd considered just offering her protection, but his ingrained honour-bound sensibilities had baulked at the idea.

He refused to keep a woman for the purposes of pleasure—sex—no matter the sentimental feelings that would accompany with Ellen. He loved her. He couldn't place her worth beneath his. Guilt had struck him even at the thought. His new-found happiness was in re-building her self-esteem not shattering it. He refused to insult her.

No, he'd decided he wanted to keep her, and if he wanted to keep her he could only offer her an honourable route — marriage. After all he was a second son with no fear of insulting the *ton*'s bloodlines. Heirs were his brother's worry. The blessing of a second son was you could walk away from status if you chose. He'd chosen.

His only problem was an independent income; he'd been living off Robert's estate all his life. He'd need to find some other way to support her. But having managed Robert's land for years he presumed he could easily find a position as a steward. His mind made up, he'd been walking on air anticipating her gratitude, expecting to be hugged and cried over, with happy tears. Not Ellen, no, only Ellen could see a marriage proposal from the son and brother of an Earl as offensive.

He stood up, impatient, and struggling to understand her unjust response, caught her shoulders and stilled her. "Ellen, I'm serious. Think about this. Surely you would rather be with *me*? I don't want you as my mistress. I want you as my wife."

Anger was apparent in every taut muscle beneath his touch. She turned away, her eyes full of pain, and continued dressing. "I know you mean well, Edward," she said as she moved, her words clipped and tight, "you are honourable and good, and for that reason alone I would *not* accept you. You need a decent woman for a wife. Not me." Her arms in the sleeves of her dress, she slid it over her head and then turned back, meeting his gaze as her dress dropped, sheathing her slender frame. "But even, despite that, I cannot. He'd kill you."

"Thank you!" he thrust back, lifting his hands, palms upwards, expressing his frustration as he reined in his fermenting ire. "It's nice to know you have no faith in me. I am able to protect myself, *and you*, Ellen. And if I cared about your status I would not have made the offer."

In answer his shirt was thrown at his chest. "Just get dressed, Edward."

"I wouldn't let him reach you!" he yelled, throwing his shirt to the bed before bending to collect his underwear from the floor. Pulling it on, he looked back to see her sitting in a chair, putting on her stockings.

Intensely angry he pulled on his breeches and buttoned them, then bent to collect his stockings and boots and sat to put them on, grumbling as he worked. "Stubborn, bloody, woman. I cannot see what is so important to you that you would stay with him. I saw the bruises he gave you with my own eyes. Why would you stay with a man like that?"

When his eyes lifted back to her she was fully clothed standing a few feet away and watching him. As their gazes met she walked forward. He sighed and she picked up his crumpled shirt from where it lay beside him.

She rolled it up while he watched her and then set it over his head.

He slid his arms into the sleeves, his eyes not leaving hers, waiting for an answer.

"Because I have to. There is nothing you can do about it except believe me. Just accept it, Edward."

Frustrated he stood, and his hands bracketed her waist, but the storm of his anger began blowing out. "Then for God's sake tell me why? If I understood perhaps I *can* find a way to help you."

She pulled away again, turning her back and reaching for his waistcoat and his morning coat. "You can't. Just leave this, Edward. Please."

His brow furrowed as she turned back with his clothing, her gaze pleading. He put his morning coat aside and drew on his waistcoat. He was confused. When he'd decided to marry her, he'd thought it the perfect solution. She obviously did not.

"Ellen, if you are worried over my brother's opinion I don't care for it. We could move away, somewhere no one will know your past and Gainsborough would not even think to look for you." His waistcoat secured, he looked back up.

She was standing before him with a well of tears glittering in her eyes.

Cut by her pain, his frustration burned completely out as her forehead fell against his shoulder as if every good thing he'd given her in the last few days had ebbed away. "Ellen." He embraced her. "I didn't mean to make you cry."

He longed to be able to defend her. Yet how, when she would not explain her reasons? Through his hands resting on her back he could feel her crying but there was no sound. Then she pulled her head away drawing herself up, re-establishing that bloody shell of defense he'd fought so hard to dispel. It hurt him to watch it.

"He *can* reach me, Edward, *wherever I go.* I cannot leave. If you cannot accept things as they are then perhaps this should end." She turned away to collect his cravat.

He shook his head, refusing her words. He would not allow this to ever end. He caught her arm and turned her back. "Not if—" Her fingertips covered his mouth again.

"There are reasons, Edward, reasons I cannot explain, I can't leave." The absolute belief in her voice furrowed his brow in question as her gentle, slender fingers began wrapping his cravat about his neck. Yanking it from her hands, her touch too much to bare at that moment, he took over the task.

"Reasons you will not explain, not cannot."

At that she just shook her head.

What on earth could she be holding back? He had been so certain of her answer. He had chosen her over everything else and she'd refused him—chosen Gainsborough over him. The woman had cast him a death blow.

The champagne stood untouched on the tray.

His fingers tying off his cravat, anger easier than pain, he turned back to face her, his anger broiling again. "Is it because of his money?"

His reprisal hit. Hurt twisted her lips and narrowed her beautiful eyes. Instantly he felt remorseful.

"How can you even think that!"

"Then tell me what I am supposed to think, when you will not say?" His voice was strained with his frustration, and straightening unconsciously he stepped towards her, his fingers balled in a fist holding on to his temper. She flinched and stumbled back, her arm lifting in defense. His anger drained again in the cold realisation that she thought he would hit her. In its place mortification struck him like a frigid dunking in a bath of ice.

He reached for her. She backed away.

Opening his palm, he beckoned her to come to him. "God, Ellen, I would *never* hit you." Shaking, sobbing without restraint now, she came to him, her arms reaching to cling about his neck as if she never wanted to let him go.

He was certain her tears were over whatever it was she wouldn't speak about. But if she wouldn't speak, what could he do to help her? Nothing. Nothing, except hold and comfort her, and keep her close.

His fingers tucked her hair behind her ear. "You cannot leave him, and I cannot leave you, so we shall have to go on as we are, and when he comes back you will send word to me of when we can meet, as you did before. Don't cry, sweetheart, please? Let's not spoil what time we have left."

His eyes closed as she continued to cling to him, and he could feel the beat of her heart against his chest as her sobs eased. Of course it would take her longer to trust him when she had known that brute as a teacher of trust. He wondered again at the things she would not say, what the hell did Gainsborough hold over her? Lord, he hoped one day she would trust him enough to speak.

He set her away from him a little and lifted her chin with his fingers. Her eyes were as mournful as they'd been that first night. God he hated himself for hurting her more. Placing a single light kiss on her soft lips, he then rubbed his nose against hers. "I'm sorry, sweetheart, smile for me again."

She did. Though it was obviously forced, and then her eyes still shining with sadness she lifted up onto her toes and kissed him, her tongue sweeping into his mouth. She tasted of cake and chocolate. He took her olive branch, his heart bleeding over the need to be loved he could feel in her kiss. She'd refused him, but she wished to accept, she said it with her body though she refused to say it in words. All too soon she pulled away, her gentle touch bracing his neck.

"Will you play lady's maid and do my hair? Then would you walk me home? I would like some fresh air." His lips compressed and then lifted to a smile, acknowledging the lightness she infused into her voice, as though seeking to set their argument aside.

"Yes, I will play lady's maid, seeing as it is you who asks. And, yes, I will walk you as far as St James Square, but I doubt you shall find fresh air in the city. For that you should have accepted my first offer and come to the country to live."

She smacked his shoulder with the heel of her hand, but laughed. "Does this mean, Lord Edward, that you intend to become an incessant nag? For if you do, I shall most certainly review my decision to see you again."

The sound of her teasing and laughter clasped a vice-like grip about his heart. A moment ago he had feared never to hear it again. She turned her back to him so he could put up her hair. "Has no one ever told you, men do not nag, they merely ask, Ellen. It is the fairer of the sexes that nags, men are above it."

She laughed. The sound warmed him to the very depths of his soul.

Later, dressed and ready to leave the room, Edward looked back at the bottle of unopened champagne, while his fingers slipped to touch the special license and ring hidden in his inside pocket. How different he had expected things would be today. He'd thought he would never let her go again. He'd thought by tomorrow she would be his wife, with no risk of their parting, no need to say good-bye. Instead here he was, handing her back into a circumstance neither he nor she could control, again. She must dread it. *Then why the hell was she going?* He couldn't work it out.

He turned, waiting while she pulled on her cream kid leather gloves and tied the ribbons of her serviceable dark green winter bonnet. It matched the heavy woollen pelisse she wore today. Instinctively the palm of his hand slotted beneath her elbow to guide her from the room and downstairs.

When they reached the street she fell into step beside him as his hand left her arm. And glancing sideways, he only had a view of the funnelled brim of her bonnet. If he were sensible, he wouldn't touch her, minimizing their risk of being observed as a couple. But he was not in a sensible mood. Catching up her fingers, he clasped them in his own. It seemed she wasn't in a sensible mood either, she didn't pull away. But then if she was of a mind to err on the side of caution she would not have dared to walk through the streets with him.

It felt good. He felt normal, in a way he had not done for days. He should probably go to White's tomorrow and seek out Rupert. No doubt his presence would have been missed. There was not being cautious, and not being sensible, and at the worst extreme being blatantly bloody obvious—he didn't want to go that far, and if the need for discretion must persist then he had better learn to be a little more prudent.

They crossed another street, drawing no undue attention. To the people passing them by, they must appear like any other promenading couple. As they continued Ellen stopped by a shop window and pointed out some piece of frippery with a silly sally, making him register for the first time her lack of vanity. He made another game of her nonsense. Stopping at a different window and picking something he would buy for her, at the next she chose something for him, it continued, no matter what the shop. But when they reached a ladies hat shop and it was her turn to pick for him, suddenly she turned.

The funnel brim of her bonnet framing her face, he saw her skin blanch, and her eyes were wide while her fingers tightened about his.

"Is something wrong?" She just held his gaze but said nothing. "Ellen?"

Her fingers squeezed his more tightly as her eyebrows lifted in a communication he didn't understand.

Behind her two women left the shop; Her Grace, the Duchess of Pembroke with her eldest daughter. They didn't notice him, they didn't know him well and he made no effort to be seen, not that he need fear they would recognize Ellen.

Tugging at her hand he pulled her into motion with a smile. "What, you don't fancy seeing me in a frilly hat?"

Shaking her head, with a hesitant smile and an air of someone who cast something aside, her fingers squeezed his hand again as she answered, quietly. "You're incorrigible and just for that I would buy you the pink one."

He laughed, pointing out a garish bright green waistcoat in the gentleman's shop next door, saying it would do her well in return. Yet when he looked up she'd turned to watch the Duchess of Pembroke climb into her carriage. "What is it?" he prompted.

She turned back and shook her head, her fingers pressing to her eye. "Nothing, I just have a speck of dust in my eye."

Shaking his head at her too, screwing up his nose in playful severity, he said, "What? You don't like my present? Well then, I'll have to find you something better." And tugging her to the next shop he then told her what Madam needed was a good cigar. It made her laugh again. But he didn't believe she'd had something in her eye. He did believe she thought the Duchess of Pembroke may recognize her.

But why? Had she been Pembroke's mistress once? His imagination began to roam while she pointed something out in another shop, his mind developing all sorts of tales. Had she lived locally to Pembroke when she'd fallen from grace? Or worse, what if she had been in service in Pembroke's household? How much older than his daughters was she? Perhaps she'd been a governess? It would have seen her dismissed and disgraced without reference. She would not have found another position. What if Pembroke had been the one who forced her into this life? The man was certainly cold enough.

When they reached the corner of St James Square, keeping out of sight of the bay windows of White's, she stopped and looked up at him, her eyes in the shadow of her bonnet.

Lord, he wished she would just tell him what had happened before, or at least what secret kept her under Gainsborough's thumb. Not knowing left his mind making things up to fill the gap. It was quite likely to drive him mad.

"I'll leave you here," she whispered, her smile telling him she longed for a kiss.

He nodded, his thoughts probably written in his eyes.

She smiled more broadly, playfully swatting at his arm. "You could at least show a small measure of sorrow at our parting, my Lord. Less than an hour ago you did offer for my hand."

It did what he knew she'd intended and drew his attention fully back to her. "The offer is still open if you choose to accept it."

"Are you nagging again? It is not at all polite to do so as we're parting."

He gave up a smile at her teasing, aware she was doing it for his benefit, to ease the blow of her refusal. Taking both of her gloved hands in his, he said, "As I informed you earlier, Ellen, a gentleman does not nag but merely asks, and I shall continue to do so as I will." Then leaning a little forward he whispered, "Until tomorrow, sweetheart. Will you meet me at the same time?" His grip pulling her closer with a sharp tug, he successfully surprised her into lifting her face, giving him the opportunity to reach beneath her bonnet and bestow a final quick parting kiss on her lips.

Pulling away, she nodded. "Yes, tomorrow. Do not be late." Her voice was a little shaky.

"Am I ever?" She didn't want to go back, he knew it. It was the same every day, her confidence shattering at the last. But he had no choice other than to let her go. He had given her another option and for whatever reason she had not taken it.

"Tomorrow then, Ellen." He let her go, watching as she turned away and weaved through the people in the street.

He followed at a distance, to ensure she made it safely to Gainsborough's, but stopped at the corner, watching while she climbed the steps. He saw the door open. Ellen stepped inside. Turning away he had a feeling that she'd left him for good but he laughed it off, thrusting his hands into his pockets. It was paranoia. They'd had their first argument that was all. They'd agreed on tomorrow. He would see her then, and he would have a second chance to make her understand what she had to do. Accepting his proposal was her best and only choice.

As he wove a path through the crowds his thoughts went back over their conversation. She'd said she loved him. He didn't think it was just words. The warmth of it filled his chest, but did nothing to waylay his confusion. If she loved him, why on earth was she not willing to accept his offer?

And if she stayed with Gainsborough and never left, what the hell would he do then?

Shrugging his shoulders he walked on, turning his concentration to the street. He wouldn't contemplate it. She'd accept him at some point. He would make certain she did. His memories turning to their love-making, he felt a self-satisfied smile lift his lips. He'd make damn sure she couldn't refuse him.

Chapter Five

Edward rounded the street corner whistling as he walked and acknowledged the lightness of his mood. It had returned to optimism overnight. He'd see Ellen in two hours. That alone made him smile. And when he saw her, he was going to ensure she accepted his offer of yesterday. He'd spent the time from dusk until the early hours of the morning sitting at his brother's desk thinking things through. Just before dawn he'd made some decisions and planned his assault with a more circumspect approach. Today he would pick the moment when she was languid and satisfied from their love-making and he would hold her close until she listened. He would declare his love and refuse to take no for an answer, he'd deploy every element of persuasion he had in his arsenal to get the girl to comply. Nothing Ellen could say would deter him.

The smile of anticipated victory still on his lips, he jogged up the steps at the front of White's and tipped his hat to an acquaintance who was leaving.

A footman stood in the doorway. Edward handed over his hat, gloves and greatcoat before walking on, and then called for a cup of strong coffee as he passed another footman. His cousin, Rupert, was sitting alone at a table in the middle of the room. Lifting his hand, Edward hailed him.

Rupert folded his paper, tossed it onto a low table and stood as Edward strolled towards him, smiling.

Edward offered his hand and Rupert accepted it, also clapping a palm on Edward's shoulder.

"It is bloody good to see you. I'd begun to think something was wrong."

Edward's smile lifted. "Nothing is wrong, Rupert. In fact quite the opposite, life is being particularly good to me."

Their greeting over, Edward sat.

Rupert did too.

Edward surveyed the room through the haze of pungent tobacco smoke which hung in the air like a high mist, noting the various occupants of the club, including the Duke of Pembroke in the far corner. Edward turned back to Rupert. Pembroke was the last man he wished to see after Ellen's reaction to his wife the day before.

In general, the club was quiet, but there was always an air of restraint about White's. Conversations progressed about them in deep hushed masculine tones. Across the room, there were several vacant seats by the window niches, those which tended to be populated by London's later risers, men like Edward's brother, the self-absorbed, who liked to pose for the benefit of the women in the street beyond.

Edward's eyes turned to the footman approaching with a pot of coffee and a cup balanced on a silver tray. It was the footman who'd passed Edward the note from Ellen the other day. As the man set down the tray he slid something from beneath it, just slightly, and cast Edward a meaningful look.

Edward's brow furrowed and he eyed the folded corner of paper peeping from beneath the tray and felt his heart stop for a moment. Without thinking he reached down and slid it free.

Why on earth would Ellen write? On the front of the paper it was just his name. Ignoring Rupert's blatant curiosity he opened it. She had written just three words. *He is back.* And then below the letter *E*, and *I will contact you when I can.* He could see she had struggled to find the privacy and opportunity for the simple note. His stomach solidified to stone and his fingers folded and refolded the piece of paper while his mind raced through what it meant—what he could do. He could not see her this afternoon that was certain. So how the hell could he persuade her to run away with him? The one thing he knew was, he was not going to sit idly by and watch her with that bastard. He shoved the note into the inner breast pocket of his morning coat and reached for a coin, then passed it to the footman and accepted the cup of coffee the lad had poured before leaning back in his seat to brood, resting one booted ankle on the opposite knee.

"What was that?" Rupert asked.

The shock and confusion must have shown but Edward met Rupert's gaze and answered, "Nothing of any import," in a tone that was a very poor impression of off hand. Prior to meeting Ellen, Edward had had no need to prevaricate, he was not accustomed to it.

Ignoring the sceptical look Rupert gave him, Edward sipped his coffee, his mind racing through his revised options. The first was to go to Madam's, the gambling-hell Gainsborough favoured. It was the only place he could anticipate seeing Ellen.

His gaze locking with Rupert's, he proposed, "Do you fancy a game at Madam Marietta's this evening?"

Rupert's eyebrows lifted in an obvious expression of disbelief. "I have not seen you for a bloody week. Do you really expect me to drop everything for you now? I am not your lackey, Ed.

"Do you even know how odd you've been acting? I wrote to Robert to tell him. I've called more than thrice at Bloomsbury Square to be turned away by Jenkins with excuses, and you are never where you're meant to be. Anyone would think you do not want to be found. In fact it is ever since you closeted yourself away with Gainsborough's little piece of muslin that you..." Rupert suddenly stopped speaking, his eyes widening in apparent dawning understanding and Edward watched with trepidation. He could see the puzzle slotting into place in his cousin's head and then Rupert's forefinger lifted and pointed accusingly.

"That is it. Is it not?" His growing excitement transmitted to the pitch of his voice. "You sly bastard, you've been rutting Gainsborough's whore!"

Edward moved like wildfire, his coffee spilling, his cup and saucer rattling, as he carelessly thrust them aside in a rush of anger and leaned his hands on either arm of his cousin's chair. Looming over Rupert with a sneer of irate disgust, he snarled, "Shut up you fool," in an abrasive hoarse whisper.

Clearly unperturbed, holding Edward's glare, Rupert's head shook once, in obvious disbelief. "You lucky devil, that's out of character for you."

Edward felt his lips twist in distaste, but his anger already cooling he realized they'd drawn the attention of the entire room. He looked at the table beside them and recognised Lord Banks and Bower, watching, among others of influential standing. Their eyebrows lifted. Edward stood, straightened his cuffs and nodded in their direction as though nothing was amiss, then turned to collect his cup, ignoring the equally interested stares he received from other areas of the room. Even Pembroke had looked up.

Rupert's hand rested on Edward's shoulder and Edward turned back, meeting his cousin's probing gaze. "So that's the way of it," Rupert whispered knowingly, smiling, visibly congratulating himself for guessing correctly.

Edward drained his cup and set it down, his anger flaring again at the sordid conclusion in his cousin's eyes. Then he gripped Rupert's arm and drew him across the room. "That is not how it is." Reaching the quieter space by the windows, Edward let Rupert go.

"Robert will love this," Rupert hissed.

"Keep your voice down," Edward snarled, out of patience, he did not give a damn what his brother would think. "This is not one of Robert's flirtations. And *no*, for your information I am not *rutting her*." He spat the vulgar word in Rupert's face.

"You are not telling me you've fallen for the slut?"

Within seconds Edward held Rupert by the collar and Rupert's hand had wrapped about Edward's wrist, pulling at his grip.

"Call her that again and you will be looking into a pistol." Edward shook Rupert once then let go and glanced across his shoulder to see if his outburst had been observed. It had not.

For the first time since meeting Ellen, Edward admitted to himself just what a tangle he was embroiled in. Heaven help him, had he really just threatened to call out his cousin? Rupert had been Edward's best friend for half his life. Edward cursed mentally, ashamed, and his fingers swept through his hair, his hand shaking. After reading her note, he felt like he'd been bodily put through a wringer, his emotions were in shambles, and he was in no mood to tolerate Rupert's slanderous and ill-informed opinion. But nor was it appropriate to threaten bloody murder.

"I'm sorry," Edward breathed. "I should not have lost my temper, but I will not listen to you insulting Ellen, Rupert. Do not."

Rupert viewed him with what appeared furious disbelief, tugging his morning coat back into place and then straightening his rumpled cravat. "*Ellen?* What the devil is going on, Ed?"

Edward sighed. "Gainsborough's been out of town. I've met her a few times."

Reproach burned in Rupert's gaze. "To what end? You'll not draw her away from Gainsborough. He's worth a fortune. You'll never compare. Women like her are in it for the money, Ed, she's using you for fun."

Edward shook his head, disgusted. "It isn't like that."

"No?" Rupert's eyebrows lifted again, clearly disputing Edward's answer, as he signalled to a footman across the room. "What is she in it for then? She is hardly with Gainsborough for pleasure.

"Shall we sit?" Rupert prompted in a brisk voice, moving towards a vacant table by the window.

Edward followed. "She never wears jewels. He gives her nothing." As Rupert sat, Edward did too, leaning forward and gesturing with a hand. "He knows if she had the means to leave she would. She is not avaricious."

"But *you* intend to give her the means to leave him, I suppose. You're mad. You do not fight against such men as Gainsborough, Edward. His money has too much influence among the *ton*. You'll never be accepted again. You'll have no hope of a reasonable marriage for yourself after such a debacle as that. And a debutante with a dowry is what you need as a second son, not a second-hand whore."

Edward glowered. "Shut-up, Rupert, I'll not listen to you insult her."

With a smile that said he was not intimidated, his cousin turned to the approaching footman and called for brandy. Then facing Edward again, looking earnest, Rupert pursued, "So what *is it* then, Edward, if not a mutual affair for the benefit of sexual gratification?"

Lifting an eyebrow in silent reproach, leaning back, Edward waited as a footman brought the brandy and glasses, and filled them. Rupert passed the man a tip. When the footman moved away Edward answered, his eyes fixed on his cousin. "I like her. She likes me. You ought to know I have no interest in debutantes. It's not an affair, Rupert, I've offered for her."

Rupert choked on his brandy, lifting the back of his hand to his mouth. He coughed and swallowed. "Offered *what*, Edward?"

"Marriage, what do you think?"

"You are insane. She's a courtesan! If you had offered her carte blanche I doubt you would have succeeded with Gainsborough's wealth still in the offing, but marriage? What did she do? Laugh in your face? I doubt she liked the idea of domesticity no matter how much she likes you in bed." A bark of laughter escaped his cousin's throat. "I thought so, she turned you down. The woman's bewitched you. God, she must be good!"

Edward's lips twisted with distaste.

"Ed!" Rupert lifted his palm to stay Edward's response. "What is wrong with you?"

"That note was from her. Gainsborough is back. We were due to meet but she can't get away."

"Ah." Rupert's eyes scanned his face. "The jigs up then, she's turned you down and deserted you. I suppose you wish to go to Madam's to have it out with her." Shaking his head a little, Rupert concluded, "I *will* come to Madam's with you tonight, Ed. For no other reason than someone needs to keep an eye on you, before you make a fool of yourself. As for this woman, just think very carefully before you do anything more. Do not take any steps you will regret. And remember I have a sister who is unwed. If you ostracize yourself from the *ton* you ruin this family's reputation and you ruin hers."

⋙⋘

Resting back in his seat, Edward's grip tightened on his hand of cards, holding them up before him, but his attention was not on them. Looking past the cards he could see Ellen on the other side of the room. She and Gainsborough had arrived an hour ago while Edward had been here for three, waiting, hoping Gainsborough would bring her, and getting more and more impatient. And Edward had lost money, a considerable amount which he could ill-afford, but his concentration would not turn to the game.

She looked at him. He longed to acknowledge her. He felt so damn impotent. He wanted to just get up and go to her, take her out of here and take her away, as far away as possible from Gainsborough. Only one thing held Edward back from it, Ellen.

Until she agreed, until she told him what tied her to Gainsborough, so Edward could persuade her to rely on him, he would not risk the man hurting her again.

She was watching still and Edward could tell she was trying to discern what he was thinking. They had known each other barely a month and yet he felt as though he understood her every look. His lips lifted to a smile as he thought of all the places on her body which would deliver an unconscious response. The intensity and direction of his thoughts must have reflected in his face, because, blushing, Ellen looked away. Desire shot to his groin, a pain that ran from his stomach down.

The pain of a sharp strike hitting his ankle beneath the table cured his building arousal. He shifted, leaning forward to rest his elbow on the table while his gaze fell back to his hand of cards.

"Careful," Rupert leaned to whisper, "the entire room can see what you are thinking." He was sitting beside Edward.

Edward smiled, not looking at his cousin.

"Gainsborough might be old, ugly and a cold-hearted sadistic bastard, but what he is not, Ed, is an imbecile. If you want this affair of yours to remain a secret you are going about it ineffectively."

Despite his cousin's counsel Edward's gaze lifted instinctively back to Ellen. He couldn't help it. Proving Rupert's words, Gainsborough smiled viciously at Edward from across the room, caught Ellen's wrist and pulled her down onto his lap. Edward's stomach twisted in disgust. Looking back at his hand of cards, he struggled to control the anger which sent blood racing into his limbs. It was done to rile him. Gainsborough was aware of Edward's interest if nothing more and was flaunting the fact that Ellen was *his*. Well not if Edward had any bloody say in the matter. But for now—*for now*—he must do as Ellen desired and let Gainsborough have his way.

"Your turn," Rupert barked.

Edward realized the entire table was waiting for his response. He hadn't a clue what cards had been picked up and laid, or what bets had been called. He threw away a card, any card, he didn't particularly care. Rupert groaned, clearly the wrong card then. Someone else collected it from the table.

Why didn't she find a reason to get away from Gainsborough so they could talk? Edward glanced at Ellen. Gainsborough was watching, and smiled.

Edward focused back on the game, forcing himself not to look at her for a couple of rounds, until he couldn't resist the urge any longer. Deeming it safe by now, his gaze crossed the room. Gainsborough was leaning to say something in Ellen's ear, with one fat palm resting over her breast.

Bastard! Edward couldn't look away. The air trapping in his lungs, his heart missed a beat.

Then Ellen rose and walked away on her own, crossing the room, weaving between tables.

His eyes followed and taking a breath he leaned forward. He should be careful, discreet, but he just wanted a moment with her. *Damn it*, he was not going to miss a chance to speak to her.

"I'm done." Looking at the men about the table, he threw down his folded hand of cards but Rupert caught Edward's arm as he began to rise, pulling him back down.

"Is that wise?" Rupert spoke for all to hear, his inflection telling Edward plainly Rupert was not speaking of the card game. He knew exactly where Edward was going.

Edward smiled, nodding to the rest of the table. "I'm playing poorly. What is the point of continuing and losing more?" He shrugged, looking at his cousin, acting the part of a man losing interest in the game.

Rupert frowned, clearly not fooled. "Just be careful," he said, more quietly, and lifted his hand from Edward's sleeve.

"Am I not always?" Edward replied, his own voice low, his eyes already turning to the door Ellen had gone through, as he rose from the chair.

"No, and I should say your current behaviour proves it," Rupert answered to Edward's back.

"Ellen." Her name was whispered with urgent insistence. *Edward.*

She couldn't believe he'd been foolish enough to follow.

The hallway was dark and all she could see was his silhouette against the light spilling from the main hall.

Her traitorous heart swelled. Just to have him in reaching distance caused a lance of pain to strike through her chest.

She'd felt empty without him, and her body instinctively craved the comfort he could offer, his solidity, security. She'd spent the last hours wishing for his hand to clasp for reassurance and his strength to defend her but now he was here she wished him gone. How could he be so stupid and endanger them both?

"Where are you going? How long do we have?"

Her heart closed against the desire to step into his arms and cling to him. Instead she whispered harshly, "Go away, Edward."

Trying to behave as though he was not even there, she moved to sweep past him, her pale green satin skirts brushing his leg.

He caught her arm. "Ellen, what is it? What's he done?"

She'd spent the last dozen hours in fear of Lord Gainsborough's reprisal. She was scared. The man had been asking her questions for hours, and it was a game of roulette as she scrambled together answers which she would never remember if she had need to repeat them. She'd been so silly. She ought to have known Wentworth would tell him about her absences.

She looked at Edward's fingers on her arm and then at his face. She could not remember the last time she felt this afraid. "Let go, Edward. I need to get back." Years had passed since she'd feared Lord Gainsborough would execute his threats, because she'd learned her place. But Edward had changed everything—he'd shattered it.

God, I've been so selfish.

Warring emotions of fear and pain clashed into despair. Her desires were irrelevant. Anger welling inside her, it rose up in a tumultuous whirlpool of regret. She was unable to control any of this. And now it appeared she could not control Edward either. The only thing to do was end this, then Edward would be safe and she would have no need to fear.

"Ellen?" He let her go, a note of pain in his voice.

This would hurt him. It would hurt her. But she had to end it. Facing him, fists clenched at her sides, restraining her pain, shaking, she pushed the one man she wanted to be with away and threw her anger for Gainsborough and fate at Edward, to make him believe. "Are you stupid? Why did you follow? Leave me alone, Edward. I have to go back. I said I would contact you."

Her voice was a harsh whisper, and the rasping tone was enough to tell him her anger was genuine.

He lifted a hand to touch her. She knocked it aside.

What on earth was going on?

Fear lodged in the pit of his stomach. Had Gainsborough struck her?

Ignoring her verbal and physical denial, gripping her arm he pulled her into Madam's private parlour, where this had begun.

A single candle burned before the mirror above the mantle, spreading a soft flickering light across the room.

Clicking the door shut behind them, with a care for silence, he then let her go.

Immediately she launched at him, slamming the sides of her fists at his chest. Her blows had no more effect than a bladder ball bouncing off a wall, but her distress moved him.

He knew she wasn't angry with him. He could tell she was just feeling trapped. His arms surrounding her, he held her. She fought for freedom and then suddenly, like a mare breaking to the saddle, he felt her energy to fight drain away and she clutched the sleeves of his evening coat over his biceps, holding on for a moment as if the torrent of her emotion would wash her away. Then a sob, overflowing with desperation, escaped her lips. The sound struck him with more force than any of the physical blows she'd thrown and when she lurched and tried to pull away again, he let her go.

A single flat palm struck his chest in reprisal before she backed away, tears shining in her eyes. "Let me leave, Edward. This has to end."

Stepping forward, following her retreat, his eyes scanned her face. She wore no makeup. She had no visible bruises. "Has he hurt you?"

"No! *But he will, if I don't go back.* Please! He only sent me to order a drink, I have already taken too long because I used the retiring room. Stay away from me, Edward. If you want me to be safe, *let me go!*" She tried to sweep past him, but he blocked her path.

She was scared, he could see that, but if this was to be his only opportunity to find out why, he was not letting her go.

Her palms lay flat against his chest, white satin resting on his black evening coat, holding him at a distance. He could change nothing. It had to end. If he would not do as she asked, it was better to push him away. She'd spent all her adult life hiding her emotions, why must it be so hard now. Biting her lower lip, she fought for control as her hands fell and she saw the candlelight catch in his stormy blue-gray eyes.

She forced a cold note of determination back into her voice. "I need to get back, Edward."

He gripped her shoulders and held her still, as though he was afraid she'd run. "Not yet. Just give me a moment. I need to speak to you." The handsome strong lines of his features showed restrained emotion.

This was breaking her heart and his, but she had to do it. "Edward, if I do not return soon Lord Gainsborough will ask questions. He already suspects." Laughter rose in a room above.

She glanced up, and then faced Edward again.

"All I want is a minute."

She gave up, seeing no way to persuade him otherwise, it seemed quicker to simply let him speak. "Say what you must then, quickly, and let me go."

Her voice hit him like a stone in his chest, it was dismissive and matter of fact now her emotions were harnessed.

"You're withdrawing from me?" he challenged, astounded. *What the hell is this?* "Ellen, do not..." He cursed out loud, and stepping closer, felt her physically recoil. His grip dropping from her shoulders, he stood before her with all the confidence of the callow youth loving her made him. She *was* casting him off. Rupert's words lanced Edward's brain. *Had she been playing after all?*

"Yesterday you said you loved me."

"Yesterday Lord Gainsborough wasn't in the other room, Edward. Say what you want and then let me go. But I will not meet you again, not when I can't trust you. You cannot pull a stupid stunt like this."

Disbelief and anger warring, his eyes narrowed. "Ellen? I offered to get you out of his reach. If you'd accept me..."

She laughed. A horrible vicious, cold and hollow sound. "Is that all, Edward, is that why you dragged me in here, to repeat your ridiculous offer."

Watching emotions play across his face, hurt, anger and hatred, Ellen knew what to do to end this. She thrust the knife into his heart to kill his affection.

"Why would I accept you? You're penniless, living off your brother. Could you buy me furs? You cannot *afford* to keep me, Edward." She could see he was stunned by her words. Her fingertips pressing against his chest she pushed him aside, feeling the firm muscular contours beneath his coat, contours she had spent the last week learning. Then walking past him she tossed the final blow. "It's over." Playing the perfect courtesan her skirts swishing with the undulating sway of her hips she walked out of Edward Marlow's life.

"*I won't let him win,*" he called behind her.

God, the fool. Anger returned in a rush, an easier emotion than the one which caused such pain. Her fingers fell from the door-handle and she turned back, her eyes narrowing on his brooding face.

"I am not a hand of cards, Edward." Her voice, like her heart, was cold, void.

Men! Was he truly no different? Did this all have to be about him?

"This is not about winning or losing. Whether you and I love each other or not? Whether I accepted your offer of marriage or not? You do not have control over this, nor do I. Nothing makes any difference. Whether *you* win or lose. Whether he was to win or lose, as you put it. I will always lose." She turned to leave. Then thought again and turned back. He looked bewildered, guilty and angry.

"Because you would not have his money?" he questioned, clearly insulted.

She could hardly be angry with him for saying it, she had planted that seed again, but it still hurt to know he'd believe it. Sighing, she carried on. "Yes. You said you loved me, but if you truly loved me, you would think of me above yourself. I am ending this because there can be nothing more. Surely it is better for us both to simply admit it, rather than go on. You will win, Edward, regardless. You are left with your life as it was before you met me, intact. Congratulations." With that, she did leave, shutting the door on any hope of a future without fear.

Edward's shaking fingers ran through his hair. She had dropped him, just like that. Thrown him off. Only yesterday she'd declared love. Stunned, in shock, he thought of his cousin's warnings. But he didn't believe it.

Why would she do it now? Her body writhed beneath his when they made love and she clung to him when they lay sated. She'd laughed with him, a dozen years younger. She had told him before it was not about money. She had told him too, she could not get away from Gainsborough. Then there was only one answer, whatever tied her to Gainsborough had made her run from *him*.

God, she was cold when she wanted to be, she had stuck a knife in his ribs just where she knew it would hurt the most, and twisted it. But he realized now, she'd only done so because she knew it was the one weakness that would make him believe. Low, was what it was. A bloody blow beneath the belt. Clearly no one had taught her the etiquette of boxing. They'd taught her how to annihilate with one swift punch.

What had she meant? You will win? I will always lose? She was not happy in the life she had, but she'd said she had no choice. She wanted to leave then, but she didn't trust him to help her do it.

His decision was unchanged. Despite her best efforts to rebuff him. All he had to do was convince her he was serious, constant. She was pushing him away to test him and he was not about to let her succeed.

Angry but determined Edward left the quiet parlour.

He noticed no one watching as he abandoned the darkness of the narrow hall. Ahead he could see Ellen re-entering the room where Gainsborough played. Edward did not follow. He had no intention of prodding Gainsborough's ire unnecessarily, especially as it was Ellen who'd suffer, but nor was he walking away. Sauntering languorously through the club's various salons he watched the play with a distracted air. But like a magnet it was inevitable his mental focus stayed with Ellen and eventually he could no longer physically stay away. He strolled back past Gainsborough's table not far over half-an-hour later.

Gainsborough had Ellen on his lap, her arms around his neck and his hand on her thigh. Edward threw her a disgusted look, which Gainsborough caught and returned with a lewd grin. Shaking his head, Edward's gaze passed to Rupert who was hailing him from across the room. Rupert looked to be having better luck than Edward, a pile of notes lay on the table. Walking past a footman Edward called for a glass and brandy bottle. He needed to put himself out of this bloody misery, and what better way to numb the pain.

When he reached Rupert, his cousin beckoned him to lean down and asked if Edward had spoken to her.

Nodding Edward made no effort to expound. Instead he pulled up a seat behind his cousin to watch the game, and when the footman brought the brandy, took the bottle and glass. He filled the glass up and knocked it back, then did the same again. But Edward's eyes never went near his cousin's game. Instead they fixed on Gainsborough and Ellen, and their performance. It was obviously played to spur Edward's anger. Staring, he kept drinking to deaden the blow of being forced to watch the woman he loved in another man's hands. But he was not going to let Gainsborough bully him into leaving the club. If Edward did, he'd fail her. No, he had to prove he was in this for the long haul, and he'd not do it by turning at the first hurdle. So holding the bastard's bloody gaze, Edward warned the son-of-a-bitch he would not be chased off.

⊰ჼ⊱

Three triple armed candelabras burned behind Ellen and two more stood across the room, flooding it with light, illuminating Lord Gainsborough's sadistic, lecherous glance towards the four poster bed. It dominated the bedchamber, fearsome and threatening. Her personal hell. Leering at her like the man before her, taunting her with its thickly carved pillars, head and footboard.

I cannot do this anymore.

Lined with paintings of women in a variety of nude poses, the bedchamber was a masculine room, his not hers. Its ceiling was adorned with a vibrantly colored mural of the naked Gods at play. The dark red walls intimidated her. She hated this space in which she was forced to suffer evil. She felt sick.

Lord Gainsborough's eyes turned from the bed to her.

Forcing herself to stand her ground, her fingers clasped the skirt of her evening gown, desperately clutching the fabric as though she clung to the edge of a cliff. Her palms were cold and clammy with fear as he reached to touch her.

She shivered with intrinsic revulsion.

She wanted Edward. She wanted love and security.

Ritually, this was the moment her mind gave her body into Gainsborough's hands and left it. But it was too hard this time. Edward had melted the ice about her heart—she couldn't not feel anymore. Her emotions reeled and utter despair burned inside her. She wanted to weep from the sadness of it, but she refused to let this man see how much he hurt her, it would only increase his satisfaction.

Pain formed a lump in her throat and she tipped her eyes to the ceiling, to hide the glassy shimmer of unshed tears, as Lord Gainsborough's fingers slid across the fabric of her gown, over her breast.

He knew about Edward. Gainsborough had been playing her like a fish on a line all night, tormenting her, threatening her, letting her think he had let it go and then returning to the point. In the carriage ride home he'd openly sneered at her, casting questions about Edward's ability, asking for details. He wanted to know what they'd done in bed, what she'd done, and what Edward had done to her. She had answered none of them, but even so Lord Gainsborough was more aroused.

Her stomach turned over and bile rose in her throat, she swallowed it back.

He wanted to see her cry, to make her beg him to stop. He would use her anyway. Her pleading would only increase his pleasure.

She had taken the risk of seeing Edward and this was the price.

But it was costing too much.

At the club, when Edward's gaze had locked with Gainsborough's, she'd known Edward understood. Gainsborough had mauled her as a taunt. Thank God, Edward had done nothing in response bar stare, and drink. Yet she'd endured his pain with mortification, feeling her heart break. But what could she do? What could *he* do? *Nothing.* She could not protect Edward any more than she could protect herself and he could not save *her*.

But she couldn't endure this, she couldn't, and yet she had no choice.

"What do you take me for, Ellen?" Gainsborough's whisper was low and threatening. "Did you think I would not know of your dirty little affair? Like a bitch-on-heat you ran to his bed the moment I left town. Was he good, Ellen?"

She let her gaze fall to the floor, standing motionless and silent, her heart racing in a sharp unfaltering rhythm. His fingers suddenly, painfully, gripped her hair, tipping her eyes to him.

"I like the thought of you behaving like a slut for him. Did you learn new tricks? Teach me, and play hussy for me, and perhaps I'll not choose to kill him. But it ends now, do you hear me? And to be sure of it, I've decided to fetch the boy." The threat was spoken in a honeyed tone, as though he was offering her sweet incentives, not cruel intimidations.

Her heartbeat faltering, the blood drained from her vision in a rush as she grasped his arm to stop her fall. Fear raced over her skin, lying like ice across a lake. She was trapped beneath it.

His face inches from her own she smelt his vile breath, stale with cigars and brandy. Her stomach revolted, turning over, while sheer panic pumped a surge of energy into her limbs, she wanted to fight, *or flee.*

"Violence never seems to serve its purpose with you," Gainsborough groundout in a deep growl against her ear. "I am sure if it was the boy I threatened you'd obey my every word, wouldn't you? I have sent for him, Ellen, and if you do not want him hurt you had better be especially nice." His grip in her hair twisted painfully. "No affairs, Ellen. You're mine. Remember it." Releasing his grip, he flung her away and his cruel, callous laughter filled the room. Ellen hit the floor hard, her head striking the boards and pain piercing her skull. Confused and dizzy, her fingers touched an open wound and felt warm sticky blood. She tried to think.

The urge to fight or flee swept through her veins again.
Fight? Flight?

Completely cold within, her limbs felt like stone as her body waited for her decision.

If he thought for one minute she would try to escape, if he knew she had the possibility of help, he would lock her up for good. But she did, and he did not know. She had Edward, and Lord Gainsborough thought her too cowed, too tied to him, too afraid to risk running. But if Edward loved her as he'd said, then he would help, and she would give him the chance. Edward wanted to know her demons, well now he would have no choice, he was about to meet them at their full force. She had to trust him.

Lifting her gaze back to her tormentor, Ellen saw Lord Gainsborough watching her with a lewd, self-satisfied smile. She could see he knew his threat had hit its mark. "Ellen." He beckoned her to rise. "Come show me what a good woman you can be when you wish. If you are good, very good, as good as you were for Marlow, perhaps I may be lenient with the child."

She felt sick. Her stomach clenched and heaved, retching bile, she couldn't control it. She was sick. Instantly, her arm wiping her mouth, she scrabbled backwards, away from the terrible storm she saw in Lord Gainsborough's eyes.

"Disgusting bitch! Wentworth!" His holler bounced back from the immoral images about the room and the door burst open so violently it flung back to hit the wall. She knew instinctively Wentworth had been listening to every word from beyond it, obtaining his own gratification by eavesdropping on Gainsborough's abuse.

"Clean up this filth! Send for my carriage! I will not be staying! You will regret this, Ellen!" He flung the last at her in a final warning, his forefinger thrusting in her direction, a promise of retribution in his eyes.

Ellen watched him walk away, feeling as though she was suspended in mid-air, poised above her body, her blood racing into her arteries. She would run. She had to run. She had to reach John first and she had to rely on Edward. He would help her. *He would.*

Edward lived in Bloomsbury Square. He'd told her where. It would take her half-an-hour to reach him, if they rode from there then perhaps an hour or two more to reach John. Could she reach her son before that bastard had him? If Gainsborough had already sent someone, would that be soon enough? Her racing heart missed a beat and turned her blood to ice again.

Ellen rose from the floor, her body shaking, and turned her back on the maid who came to clean the floor. Not Millie. She hadn't seen Millie since returning. Ellen crossed the room, going to the jug standing on her chest and tipped some water into a bowl beside it, then splashed her face. They'd turned Millie away. Ellen prayed her maid was unharmed. Did Gainsborough know about Ellen's letters to John too? She had been so selfish.

Ellen picked up a square of linen and dried her hands and face, then put it aside and turned, looking for her cloak. It lay over the back of a chair near the door. Her heart beating with a deafening pulse she crossed the room, and picked it up, allowing it to hang at her side. She said nothing to the girl who knelt beside a bucket, scrubbing the floor with a cloth, and walked from the room. The girl did not look up.

Outside her room, Ellen ran along the hall, neither hearing nor seeing anyone. They were all so convinced she would never have the courage to run, no one watched. When she reached the stairs, she hurried down, her eyes glancing about the hall below and above. She saw no one. But as her foot touched the bottom step a bark of laughter rang from the shadows beneath the stairs, then she heard footsteps moving away and the servants' door closing. It was Wentworth and one of the footmen. They laughed again but this time it was more distant, they were heading below stairs.

She waited, unable to hear their words as they drifted away, growing more and more distant. Then she heard a second door open and close. The sound disappeared.

She waited no longer. Running across the hall to reach the front door, she prayed it was still unlocked. The handle turned beneath her fingers and as the door opened cold night air rushed in. With just enough space to pass she slid out around the heavy wood and pulled it shut behind her, slipping into the darkness of the city and the chilled late winter air, into a new life that would lead her who knew where.

Chapter Six

Edward woke from a deep sleep, induced by the significant amount of brandy he'd imbibed to dull the pain of watching Gainsborough's evil games. He didn't like playing puppet, but the man had held him on a bloody string. God he was sickened by the things Gainsborough did while he'd looked on. And to watch it, knowing she didn't want him to intervene, had been like sitting before her with his hands tied behind his back. He'd wanted to stop it, to drag her away and send a satisfying fist into Gainsborough's jaw. But instead he'd played audience — impotent. It lay on his conscience. The lead-weight of it was now a hole in his chest and an ice cold stone in his gut.

His head was pounding.

No, it wasn't in his head. Someone was banging on the front door beneath his window.

Where the hell was Jenkins?

Sitting up, his fingers rubbed the sharp pain pounding in his temple, to the same tune as that persistent bloody knock. God, he'd have to go himself, the din was unbearable.

Sliding his legs over the edge of the bed, he hauled himself upright. His brain was thick, like treacle, his thoughts sticky, still fogged with sleep and the overindulgence of drink.

"Edward!" *Ellen?*

God.

She hammered on the door again.

The fog cleared from his mind instantly, his heart lurching into a fast kick. He grabbed his robe and thrust his arms into the loose silk sleeves. Already in motion, he left the room, tying off the belt to clinch the fluid fabric tight at his waist.

"Edward!" The high pitched panicked strains of her voice pierced the silent house.

He ran along the landing and was at the top of the stairs in moments. "Jenkins!" He hollered for his brother's butler. The man was at the door, in his breeches, his shirt tail hanging out, a single lit candle in a stand gripped in one hand, his other was about to open the door. But at Edward's call Jenkins stopped and looked back.

Lord Edward? Do you wish me to answer? The look said.

"Edward!" Ellen screamed from the other side hammering on the wood again, striking it so hard the sturdy door actually jolted. Jenkins's eyebrows lifted. No one knew of Edward's affair with Ellen but Rupert, and Edward had never been in the habit of introducing women to his brother's home. Undoubtedly Jenkins was bewildered by this out-of-character intrusion but he would have to deal with it. Halfway down the stairs already, Edward nodded sharply for the man to open up.

"*Madam.*" Jenkins barked as Ellen pushed her way through the narrow aperture, knocking the elderly butler out of her path.

Her wide shining eyes swept about the hall, onyx and silver flashing with uncertainty. Her skin was starkly white and the ebony tresses of her hair in chaos, half pinned, half fallen. Her black cloak and pale gleaming green satin dress were clutched up at one side, in what appeared a terrified grip.

She had an ethereal air. But God she was a beautiful, precious sight. His love for her was an ailment from which he never wanted to recover.

Jenkins a-hemmed, with a false little cough into his clutched fist as Ellen stood frozen for a moment, as though she was lost in the height and size of the grand hall.

She did look very small within it, and dazed.

"Forgive — me."

She'd regained command of her voice, but her breath was still untamed. Her chest heaved as she fought to speak, her fingers slackening their grip on her dress.

The fabric of both cloak and gown fell to the floor as Edward watched.

"Is Lord Edward — home? I need — to see him." A ridiculous reverence sounded in her breathless whisper, he presumed it was for the sage like butler and the opulent hall. "Please, Sir," she pressed again, her voice more urgent.

Looking upwards, Jenkins visibly waited for Edward's response.

Edward descended a few more steps, bemused, wondering why she'd come, and she'd come on foot, from the state of her evening slippers.

Her fingers pressing to her chest, he saw her struggling to catch her breath. Her eyes were wide.

Something was seriously wrong.

"Ellen, I'm here. What is it? What's happened?" Holding his hand out towards her, he descended.

A sharp look of relief crossed her face when she saw him.

"Edward!" She rushed towards him, meeting him at the bottom step and casting her arms about his neck, hugging him momentarily. Then instantly she drew away, grasped his fingers and tugged his hand, trying to pull him towards the door. "He knows about us! We have to go!" Panic had darkened and dilated her eyes, they were intoxicating orbs of pitch, surrounded by a ring of silver light, emphasised even more by the black frame of long sweeping lashes.

"Please come, Edward," she urged, pulling at his hand, without any recognition of the fact he was not dressed.

Gripping her hand more firmly Edward held steady, while Jenkins looked on, obviously outraged and astonished. "What is it, Ellen, sweetheart, tell me?"

"Edward, we need to go. *Please*. Have you horses?" Her hand pressed to his chest, holding him away as he tried to draw her closer, desperation burning in her eyes.

"Ellen, you're safe here, darling." One hand still gripping hers his other lifted to comfort her, but before he could touch her she drew back. His hand slid across her hair. It was matted and damp. Extending their joined grip to its full breadth, she tugged at him to make him move and follow her, while he lifted his hand to see what the sticky liquid was on his fingers. *Blood. Oh God. That bastard.*

"You're hurt," he said, tightening his grip and pulling her back. She flinched when his fingers found the wound yet let him touch it. But he couldn't see it beneath her hair, with the light so low.

"Fetch some warm water and clean cloths, Jenkins," he ordered, thinking she'd quietened down at last. But as his hand lifted she suddenly bolted, letting go her grip on his fingers. She stopped three paces back from him and her fingers curled into fists as her chin tipped up, ready for battle. It was the same look he'd seen in Madam's parlour in the club, and in the room of the inn yesterday. It was determination.

"Edward, we have to go! If we don't leave soon he'll get there first." Her voice was filled with pain though, and desperate.

"Where Ellen? For what?" he sighed, growing more confused.

"Edward. Please. I don't have time to explain! We need to go!" Her last words were frantic, her pitch becoming desolate. *"Help me!"* Her voice cracked. "You said you would."

Her tone said she thought he was failing her. His will to fight her crumbled. Wherever she needed him to go it was important to her. She'd not asked a single thing of him before. She must be asking him for a reason now. Finally understanding hit him like a punch. Gainsborough was playing the hand she'd feared. He was carrying out the threat he'd held her by.

Edward's mind was suddenly fully awake and his thoughts formed with deeper clarity. She'd run to him for help; she trusted him; even if it was because Gainsborough had turned on her again. This was his moment to prove himself. His chance to show her he could break Gainsborough's hold. *Time to pay the piper, Edward, old boy.*

He held out his hand and she came to him, catching it. Shifting the grip, he laced his fingers between hers in an intimate statement of just how thoroughly their lives were now linked. He had her now and he wasn't going to let her go, nor let her down. If Ellen asked, he'd follow. Lord, if the woman asked him to step off a cliff he'd follow if it meant she believed in him and would ultimately accept him — and stay.

"Jenkins, we need the water, cloths and the carriage. Have it brought out front."

"*My Lord?*" The pompous man who'd stood guard over the family for two generations looked aghast.

"Jenkins! My orders," Edward prompted.

Ellen pulled at his hand again. "Not the carriage it will take too long, we need horses, I can ride."

Edward looked from the butler, to her, and back. "My horse then, Jenkins."

"My Lord," the elderly servant acknowledged with distaste in his voice, about to turn and pass the order on.

"*And another,*" Ellen called at the butler and then looked up again. "If I ride with you, we will be too slow."

Edward squeezed her hand in reassurance.

"As Miss Harding says then, Jenkins. Have Tom pick one of the steadier mares."

"No, we need the fastest." She looked at the butler and then back. "Gainsborough's men may already be on the road, I don't know how long ago they left, if—"

Edward lifted their joined hands and kissed the back of hers, silencing her frantic words. He got the point, as did Jenkins, they needed to hurry. "So the fastest, Jenkins, with utmost haste."

Jenkins nodded and bowed briefly, throwing a haughty, holier-than-thou glance at Ellen before striding off. Then he stopped suddenly and turned back. "We've no side-saddle, my Lord."

"It matters not," Ellen answered, "I will ride astride." The look she cast the man in return for his slanderous glare, even Edward's mother would have been extremely proud to command when handling servants. "And do *please, hurry,* Mr Jenkins." She delivered these last words in a regal, irrefutable request, and then shocked Edward further by adding. "I'm sorry I disturbed you, but I am very grateful for your aid."

Jenkins's lips twisted in an instantaneous smile, his haughtier vanishing beneath a vapour of approval. It seemed the fact that the woman Jenkins had deemed a hussy on sight, had stood up to him with the grace of a duchess then thanked him regardless, had the butler nonplussed and mystifyingly mellowed. Edward's eyebrows lifted in silent applause. Jenkins never bloody smiled.

"Miss." Jenkins bowed swiftly and then departed.

"I need to dress," Edward declared, keeping a tight hold of her hand as he started leading her upstairs. He took them two at a time while she ran up each step.

When they reached his room, before he let her go, he pulled her close and kissed her firmly but briefly. Yet not brief enough.

She pushed him away.

"Dress," she urged him. "Please. We must hurry."

"Yes, Miss," he said, laughing and pulling away with a tug of his forelock. He smiled as he turned to find his clothes, unable to hide his pleasure. He had her now, and he was damn well not going to let her go again.

He hurried then, as she wished, and pulled open drawers, churning up his clothes to search for stockings, buckskins and a shirt and tossed all his finds to the bed. Then he tugged the tie of his robe loose and let the silk cloth slither in a light airy flow to the floor. He heard her sigh and turned to see her hovering beside the door. Despite her haste and fear, her eyes shimmered in open admiration. His smile broadened as he stood upright and, blatantly showing off, he walked to the bed to collect his clothes. He felt like a king with the world at his feet now he had her here, and as he dressed he swore to himself, whatever it took, no matter what this threat to her was, he *was* keeping her.

Buttoning his buckskin pantaloons he turned to look at her again. "So are you going to tell me where we're going and why?" he asked, sitting back on his bed to pull on his stockings.

"You'll find out soon enough," she answered, with a shrug. "If I explain, you will want to ask questions I haven't time to answer. Just hurry *please*."

A knock struck the semi-open bedroom door and Ellen jumped half out of her skin and turned swiftly, obviously ready for flight. If she'd had a gun, he thought his poor valet, Cooper, may have been dead.

"Come in, Cooper," Edward called to the man who stood gaping at the woman in his room. "Ah, I see you've brought up the water. Miss Harding cut her head, clean the wound for her while I dress, she's in a rush."

Cooper's eyes spun to Edward and he nodded agreement.

"Ellen," she'd paled again, significantly, and stood motionless, "sit down over there." He pointed to the stool beside the dressing table where his shaving equipment lay. "Cooper is my valet, let him clean you up, I shan't let you go anywhere in any case until I know how bad that wound is."

She nodded, hesitant yet compliant and moved warily about Cooper, who crossed before her to set down the water and linen strips, but brave as ever she sat down before the man, back straight and hands clasped in her lap.

Observing her in silence, Edward continued to dress as she struggled to hide a wince when Cooper touched her injury with the damp cloth.

She was scared out of her wits by whatever threat Gainsborough was delivering on, which meant Edward should at least be a little concerned about what she was leading him into. But at the moment, in comparison to what he was gaining, namely her, he didn't give a damn. To have the woman he wanted right where he wanted her was payment enough for any ensuing danger. His spirits were on a soaring ride to the stars, his hangover forgotten, or perhaps it was that which edged his excitement and sparked his restless, too-long-idle blood.

Shoving his foot into his hessian boot with a final tug he then stood and grabbed a warm, worsted riding coat from his cupboard, a smile splitting his lips. Turning, he saw Cooper had nearly finished. The water in the bowl was bright red.

"Is it bad?" he asked of Cooper as Ellen looked up too.

"No, my Lord, 'tis less than an inch, but you know how head wounds bleed."

"Then you think she is safe to ride?"

At that Ellen stood. "I'm not staying here, I'm coming. I have to go."

The damp, red stained linen in his hand, Cooper looked from Ellen to Edward appearing puzzled, clearly wondering what this was about.

"Cooper?" Edward pushed again.

"She'll do."

"Come on then." Edward held out his hand. She rushed to him, as though he was an island in a stormy sea, grasping it.

Sending a grateful smile to his valet, Edward caught up his riding gloves and then led Ellen from the room.

In the hall Jenkins stood with Edward's greatcoat in hand, holding it up for Edward to slip into quickly, while Ellen hovered, glancing back to the ticking hall clock.

Catching up Ellen's hand again, as Jenkins pulled open the door, Edward thanked the man, Ellen did too, and then they rushed out into the night. In the street, two of his brother's best hunters, which Robert had brought back from Spain, were prancing in eager anticipation of their unexpected late night jaunt. While above them a slender, sickle like, crescent moon hung in the night sky, watching their hasty departure, surrounded by a million sparkling stars.

He hoisted Ellen to the saddle and steadied her as she lifted her skirt and slid one leg across the pommel. Her magnificent gray's coat was almost luminous in the moonlight. As Ellen took the reins he corrected the length of one stirrup while the groom who'd held the horse moved to set the other into place. Ellen patted the mare's neck, confidence on a horse showing in her grip on the reins. The attentive touch was answered by a steamy snort into the frigid wintery air.

Edward's mount was a black, a fierce looking beast, with sleek muscular definition. Edward set a foot in the stirrup and hauled himself up to the saddle, sending his other leg across the animal's rump, then sat back and took the reins from the groom.

Edward nodded his thanks before turning to Ellen.

She tapped her heels against her mare's flanks with a sharp kick and jolted the horse into motion.

Edward spurred his stallion to follow her, matching her mare's pace.

At this hour the streets were virtually empty, apart from the odd vagrant, drunk, or dandy on his way home from a brothel, so they need not mind their pace. Their horses' hooves struck the cobbles with a sharp metallic ring. The sound bouncing back in a harsh echo off the terraces of brick buildings which flanked the streets, like a minute bell chiming out the time as they rode out of London at a canter.

꧁꧂

Kicking his heels again, Edward pressed his stallion on.

Ellen had led the way from the moment they'd left London. She'd forced her mare to full gallop and not slowed. Her cloak was flying behind her, undulating in the swift breeze of her fast pace. Her hair was caught in it too, long ebony tresses catching the air like flags, thoroughly untamed. Her dress had risen up to her thighs—her slender, feminine calves, coated in white stockings, hugging the animal's flanks. But the most intriguing, nay charming, sight was the line of pale flesh above the perfectly turned shape of her delicate knees where her stocking tops ended in a seductive taunt, and the emerald green ribbons of her garters danced on the breeze. The next time he made love to the woman he was going to leave her stockings on and run his tongue over that tantalising flesh which tormented him now.

She, however, was clearly oblivious to the lustful turn of his thoughts; she rode like a woman possessed—a skilled equestrian—as though the horse was a part of her and she an integral element of its broad muscular strides. She was a hell of a woman. And she was his. His mind just kept coming back to that one grounding thought.

He heard her urge the mare on again, calling the animal to reach for another wind in a soft whisper of assurance. The silence of the clear night air was broken only by the thundering thuds of their pace and the heavy breath of their animals. Their out breaths a surge of steam, rising in the sharply cold winter air, only to be ripped away by their pace, as was the mist of his own and Ellen's breath.

Ellen was pushing the mare on with such single-minded determination anyone would think all the demons of hell were tearing after them.

The unanswered question, *why*, raced back into Edward's brain as he kept his eye on the turn of her leg, and his body on her focus for speed. Steering the hunter to match her mare's pace stride for stride.

He had so many unanswered questions. Where had her life begun and how had it come to this, were just two of them.

And now he'd seen her ride, those same small miss-matched quandaries which had made him first ponder those questions struck him again. She was either a woman of extreme rarity, born with a natural skill in the saddle, *or* she'd been sat upon a horse from the moment she could walk. That was not the case for the daughter of a poorer family, even a gentleman's or merchant's daughter. Girls like that came from old money or new.

So had they fallen on hard times? Had she been orphaned? Or *had someone, not something,* forced her to this?

They were questions he would soon have to face the answers to. Whatever occurred from this day forth, wherever she was taking him, as he had so boldly sworn in the club, he was in this for the long haul. And if he was going to make her his wife, look after her, protect her, he needed to know and face the demons she was currently sprinting from with headlong speed.

The sharp thud of hooves, on compact, frost-bound earth, ran on in a steady unrelenting rhythm.

His eyes lifted to the sky, the endless blanket of inky black, with its scatter of diamonds, and the burnished sickle moon. At least the weather had played into their hands. The clear night giving them enough light to follow the road by. Even if he could not see the exact rise and fall in the black chasm hiding the track beneath them, as each long stride of the horses reached out in a statement of belief.

His gaze passed back to Ellen. They would have to stop soon. He touched the neck of his stallion and it was damp with sweat. The animals had run their length. If her destination was much further, then they would need to change mounts or let them rest.

"Ellen!" He spurred the stallion into a longer stride to catch her. "Ellen!"

Fully focused on the mare's pace, leaning low in her saddle, she didn't hear him, or ignored him.

"Where are we going? How much further?" he shouted over the rhythm of the horses' hoof beats striking the frost-hardened ground, the creak of leather and the jangle of brass tack.

Turning her gaze to his for a second only, determination in the silver glint of her eyes, without slowing their enforced pace at all, she answered, "Windsor! Not far!" Her gaze reaching to the distance again, she looked as though she would get them there before Gainsborough by sheer will.

He didn't want to have to challenge her, but knew he must. "It's *too far*, Ellen! The horses will be run ragged before then! We need to rest or change them!"

Her gaze spun to him across her shoulder. "No! We can't stop!"

"Ellen, you need to stop at the next inn and at least change horses! The horses have long passed their second wind!" He saw her heels tap the mare's flanks in answer and pull away.

"Ellen! You will not get there at all if you over push the horse! At the next inn we are stopping and I shall procure a change if you are so urgent to go on!" It was a statement, not to be argued. Her answer was a scowl thrown over her shoulder as she pulled ahead. But he knew she'd concede. The skill with which she rode told him she knew enough about horses to realize what he'd said was true.

Quarter of an hour later, Edward stubbornly ignored Ellen, who was clearly frustrated and fractious as she paced the courtyard of the inn. She'd refused point blank to take any refreshment. Instead she was waiting for him, restlessly watching one of the stable lads walking their horses to prevent any injury, while he selected their replacements. Running his hands over the animals' fetlocks, he asked the grooms to walk them a pace or two to ensure they weren't lame, continuing to willfully ignore Ellen's unspoken impatience. Once they'd done so, he pointed to his chosen animals and ordered them saddled, then turned back to watch her.

She was beautiful, even in her distress, and looking thoroughly dishevelled, her gown creased, her hair wild and tangled. He loved her best dishevelled. *And this dishevelled beauty is mine now.* He couldn't believe the level of emotion stirring in his chest each time he looked at her and had that thought. Yet he still wanted to know what this was about. The closer they got, the greater his unease. The question was, what was she leading him into? Surely he ought to be prepared for what he faced. From the way she now stood, looking ahead up the road through the open gates of the inn's yard, visibly wishing them already there, she was not running from Gainsborough, but running to something—or someone.

Suspicions had been racing through his thoughts from the moment she'd declared their destination. He wanted—no—he needed—to know the truth. He wanted to prepare himself for whatever this great secret may be. If she'd been too afraid to speak of it before, it must be something she thought he'd disapprove of, or fear.

Sighing in resignation, physically prepared to look her demons in the eye without flinching, he strode to her side, his steps firm, as determined for the truth as she appeared to be to get wherever she was leading him. Standing behind her, he rested his palms lightly on her upper arms. She was freezing.

He'd forgotten she was still in her evening gown with its short sleeves. As she leaned back against him, he rubbed her arms briskly to warm her for a moment until she pulled away and turned to face him.

"You should have told me you were cold." As he spoke his fingers dropped to the buttons of his greatcoat, slipping them loose swiftly. "Wear my riding coat beneath your cloak. I have my greatcoat to keep me warm."

He shed his greatcoat from his shoulders and passed it to her, before freeing the buttons of his riding coat too. "You should have said something," he reiterated as he shrugged it off.

"I didn't want to slow us down. Will they be quick?"

He glanced at her in exasperation and took his greatcoat from her hands as her pale gaze lifted to his face, looking desperate and pleading.

The glow of a distant single lamp warmed her skin on one side of her face while the other was in shadow.

He slipped his greatcoat back on, not answering, then undid the clasp of her cloak and slid the garment from her shoulders. She watched his face intently, waiting.

"They will," he said, as he hung her cloak over his arm before he took his riding coat from her hands and held it up for her to slip on. "I've told them we need to hurry. Will you tell me now where we're going?"

His coat hung loosely on her slender, smaller frame, swamping the woman and enhancing her fragility.

"Eton," she answered, in a quiet, hesitant voice, still with her back to him. He took her cloak from his arm. "We are going to one of the school houses there." His hands paused for a moment, stunned, before he mentally forced them back into motion.

He set her cloak into place and then his fingers rested on her shoulders and turned her, to re-secure the clasp.

She hadn't breathed and her eyes watched his face.

A child. His heart was slamming against his ribs. His eyes met hers.

She and Gainsborough had a child.

Is that what she'd meant about this being more than money? God, it all slotted into place, forming a picture which made perfect sense. That was why she wouldn't leave. He said nothing. The open courtyard of an inn, with others to hear, was not the time to press her. There would be time enough later.

"They're saddled and waiting, my Lord!" a groom called.

Glancing across he gave the man a nod, then turned back. She looked so vulnerable, as though she half expected his rejection. He caught up her hand. "Come on, Ellen, we need to hurry." Her fingers clutched tightly about his, gripping hard as he led her to the mounting block where the inn's groom stood holding the bridle of the stallion she was to ride. As he handed her up he brushed his lips to her gloved knuckles before letting her go. "We'll not be much longer."

Now he could understand her haste.

Ellen felt the very pleasant pain of loving Edward, a pain she'd learnt so well in the past week. It punctured her heart each time he moved her with an act of absolute trust and tenderness. The warmth of his body seeped from his coat deep into her soul, wrapping her in his security.

He knew the reason for their urgent flight but he hadn't turned away, nor grown angry or berated her for not telling him she had a son. He had simply accepted and reassured. There was no other man like Edward.

Her hand touched his shoulder before he turned to his own mount. "Thank you."

That he knew why she thanked him was clear as she received a repeated look of reassurance. "All will be well, Ellen. I promise."

She wished she could believe it, but she would only feel better once she had John back in her arms, safe.

❧

Edward struck the knocker hard for the fifth time and took a step back, waiting before the oak door of the large Elizabethan House. Ellen's hand clasped in his, he looked upwards, his eyes passing over the external ebony timbers, reaching like fish bones in a skeleton across the whitewashed exterior. Carved figures taunted him from the gables beside the door and he took a deep breath, not knowing what to expect here.

At last a light flickered in a room above.

Ellen's hand slipped from his and she stepped forward, pulling her cloak tighter about her and hiding her inappropriate attire.

Edward stayed behind her and rested his hand at her waist offering physical support.

They had tied the horses to a tree further back along the drive and he could hear the animals whinnying behind them, restless, pacing and pawing the ground with impatience having not yet broken their first wind.

His gut turned over as light spread about the stirring house, finally appearing in a window to their right, and as he heard the door's locks shift, Ellen's fingers pushed his hand from her waist.

When light spilled from the entrance onto the gravel drive Ellen stepped forward again. Edward didn't move, watching as the door opened to reveal a stiff lipped man, his tailcoat buttoned askew and a woman of large build behind him with a ruddy, round face. Both looked at them in questioning accusation and suspicion. Well it was, what, about five hours after midnight; certainly a little early to be calling.

He heard Ellen's swiftly indrawn breath. "Mrs Falkes? I apologize for waking you at such an early hour. I am Mrs Harding, John's mother."

While the Dame's expression shifted to utter shock, Edward set his jaw, refusing his instinctive reaction to Ellen's words. *Mrs. Not just a mother then, a wife too.* No wonder she'd refused his marriage offer, 'I can't.' Of course she could not, if she was already married.

"Mrs Harding? We thought—"

"As you may see, you were wrong," Ellen interjected with the sharp pitch that had sent Robert's butler jumping to do her bidding, "and I have come for my son. I will be taking him home."

"You do realize, Mrs Harding, the boys are sleeping?" The woman's chins wobbled with her chagrin.

Edward saw Ellen's fingers grip together before her waist. "We would not have come, Mrs Falkes, unless the matter was urgent. Please fetch my son?"

"And who is we, Mrs Harding?" The woman's piercing gaze turned to Edward. How much did she know of Ellen's life? Could she guess how things stood between them? How much authority did Ellen have to take her child?

Letting none of his thoughts show and setting authority into his voice, Edward eyed the woman with condemnation, for daring to question Ellen's right, and stepped forward. "I am Lord Edward Marlow, Madam, second son of the tenth Earl of Barrington. I have accompanied Mrs Harding to ensure the safety of herself and her son." At the mention of a title, most commoners crawled.

"Then where is your carriage, my Lord?" But this one it seemed was not so insipid.

Impatient with the woman's arrogant defiance, his instinct was to tell her it was none of her damned business, but as she appeared to be the gatekeeper to Ellen's son, he answered with restraint. "Unfortunately, the urgency of the matter meant we had no time to await the preparation required for a carriage and I am sure you would hardly expect me to allow Mrs. Harding to ride out alone at this hour of the night. Now, Madam, if you would fetch the boy, the matter cannot wait."

"And the Duke? How am I to know who you are, you could be anyone?"

The Duke?

"My son will know me. Send for my son." The conviction Edward heard in Ellen's voice, finally prevailed and drawing back the woman beckoned them over the threshold.

"Fetch the boy, Pitt, then we shall see." The Dame tossed the order to the man beside her.

Holding a hand forward Edward encouraged Ellen to enter before him.

While Mr Pitt went to fetch the boy, the Dame ushered them into a small parlour and bid them sit.

Ellen instantly dropped into a chair, acting pliant and patient, which Edward knew she was anything but. He could see her restless urgency as her fingers tucked her cloak tightly about her, then dropped to her lap, clasped and unclasped.

Edward remained standing and moved to a place where he could survey both women.

"A drink, my Lord?" the House's Matron asked him, giving him the distinct impression she was now, finally, pandering to his status.

"No thank you, Madam."

"Have you some word from the Duke? His seal? Without his say-so I should not let the boy go." Or perhaps she was just playing to his vanity in order to get to the truth.

Whoever this Duke bloody well is?

He fought to keep his voice level and his expression impassive, "I am afraid there was not time," refusing to show the kick he felt in his stomach when she mentioned the title.

He could do naught now but accept the child must not be Gainsborough's but this Duke's. The sharp pain in Edward's chest was undeniable, but he refused to heed it, refused to contemplate the questions racing in his head again. There would come a time for him to ask them and have the answers, but for now his role was simply to support Ellen.

Rising, Ellen's trembling hands held her cloak closed as her chin tilted up. "Is my word not good enough, Mrs Falkes? My son may be lodged with you at His Grace's behest, but I am still his mother."

Her determination made the Dame back down. He was stunned into silence too. He hadn't really seen this side of Ellen until tonight. Mrs Falkes turned and disappeared from the room, mumbling about the choirmaster being unhappy. Apparently the boy had a solo to perform in the King's chapel.

Ellen's eyes turned to him as the woman's footsteps could be heard on the stairs, "I'm sorry, Edward," she whispered. "I never intended for you to be drawn into this. I did not wish to make you lie for me."

Stepping towards her, his fingers lifted and brushed her cheek. "You know I would do anything for you."

His words were interrupted by the sound of light quick footsteps hurrying down the stairs. "My Mama has come?" The voice was high pitched and still croaky with sleep.

"Master Harding, do remember your manners. Your mother is in haste. She will not want you to make a fuss over her."

Edward felt the breath catch in his lungs. This was Ellen's son. His whole existence tilted on an unsteady axis.

The door opened wider, readmitting Mrs Falkes, and before her stood a boy, about four foot high, slender, with dark hair and astonishingly pale blue eyes like his mother's, rimmed with long, black lashes. Those eyes stared at Edward, widening in lack of recognition, then the boy blinked and lifted his fisted knuckles to rub the sleep from his eyes.

"John? *Darling*," Ellen spoke, dropping to her knees. "You've grown."

Edward watched the boy's face transform from mystified tiredness to utter delight.

"Mama!" The boy pulled free from the Dame and ran to his mother, throwing his arms about Ellen's neck and pressing his cheek to her temple. Ellen hugged the boy in return, tears staining her cheeks.

All caution and concern slid from Edward's thoughts as he watched Ellen hold her son. His fears were irrelevant before the joy of this reunion. In its place he felt only overwhelming satisfaction and pride. His eyes turning back to Mrs Falkes, he found the woman watching him. His look of fondness for the scene had perhaps revealed too much.

He looked back at Ellen. "Come, Mrs Harding, we should not delay."

Ellen gave her son one last squeeze, as though to confirm the boy's solidity and reassure herself this was not a dream, then rose. Once standing, she captured the child's hand in hers in a way that suggested she was making a mental vow never to let go. "We're ready. John, we are taking you home for a while, I will explain on the way." As Ellen began leading the boy towards the door, Edward turned to Mrs Falkes.

"Thank you, Madam," he acknowledged with a nod. The woman bobbed a shallow curtsy.

"You will keep me informed of what is happening, Mrs Harding?" she said as she rose, following the pair of them with her eyes.

"Of course," Ellen responded, but Edward could hear in her voice that her mind had already turned to getting as far away from here as possible.

"Madam," he acknowledged as they reached the front door and Ellen took the boy out.

"My Lord," the woman replied with a look of caution, her eyes again darting from him to Ellen. She was having second thoughts. He turned, ignoring the risk, and strode off along the drive. Their horses whinnied and stamped, their breath misting in the cold dark air. Glancing back he saw the woman still standing in the doorway, framed by the light of the house. They needed to get the boy away from here, quickly.

As he reached the horses, he met Ellen's gaze and spoke in a low tone. "I'll take the boy up before me. Mount up quickly."

"I will take him. I want to."

He nodded agreement and offered her his cupped hands.

Her dainty dancing shoe pressed into his makeshift step and he boosted her up.

Then while Ellen settled into the saddle and arranged her cloak to cover her exposed legs as her dress rucked up when she sat astride, he turned to the boy. "Ready, John?"

The lad nodded, looking wide-eyed at Edward, clearly still sleepy.

Edward smiled.

The boy smiled back, silver moonlight illuminating his face—so like Ellen's.

"Ready, Sir," he answered.

"Up we go then," Edward caught the child about the ribs, before lifting him up to the pommel of Ellen's saddle.

Ellen's arms surrounded him and he shifted to sit astride.

Edward untied the animals' reins and passed hers up. When his fingers brushed hers she caught them briefly. He glanced up and met a look of gratitude.

She smiled, let go, then turned her horse and tapped her heels, stirring the animal into a trot.

Edward smiled to himself, clasped his reins in one hand, set a foot in the stirrup and swung up. At least he was earning her trust. With a quick directional tug on the reins he turned the animal, prodding the horse into a canter to catch up with Ellen.

When he reached them she was pulling her cloak tightly about the boy to keep him warm. Edward mirrored her animal's pace and made a decision not to look back as he sensed the Dame still watching. Instead his eyes turned to Ellen and the boy. The child's expression was lit by exhilaration as he looked up at his mother with a broad grin.

When they rode out of Eton the sky gradually paled to the light sapphire blue of dawn, while a blushing shade of red stretched from the horizon in the east. The trill of birdsong rose, lifting to its crescendo in a mass chorus to serenade the breaking dawn. The whole night had been surreal.

"Who are you, sir?" the boy twisted to ask, looking sideways in Edward's direction.

Before Edward had chance to answer, Ellen's voice filled the distance between them.

"This gentleman, John, is Lord Edward Marlow. He is a very good friend of *ours*."

Leaning from the waist Edward bowed slightly, "I am at your service, Master Harding," and then formally reached to offer the child his hand, their animals' paces a steady canter. Accepting the gesture with what appeared a keen for excitement smile, the boy took Edward's hand firmly.

"I am pleased to meet you, Lord Edward. Thank you for escorting my Mama." The boy's voice mimicked the severity of an adult.

Edward smiled and let go of the boys hand "You're very welcome," then added, "I hope we shall be friends," before looking back to the road.

"Where to now, Ellen?" In the distance a crossroads loomed.

No answer.

"Ellen?" he encouraged again, but glancing across his shoulder for her response, what he saw was uncertainty, she'd thought no further than this point.

There was only one place he knew they could go where he would feel safe.

His gaze falling down to the child's he concluded, "We're heading for the Earl of Barrington's estate in Yorkshire, my brother's home, John. But first there is an inn in Guildford I know. We will stop there to break our fast and hire a carriage and then travel on."

"I've never been to Yorkshire, Lord Edward," the boy countered.

Edward reached across and pressed a hand on John's forearm briefly, the weight of this new responsibility settling firmly on his shoulders. It instilled a revived sense of purpose in him. "Then we will have an adventure will we not, Master John? Come, we have a long way to travel." With that he looked forward and tapped his heels urging his stallion to a gallop, throwing Ellen a look over his shoulder that called her to follow and match his pace. In answer he caught another look of gratitude.

"Can we gallop, Mama?" He heard the boy call behind him.

Chapter Seven

Edward watched, waiting silently in the hall of the inn, as Ellen glanced backwards to her son who was still breaking his fast. When she turned to face Edward again she clicked the door of the private parlour shut and leaned back against it, one hand still tucked behind her, no doubt resting on the handle. Always cautious, especially when she felt pressured, he'd noted Ellen seemed to feel better when she knew there was an escape route. The obvious conclusion to be drawn from her pose was that she was still terrified of something, probably losing the boy.

She looked up and met Edward's gaze.

"How is your head?" She'd shown no sign of concussion but even so he would be happier once she was in the carriage, resting.

"Sore," she answered with a hesitant smile, "but not a problem," she continued; then broke into a babble of apologetic words. "I'm sorry I put you in this position, Edward. I did not mean to. I can't even begin to tell you how grateful I am, but won't your brother dislike you taking us to his home? I don't want to be—" He pressed the gloved tips of forefinger and index-finger to her lips, suspecting these apologies had been damming up in her head for hours. He neither expected nor wanted gratitude. He'd offered to protect her—to help her. He loved her, and with love came responsibility and dependence. She was his responsibility now and so was her son. And he would not admit to longing to know who the child's father was, not now. The hallway of an inn was not the place for such a conversation.

"My brother is not my keeper, Ellen, he owes me this at least, and Gainsborough cannot reach you on his property. Once there we can plan what to do next in safety. I have hired a postchaise with a postillion rider to speed the journey and four men to accompany us. We have enough to change the driver and rider regularly so we can keep moving, weather permitting. They'll be armed, and we'll have at least two outriders just in case Gainsborough plays any unexpected games, so you have no need to fear." Completing the explanation of his plans, he let his fingers fall and smiled.

She looked at him, visibly nervous and uncertain.

If he'd lived her life he supposed he'd be cautious too.

"How is your son? He's well? Content?"

"I should have told you, I—" She started apologising again.

Edward shook his head. He did not want to hear it. The only thing he wanted to know was the whys and whose, but it was not the time to ask.

"You had your reasons, Ellen. I'm just glad you came to me in the end. We'll talk later. For now we should hurry. We aren't far from London, and we've a long way to travel. Have John bring some food with him if he's still hungry."

"Edward, you've not eaten." Her eyes held his, full of insecurity.

She must know he had questions.

"I'm not hungry, Ellen. I need to see the horses saddled."

"You are riding?" She sounded relieved.

Don't tell me there are even more secrets you fear the boy could tell? The possibilities he'd patched together in his head were now shambolic. He daren't even try to imagine what more there could be, but if there was more, he wanted to hear it from her, not her son. "Yes, Ellen, I'll leave the carriage to you and John. I am sure you will prefer to be alone."

Ellen felt a chill grip her heart. She'd pushed him away.

He was angry, even though he was helping. But he *was* helping, that was what mattered.

I have John.

Turning back to the door, resting both her fingers and her forehead to the wood she listened to Edward's footsteps striking the bare floorboards in harsh, brisk strides as he walked away.

She had her son. She could barely believe it. Yet she did not want to lose Edward any more than she wished to be parted from John again. Her fingers turned the handle and released the door.

John's eyes lifted to her and he smiled.

She smiled too. "Lord Edward asks us to make ready. Shall we pack some bread and cheese into a napkin and take a picnic?"

She'd not seen John for two years. He was so much taller, older. She had only seen him a few times since the day he'd been taken from her, hardly more than a baby. Blinking back tears, she crossed the room to him.

He stood. "Mama, is something wrong?" The concern in his voice reminded her of his father, all bristling honour and pride.

"Nothing is wrong, John, *nothing*." *Everything is right now I have you.* She lifted his chin and kissed his cheek. He was growing up. One day he'd be a man—a man she feared would not respect her once he knew what she was. Casting the thought aside, she hugged him firmly. She would think of the time they had together and nothing else, she was going to make the most of it, however long it lasted.

A few minutes later they stepped from the inn into a sharp wind which swept at her cloak and her skirt, spinning the dust of the courtyard up in a whirl about her feet. Edward was waiting by the carriage door. Clutching John's hand she ran to it and handed him up, but when her foot touched the step to follow, she felt Edward's fingers rest under her elbow.

"If you need anything, or need to stop, just knock on the roof by the driver's box." His words were a brusque statement, hiding any undercurrent of emotion.

She stopped, looking over her shoulder, opening her mouth to speak, but could think of nothing say. His gaze had turned to the outriders. She'd apologised to him already, more than once, and he'd dismissed it. He didn't want an apology, yet he probably wanted explanations she didn't wish to give. When he looked back, all she did was nod her agreement, before climbing into the carriage.

Edward shut the door in her wake and bowed slightly, possibly out of habit. He had no need to bow to a courtesan. He'd not done it before, not unless he'd been jesting. And actually, if he'd slipped into formality, it implied he'd set a distance between them.

Did he no longer feel close to her?

He turned and strode away.

She felt like crying as she leaned back into the carriage's leather seat and watched him walk across the courtyard, tall, strong and dependable. Confidence and command in his every movement, he called his final orders to the men he'd hired, then slipped his foot into his stirrup and pulled himself up into the saddle, as though it was the simplest thing to do.

The man was beautiful but there was an air of risk about him today — danger — with his jaw unshaven and his dark brown hair ruffled by the chill wind that had caught up while they'd eaten. His hand lifted, signalling to their entourage, and in answer she felt the coach roll into motion. As the carriage pulled away, she leaned forward to keep Edward in view for as long as she could, until he finally disappeared behind them.

John hugged her, drawing her attention back to him. Collecting a blanket from the far seat, she laid it over him. There were hot bricks on the floor to keep them warm.

She had thrust them both upon Edward's charity when he'd not even known of John's existence. Now she was obligated to Edward. She felt vulnerable. The circumstances were too similar to when she had lost John. She didn't know how this would end; what Edward thought.

Her fingers gently caressing John's ebony hair, she felt his weight increase as he fell asleep. She pulled the blanket up across his shoulders then rested her brow against the side of the carriage, looking out the window.

Edward was riding at their side, slightly ahead, his seat in the saddle perfect, the horse a part of him. He'd thought of everything when he'd organised this, in less than an hour. The thought did not reassure her. If he liked his life so well ordered it was hardly a positive thing, she had foisted herself and John upon him and thrown it out of kilter. He'd hired the carriage and the men. He was taking them as far as Yorkshire. But what then? She didn't want to think on it. She dare not guess the questions and emotions circulating in his head.

He'd offered her marriage but he'd not anticipated a child to support. He'd told her he loved her, but had John's existence changed his feelings?

A tear streaked down her cheek. She wiped it away. Now was not the time for self-indulgent tears over a life she'd lost years before. She had John. She must take things as they came, yet she could not help but hope she would not face the future alone but with Edward.

&ஒ&

Edward was jolted awake as the carriage hit another rut in the road. His gaze on Ellen and the boy, he lifted his head from the padded leather squabs, stretched his neck and arms, and took his feet from the seat opposite to set them on the floor. At their last stop, for dinner and a change of horses, when he'd told her his decision not to stop but press on as the night was bright, she'd insisted he take a rest and sleep. They had fallen asleep too. The boy was cradled beneath her arm, his head resting on her breast.

The child had clung to her all day, or perhaps it was Ellen who'd clung to the boy.

Edward recalled the moment she'd asked him to stay with John while she'd sought out the necessary after they'd eaten luncheon. Edward remembered the feel of a small uncertain hand clasping his. He'd been struck dumb when the child asked how Edward knew Ellen. He'd given a diplomatic answer, which was not an outright lie, explaining that they'd met through a mutual acquaintance.

The boy's inquisitiveness moved on then to questions on the horses Edward had hired, and Edward had agreed to let John ride for an hour rather than return him to the carriage. A promise Ellen had not liked but did not refuse.

Edward felt a smile twitch his lips, inspired by the boy's pleasure at the merest thing. It amused Edward. As they'd ridden together, the child on the pommel of Edward's saddle, observing the wildlife and sharing anecdotes of boyhood carousing, Edward's own renewed zest for life had grown. He had purpose again, Ellen and this child.

But there are still so many unanswered questions.

His mind searched through the possibilities as he watched them sleep. The boy was like Ellen in looks and nature. He was certainly not Gainsborough's; he knew Ellen had only been with him five years. Who *had* sired John? How many men had there been in Ellen's life? He took a breath. 'The Duke.' The Dame's words still haunted Edward. His brain had been cluttered with unendurable conclusions and suspicions for hours, that torturous emotion, envy, roiling in his veins. He hated thinking of her with others. He'd borne Gainsborough's taunting, even though it had made Edward feel physically sick, because he'd had no choice, but to think there were others who'd touched her like that was like having a knife driven into his stomach.

Does it mean I love her less?

No.

He looked at her, his sleeping beauty. She stirred the same longing as before in his chest. But he wished she'd not held this from him, and he wished he had the answers to his questions so he could perhaps understand and at least clear his head.

Who was her husband? Who was the father of her son?

These thoughts would get him nowhere. He was merely torturing himself. The fact was she was his now and he intended to keep it that way. That is what he should focus his thoughts upon. But he needed action. He could not battle the imaginings of a latent mind sitting here idle. At least while riding he was not haunted by images of Ellen with other men. Frustrated, a little angry at her, and restless, Edward reached to tap the roof twice, signalling for the carriage to halt.

⊰⊱

Just after breakfast on the third day the carriage climbed steeply up onto the first plateau of the Yorkshire moors, and leaning down from his horse Edward tapped the carriage window; signalling to her that they were nearly there and riding through his brother's lands. Since then the carriage had swept through undulating hills and dales. It was a county of emerald, with meandering brooks, heather clad moors and sweeping valleys; where a blanket of fog rested, hazy in the early sunshine and flocks of sheep grazed, the first young lambs of spring bouncing and skipping about them.

Finally, the carriage crossed the brow of a hill and the road began following the line of a high stone wall. After another few miles the wall turned back from the verge, opening onto a large gray stone gatehouse and a set of broad iron gates, which rested open, the carriage turned.

The entrance was guarded by two formidable lion statues with the Barrington family crest resting before their paws. The carriage swept through and stopped just inside the gates as Edward leaned forward in his saddle to speak with a man in maroon and gold edged livery. On the other side of the carriage, John twisted to kneel on the seat by the window and pressed his brow and fingers against the frigid glass, his breath forming an area of fog on the translucent pane while he watched the gatekeeper remove his hat and bow. Then, lifting his hand, Edward called the coach back into motion and the man stepped back.

"Mama, may I open the window to see?" At her nod John slid off the seat and crossed the carriage to climb onto her lap, then tugged the window strap to jolt it down. The cold winter air rushed into the small carriage and she slipped her arms about his lean midriff, holding him securely as he leaned out the window.

The carriage rumbled along through a long avenue lined with towering horse-chestnut trees and at a turn in the gravelled drive she saw it snaked down into a valley and back up the other side.

When the coach reached the next brow and crossed over the top, in the distance she saw the first glimpse of Edward's home, Farnborough, the Earl of Barrington's country residence, Edward's family seat. The carriage continued on a downward slope into the valley where his brother's property stood.

The place was vast, fronted by in the region of two dozen windows or more. At the heart, an ancient Norman keep reached skyward, surrounded by towering turrets. It was flanked by two large wings, built in a gothic style, gray stone, to blend in with the old, although their appearance was more histrionic than historic.

Her feelings of trepidation grew, her eyes never leaving the building as the carriage drew closer. Then they swept beneath an archway and a raised portcullis into a central courtyard. The noise of iron horseshoes ringing on the cobbles filled the air as the carriage and outriders came to a halt. Edward dismounted before a large fountain which splashed in the center of the courtyard.

No wonder she'd heard people say he was at a loss for what to do in London. He'd managed all this on behalf of his brother for years. It was his home. A cold shiver ran across her skin. What if they were not welcome? She'd had days to fret over it and when she'd tried to speak to Edward he'd merely dismissed her concerns. They'd had no opportunity to speak in private. She still had no knowledge of his feelings and feared he was only helping them to fulfil his promise. A gentleman's word was his honour. *Honour. That godforsaken word.* Oh, she knew all about that cold-hearted sanctuary of reputation. She didn't want Edward to help them because he'd made a promise before he'd even known of John. She wanted him to help them because he *wanted* to. She wanted to know how he felt about her now and what he felt about John.

When Edward opened the carriage door, he smiled and lifted John down. "Welcome to Farnborough," Edward said, pleasure and pride in every syllable as he set John on his feet.

Then Edward turned to her, while John beamed, his eyes skimming over the buildings about the courtyard, wide with expectation.

"Ellen?" Edward offered his hand to help her onto the step which a man, clothed in the same livery as the gatekeeper, had dropped into place. "We are home." Edward's whole demeanour was flooded with pride. But it wasn't her home.

She accepted his aid and stepped down, aware of her travel-stained clothes and the increasing number of servants filling the small courtyard. She still wore the evening dress she had fled in. Pulling her cloak about her more securely, she found herself facing an approaching servant.

"Davis!" Edward acknowledged, his voice full of affection.

"Lord Edward. The Earl will be pleased you have returned, but I am afraid he is not here. He's gone to London, my Lord. I had believed his Lordship's intention was to speak with you. He received an urgent letter from Lord Rupert."

Ellen felt the servant's eyes scan her in assessment and saw Edward's expression darken. "Rupert? When did Robert leave?"

"Two days ago, my Lord."

"Then it could be a week or more before he returns.

"Davis, I must introduce Mrs Harding and her son, Master John."

As the servant gave her a slightly austere and judgemental look, Edward added, "They are to be made welcome, they are my guests, Davis. Give Mrs Harding the yellow room with the view of the lake, John may have full use of the nursery floor. I believe our collection of soldiers is still up there." He cast a smile to John. "Margaret can take him up. And we all require baths and refreshment at once, Davis. You may ask Jill to attend Mrs Harding." Edward turned to Ellen then, as John tugged her hand, urging her to follow the servant.

"Go with Davis. I'll see to the horses and men, Ellen. Take John in."

Meeting his gaze, Ellen felt herself dismissed in the same way he'd dismissed his brother's servant. She nodded and turned to face the sober, challenging gaze of the man he'd called Davis. She'd encountered this judging look most of her life, but not before her son. She pulled John close, her instinct to flee, but without Edward there was nowhere they could go. She did not even have a farthing to her name. There was nothing else to do but follow the scowling servant.

He led them into the house to a family sitting room. It was dark, wreathed in shadow, but homely, panelled with aged oak and cluttered with well-used furniture. Two red sofas flanked the unlit fire, and three chairs stood further back.

Her gaze lifted to a full-length portrait of a man above the mantelpiece, he had the same coloring and imposing stature as Edward. His hair was swept back in a queue, with gray shadowing his temples. Edward's father she supposed. She could see the mansion painted in the distance behind him.

"Master John."

A woman in perhaps her fifties, or early sixties, stepped in through the open door, dressed in a gray uniform with a starched white apron and mobcap. As Ellen turned to face her John pressed close to her side and the woman bobbed a shallow curtsy. "Mrs Harding? I am Margaret. I was asked to take the young master up to the nursery."

"Mama?" John's hand gripped more tightly about Ellen's.

"Perhaps I should come too," Ellen responded, squeezing her son's hand in return.

In answer, drawing closer, the woman dropped into a chair, facing John at his own height. "Now then, Master John, there's no need to bother your Mama, is there? She will want to have a bath and change after your journey too. If you come along with me we can sort out a tub for you, and I can find all of Lord Edward's and Lord Barrington's old toys. Then perhaps we could toast some crumpets by the fire and have some sugared tea?"

John let go of Ellen's hand and drew away. The woman had won over her son in a moment. Warring relief and concern possessed Ellen. She did not really want to let him go, she'd only just got him back. The nursemaid stood and took John's hand as he came to her. "No need to worry, Mrs Harding, Master John and I shall get along just fine, and as soon as you are ready you may ask Jill to show you up and pay a visit. If Master John needs you before then I will send word."

"Thank you, Margaret," Ellen answered, clearly requiring more reassurance than her son. She still felt bewildered, afraid, knowing she should not be here. As they turned to leave, John immediately started telling the nursemaid tales of their journey, talking of Edward. He'd spent hours riding with Edward as they'd traveled and was beginning to idolize him.

Left with nothing to deny her confused thoughts, crossing the room, Ellen studied a group of miniatures. The small ivory ovals, trimmed by polished brass, hung in a cluster. There were five. Three were children. Her fingers touched the one in the center she believed to be Edward, an impish smile on his face. Beside him was a girl who looked younger than him, but she did not remember him mentioning a sister. The two miniatures above were of his parents. One was identical to the portrait above the mantle, if perhaps an impression painted at a younger age, and the woman beside him was stunningly beautiful.

"Madam."

Ellen turned and blushed, caught prying. A young maid stood in the doorway. She too bobbed a curtsy, although her eyes surveyed every detail of Ellen's appearance, wide and assessing, studying her as an interloper in Edward's life. Gentlemen in general kept their mistresses at a distance from their family. Edward had stepped across a boundary in bringing them here. The servants knew it, even if he did not. Again she feared his brother would cast them out, her and John, when he returned. She had a few days though, to think, to plan—to talk.

⁓⁓

Pacing the small drawing-room, which he'd always used as his private retreat, Edward drank the last of the brandy in his glass. His gaze lifting, he met the eyes of his father as they looked on in measured, imperious, judgement from his portrait.

His father would not have liked him bringing Ellen here. He would not have liked her immorality. But he would have appreciated his chosen bride's remarkable beauty, her demure yet immovable courage, and if none of the former had won him over, he would have fallen for Ellen's charm in the end, Edward was sure. Who could not? After all she'd tipped Jenkins's stubborn, thoroughly English, stiff upper lip into a smile, and now Davis had seemingly been swung about from north to south. His frosty welcome had thawed to a silent almost pitiful adulation as she oh so carefully minded her p's and q's with the man. Throwing at him the occasional sweet as sugar smile in gratitude for the way he fawned over her son.

In contrast Edward had been out of sorts, unable to look at her during dinner, knowing the moment had come for him to ask his questions, though he did not wish to hear the answers. They'd barely spoken on the way up here, the chasm between them widening with every mile, unasked and unanswered questions hanging between them.

She'd been silent through dinner, pushing her food about the plate with her fork, while John had rattled on about all sorts of nonsensical balderdash, wants and wishes. Edward knew the child was excited over his new home and hungry for adventure, and Edward liked John's company, but wanted to speak to Ellen. Now she'd taken John up to bed, with a promise to return. When she did, Edward had not intended to push for answers immediately, but he knew he must, he needed to put her past aside.

He heard the door hinges creak behind him and turned back. She was standing there.

"Come in, Ellen. Shut the door. Can I pour you something to drink?" His voice sounded clipped, lacking in emotion, even to his own ears.

"No, thank you." As she stepped into the room he watched her gaze skim over him, looking from his polished evening shoes up to his clean shaven jaw and then at the lock of hair which he'd felt fall forward onto his brow. He set his empty glass down on the silver tray with a hollow clink and lifted his fingers to slick back the errant lock.

She closed the door, crossed the room and occupied a single chair, as though she was entering a court, casting him as judge and jury.

He didn't wish to intimidate her. Folding his body into a seat opposite he slouched back, his fingers gripping the scrolled leather arms, in an attempt to set her at her ease. It failed. She remained ramrod straight, her fingers clasped in her lap. He had the strong impression she was not going to make this easy no matter what he did. And thus there was only one thing to do and that was to come right out with it and damn the consequence. Suddenly he felt immensely younger, all of the four years that parted them in age.

"I do not wish to force you in to speaking—"

"But you wish to know who John's father is?" she interrupted, her gaze meeting his—challenging him—daring him to deny it. He said nothing, waiting on her words. He wanted to know who her husband was too. Were they one in the same?

On a sigh she began the tale, a slow yet deliberate note to her voice, "Very well. He was, *is*, the son of my husband, Major Paul Harding." Edward sucked in a breath. "He is dead, Edward," she said in answer to his response. "I met Paul when I was sixteen. We married in my seventeenth year. I followed his regiment with other wives." Her gaze left his then, falling away to a memory Edward would never see. "He died at Waterloo, before I'd discovered I was carrying John. Paul never even knew." That pale crystal-blue all absorbing gaze, met his again, sharp, unbending.

"If you would know the rest?"

Of course he wanted to know. He had always wanted to know, ever since he'd met her, before he even knew about the child. He wanted to know every man who'd been before him and then he would call all of the bastards out, one by one, for bringing her down to something he was certain even she abhorred. Fighting a vicious battle with his emotions, he said nothing but gave a stiff decline of his head bidding her go on.

With a little shrug, implying she was throwing caution to the wind and risking his judgement, she continued, "Paul's Lieutenant Colonel took me under his wing. I had to eat. I had no way to get home. He offered me both. The army had not paid Paul in months, his Lieutenant Colonel knew it. He asked for nothing from me at first, but after John was born he wanted something in return. You understand there was not only my mouth to feed then but John's too. And as he so forcefully pointed out I was already indebted to him—obliged. There was only one way in which he would accept payment. I knew it was wrong of me, but I was out of my depth." Her bright eyes flashed a spark in his direction, visibly daring Edward to condemn her in word or deed.

He did not, instead he gave her an understanding smile. He'd always known she'd never chosen to live as she'd done. It belied his desire to tear the bastard limb from limb.

She smiled back with a bolstered, more confident, look. "I was terrified, but didn't know what else to do. All I thought of was John. And then one night the Lieutenant Colonel came home and told me he'd lost me in a game of cards to another man, a

General. I argued and fought against it, but in the end, again, I had no choice. I had nowhere else to go. From that moment on I have been passed from one man to another as a possession, bought and sold."

Including some Duke, who must have somehow got his claws into her son.

Her shoulders lifted and fell again, this time the gesture implied her bitter acceptance of the fact and her helplessness. And it did not escape Edward that she'd first passed to him via a card game too. He felt ashamed.

"I could not change it, so I learned to live with it. That is my tale." She delivered the simple statement in the way another woman would accept a green trim for their bonnet instead of pink.

Endured it, yes, and established her shell.

Oh yes, he'd seen how she guarded herself from hurt—from the mental intrusion if she could not protect herself from the physical. But she had not succeeded in hiding her pain from him. Her situation had stolen her life from her, stolen her son.

She looked tired, worn and bleak suddenly. She didn't like the woman she'd become, nor the choices she'd made, he could see. Yet that was the point, was it not? The whole point of what she'd just told him. This life had never been her choice. It was where the dice of fortune had cast her. She was driftwood on the tide of fate, nothing else. That tide had brought her to him.

I am her choice and she is free to accept my offer, a widow not a wife.

He could give her the power over her future now. Let her play with providence for a change instead of providence tossing her about on its own whim. He could free her from that life for forever.

"Ellen." Her gaze piercing his as sharply as the sun reflecting off an ice encrusted lake her eyes dared him to judge again. "What of your family? Did neither your own, nor your husband's offer help?"

Her skin reddened in a deep crimson blush. For a fleeting moment he thought there was something more she held back, but when she spoke his assumption was forgotten. "I wrote to them both, there was no reply. They have never helped me." Her gaze falling away from him, she stood. "If you have heard enough, I admit to being tired."

"Ellen, wait." He rose. "I will send word to the vicar and ask him to meet me first thing in the morning. We can be married tomorrow."

Her gaze flew to his face, astonishment and accusation in her eyes. "You are not asking me? Am I not a part of the decision, Edward?"

Lifting his hands, palms outwards, warding off her anger, he responded. "I know you said no before, but surely things are different now?"

"You mean now I am pushed into a corner again."

She would have turned away, but he caught her arm. "Ellen, I won't force you into anything you don't wish for, but I thought you would understand. This is the best way in which I can offer you protection. Now I know of John, does it not make even more sense? It is still your choice, but I can only truly protect you if you accept my offer, if—"

Her arm tugging loose from his grip, she broke his sentence with fury in her voice. "Were you not listening? I have heard this argument before! Without me what else will you do! It is of course your choice, but you have no other option!"

She verbally punched him in the gut with her words. He was not those men. He was offering her his name, not just his protection. God, could the woman not see and hear how much he loved her. He needed her. He could not bloody breathe without her. But perhaps that was the only way to prove the sincerity of his feeling. To persuade her he was in earnest perhaps he had to be prepared to let her go. He remembered his silent promise of but moments ago, to give her, her freedom.

His hand dropping, as though a lead-weight hung from it, he answered, "I am not like them, Ellen. Have I treated you like them? I am offering you my name and my home if you marry me. Gainsborough cannot reach you then. No man can have a hold over you ever again if that is what you wish. How you live afterwards can be your choice. I'll claim no right over you."

His eyes fell away from her vivid gaze, which assessed him so acutely. "If you don't agree to my offer, you may stay here as long as you wish. I will ask for nothing in return, *ever*, whether you accept my offer or not. Your future is in your hands either way, Ellen. Do as you wish and I'll abide by your decision."

Her mouth had fallen open as she listened to him, her palm pressing to the expanse of bare flesh at her chest, index finger and thumb resting along her collar bone, as though controlling her quickening breaths.

When she made no effort to speak, "Ellen?" he pushed her, meeting her gaze again, impatient to know his sentence. If he was to be cast aside into purgatory he wished to know it. When still she merely stood staring at him, he pressed again, unable to keep the anguished croak from his voice. "For God's sake, Ellen, put me out of my misery. I feel as though I have just lain my head beneath the guillotine. Aye or nay? A false marriage, a true marriage or nothing at all?"

Her eyes suddenly sparkled like fine diamonds, glinting with the light from the candles in the wall sconces, and tears. Her silk glove coated fingers touched his cheek, the pad of her thumb falling on his lip. "You misunderstood me, Edward. I love you. I want to be with you. *But marriage?* It's such a big step to make, and, and I am not the sort of woman a mother would wish a man to wed. Won't your brother disapprove? What if he were to disown you? What then? What if all your friends and family cut you? It is not just me I'm thinking of."

His fingers captured hers, drawing them away, as his thumb brushed across the fabric covering her palm.

"Ellen, I cannot offer you the opulence of an address like this, nor do I have Gainsborough's money to put you up in a smart townhouse, but I have run Robert's estates for years, I can take a steward's post, we will have accommodation and no one will know of your past. If my friends and family cannot see the good I see in you, Ellen, then let them cut me." He must have said something right for she rose up on to her toes and kissed him on the cheek tenderly.

"You would give up your family for me?"

"I will give up everything if I must. You and John will be my family. I swear to you I will treat him as my own son." His hands spanning her tiny waist, he continued. "Ellen Harding, I love you, become my wife and you will make me the happiest man." His lips descending to hers, he kissed her, trying to show her how he felt.

She broke it. "Yes." The single word was breathless, barely a whisper against his lips.

Pulling away, his gaze met hers. He saw surprise, relief and joy, in her face.

Opening her lips, she laughed, as though she astonished herself. "My answer is, yes, Edward. I will marry you. But not tomorrow, the banns have to be read."

Picking her up by a tight grip on her waist, while her fingers gripped his shoulders, he twirled her once before setting her back onto her feet with an august laugh. "There, my dear, is where you are wrong. I obtained a special license when I asked you before in the sincere hope you would say, yes, and leave with me then. I have it still. We will be wed tomorrow."

Her fingers framing his face, she said, "You are mad, and the most gallant man I have ever met. What did I do to deserve you? I have no idea. This is foolish. But if you are truly happy to have me as your wife I will not say, no, again." Her touch lingering on his skin, her eyes sparkling with a hope he'd never seen there before, he felt the warmth inside him surge, the heat that was pure love and naught to do with sex.

But when you had one, why not take the other.

Kissing her deeply, he tasted salt on her lips, joyful tears.

He was nothing without her, he knew it. Together they made a whole. Their wedding would be no more than a certificate.

"Come to my room," he whispered across her parted lips, and then felt her mouth break into a smile beneath his, before she slipped beneath his arm and out of his reach. The smile still toying with her lips, she was the Ellen of those carefree days in London.

"No, my Lord, I think such a thing would be terribly bad luck. You must wait until your wedding night."

Edward laughed as she ran from the room, revelling in her joy as the years slipped away from her again. He liked seeing her smile. He wanted to make her smile every day for the rest of her life.

Chapter Eight

Ellen stood before the altar in the little church, beside Edward. He'd tossed her life up in the air and caught it in his steady, sensitive hands.

John was in the narrow box pew to her left with the Earl of Barrington's butler, Mr Davis, and his housekeeper, Mrs Barclay. The servants had attended to bear witness.

Ellen's first wedding had been a similarly fast affair. A long ride to the Scottish border and vows shared over an iron anvil, but the time she'd had with Paul had been gold to her. She remembered it with a dreamlike distance. She'd been innocent, a virgin, beholding Paul with glowing expectation and no fear of fate. This time she was neither innocent of life or death, and she was afraid of fate.

'It is how it is,' her father had once told her. 'What will be, will be; we must just make the best of it,' she had often heard Paul say.

Still, she'd always wished she could divine the future and know what faced them on the road ahead, beyond the next brow of life's journey. She wanted to have choice, to be happy. This morning, when she'd woken at first light, she'd risen and gone to the window, drawing back the heavy curtains. The first rays of the rising sun had caught the veil of white frost covering the ground, casting diamonds, like seeds, beneath her window. It felt like a gift from God, a peace offering. The morning chorus, resounding across the pleasure gardens below, a serenade to the dawn, had felt like it was sung for her. Her heart full to the brim, she'd looked to the distance and clutched her hands together, taking hold of all her hopes and protecting them.

No one knew as well as she did, how hopes could turn to ashes in your hands. She knew the force of the demons chasing her. Edward did not. They'd damned her to hell before. She prayed Edward would have the strength to fight them off, urging herself to have faith in him. She was building castles in the air, marrying him — writing her own fairy tale. But life was not like fairy tales. Life did not play fair — evil won. And fending off Gainsborough was one thing — fending off her father was entirely different.

She looked up at Edward. He was watching her, tenderness in his eyes. He had the strength, goodness and courage to care. She loved him and he loved her. She'd disbelieved him once, he'd proved her wrong. Edward Marlow *was* her saviour and her hero. All her faith was thrown into the pot. Win or lose, this *was* her choice — her gamble. Just as it had been with her first husband Paul, only then fate had dealt her a bad hand. Now she hoped, she prayed, here, before God, *that her luck would change.*

Tears in her eyes, she said, "I will," and Edward took up her left hand to slip a narrow gold ring onto her finger.

"I give thee…"

She had John, and she had Edward. She would not think of anything else, not yet, not until the moment came when she must. Until then she would take every chance of happiness life gave her. Her eyes took in the glinting light from the tall plain glass windows which shone down on Edward's hair, reflecting back like a halo.

"I now pronounce you man and wife." The vicar's sharp, shrill, words rang out against the bare stone of the small parish church and rising to her toes she wrapped her arms about Edward's neck, hugging him tightly, wordlessly begging him to never let her go.

"I love you," he whispered into her hair and as she lifted her head to answer he kissed her.

"And I you, *husband*," she spoke against his mouth, close to crying. Blinking back the tears, she smiled, laughing at their folly. "Marrying me is madness, but I love you more for it."

"Mama!" John came rushing to her side, barrelling into her and wrapping his arms about her waist, hugging her tightly as Edward released her.

"And now Lord and Lady Edward we must sign the register. If you will come this way?" the vicar said, shepherding them to the vestry. Edward signed first, before taking John's hand from her so she could sit before the broad record book. While Edward spoke to the vicar she quickly wrote her father's name, sans title and signed her own. The witnesses then made their mark, while she watched, hoping neither would recognize her father's name, neither appeared to. Feeling Edward's fingers slide into her own she turned, forcing a smile, though it was not hard to do as she met his.

"*Husband*," she whispered up to him and squeezed his hand. It was not a word she'd thought she would ever say again.

"*Wife*," he answered, his fingers tightening about hers, as his lips parted more broadly, clearly indulging her, his eyes shining.

A small part of her felt a nagging twinge of guilt. Was this wrong, to accept his offer of security when he didn't know the truth? If only he'd not sought to persuade her, but everything about Edward was persuasive. He had offered, she had accepted, and that was that. She had committed far worse sins than telling half the truth. She hoped he would never know the rest.

"Come then, on to our wedding breakfast." He began walking backwards, his grip on her hand pulling her with him.

Ellen laughed, all they had awaiting them was a very normal luncheon, just the three of them.

"Am I to call you Papa now?" John asked, gripping Edward's other hand, as they turned to leave the church by the small exit from the vestry.

"You may call me what you wish, John. If you like it can be, Papa, or if not then it shall be, Edward."

The boy smiled up at him. "I would like to have a Papa, I cannot remember mine." Ellen's teeth caught her lower lip.

"Then you have a Papa now, John." Edward's hand slipped from John's and instead rested on John's shoulder and pulled John to his side. They were a family in every appearance, Ellen thought, as they followed the path from the church back to the house, the servants behind them.

"My real father fought in the war, but no one will speak of him." John continued, with the innocently blind speech of a child.

"From what your Mama has told me, John, your father was a very brave man, who you have good reason to be proud of."

Clutching Edward's hand more tightly, Ellen expressed her gratitude for his consideration. In response, looking back at her, he lifted her knuckles to his lips and kissed them, as though he truly understood.

She knew he did not.

John had been brought up to ignore the existence of both his parents. How was Edward to imagine that?

"I would like to know about my real Papa, Mama. Would you tell me?" John urged.

She smiled, looking at Edward in case he would not like it, but he never flinched. *Amazing man.* Her gaze passed back to her son. "He was special, John, brave, and you are very like him."

She went on to talk of nights about the campfire. Of tales Paul had told her about his battles, of how Paul had helped his wounded friends. The simple, difficult but happy life she'd known before his death. And as they walked together back to the Earl of Barrington's country residence, she felt as though she was in that blessed place again. Only this time it felt fragile, like a bubble that would burst, or theatre, a performance in which she was merely acting. It could not be real. But as the day progressed she tentatively let belief and joy seep deeper.

Over luncheon they talked of things they would do. Edward, asking John about the things he enjoyed, promised to find the boy his own pony so they could ride together in days to come.

In the afternoon they played cards with John, using imaginary pennies as a stake, at the end of which her son was wealthier by more than a dozen promissory notes.

Later, when she walked John upstairs to the nursery for supper, Edward followed, and in the end they stayed, sharing a plate of cook's crumpets with butter and honey instead of dining downstairs.

Afterwards, when she tucked John into bed and told him another story of his father, Edward watched, leaning against the door frame.

"He's a good lad," Edward told her as they left John to sleep, his hand resting on her shoulder as they turned to the stairs.

Ellen smiled. John had been her only reason for living until Edward. "I wish Paul had known him. He would have been proud. But I am grateful for your kindness towards him. You cannot know how much it means to me."

"Ellen, no gratitude." His hand slipping to her waist, he drew her closer as they reached the stairs and began to descend. "I promise I will treat John as my own son. Whatever I can do to heal the wound of losing his father I shall, but I don't expect to be thanked for it."

Stopping on the stairs Ellen hugged him. "You are too good for me, Edward Marlow. God alone knows what I did to deserve you."

"Ellen, darling, you deserve everything good. You've been through enough hardship. Come, I believe it is a bridegroom's prerogative to carry his bride across the threshold." With that she was swept up effortlessly in his strong arms and carried to his bedchamber, while she clung to his shoulders, laughing.

"You've made me wait for this," Edward spoke as he kicked his bedchamber door open and carried her into the masculine room of dark oak and royal blue hues.

"But now you have the luxury of making love to your wife," she answered, her gaze skimming across the room. It was welcoming and warm, with a fire burning in the hearth and several candles alight.

The room was Edward, not in the least austere.

He laughed, his voice deep and teasing. "And you were right." He dropped her onto his bed and leaned over and kissed her, one knee beside her on the quilt, his hands on either side of her shoulders. "I will appreciate it far more." His dark blue-black gaze sparkled with a look of adoration.

The sight of it melted her heart as her fingers worked free the buttons of his evening coat.

"And I will keep my vow. I am going to honour and worship you with my body." His lips nipped at hers. "It will hardly be a chore."

She smiled in answer as he allowed her to free him from his coat. And then her fingers were at the buttons of his waistcoat, and it was like the days they'd spent in London.

"*Wife*, give me the chance to undress my bride."

"*Husband*, I will give you the opportunity, but first allow *me* the pleasure of viewing your glorious chest."

"Lord, but I married a cheeky hoyden."

Ellen felt laughter bubble from her throat. "If I desire my husband, pray tell me what is wrong with that?"

His lips brushed at hers again before she pulled his waistcoat from his arms and threw it to a chair. Then his hands were drawing her up to free the buttons at her back.

Having loosened his neckcloth, pulled it free and then thrown it to the chair too, Ellen jerked his shirttails from his breeches. Once she'd stripped him to the waist she traced her fingertips across the contours of his muscle. He was such a remarkable man, *her Edward*, hers, to have, to hold—*to keep*. The thought of it made her heart thunder and a delicious ache reach from her breast as he kissed it through the thin cotton of her chemise.

His fingers fumbled over the laces of her light corset at her back.

"Ellen, sit forward." The command was a deep resonating, impatient growl, as he tugged at the stubborn knot.

A wicked streak gripping her, complying, she ran her fingertips downwards.

Edward's responsive groan was rough and rasping as his fingers pulled loose the lacing threaded through her stays. "What are you doing?"

Ellen laughed. "I promised to have and to hold, husband. I am merely obeying."

"Well, for tonight, my very dear, wife," his kiss caught the edge of her mouth, and then the end of her nose, as gripping her shoulders, he pressed her back to the bed, "I would rather you have than hold."

His kiss was deep and all consuming as his hand covered hers and gripped. Then she was full of him, gasping at his impatient onslaught.

Both her hands were captured in his and pinned above her head as his weight pressed her down thrusting through the slit in her drawers. This was what she craved whenever Edward was near.

"Will you obey me always, wife?" He spoke into her mouth.

"I will, when you ask me to do what I wish."

His loving was playful and taunting and he smiled at her, his gaze shimmering with heat. She was smiling too, her muscle tight, her heels pressing into the mattress and her hips arched. It was sweet torture and her breathing reduced to shallow pants.

He was everything to her. She wanted to grip his shoulders and hold on for dear life but he wouldn't let her hands go.

"Ah! Edward!"

"Edward!" she was pleading now.

Then she fell from a precipice into open air, all her senses lost.

"*Edward?*" He'd withdrawn but only to strip her of her flimsy underwear.

She lay naked in only her stockings and garters when he returned and she would have complained about him still wearing his breeches and boots but then his lips touched her stomach.

Utterly intoxicated Ellen's eyes were closed and her head pressed back into the pillow. "Oh, Edward!" Her fingers gripped in his hair.

"Do I do *you* honour wife?" The warmth of his words spun tremors through her as his fingers toyed with her stocking top, sliding in and out while his tongue played a similar game.

"You do! Edward, ah, you do!"

His answer was a very self-satisfied chuckle.

Then he was kissing a path back up her body to claim her again.

She thumped his shoulder with the heel of her hand. "Take off your boots!"

At that he leaned back and then shifted to sit on the edge of the bed letting his legs hang over. Ellen climbed down to take off his boot, still wearing only her stockings and garters.

He lifted his leg.

"That is a nice view," Edward drawled his fingers touching her hip.

The man was insatiable. "Edward!" But as she spoke his boot loosened and slid off. She pulled off his stocking too.

He lifted the other foot for her attention and his lips touched her back as his fingers busied themselves enchanting her and stealing her concentration.

His second boot loosened and fell to the floor along with his stocking. But his hand gripped her hip and stopped her sitting back as he stood instead.

With his breeches at his ankles, his tall strong body embracing her and his clever hands working their art she fell into oblivion again, leaning on him and letting him have his way. Then they were seated, she on his lap, her legs about his, her back against his firm chest as he loved her with slow determination.

He was the key to her existence this man, filling her completely, so deeply inside her in every sense, body and soul. It made her feel wickedly erotic, indecently so, the scandalous being she had seemed but not been for the past years. In Edward's arms the feeling excited her.

When he rose he turned her to the bed and kissed her back as he showed her how he wanted her to kneel, on all fours. She could barely breathe, hardly think. *Dear Lord.* His muscular thighs pressed to the back of hers and his hips struck her buttocks. A cry of ecstasy escaped her throat, rising from the bottom of her lungs.

There was tension in his grip and an element of ruthlessness, but there was devotion and respect too. She felt adored. She ascended into blissful rapture and felt him follow.

That was his last gift to her today. There could be a child now. She was not unclean anymore. She was his wife.

After a moment he tumbled her to the bed, pulled her into his arms and rained what felt like tender, cherishing kisses across her face. She captured his nape, and pulled his lips back to hers, feeling victorious and then smiled and whispered. "Does it make me wicked if I liked making love as we did? I have been the mistress of three men and none of them used that pose."

His forefinger traced the line of her jaw. "Sweetheart, you could never be wicked. You do not have a single wicked bone. But I'm glad that at least I am the first in some form on our wedding night."

Ellen felt her eyes fill with tears which brimmed over. His thumb wiped one aside.

"I didn't mean to distress you by saying that. I'm sorry. I don't care about what's happened before, Ellen, its past. From today, we've no history, we'll make our own."

Ellen held her breath. There was a past she could not escape, not when she had John, but she would not burden him with it. She trusted him, but she refused to let him look that demon in the eye on their wedding night. She hoped he never would. And if he did she would cling to her rock, Edward. She would hold on for dear life if she had to, no matter how bad the storm grew about her, or how much the tide pulled her back. She'd fight to keep him. He'd hauled her from the wreck she'd made of her life and she was holding fast to him until they reached calm water; if they ever could.

"You're sad?"

"Happy," she answered. "I was thinking about the things that have happened. I feel as though this is all a dream. Don't pinch me. I don't want to wake up."

His fingers gently slipped to pinch her earlobe in response. "It's no dream, sweetheart, you're here."

"Yes, still here," she whispered back.

⚭

Waking with a start, Ellen heard someone tap on the bedroom door, the instinct of years and restless dreams,

172

throwing her into a place of fear. Moving to rise she realized her body was weighted down, restrained by a muscular thigh bracing her legs and an arm which lay idle across her midriff, its palm resting on her naked breast.

Edward, she hadn't dreamt this.

The slight knock struck the door again. She lifted Edward's hand trying to wake him. "*Edward.*"

"Mm."

His hair was tussled and stubble shaded his jaw. His long black eyelashes flickered and lifted, and his dark blue gaze focused on her. He smiled.

"Wake up." she urged, as his fingers slipped from her hold and returned to squeeze her breast. "Someone is knocking."

"Mama? Papa?" John's call came from beyond the door.

Ellen threw Edward's hand aside, scrambled off the bed to retrieve their clothing from the floor and set the cluttered pile on a chair, then hurriedly pulled on her underwear, glancing at Edward who'd risen and was slipping on a dressing gown.

"Mama!" John called again.

"Just a moment, John," Ellen answered as Edward moved to unlock the door, waving her back to bed.

She slid beneath the tussled sheets and was smoothing them out across her lap as Edward opened the door.

"Good-morning, son."

Ellen's heart skipped a beat at his words. They were not pretense, he was still half asleep. They'd been spoken from the heart. She watched Edward lean forward to look out the door, his head turning right and left. "No nursemaid, John?"

Still in his nightshirt, John frowned and grunted. "I am not a baby. I came down on my own."

"Did you indeed." Edward spoke with a smile on his lips and in his voice. "Well then, young man, you had better come in and see your Mama while I ring for some chocolate."

A broad grin stretched across her son's face as he glanced upwards, sending a look of hero-worship at his new Papa. *Heavens*, Edward was turning out to not only be her rock but her son's too.

If Edward knew how much he had truly taken on his shoulders, he may not be smiling then, her conscience whispered. But Ellen refused to heed it. Instead she gave the man who *was* her saviour a closed lip smile of thanks and was rewarded with a broad answering grin in acknowledgement, as he tugged the damask bell rope.

"I suppose breakfast in bed is in order," he laughed as John launched himself on to the bed and snuggled up to her, his arms reaching about her neck.

Giving her son a squeeze she kissed the crown of his head, as Edward slid beneath the sheets beside her.

"What shall we do today, Papa?" John chimed, animated with excitement.

Could a heart burst with joy, Ellen wondered. But not wishing him to overwhelm Edward she sought to pacify him. "Perhaps your new Papa shall want a day to himself, John. He has been travelling for days remember."

"Hardly," Edward scoffed. "It is our honeymoon, Ellen. No, I think today we shall go shopping, you need clothes." Edward's arm then slotted about John's shoulders pulling him from Ellen's hug to hold him in a more masculine, confidential and exclusive embrace. "And then we can look for something for you, John, a pony perhaps?"

"A pony!" Bouncing up John turned about, kneeling to face them both, full of enthusiasm.

"You need not spend your money, Edward." Ellen began to rein this in. Edward was a second son after all. He'd freely admitted he would need to work to support them. She did not want him spending rashly just to please her and impress her son, nor did she want to place him in debt.

His gaze met hers, visibly reading her thoughts. "I have enough for this. I wish to treat you and John, and I expect you both to enjoy being spoilt."

With that the door was tapped again and bidding the maid enter, Edward ordered breakfast.

An hour or so later the bed covers were sticky, and John also, after drinking three cups of chocolate and eating three slices of bread with jam. Taking her son's sticky fingers in her hand, Ellen led John from the room and back upstairs, to pass him into the care of his nursemaid.

"I like my new Papa, Mama."

"I know, sweetheart. Are we not very lucky to have him?" Unexpectedly John spun about, securing his arms about her waist.

"You won't send me away again, Mama, will you?"

Ignoring the instant rush of tears to her eyes, Ellen held him tight in return, the two of them clinging to each other in the way only two people who'd known separation could. "No, John," she lied, unable to face the possibility of the truth. She would never let him go by choice, but so many times the choice had not been hers. Then bending to kiss his sticky cheek, she prayed she would have control over it, but even as she did so, she felt the web of lies, of half-truths, weaving about her, hemming her in. "Never willingly," she said more quietly, then in a more bolstering voice, rising back up she patted his shoulder, "Now run along to your room, the quicker we are ready, the quicker we may look for that pony of yours."

She was going to enjoy today. She was going to relish it and not feel guilty. She was going to look for dresses and be Edward's wife and thumb her nose at fate. And if her father came—when her father came—she was not going to hide from him anymore. She was going to make him face her—face what she'd become. She wanted to be visible again.

◈◈

Edward glanced at Ellen. She was seated on the other side of John. The three of them squeezed onto the seat of the trap as it jolted along and John held the ribbons. Edward had let the boy take the reins when they'd left the busy road.

They'd spent the morning shopping and John had been bored, despite Edward taking him to buy some sweets while Ellen purchased her unmentionable things. She was wearing a ready-made day dress now, which had been quickly tacked to fit, and she'd been clearly glad to get out of the tired, conspicuous, evening dress. John was wearing old clothes, which Margaret had found in the attics, his or Rob's, to save the necessity of purchasing another full wardrobe. Ellen had needed everything of course. He'd even insisted she purchase a ball gown, and she'd chosen a daring style and requested that it be decorated with red ribbon, a light of marked decision in her eyes. It had cost a considerable amount, but he refused to baulk at the expense, and he was not going to avoid the next expenditure either. He was looking forward to seeing both their faces. He'd sell the phaeton and the matching pair of horses he'd left in London to cover it, he'd have no need for a flash racing vehicle as a steward.

Firmly grasping John's smaller hands, Edward helped steer the curricle through the gates of Park House.

"Where are we?" Ellen asked, warily viewing their surroundings.

Meeting her gaze, he smiled. "At Park House, the home of my dear friends Lord and Lady Forth." At that statement, she blushed crimson. She'd seemed in a defiant mood in the shop, purposeful, although he didn't understand what had charged her up. But her confidence and motivation apparently ebbed now, she looked at first deflated, as though struck, and then angry as her manner changed again and became coldly rigid. She was steeling herself, setting up her damned armour.

Blithely ignoring her reaction Edward continued, looking at John. "Forth just happens to be brilliant at breeding horses."

The drive opened on to the circle which fronted his friend's property and Edward helped John draw the curricle to a halt, congratulating the boy.

They were met at once by a groom in smart royal blue livery who took the horses' bridals.

Edward jumped down and then lifted John down after him, saying, "Shall we see what we can find, young man." John grinned, nodding and Edward offered his hand to Ellen. In contrast, she was unsmiling and looking starkly toward Forth's large fashionable house.

"Edward! I cannot tell you how excited Julie has been ever since we received your note." Edward looked to his friend. Forth had come out of the house and strode across the gravel. "I know you have come for business but she has already sent for tea. I presume you will allow her an opportunity for introductions before we visit the stables? I have to say you surprised us. It's certainly out of the blue." He was smiling profusely beneath his waxed moustache and a lock of wavy short blonde hair hung over his brow. A true country gent was Forth. He was shorter than Edward and half a dozen years older. Their friendship had been forged in the first years that Edward had taken on his father's estates. While Robert wasted his time abroad, Casper had been a guiding force, the brother Edward had lost.

"Are you not going to introduce us?" Casper prompted with a look that shifted from Edward to John and then Ellen, at which point Edward watched his friend physically step back.

"My, my, you captured a beauty in the capital." Then remembering his manners, Forth extended his hand. "My pleasure, Lady Edward."

Dropping a shallow curtsy Ellen set her hand in Forth's. "My Lord," Ellen responded, clearly reticent, her skin still deep red.

"And this is my son, John," Edward stated.

Stepping forward, John bowed deeply. When he rose, Edward found his hand resting on the boy's shoulder, pride swelling his chest and broadening his smile. The lad was well-bred.

"I am pleased to meet you, John." Forth acknowledged the boy with a friendly smile. "We will of course pick you out the very best pony I can find."

"Thank you, my Lord," John responded quickly.

"Have I missed the introductions?" Julie's voice rang out across the drive and in an instant her arms were about Edward's neck in a jubilant welcome and she pressed a kiss to his cheek, before pulling away.

"Edward, what news!" Breathless with enthusiasm, she turned to John, bracing his face in her palms and bending to press a brief kiss atop his head, thereby stunning the boy to silence and turning his skin as crimson as his mother's.

"But I know who you are," she said straightening up still gripping the boy's face in her hands, "you are, John. And, my dear…" Her hands fell away from the boy as she turned to Ellen, stopped and stared, her mouth falling open, momentarily silenced. But not for long, quickly recouping she stepped forward and took Ellen's hand between her own. "You must be, Ellen. You can have no idea how happy we are for you. You shall find no better husband than Edward. You will come in for tea?"

Edward watched a strained smile form on Ellen's lips and taking up John's hand again, he moved to stand at her side and pressed a hand to her back. She was clearly uncomfortable. Julie's exuberant greeting had daunted her.

"Thank you, Julie, we gladly accept," he acknowledged.

"Wonderful," Julie breathed and instantly slotted her arm through Ellen's, to draw her away.

Ellen looked back across her shoulder, passing Edward a disconcerted glance as he and John followed behind. He could do little but smile in answer as he wondered at the cause.

While they drank their tea it became more and more obvious Ellen was extremely uneasy. The atmosphere was thick with tension. As the cliché said, he could have cut it with a knife.

Julie went to extremes to ingratiate herself, while Ellen simply refused to engage.

Then when Julie mentioned Eton she inspired an indiscreet show of emotion from John who announced bluntly, he did not wish to go back. Following this Julie changed the subject and asked about Ellen's family, saying Ellen looked familiar.

Even though he didn't know the truth, Edward would swear his wife lied when she said they came from the Cornish coast, pronouncing Julie would certainly *not* know them.

The conversation then progressed to how *they* had met, and Ellen left it to him to answer with a look that said, you got us into this. He told Julie they had met at an entertainment event in

London, and the moment he'd seen Ellen across the room it was love at first sight. It was true after all.

Obviously not amused, Ellen apologised for not inviting his friends to the wedding in a stiff, cold voice and said she'd wished it to be quiet.

The conversation similar to systematic torture, Edward made the decision to remove to the stables.

When they reached there, things eased a little as their attention turned to the horses, and John picked out a piebald pony. But then Edward turned Ellen's attention to the surprise he'd planned for her.

The gray mare he'd picked was beautiful in looks, temperament and speed. He'd admired the animal for months but it wasn't a man's horse. Now she was going to be Ellen's.

When Ellen saw her he felt her grip tighten on his arm. He did not meet her gaze. If she was reproachful he didn't want to know. This was his indulgence, a wedding gift. Edward lowered his arm and clasped her hand instead, drawing her towards the stall, from which the gray was being led. With a pearlescent white coat, the mare was a magnificent looking specimen of horseflesh, standing at fifteen hands, and although good tempered, she had a considerable pinch of spice to her personality. She and Ellen would suit so well.

He felt Ellen being drawn to the animal as her hand slipped from his. "*Edward*, she's beautiful." Her voice was quiet and reverent, her eyes on the mare, glittering with childlike want, she pressed her palm against the horse's cheek. It turned its head into her hand.

He'd known when they left London she had an instinctive or excellent knowledge of horses and now it was proven again as she seemed to immediately connect with the mare. Her gaze sparkled with uncontrolled pleasure. Whatever had made her uncomfortable here had clearly slipped from her mind on sight of the mare. After a moment she turned to look back at him.

"You've bought her for me?" she said, her voice full of wonder.

He stepped forward, closing the distance between them, and rested a hand on her hip, patting the mare with the other. "She's a wedding gift. I knew you would appreciate her."

"Oh, yes," she breathed, her voice broke, but then she continued on a whisper, for his ears only, "I've not had a horse since I was young. Thank you. I'm truly touched. You've done too much for me, for us, far more than I can ever repay. I have nothing to give you."

Pulling her closer to his side, her buttock brushing his hip, he bent and kissed her temple, then whispered back, "I have you and John. There's no debt Ellen." Then more loudly he added, "I'm glad you like her."

"She is to your satisfaction?" Forth asked from behind them.

Ellen jumped and moved away, running her hand over the mare's winter-coat as Edward's fell to his side. She was clearly uncomfortable with showing any intimacy before his friends. He wouldn't needlessly disturb her. But the memory of watching her intimacy with Gainsborough in the club that last night suddenly thrust into his thoughts. He threw it aside, refusing to let it haunt him. He did not wish to remember it. Yet the memory made him realize dozens of moments like that must be scored into her mind. He felt cold for a moment, unable and unwilling to imagine *all* she'd endured.

"Yes, she's wonderful," she answered Forth, then looked back. "Has she got a name?"

"Pearl," Forth responded.

"Pearl," Ellen tested the name on her tongue. "It suits her." She turned her attention back to the mare and spoke as if she truly thought the animal could reply. "We are going to be firm friends you and I, Pearl."

Discarding his disturbing thoughts, Edward laughed as the horse whickered. As though the damn thing could really understand and talk back.

"What a match," Casper commented, as John called from across the courtyard.

"Papa, Mama, look!" Edward looked back at John. He was rising and falling in a neat trot, riding in circles as the pony was held on a lead rein. Perhaps Ellen's talent *was* instinct for the boy was equally blessed. Either that or he was extremely used to horses too, which Edward doubted would have occurred at the school. No, the boy was like a duck to water.

"You are an excellent horseman, John!" he complimented, lifting his hand in acknowledgement of the boy. "I'm impressed!"

A broad proud grin lodged on John's face.

Edward looked back at his friend. "Casper, can you have the horses brought over later? We should be going really." Turning back to his new son, he added, "Then we can go riding tomorrow morning, John! If you'd like to?"

"Oh yes!" John stopped the horse easily, swung his leg across the saddle and jumped down. A move it looked as though he had done at least a thousand times before. Then the boy ran the distance from his pony and launched himself at Edward, hugging his waist. "Thank you, Papa."

His hands settling to return the embrace, Edward felt his heart clench. "You are very welcome, John." *I love my son*, he realized in answer, *just as much as I love my wife*.

"We are both very grateful. Thank you, Edward." Ellen's voice came from beside him.

"It's nothing," Edward responded as he turned to receive her words and John pulled away, but seeing her cloaked look had returned to shadow her eyes he left his response there.

"Should we get back?"

His brow furrowed at the note of censure in her voice. Though he agreed, "Yes," and smiled to bolster her up, wondering again what was going on as Ellen's fingers slipped about his elbow.

She gave him a sharp look, her eyes darting to the Forths, he assumed to remind him of their audience. She must have seen the question in his eyes.

Broadening his smile, developing his own mask, he turned back to face his friends just as Julie moved forward to say her goodbyes, offering her customary parting hug. He bent a little to receive it and bestowed a kiss on her cheek, his hands sensitively gripping her upper arms before he let her go and she passed on to Ellen. Forth offered his hand and Edward shook it.

"May I call on you one day this week?" Julie asked of Ellen.

"If you wish. Please send word when you will call. Thank you for tea." Ellen's polite, clipped words implied it was the last thing *she* wished.

"You are welcome, Ellen," Julie responded, her voice infused with warmth. Of course Ellen wouldn't know the woman was desperate to be her friend, but Edward did. "And I hope you will call on us, *often*." Julie leaned forward and kissed Ellen's cheek. Ellen stiffened. He knew Ellen was uncomfortable, but he also knew Julie was suppressing her instinct to embrace Ellen.

"Come, we will walk with you and wave goodbye," Julie stated when she pulled away, casting Edward a look that said, *what have I done*. He smiled in apology and shrugged. He hadn't a clue.

Smiling brightly, and Edward guessed falsely, Julie turned to Casper.

Ellen had them all dissembling now.

As he walked arm in arm with Ellen, Julie and Casper beside them, Edward discussed livestock to avoid silence. When they reached the curricle, he thanked his friends again, as did Ellen and John and then they parted.

On the way home Ellen spoke not a word, while John chatted constantly about his pony.

Chapter Nine

Edward watched Ellen step out of John's bedchamber beside the nursery and pull the door shut quietly. "Is he settled?" She jumped.

Ellen had escaped the dinner table to take John up to bed while he was drinking his port. He'd followed because he feared she was avoiding him.

She'd been uncommunicative all afternoon, claiming a headache and retiring to bed, leaving John in Edward's company.

He had entertained the boy with a game of backgammon and Ellen had rejoined them for dinner, but she'd hardly talked.

He hadn't a clue what he'd done to deserve her cold shoulder. He wanted to know.

"Yes." Her gaze fell away from him as she moved to pass him, showing no inclination to explain her ill-mood.

Exasperated, his temper on the verge of breaking, Edward touched her arm to stop her. "What's wrong?"

"Nothing." She pulled her arm free. But the note in her voice told him if he hadn't already known, it was something.

Lowering his voice to a whisper John would not hear through the door, determined not to lose his temper, Edward responded. "Ellen, do not lie to me, I'm not a fool. Your manner has been different all afternoon. You've hardly spoken to me. Something is wrong. I won't know what it is unless you tell me."

Her pale blue eyes, swept up to his, in a look that clearly stated he was out of favour yet her words again defied him. "If there was anything I wished to say to you I would have spoken of it."

"So that is it then, I am to be excluded from what is really going on in here." His index finger touched her temple. Her eyelids fell, cloaking her response, her eyelashes fanning across the white skin of her cheek, so black.

She was a woman of contrasts, and all those contrasts were the things that made her beautiful, pale skin, ebony hair, black lashes framing pale eyes, and beneath her hard shell, a soft heart. These were all the things that made him love her. He brushed the pad of his thumb across her closed eyelid his fingers against her cheek. "*Tell me*. We cannot live together if you will not discuss things openly with me? Don't throw me scraps of how you feel. Don't make me beg."

Her eyelids lifted, her emotion clear now — anger. Her hand knocking his aside, she took a deep breath, as though she'd not breathed for hours. "Yesterday you offered me choice and then again you did not consult me." Her voice was a whisper, but it was harsh and bitter with resentment.

"Ellen?"

"Did you not even think to ask me before you took me to meet your friends?"

On the defensive, the volume of his voice increased. "I thought you would welcome the friendship of another woman. Julie is the easiest, most welcoming woman I have ever met but *you* managed to insult her. I never thought for one moment that you would not like her. No one dislikes her!"

"The problem is, *Edward*, you do not think!" Her voice rose too; her anger now equally audible. "Do you not realize what that poor woman would think if she knew the truth? Or your friend, Lord Forth? They would be outraged, disgusted, if they found out you had brought a whore into their home — *to socialise*. He would never speak to you again! If Lady Forth passed me in the street and knew who, or *what*, I am, she would cross the road to walk about me! They would not want me sitting in their drawing-room drinking tea!" The breath she stopped to take dragged into her lungs, pushing her breasts tighter against her bodice. She was shaking.

Her pale crystal eyes sparking in the low candlelight of the narrow hall, she continued, "I know I accepted your offer. Perhaps I was wrong to do so. But you cannot forget who I am, *what* I am, Edward."

The thrust of her words cut into him like a knife and in answer his blood instantly boiled, his temper soaring. She moved to turn away, that instinctive desperate reaction he'd seen her have to anger, he caught her arm, he was not letting her walk away with her words of self-condemnation ringing in his ears. "What you are, Ellen, is my wife! And the sooner you remember it and stop setting yourself down the better!"

"Mama, is something wrong?" Edward's gaze spun from Ellen to John. He was on the landing, dressed in his nightshirt.

Letting Ellen's arm go instantly, Edward felt guilty, he'd no idea how much John knew or had heard. Ellen was obviously concerned, no beyond that, bloody mortified, as she rushed to turn John about. Edward felt even worse. No matter that it was her lack of self-worth that was the issue. He recalled his earlier thoughts, his memory of that last night in the club. One memory haunted him, two when he thought of her bruises. Hundreds not dozens must haunt her. No wonder she felt like this—unclean. He'd felt unclean to watch it. He did not wish to add to her pain. He'd hurt her emotionally if not physically, and that was hardly likely to improve her opinion of herself, or him.

He had an apology to make.

"Nothing is wrong, John." He listened to her whispering to the boy as she led him back to bed. "I am sorry we woke you. We were just talking too loudly. You must not mind us. Come on, I shall tuck you back in and then you must get some sleep to have the energy to ride tomorrow."

Edward moved behind them and leaned against the doorframe, his arms crossing over his chest, watching her tuck John in and bend to kiss his forehead.

The look she gave Edward as she came back across the room clearly blamed and chastised him, warning him to hold his peace until they were out of earshot of the child.

"Ellen." he spoke as she closed the door.

Her eyes narrowing in what appeared impatience, she put a finger to her lips, giving him a similar chiding look to the one she had given to her son when she had corrected his behaviour at Forth's over the Eton outburst, then whispered, "Downstairs."

Holding out his hand for her to go first he dutifully followed, his anger dissipating, a smile tugging at his lips. Being treated like a scolded child amused him. At least he could sympathize with his son in future. But when they reached the drawing-room, clicking the door shut, he strode towards her, determined to get the notion out of her head that her past made any difference to their future.

With a deep breath, fixing his eyes on the woman who defiantly stood before him — Ellen, buried deep behind her defensive shell — he sought for the words that would convince her.

He understood her reason for being upset, he was no longer angry, but he was not going to continue to let her belittle herself. And her hard as rock expression said she was refusing him access to the pain hidden beneath it.

A month ago, he'd not have thought he could possess the strength of feeling stirring in his chest.

He shrugged, expressing his inability. Where to begin? How to shift her perspective? "As I said, Ellen, what you are, is my wife. Nothing more. Nothing less." He willed her to believe it, putting all the love he had for her in his voice and his gaze. "Forget the past. I will not allow anyone to reject you. I shan't publish it, but if people find out about your history, so be it. No one is without fault. *I* respect and love you. I don't care what others think."

She turned away, her palm pressing to her midriff.

Unrelenting he pushed on, refusing to let her escape this, he had to make her face it, but his tone gentled a little as he continued, his voice understanding, but insistent. "You told me the very good reasons that left you where you were, but whether it was your choice or not is no one else's business. Let people think what they like, Ellen. You have me now, and I think you wholly worthy of befriending my friends. I know them far better than you and I happen to think that my friends care enough for me to like who I love, regardless. Even if Julie knew your past she would not cut you, I would bet my life on it." The assertiveness suddenly fell from his voice, as she turned back to him looking lost. Then she was in his embrace, her slim arms enfolding his ribs, holding him tightly, her cheek pressed to his shoulder, her unsteady breath and her soft hair caressing the skin of his jaw.

He kissed the crown of her head, whispering to her hair. "I will hear no more of this self-judgement, Ellen."

And now she cried. Good, perhaps she needed cleansing.

He stroked her hair for a moment, then picked her up and moved to a chair, sitting her on his lap and enfolding her in his love, in his highest esteem, letting her cry it all out.

Crying served no purpose. It solved nothing. But Ellen was so out of control of all of this, tired, exhausted and desperate. The strength she'd held on to for years, was worn down to the very marrow of her bones. Since Edward had broken the ice about her heart and unleashed her emotions, she seemed unable to hold them back anymore. She had seen more of John in the last week than she had for years, but she was terrified of what was to come, of losing him again. Perhaps there could be another week or two before her father came. It was her father who'd opened her eyes to the person she'd become when John was born, holding a metaphorical mirror to her face and making her look at the woman he called a whore. She knew how soiled her life had been, she felt it eating at her soul every day and Edward could never understand that. But what she couldn't comprehend was that he didn't even seem to care about what she had been.

Her head still bent to the lapel of his evening coat Ellen whispered, "I have to look into John's face every day knowing the things I've done. How can I teach him right from wrong when one day he may find out the truth and judge me? I do not feel fit to face my own son, let alone look into the faces of your friends, knowing how false I am."

His palm brushed over her hair, the deep timbre of his voice rumbling in his chest beneath her ear as he spoke. "You are not false, Ellen. The false woman was the one forced to live with Gainsborough. That part of your life is over. You are not alone anymore, sweetheart, *you have me.*"

His voice was a soft deep caress, his words a balm which touched places inside her she longed to be healed. Hope, was the one word, she longed to wholly claim. She wanted to believe in a future in which John would be hers. She wanted to look at herself in a mirror and not feel disgust.

"I love you, Ellen. You are a good woman, with a good heart, despite everything you have endured, that makes you a better person than most."

He was her rock. Lifting her head her fingers flattened his crumpled, tear stained lapel. Then his fingers crooked beneath her chin, urging her to lift her head. Her gaze met the glinting dark blue-gray as it caught the candlelight, the onyx circles at their center a mirror which reflected back her pain.

Did he understand after all, had she misjudged him in this too?

"I know I should have spoken to you before I took you to Forth's now. I understand why you are upset. I'm sorry I did not. You're right, I do not stop to think of things from your perspective. I promise I shall try to in future, if in return you promise to do something for me—stop judging yourself so harshly? Let us leave the past where it is and move on." His gaze seemed to reach into her thoughts, waiting for her response, appearing to desperately will her to be happy.

What on earth did I do to deserve you? Instead of speaking this she lifted her chin from his touch and dropped her gaze and her head, focusing her eyes on his lips so she did not have to see the hurt she knew would settle in his eyes. Then she uttered in a broken whisper a thing she hadn't even known until now had been a burning pain inside her, she had buried it so deep, "I cannot bare it that you saw me with Gainsborough; that you know what I was before; that you watched him touch me that night. I hate knowing you saw me like that. How can I face your friends, when I find it hard to face you, or even my reflection in a mirror? I wish I had met you long ago, before this all began." Tears welled in her eyes again and tumbled over her lashes.

The hug he gave her in answer was fierce and her face turned into his neck, now soaking his starched cravat, while her arms clung about his shoulders.

The weight of his strong comforting palm fell atop her hair, cradling her head. "Oh darling, how am I going to convince you? *I don't care.* You were trapped. It was painful to watch it, but all he ever had of you was your flesh and bone, I know that. If I wondered before how he tied you to him I know now it was through John. He abused you, Ellen, it was not your choice, nor your fault, but if you cannot accept that, how can I help you be free of him. He still has a hold of your thoughts. Forgive yourself. Forget it. It's finished now. Let your mind be free of it, of him and all the others."

When she didn't answer, but kept her face pinned tight to his neck, she felt him suck in a deep breath and let it out on a sigh. "I want to help you, Ellen." He spoke with absolute conviction, his tone reaching into the very depths of her heart, filling the cold, sore and wounded hole in her soul with warmth. "But I don't know how. I don't think I can bear to see how hurt you are and not be able to help you heal."

I want to heal. I want to hope.

His hand stroking her hair, he finished, "Please let it go, Ellen, for me, and for John."

She lifted her head and pressed her lips to the strong line of his jaw, then to the corner of his mouth and then his lips as he turned to face her, while her palms pressed to his cheeks, framing his face. She could not love this man more. She loved him with a passion, her hero, who fought with her demons and won. Oh how she hoped he could win against the last and worst. His firm gentle lips answered hers, kissing her back. Fresh tears tumbled from her eyes as she pulled back a little to see his face. He smiled. A choke that was half sob, half laugh, left her lips as they broke into a hesitant smile too.

"I'll try," she voiced. The look he gave her in answer was turbulent with emotion as his palms and fingers pressed to the sides of her head and brought her lips back to his. He kissed her ardently, as though seeking to portray all he'd said about his feelings for her.

When she felt his emotion dissipating and his kiss gentled, a smile lifting her lips, she whispered to his mouth again, "I love you so much."

He pulled away and smiled too. Lord, he was beautiful when he smiled. Her heart swelled. He'd let her argue and listened. He had let her lose her temper with him and apologised to her. Even Paul had not liked it when she was angry, and sorry had never been a word he knew. "You are a wonderful man. Thank you. I'm sorry I offended your friends."

Her arms slipping from about his shoulders, she sniffed as reaching to the inside pocket of his evening coat Edward withdrew a handkerchief and offered it.

Accepting it she gave him another uncertain smile.

Then his fingers gently tapping her under the chin, a deep gravelly grunt of humor escaped his throat. "I love you too, more than I ever thought it was possible to love anyone. And I love your son as though he is my own. But you shall not just *try* though Ellen. Do you understand? I shan't accept *trying*. You will let it go, I insist."

Chapter Ten

Ellen laughed as John tossed the ball to her. Edward, as the piggy in the middle, tried to catch it and made an awful impression of failing. Ellen caught it and threw it back, arcing it across the background span of azure blue sky.

The thaw of spring had come, at last. The wind turning from the north to west winds that brought the frosts, to the warmer south to east breezes which opened up the growing buds of blossom on the trees and sank its tepid warmth into the earth, bringing to life all the hibernating bulbs and plants. And the renewal, the expectation, of the blossoming season had seeped into her and John too, thanks to Edward's generous love which had formed and now fuelled their little family. In her heart it felt like spring too.

Reaching tall John caught the ball securely with a shout of pleasure as Edward made another playful lunge to capture it. Then dodging from one side to another, John teased Edward, trying to trick him into darting the wrong way to block the ball.

Ellen watched them with a heart so filled with happiness it was painful. John's internal joy literally shone from him. It was thanks to Edward's constant care and approbation.

When John finally gave up teasing and tossed the ball though, Edward reached up and easily caught it.

"Papa!" John yelled in complaint.

Edward merely laughed, "I call an end. I am hungry for my luncheon. I say we eat!" The proposal was to John, who, grinning, then ran across to the picnic blanket.

Edward stole the moment of John's distraction and turned to embrace her suddenly, claiming her lips with a kiss. She was breathless and hot when he broke away, and no doubt blushing, the kiss had expressed all of his love and desire for her.

He gripped her hand firmly, his hold feeling possessive, again suggesting much more than the simple touch it was as he walked her to the blanket.

"What do we have?" he spoke to John as the boy began unloading dishes.

"Hot chocolate." John grinned, as he lifted out a corked porcelain canister. "Rabbit pie," he continued, as he pulled each item out and set it on the rug. "Boiled eggs, curried rice, *scones and whipped cream, Mama.*" John looked up to her with a smile knowing they were her favourite, and no doubt why cook had included them.

"Sounds like a feast to me," Edward responded as she knelt and began to lay out the plates and cutlery, before starting to serve out the dishes.

This had been the pattern of their days for over a week, a long ride in the morning, to a destination Edward had planned the night before so that the footmen could bring out a picnic. Then they would idle in play for an hour or two, eat lunch and return home. The afternoon was equally lazy, with card games, chess or backgammon, before a warm fire because the spring air had not yet heated enough to completely sweep away the chill of winter. Often leaving her boys to play, Ellen would curl up in a chair with one of the books from his brother's library.

Life was heavenly.

Of Edward's brother there had been no sign, nor word, which did not seem to bother Edward at all. But more importantly no one had come for John and they had now been here for what, twelve days, nearly two weeks. She was beginning to progress from hope to a burgeoning belief that they were truly safe. Some of Edward's endlessly positive nature was perhaps rubbing off on her. Leaning back onto her hands, her feet stretched out before her, crossed at the ankles, she was quite snug within her new sapphire blue riding habit with its smart black fringe and trim. She smiled. Then sensing Edward watching, she turned to receive a dark assessing look which broke into a smile.

The man was unceasingly randy. He would have her in bed all day long if it was not for John. When she had made that wicked accusation to him the night before, he had merely laughed and told her bluntly that 'it was after all their honeymoon, and why should he not appreciate her beauty and sate his appetite. Surely she would be more concerned if he did not.' She'd smiled at him in answer.

Besides she had no weight to her words, he knew how much she enjoyed making love too, as if to prove it a little fission of desire curled inside her tummy.

As she finished her mouthful Edward reached for a scone, broke off a piece and dipped it into the whipped cream, lifting it to her lips. Ellen bit off the end. He was being wicked. Confirming it he leaned to her ear. "Perhaps I should ask cook to send us some cream up for supper."

"*Edward.*" She slapped at his arm and sent her gaze to John in warning. In response he kissed her lips briefly licking the cream from her lower lip before he drew away.

"Now, John, what shall we do this afternoon?" Edward said, looking at John.

"Can we play backgammon, father?"

Father. That word sounded so natural on John's lips now. It had become common place, a fact, the truth.

She looked at John. For his age he was a needy child, not for things, but for love. He'd been so starved of it through the years. She had tried to offer it in the written word but it was not the same as her physical presence in his life. He'd clung to her through their journey here and accepted Edward without hesitation. John had longed for a father as much as his mother and Edward had fulfilled John's wish. Edward's willingness to give often overwhelmed her, and her son soaked it up.

Edward had wanted to heal her and he had. She could feel the wounds and scars in her soul mending, disappearing, thanks to Edward. But he was healing her son too.

Ellen turned to Edward, who was sprawled beside her, resting on one elbow, and hugged him. Pressing his head to her chest, she summarily cut off the conversation which had continued between him and John.

He freed himself, laughing. "What was that for?"

She didn't deem to give him an answer. Instead holding out an arm, she encouraged John to come for a cuddle too. He did, accepting her possessive and comforting grip.

Edward shook his head, smiling, sat upright and brushed crumbs from his coat and legs. "Tomorrow I would like us to go to church," he stated, pushing himself from the ground to his feet, glancing at her. "I have always gone. As the administering landowner, I thought it my responsibility, and as it is Mothering Sunday, I think it fitting. What do you say?" The question glinting in his eyes expressed a rare vulnerability. He'd been thinking on this then, understanding that it would be difficult for her. She lifted her hand for Edward to take, as John left her embrace rising too, and let Edward pull her up. With his fingers still grasping hers she laid her other hand over his heart on his coat.

"If that is what you wish, then we shall be more than glad to accompany you."

His answering smile said, thank you, as he gave her a stiff slight nod, as though acknowledging her courage. In response, lifting to her toes she set her arms about his neck and pressed a kiss on his warm cheek. "We promise to make you proud." The soft weight of his hand settled on her back. It was a feeling she'd grown to love.

"You hardly need promise, you always make me proud." His voice rumbled by her ear.

Julie and Casper had come over for dinner three nights ago, on her suggestion. She had apologised for her previous reticence, explaining that Edward hadn't informed her where they were going and that she was just a little overwhelmed by the speed of the wedding and settling into Farnborough House. She had then gone out of her way to play the perfect hostess. Reminding herself constantly of Edward's words she'd set her former life from her mind, and behaved as though that awful time had not occurred. It was as though it had not, to his friends and his brother's staff all she was, was Edward's wife.

The night had ended with the couples on good terms. But when the door closed on his friends Ellen had a feeling of envy for the life Edward had led before he met her, for the years he'd lived and she'd not known he was there, beyond her reach.

After they made love that night, when he drew her close, she'd asked him how he'd entertained himself in the country before he'd left for London and in turn he'd asked her about her first marriage.

Each day they seemingly knew each other better and loved each other more.

Life was perfect. *If only it would stay perfect.*

≪·≫

The heat of the spring sunshine strong on his back, warm inside and out, Edward walked along the lane leading back to Farnborough House with his wife and child, gripping Ellen's hand tightly.

Lord, he'd received a sharp shock when she and John had sung out the first hymn in a sweet, unwavering, harmony. Of course if he'd thought on it he would have known John had a superior voice. He'd been selected as a chorister to sing at Eton, in King George's own chapel, after all. *But Ellen?* Her singing voice had such clarity. It held each note with perfection. They'd taken the family box at the front of the church, and were mostly hidden from view until they stood. But when they stood to sing the first hymn and Ellen's voice together with her son's had rung out against the gray stone the whole congregation had turned in awe.

He squeezed the delicate hand in his again.

John was running on ahead, the soles of his boots grinding on the gravel path.

Looking up at him, Ellen smiled, her light blue eyes sparkling with a happiness which seemed to run very deep. A person's eyes were a window to the soul so the vicar's sermon had read. Yes indeed, he agreed, he'd always only seen good in Ellen.

If she had been afraid to go to church she'd not shown it. But if God judged a woman with such a pure, good heart as hers, for deeds that were forced upon her, then in his opinion, God was an ass. But Edward held to the knowledge of the Lord's omniscience, and if God knew all and could see all, then he must know of her innocence, her regret too, and thus he must forgive.

When they left the church Ellen had stood beside Edward greeting their neighbors, the village folk and some of his brother's tenants. Their resounding consensus on his bride was that she was 'a true gem' — 'how lucky he was', 'With such a voice' — it was added. Poor John had been patted and petted for his own sweet soprano singing voice of course, but the boy kept extremely quiet about his skill, not mentioning that he'd sung for the king. If it had been Edward at John's age, some bragging would have been in order.

In fact, Edward suddenly realized, John had said very little of his life to date, apart from asking about his father. Perhaps Edward ought to speak to Ellen and find out what had actually happened regarding John. The two of them were obviously close, but there still seemed something underlying which disturbed the boy.

"I'm hungry," John called from in front, as they turned onto the path leading back to Farnborough while he struck at the long grass on either side of the path with a stick he'd picked up from the ground.

"Good because cook promised to have luncheon ready when we return. You will be able to do it justice," Ellen responded.

Dropping the stick, John kicked into a run, racing off ahead.

"Remember you need to go to the nursery and wash your face and hands before you sit down!" Ellen called after him.

As the boy tore off out of sight Edward took the opportunity to pull her close for a long kiss, leaving her lips reddened and her cheeks rosy. He so loved her appearance when she was slightly rumpled, mussed, especially first thing in the morning, when her hair was riotous and loose, her eyes sleepy and her mouth swollen and kissable.

Smiling, taking up her hand again, he tugged her on. "Come on, I'm hungry too."

She sent him a look from beneath her lowered lashes. "For what?"

"For you always," he answered, with a guttural wolfish half-laugh. "But I'll settle for food."

"Mama!" John's urgent cry came from beyond the corner of the house and instantly the joy on Ellen's face shattered. Edward saw it. Blood drained from her face, her smile fell and fear flooded her eyes.

"Ellen?"

Without even registering his enquiry her fingers pulled from his and she turned away, catching up her skirt and breaking into a run. The sharp strikes of her new half-boots on the gravel rang with desperate urgency.

He followed and rounded the corner of the house a moment behind her nearly colliding with them both in the archway at the entrance to the courtyard. Ellen was standing rigid, one hand still holding the skirt of her new pale lemon walking dress and moss green pelisse. While John was gripping her about the waist with both arms, clinging on for dear life, as though someone sought to drag him loose.

Edward's gaze reached beyond them to see what they were staring at.

A large black enclosed carriage stood within the courtyard. It was a grand vehicle and glowing with fresh polish, its lines traced with gold leaf, and on the door was a painted embossed coat of arms he didn't recognise.

"Ellen. John," he demanded, passing them and beckoning them on with his hand. They would certainly not find out who'd arrived by standing in the driveway gawking.

He heard them follow, their footsteps ringing on the cobble of the courtyard.

When Edward traversed the steps up to the front door, in a quick light jog, Davis opened it, his manner at its most toplofty, "Lord Edward, the Duke of Pembroke is in the best drawing-room. I did say you were not at home, my Lord, but he insisted upon waiting."

"Did he say what his call is regarding?" Edward asked quietly, his heart already hammering. *Pembroke?* Ghost like memories returned in a mist, of Ellen looking at his wife. *The Duke?*

"No, my Lord."

Taking a deep breath, Edward straightened his coat and collar before turning to Ellen. She stood just inside the door. "Take John up to wash, I will see to this."

She looked in shock. No, not shock, it was terror, and she was not looking at Edward but past him. John's hand dropping from hers, the boy visibly dressed himself in armour, changing from a child to a young man, his chin lifting, steeling himself. Edward had seen Ellen do the same often enough to know.

The Duke.

Turning, Edward followed their gazes to the drawing-room door across the hall. Pembroke stood there, his pale austere look fixed on John. For a man most probably in his fifties, Pembroke still held a dominant, slender figure which defied the shading of gray in the dark hair about his temples. He was dressed completely in black, apart from his white cravat and the white embroidery on his waistcoat. His bearing and physical presence filled even the open space of the hall. The man had a menacingly powerful aura reaching from him.

"John!" Pembroke clipped out the single word as a command, and by what appeared to be an instinctive or inbred response the boy went to him.

"Your Grace," John acknowledged, crossing to the man's side, his voice grave, weighted with the sound of resignation.

No! Ominous realisation tolled in Edward's thoughts. *Pembroke? The Duke?* He remembered the speculation he'd refused to contemplate in White's little more than a fortnight ago. *She would not have done this to me? Lied to me?*

"Please, don't take him from me?" Ellen rushed forward, passing Edward, as if she would throw herself physically on the man's mercy. But then she stopped, hesitating a few feet away from the Duke, no doubt losing her courage before the look of sheer hatred and disgust which was levelled on her.

"Move this woman aside." Pembroke thrust the words at Davis, his voice as full of denigration as his glare had been.

"Mama?" John dared to speak up, in a desperate whisper, and for that he received his own rebuke.

"What have I told you? You have no mother, John. Your mother is dead."

Edward saw the plea in John's wide eyes as he looked at Ellen, his lower lip quivering before it was caught between his teeth.

"We are going home," Pembroke growled, his gaze visibly warning Ellen to stay back. "Get in the carriage, John."

The boy didn't move, braving defiance, despite his obvious fear, he just looked at his mother.

Still standing before Pembroke, her arms limp at her sides, Ellen appeared lost, bowled over by this force which she clearly had no capacity to fight. "John, I'm sorry, I…"

Edward moved and blocked the doorway, as the Duke of Pembroke took hold of John's arm and drew him past Ellen, as though she did not even exist.

"You are not taking the boy." Edward's words halted the Duke's stride and astonishment crossed his expression. It seemed Pembroke was unaccustomed to refusal.

"Who are you to order me, Marlow? You have no say in this." The arrogant dismissing look the man gave Edward would have made most men quake in their boots, but Edward was not most men.

Edward felt the muscle in his jaw contract, his teeth clenching as he restrained the surge of anger, while his right hand tightened to a fist he itched to thrust into the bastard's condescending face. But he would not be bear baited into blows which would make him the one at fault and play straight into Pembroke's hands. Instead, squaring his shoulders, he met the Duke's imposing stare, defiantly, and refused to be set aside. Schooling his voice to a deliberate, calm, clear depth, bitter with contempt, Edward answered, "You are in my home, and handling my wife's son. I have every right." His voice echoed about the hall. "Let the boy go. It is you who have no right here, Your Grace." Edward used the title with disgust.

The Duke's gaze narrowed on him, a silver-blue even paler than Ellen's, the contrast made starker by the winged dark brows which lined them. Edward knew he was being measured and there was an odd light of some other thought at the back of the monster's damningly hard gaze as Pembroke spoke. "What sort of man are you, to take a whore to wife? You'll have *nothing* from me. Do you understand? You have taken on the wrong man, Marlow. I can crush you if I choose. You stole the boy. I have come to fetch him back. The child is mine. I have the legal right here, I..."

The sudden thrusting lance of pain in Edward's chest must have shown on his face, for the man stopped talking as his mouth twisted to a sneer. Then he finished, "I see, she never mentioned that. Get out of my way, Marlow. This has nothing to do with you."

Edward's eyes left their clash with the Duke's, flicking down to John.

Head down, eyes to the floor, John stood motionless in the Duke's grip.

Edward looked at Ellen, accusation burning inside him.

"Is this true?" She was standing to one side, observing his bewilderment with a look of regret which spoke the answer, but he would have the words from her mouth. Damn her, why had she not armoured him against this? *Why didn't she tell me?*

"Ellen, is this true?" he snapped at her.

She nodded.

Taking on the qualities of a hunting wolf circling its prey, the Duke glared at her, before turning back to Edward. "Step aside."

What choice did he have? "This will not be the end of it," Edward said as the Duke came forward.

"Come near the boy again and I'll destroy you."

Edward ignored him and pressed a reassuring hand on John's shoulder as he passed. In return John gave him a forlorn look. Edward saw that John had known Pembroke would come.

John's gaze turned to Ellen.

She moved, as though pulled in their wake by a magnetic force, walking past Edward.

She'd known it too.

"John!" At Ellen's call, Edward turned to watch them in the courtyard. Ellen's reservation had dissolved, she'd rushed forward and tried to take John but Pembroke pushed her away and signalled one of his footmen to hold her back.

Edward moved quickly, striding out to where the pitiful scene was unfolding. When he reached Ellen he pushed the Duke's man aside, holding her about the waist himself while she writhed and tugged for freedom, crying out to John as Pembroke climbed up into the carriage after the boy.

The footman shut the door and her fight drained as quickly as it had come. On a sob she pushed Edward's arm away and straightened, silent suddenly and apparently resigned. But belying the tears rolling down her cheeks, Edward saw her meet the bastard's condemning gaze with a look that refused to be downtrodden.

The carriage drew into motion, lurching forward and Pembroke's footmen caught the grips at the rear, hopping up onto the footplates as it pulled away. Ellen was watching, standing motionless, as the black shiny beast of a vehicle turned to pass beneath the arch of the raised portcullis. She followed then, slowly at first, lifting her hand when Edward glimpsed John at the other window looking back, as though she thought she could still touch John if she tried. Then as the carriage swept out of the confinement of the courtyard, the driver's long whip flicked up in an outward lick at the two pairs of jet black horses' backs and the carriage pulled into a quicker pace. The strike-strike pattern of the animals trot on the gravel filling the air, the coachman called them on.

Ellen began to run, her pace increasing with that of the carriage as she clutched at her skirt to draw it from her feet, running out on to the drive behind it.

"John! I love you! I love you! Don't forget!" she called in a desperate voice as the carriage's distance from her expanded, broadening by the second.

With the carriage pulling ahead steadily, Edward doubted John heard her.

Her hand still raised in its direction Ellen stopped, now silent again, watching the snake-like black sheen of carriage and horses trail along the gravel drive and over the brow.

When it disappeared from view, she instantly turned and walked back towards the house, passing him without any acknowledgement. But despite her silence he knew she was like a dam about to break beneath a flood of emotion.

Edward followed but said nothing, letting her lead him to the private drawing-room where they and John had shared so many happy hours.

Her fingers smoothing her dress and pelisse, her defensive shell rigidly in place, securing all her dammed up pain, she lowered herself into a seat, perching on the edge of the chair.

She was his ice maiden again, the real, living, breathing, Ellen, hidden behind her wall of perfect social etiquette. Her eyes lifting to his, dared him to ask his questions.

An hour ago they'd been like any normal family.

He shook his head, turning away and taking a moment to gain control over his own feelings. It seemed he was not as skilled in setting them aside as she was, nor so experienced in dissembling.

But then he'd not had as many opportunities for need, nor practice.

She lied to me.

He moved to the decanters which stood on a chest against the wall, glinting in the spring light that spilled through the tall windows, and filled two glasses with his brother's French brandy. Then walked back to Ellen and held one out. "Take it." When she did not, he thrust it a little forward, in a gesture that warned her not to anger him needlessly.

But the chink in her armour was visible as she took the glass — her fingers shook. She lifted the rim of the glass to her lips and sipped the amber liquid, her eyes cast down avoiding his gaze.

"Is he John's father?" Edward could not keep the bitter accusation from his voice, he did not want to feel this way, but she had kept it from him. What was he supposed to think — feel? He felt deceived, betrayed and wounded.

What did I do to deserve lack of trust and lies!

Her eyes shot to his, a mocking laugh escaping her lips and he suddenly knew the answer before she spoke. "No, Edward, he is not John's father, he is mine. Everything I told you is true."

Bowled over, ice cold shock raced from his gut spreading out across his skin. He'd married the daughter of the Duke of Pembroke. He dropped into a chair opposite hers, and threw back his brandy in a single gulp, while she broke into a barrage of indignant words.

"You are not often at a loss for words, Edward. I suppose you wish to know the whole of it now?"

He stopped her with a lifted hand, angry still, perhaps even more so. Why had she not trusted him with this? "All I wish to know," he answered, "is why on earth you did not speak of this before? Did Gainsborough know?"

Her mocking laugh rang out again. "Why do you think his fortune bloomed? He was not a man of such great substance when he took me on. Have you known many other men keep their mistresses for so many years? He called me his treasure for more than one reason. He recognised me at once, and forced the General to hand me over with a sum the man could not ignore then proceeded to blackmail my father, knowing my father would not want anyone in the *ton* to know his daughter was so sullied. I think Gainsborough found it more satisfying to know who it was he fucked, than he did to actually fuck me."

"Do not be coarse, it doesn't suit you," Edward clipped out, as he rose to pour a second brandy. Of course she'd used the word deliberately to shock him — to kick him back for accusing her.

"He has been taunting the ton for years, taking me into clubs and willing someone to recognize the treasure he had in his hand," she continued. "No one ever did. He thought it a great game."

And her father had let her endure it. Her hurt and anger washed over Edward, but he was not succumbing to pity again, she had lied to him, or at least withheld the truth.

He returned to his seat, swallowing a second measure of the fiery liquid to deaden his pain.

She'd betrayed him. Slamming the glass down on a table at his side, he couldn't even look at her.

"I am coarse, Edward!" she snapped, bringing his gaze back to her angry glare. "Do you not even see it now? There is an empty casket in my family's mausoleum which declares it!" Leaning forward, she deserted her glass of brandy, leaving it on the floor as her fingers curled about the arms of her chair and she glared at him, visibly daring him to accuse her.

How did she wish him to respond to that? He hadn't a clue.

"He pretends you're dead?" he echoed eventually, the disbelieving statement spoken from his confused, tangled thoughts. He was in shock. His stomach churned.

"I told you I wrote to my family when Paul died, that was true," she began again, while his thoughts reeled on. "We'd eloped, Paul and I. What I did not tell you was that Paul was the sixth son of the Earl of Craster. He'd made an offer which my father rejected out of hand. Nothing but a first son and title would do for his exacting standards. I couldn't give Paul up. We loved each other. My father wanted me to marry a man twice my age. I refused, and he locked me up, allowing me nothing to eat until I would agree to his choice. My maid took a message to Paul and through her we planned to elope. Three nights later we were on the road to Gretna.

"When Paul died, I had no idea what to do. I wrote to his parents and mine. I never heard from them. When I gave birth I wrote again, begging for their help. My father came. When he found me I had already become the mistress of the Lieutenant Colonel. He took John away from me. *John was only a baby.*" Her last statement was spoken with a note of deep despair, a reflection of the memory visible in her pale blue eyes. But swallowing it back, as she was want to do, and hiding it beneath her thickened skin, she continued, "He forced me to sign away any right to John, and refused to acknowledge me ever again. He said I had disgraced myself, and he would not let me disgrace my family, he said I was dead to them. But he still took John. On his return he put a notice in the paper saying he had an heir, born to his daughter who had died of lung fever, following her husband's heroic death at Waterloo. They brought John up to think I was dead. Since then I have found ways to follow what they do. It isn't hard, the Duke of Pembroke's business is widely published.

"When I was mistress to the Lieutenant Colonel and the General, I found ways to watch John in the park when they brought him to London, then I sent word to my old maid who helped me meet him. He doesn't even remember the day he found out he did have a mother, he was too young. By the time my father found out, John was old enough to remember me. My father dismissed the maid. Since then I have always been in contact with John, in secret. Occasionally I managed to see him but mostly I have written. I wrote to him at the school often. For me his voice was such a blessing. When the King heard him sing once, he insisted my father enrol John at Eton and let him sing at the chapel."

"And now?" Edward found himself prompting, absorbed in her hideous tale. "John knew Pembroke would come, didn't he?" Her gaze met his, the wall down, her soul visible.

"Yes. He asked me two days after we reached here. I made a promise that he would not. A promise I knew I could not keep. But I wanted him to be happy for as long as we had. I didn't want him to spend these days living in fear of what was to come." Her eyes again dared Edward to challenge her for lying.

"But if you had told me." Edward sat forward, his voice no longer accusing but chiding.

"I thought you may send him back. My father is a powerful man. I did not want to take the risk."

Tipping his hands up in a gesture of disempowerment Edward eyed her with the hurt pain lying in his gut. "Do you still trust me so little? You wound me, Ellen. What have I done to deserve it? I've stood by you at every turn." He confronted her, injured pride heavy in his words, but his body shifted regardless, rising, itching to be closer to her as he crossed the short distance between their chairs and squatted onto his haunches before her, his hands gripping hers in her lap.

Her fingers squeezed his, in apparent acceptance of his unspoken offer of forgiveness and reconciliation. The pale, crystal-like sheen in her eyes caught the light from the window as her gaze met his. "I wanted to. I did. But Gainsborough had—"

She got no further as he pressed his forefinger to her lips for a moment. God, when was he going to stop hearing that bloody man's name from her?

"*I am not Gainsborough*," he growled releasing his impatience as he let go her hands and stood, turning back to pour himself another drink. He would not be compared to that man.

"I know." She had stood too, wishing to placate him, he could tell from her voice. "But can you blame me for my hesitation? I hardly knew you really. You are the first man since Paul—" Her voice broke for a moment before she continued. He refused to look at her, knowing if he did he would let her get away with insulting him again. *Comparing me to Gainsborough,* "—who has offered me true kindness. You have no power to fight against him, Edward. My father has an army of lawyers. There is nothing you could have done. He was right, he has the legal standing over John. I foolishly gave it to him. He would have found us sooner or later, even if we had moved on. What was the point of telling you? It seemed better to make the most of the time we had."

"If it was a *fait accompli*, why even take John from the school." Turning, his refilled glass in his hand, Edward eyed her with an expression he was sure still showed his disappointment. He'd not once let her down. He'd trusted her, but she had not returned his faith.

"Because Gainsborough knew where John was. You forget Gainsborough was not just losing me but losing his power to blackmail my father. Gainsborough would have tried to get to John first. He'd threatened to do it dozens of times if I didn't do what he wished. That night when he told me he knew about us, he said he had sent men for John. He threatened to hurt John if I saw you again. I do not like my father, but I know he will keep John safe. John is his heir you see, my father had no son. If John cannot be with me, he is safer with him."

Edward downed his drink. Another nail in the coffin then, the man would not easily let his heir go. "You have sisters, I remember."

"Yes three, younger than me, all wed now."

"You are in contact with them?"

She shook her head as though his suggestion was absurd. "As far as I know they think I'm dead. I thought it best to leave it that way. You forget how I was living. It was hardly something I would wish them to know."

"While you're left to suffer at the hands of vile brutes. Do you really think so poorly of yourself? I thought we'd begun to cure your self-loathing. It is like you are intent on doing some ridiculous penance. As though you think you deserve to be treated ill while your family live on in luxury without a care. Do you think this is all your fault?"

"I chose to run away with Paul," she answered quietly, holding his gaze uncertainly.

"Ellen." He set aside his glass and stepped forward, bracing her arms. She looked away. He shifted his grip to her face, cupping her jaw in his hands and turned her back. "*This is not your fault.* It is obvious to me now any blame lies firmly at your father's door. Give me time to think and we will work out how to respond, but I refuse to let him keep John." Her eyes opening wider, the pale blue caught the light from the window as she took a steadying breath. Her fingers closed over his then and drew them down.

"You will never cease to amaze me, Edward. I don't understand you sometimes. How can you not continue to blame me for this? I am the spurned daughter of the Duke of Pembroke, and you are not daunted by it?" Reaching up onto her toes she kissed his lips briefly, then, with a silly burst of fearful laughter and a shake of her head, she added, "If you can find a way to get John back you shall not simply be my hero, I shall bid to the church to have you sainted. And do you know what the most surprising thing is? I really think perhaps you can."

"I am known for my determination, Ellen. Perhaps *I* should have warned *you* of that." He felt a nervous laugh rise from his chest too, at the sheer audacity it would take to go up against a man like Pembroke. But God, if she finally came to believe in him it would be worth it, and it had to be worth it for John.

"You may say that again." A deep baritone rang out in empty mockery from the doorway.

Edward's gaze spun to the door at the same time as Ellen's.

Robert!

Hell.

Of all the moments for Edward's brother to return.

Edward's hands fell from Ellen's, one instead settling possessively about her waist as he moved to her side, while Robert looked her over without any impression of civility.

"It appears that I've caught you in a compromising moment, little brother. Very touching." Moving past Edward, Robert reached for the decanter. "You two have had me chasing all over London," he continued, with his back to them. When he turned around he flashed a broad grin at Ellen and then angled it at Edward, lifting his glass in a toast like gesture before asking,

"What was that egotistical bastard Pembroke doing here? His carriage nearly ran mine from the road when it turned out of the gate."

Better get this over with. If he did not, Robert would simply make Edward's life, and Ellen's, hell until he did. "That egotistical bastard, as you put it, is Ellen's father."

"*Good God.*" Robert paused, his glass close to his lips, casting Ellen an astonished look, before drinking. The glass, pulling away from his lips, he gave Edward a closed lipped insolent smile. "Done well for yourself then, Ed. Quite a prime little piece ain't she?"

Letting out a deep sigh, hinting at the lack of patience he had for his brother's obdurate and, at times, obnoxious behaviour, Edward launched into the introductions. "Ellen *this* is my brother, Robert, the Earl of Barrington. Robert, may I have the pleasure of introducing my wife."

Ellen watched as the Earl nearly spat out his drink. His eyes, rather than Edward's slate blue-gray, were brown, and the Earl's face had a few more world weary lines, but in stature and features they were alike and his hair was the same dark brown.

"I am too late then," he said, in a disparaging voice.

"Too late for what?" Edward queried, his fingers gripping harder at her waist.

"To stop you making a damned fool of yourself and the rest of us. Rupert said she was a beauty. I can see why you fell for her, *but Edward?*" The man had the audacity to look her up and down as though stripping the clothes from her body, then turned back to Edward. "As a mistress she's a gem. But a wife? *Have you gone mad?* I don't care whose child she is, she's been in Gainsborough's bed for God's sake. I had hoped, foolishly apparently, you wouldn't be insane enough to marry a whore."

Edward's hand left her waist in an instant, and in the next he'd gripped his brother's collar and flung the Earl backwards. The glass slipped from the Earl's fingers and fell to the floor, splintering and spilling its contents.

"Bloody hell!" The Earl called with a deep laugh underlying his words as he stopped his fall by catching at the back of an armchair and reached out his other palm to fend off another attack before it came.

Ellen gripped Edward's arm to deter him, and felt every muscle clenched but held in check.

The Earl straightened, an apparently defiant smile pinned on his face and when he spoke, a wicked challenging spark glinted in his dark brown gaze, "Feel better? You can hit me as much as you like, Ed, it won't make her anything other than a whore."

As Edward lunged forward with a snarl of anger, Ellen clung to his arm with both hands. "Edward don't! It doesn't matter! Let him think what he likes!"

Edward's arm fell and both men's eyes spun to her. The weight of his brother's gaze was like a physical force, assessing her.

Throwing him the sort of chastening glare she'd deployed in the London clubs she turned to Edward. "Please? You can understand why he's angry."

The Earl's lips parted in an even broader smile and looking at Edward, he said, "That's it, Ed, listen to her, she knows what she is."

Ellen felt anger brace Edward's arm again but he didn't vent it, instead a pained sound released from Edward's throat in a growl and he shook off her grip. "*God,* I cannot hold my temper with you!" he yelled at his brother. "Why are you determined to get beneath my skin? You always do it! I don't care to hear your damned poor opinion, so keep it to yourself!" His words carried the violence and anger his body held leashed. "I'll not listen to you slighting my wife for your own amusement!" Looking back at Ellen across his shoulder he finished. "Ellen, we're leaving. Go have Jill pack your things."

Ellen watched the Earl narrow his gaze on Edward. "There's no reason to overreact, Ed, you've just returned. I happen to need you here, with a whore for a wife or not." He threw in the insult at the last with a twist to his lips that deliberately tempted Edward to react.

Edward just stood, and she saw his chest rise and fall in restrained anger. Moving to Edward's side again, her hand circled his.

"*Apologise*," Edward growled.

"What? Are you joking? It's hardly slander." The Earl's insolent gaze turned to her.

"I said," Edward breathed in deeply, visibly leashing his anger, as his hand gripped hers firmly, "apologize to my wife."

The Earl shrugged, sending her a sarcastic smile. "Very well, Ellen, was it? I am sorry if I offended your precious sensibilities." His tone stripped the words of their meaning. He was not sorry.

"Luncheon is served, my Lords, my Lady." Ellen turned, as did Edward and his brother, looking at Davis who stood at the door. She saw the butler's dilemma immediately, the servants had worked for Edward for years and yet the Earl was their employer. They were in the middle of the brothers' division and Davis had come to break up the hostile reunion.

"Whether we are going or not, Edward, we should eat." Ellen cut her voice through the silence, prodding him into responding and both men looked at her again. "Edward?" After a moment he sighed and then nodded.

"Robert." Edward looked at the Earl and lifted his hand, encouraging his brother to go first.

With a privately amused look he did.

They ate in silence. The Earl sitting at the head of the table, maintaining his private smile, while Edward glowered at his plate. There was a deeper resentment between them than Edward had declared in London, she could see that much. But she was in no mood to talk or eat either. Her thoughts every few moments went back to John, wondering how far away he would be by now and if she would ever see him again.

"Considering you said you wished to eat, you are not doing very much of it." Her brother-in-law's mocking drawl reached across the table.

It was too much. She was not capable of this. "Excuse me," Ellen stated, setting down her knife and fork, "I do not feel like eating. I will leave the two of you to finish."

Edward's cutlery clattering onto his plate he rose as she did.

"No, Edward, stay with your brother, you have things to discuss."

Edward did not wish to, he had nothing to discuss with Robert. But, placed upon the spot to acknowledge his feelings and go, or stay, nodding, he said. "I'll come and find you, where will you be?"

"I don't know."

Tears shimmering in her eyes, Ellen turned away, and he was torn, unsure whether to follow or not as she ran from the room, but she'd said stay, and perhaps she wanted to be alone. Letting her go, he retook his seat hearing her footfalls race across the hall floor beyond the door and longing to be with her.

Breaking into a fresh roll to occupy his mind and hands, his heart physically feeling Ellen's pain, he challenged his brother, "Did you have to, Robert. Ellen is in no mood for your taunting and neither am I. If you have nothing good to say, say nothing."

With a sarcastic glance, his brother did not respond and said no more, holding his silence like a weapon; antagonistic as ever.

For the rest of luncheon, Edward fought to ignore the silence he'd asked for. He refused to let the anger it engendered show.

When Robert had been absent, life had been good, predictable, but since Robert's return it had become intolerable. Robert was a constant irritation, whether he spoke or not.

Bloody hell! Why was Robert so aggravating?

He was an outright bastard at times — times like this — and when he was not being a bastard, he was a self-centered, shallow, affected rake, who cared for nothing but pleasure. Edward hated that and hated him. *His own brother!* They should be close. But it was impossible.

Whoever had formed the analogy that blood was thicker than water was an imbecile. Just because you had the same blood running in your veins did not make you close. Robert had deserted Edward, used him and put upon him. As boys they'd been close, but then Robert had changed, he'd dropped out of college and become an ass, argumentative, obnoxious and intolerable and Edward loathed him.

Ignoring Robert, Edward ate. Meanwhile Robert looked as though he was amusing himself with some private bloody joke, at Edward's expense no doubt. Which of course meant Edward could not really ignore him. Physically, yes, but mentally Robert's presence was like a constant itch.

Chapter Eleven

Sitting in the circle of the rose garden in the warm afternoon light half-an-hour later, Ellen heard Edward approach. The rose bushes were bare of blooms, but the new growth was in shoot, and the narrow wrought iron seat at the heart of it had afforded her the silence and solitude she needed to think. It was a sign of how attuned to one another they'd become that he knew where to find her when no one else did.

He turned the corner of the arbour, met her gaze and paused on the threshold for a moment, offering her an apologetic smile with a slight shrug, as though declaring his inability to deliver the quick fix she longed for. "So what do we do then, stay or go?" he asked. He was straight to the point as always. She did not know the answer though. She could think no further than having lost John.

Her eyes following his movement she did not rise. She wasn't ready to go back inside. "If we go and John came back he wouldn't know where to find me."

"Is there any likelihood he will come back?" His manner and tone were solemn.

"No, none," she admitted as a shallow hollow laugh escaped her throat at the sound of her foolishness. "Am I silly, do you think, for sitting here and wishing it so?" Edward's tall frame collapsed onto the seat beside her and leaning forward, he rested his elbows on his knees, forming his fingers into a steeple as he let out a long sigh.

"I want my son back," she whispered, not even particularly to him. It was just a voiced longing that came from her heart.

He sat upright, one hand falling to his knee as the other reached about her, drawing her close. Her head fell to his shoulder and his chin rested atop her hair. "I know, Ellen, I want him back too. I will think of something. But for now, what about my brother? Do we stay here and see if he will mellow to our marriage, or do we go?"

"Where would we go?" She felt so small against him.

"To Forth's until I can find something else."

Ellen pulled up from his embrace to meet his gaze. "But then I would have separated you from your brother too."

"I was separated from my brother when you met me, before that we were separated for half a dozen years while he lorded it on the continent. You have not separated me from my brother, Ellen. That was already done by him. We are too different to be close."

The weariness and pain in his expression contradicted his words. He did not get on with his brother but she could see he *wanted* to.

"We will stay. Maybe you both just need time, and you will not have that if we leave."

He sighed. She stood, still holding his hand. And he rose then and stepped closer, his eyes glinting. "Shall we go to bed?" He clasped the back of her neck and his thumb stroked her skin.

"It's the afternoon, Edward," she shook her head, but despite her denial, the need in his eyes struck her hard, "everyone will know." The side of her that was still her father's daughter pleaded not, and yet she knew it would relieve her pain, if only for a short time she could escape it.

"And that makes us care because?" he challenged, with a rough laugh. "I need you, now. Come to bed." His voice was earthy.

"Yes," giving way to her own need as well as his, Ellen breathed the answer into his mouth.

⊰⊱

Even if their absence had not been noted, Ellen knew the tale of how they'd spent their afternoon would still spread about the servants' quarters. When Ellen's maid arrived to dress Ellen for dinner, Ellen's hair was tangled and her lips deep red. She looked exactly like the whore his brother had named her as she stood and faced the cheval mirror.

"Will you wear the white and red, my Lady."

The risqué dress I ordered in a rash moment, to torment my father; heavens, no. Edward's brother was lascivious enough.

Ellen turned. "No, the light green, Jill." The shade suited her coloring and would draw down her heightened color. The dress was Edward's choice, with a modest neckline and short puffed sleeves that flattered but did not flaunt. The material was Indian muslin, embroidered with vines and small white funnel shaped flowers. Its skirt opened from a fall beneath her breasts to reveal a plain ivory petticoat, which her long evening gloves matched. Yes, it would make a statement to his brother. She would look like a wife and not a mistress. Edward had chosen it very well.

"Will you curl my hair and set it high too please, Jill? I want to look elegant tonight."

The girl broke into an easy smile. "My Lady, I have never seen you not look elegant."

Ellen smiled also. The servants were distressed by John's loss too, and Jill had been doing her utmost to boost Ellen's mood.

Edward opened the door to Ellen's chamber, which she still used as a dressing room, and stopped on the threshold, feeling his jaw slacken at the sight.

Such a prize, his wife, there was no getting away from it, everything about her was perfect, she was like a painting, or a sculpture, whether she was dressed or undressed.

He smiled to himself at the thought of their love making this afternoon. It had been desperate, an escape into each other. But now she'd reset her defenses. He was no fool, she'd not applied this much effort in choosing her attire and dressing on any other night.

He leaned his shoulder to the doorframe as he watched her turn to sift through a drawer.

Not that he minded her making a show for his brother. He did not mind at all, he would just enjoy the sight himself. "You look beautiful."

She jumped, glancing across her shoulder. "I was just looking for my gloves. Ah, I've found them." She turned with a nervous smile, her gloves gripped in her hand.

"I like the way you've done your hair." He lifted his shoulder from the frame and walked towards her.

"Jill did it for me. According to your brother's maid it is an artful disarray."

He laughed. "Whatever it is, it suits you."

"You don't think it is too much?"

For all the years she'd spent as a mistress she was ridiculously self-conscious and unaware of her beauty.

"No, I do not think it is too much." Standing before her he curled his fingers and brushed them along the line of skin over her collar bone, then touched one of the heavy curls framing her face. "You look lovely." His eyes swept over the plait circling across her crown and disappearing into the chignon holding up her hair.

"Now you are teasing me."

His gaze fell to her parted lips and he bent to kiss them, drinking in his wife and all she meant to him. She responded like for like and his hand slid to the arch of her back pulling her closer, then moved to cup her buttock as a groan escaped his lips. At which Ellen stiffened, and he felt her fingers at his shoulders, her grip pushing him away. "If you begin this again, we shan't get down to dinner and your brother will be waiting." Ignoring the pressure of her hands he planted another quick kiss on her lips, steeling himself for the hours he could not be close to her.

"I doubt it," he answered, pulling away and taking her gloves from her hand to put them on for her. Then he offered his arm and like so they processed to dinner—to dinner and to face the sardonic arrogance of his bloody brother. He'd rather just take her back to bed.

"Ah, you did bestir yourselves to rise then. I was beginning to wonder if you would." Robert's opening shot of course was Edward's fault.

Walking Ellen to her seat, where the footman drew out her chair, Edward was not at all surprised to see her skin had turned a little pink. Another footman stepped forward with a trencher of soup ready to serve. Edward was not wrong then; Robert had not chosen to wait. Edward walked back about the lower table and took a seat facing Ellen, knowing this meal was going to be torture. However if he must face his brother for an hour he need not do it sober. As Edward sat, he turned to wave the lad who held the decanter of wine forward.

"So you two have had an entertaining afternoon."

"Leave it, Robert," Edward challenged, lifting his glass.

"What would you rather speak of then little brother? Ah, I know a subject that always gets you going—land. What I had meant to ask you, before I was made aware of your big adventure, is which of the fields are best for wheat and which for barley."

Edward dipped his spoon into the soup and began to eat, but not until his gaze had noted Ellen eating too. He had been worried at luncheon when she'd not eaten at all.

"Which for wheat and which for barley?" Robert repeated impatiently.

"Ask your steward."

"I asked Parker and Parker said you planned it yourself."

"Parker is quite capable. I should think it was the way you asked him that meant you did not get an answer."

Robert let his spoon fall to the edge of his bowl with a sharp clink, as though announcing his irritation.

Edward sighed, and then answered, "You circulate them, so see what was planted last year and ensure you do not use the same fields again. The meadows on the west are the best as they do not seem to catch the wind. The marsh meadows are better left to hay. Is that what you wish to know?"

He heard Robert pick up his spoon and take a mouthful, after a moment he spoke again. "Yes, but I would like you to write it out for me, everything you did and why."

"I am not sure I shall have time. Just ask Parker, *nicely*, and he'll tell you."

Robert's spoon hit the bowl with a harder clunk. "I have more of a mind to put the man off for not just telling me when he was asked, if he knew. I pay him well enough."

Edward drank his last mouthful of soup, left the spoon in the bowl and beckoned for a footman to take it. "Not everyone cares about money, Robert. Parker could get a job anywhere. He doesn't need to put up with your rudeness. You will get nothing from him if you speak to him as though he were dirt beneath your boots."

"That is not how I spoke to him."

Edward let his lips lift a little at Robert's defensive answer and looked at his brother. "That is how you speak to everyone, Rob." Their gazes held for a moment, as if Robert would challenge him, but then he seemed to make some decision and turned away, indicating to Davis to serve the rest of the dishes.

When Robert turned back, Edward didn't like the gleam in his brother's eye. "And of course in comparison you are perfect as usual, brother." Reaching for his drink, Robert looked at Ellen. "Ah, but now I remember, you are not quite so perfect after all. I wonder what father and mother would have said to you bringing home a wh—"

"Robert!" Edward pushed to his feet, sending his chair backwards, as he leaned onto the table facing his brother. "You've had your fun, now…"

"Sit down, Ed." Robert lifted a hand. "You're too bloody sensitive. You know I'm only doing it to rile you. Will you never cease biting?"

"Edward," Ellen whispered quietly.

Her tone chastised him, and when he glanced at her he received a quelling look, obviously calling for his temperance. A footman was already in motion to lift his chair. With a sigh Edward sat.

"What you are doing, Robert, is insulting my wife. Don't." Tossing his brother a disparaging glare, Edward picked up his glass and sipped his wine.

"Well then," Robert continued, spinning the stem of his glass in his fingers while Davis dished up the various elements of dinner. "What of you, Ellen? Is Pembroke really your father? I can hardly imagine how you came to be in your prior circumstance if that is the case."

"Yes, Pembroke is her father, and her circumstances are none of your damned business," Edward responded, leaning back while a footman filled his plate.

"The woman may speak for herself I am sure, Ed, and as she is my sister-in-law, as head of the family I think her circumstances *are* my concern, especially, if the two of you wish to live here."

"The more you talk the more you put me off the idea." Edward addressed the answer to his dinner, picking up his knife and fork.

"So what was Pembroke doing here anyway? I assume he cannot be best pleased to have a daughter whose a..."

"Stop!" Edward barked, still focusing on his food and not his brother.

"My father came for my son," Ellen answered, cutting into their argument. Edward's gaze reached to her. Of course her steel-like armour was fully in place. Her fingers reached for her glass as though the whole affair had meant nothing to her. This was the woman he'd first met. He heard Robert choke on his mouthful, and watched in amusement as Robert reached for his drink.

"A son?" He spoke at length. The words full of astonishment.

"From my first marriage." Ellen set down her glass without looking at Rob and returned her attention to her dinner.

"Your first marriage?" Robert echoed.

"To Lord Paul Harding, a Captain in the Fifty-second Regiment, he died at Waterloo. That was how I came to be alone. We had eloped. My father did not wish me to marry the sixth son of an Earl. It was not even that a military income was not enough; it was simply a matter of pedigree. Nothing but a Duke would do for me you see, my Lord." Edward watched as Ellen borrowed his brother's mocking expression and tone. "Even you would be beneath his exacting standards, Lord Barrington. My father will have nothing to do with me, but my son is his heir."

"*His heir?*" again Robert repeated.

"Yes," Ellen responded, taking a cut of meat to her mouth.

Edward's eyes left his wife as he sensed Robert turn to him. "You *are* in trouble then little brother, crossing Pembroke was not advisable. Did you have the boy here?"

Edward didn't answer but turned back to his food.

"I will take that as a yes then. And I presume Pembroke has him now. Well that is a turn up, husband and father all in one hit. It's a good thing then that I got Gainsborough off your back."

Edward set his cutlery down. He did not want to rise to this, he knew Robert enjoyed baiting, it may be a game, but Edward couldn't help himself. "What exactly did you do, Rob?"

"Ah, and now he wishes to speak. See, Ellen, I have at last found a subject that interests him." Robert's gaze shifted from Ellen to him, with a taunting look. "I made certain he would not follow, that was all."

"How?" The single word echoed about the otherwise silent room, while the two footmen and Davis stood back, expressionless, supposedly blind and deaf.

"Let us say," pausing, Robert picked up his wine, drank it and then held out the glass for a refill. Edward waited, knowing Robert itched to have him chase. The smile Robert cast on Edward as he looked back, said it all, Edward heard the unspoken words, *aren't you dying to know*, "I made the man a proposition he could not refuse."

Edward's patience broke. "Which was?" he ground out.

"To leave you alone or to face me at dawn."

"*You did not.*"

"Of course not, the man's a coward."

Turning back to his meal, Edward suddenly found that his appetite had fled. "You did not need to do that."

"Why, because it might mean you were beholden to me instead of the other way about?"

Glancing at his brother, Edward faced a look of iron. He'd not seen that determined expression on Robert's face for a long time; not since they had raced each other or wrestled as children. "Why?" Edward responded, harshly. "Because it was not your battle and you had no need to get involved."

"But, as I thought I explained, it *is* my business, Ed. I am head of the family. What you do reflects on me and you are my responsibility."

"*Funny*, you have never cared before." Edward leaned back and indicated for a footman, to take the half full plate away.

"Well I care now."

Robert did not often get angry. He'd many weaknesses but anger was not one of them. Anger was Edward's flaw. His heart thumped as he watched his brother. Robert *was* angry.

"Forget the rest, Davis, the staff can have it," Robert barked. "Just pour the port."

Edward looked at Ellen; she was blushing and silent, looking at her plate. She hadn't eaten much. She definitely did not like the turn the conversation had taken, but he wanted to know what his brother had done.

"What happened with Gainsborough?" Edward pushed, as the footmen moved about them to clear the table.

"I did not go looking for him. He came looking for you." Robert progressed, holding Edward's gaze with an accessing look. "First his bullyboys knocked at the house, and then they came to White's after Rupert, to find out where you had gone. I was not about to let the man harass us, was I? Nor did I like the idea that he should chase after you. So I faced him off, not in the seedy little club you favoured but in White's. He soon backed down. He said I had misunderstood the situation. He was merely looking for you to close some business deal, or some such nonsense. The man's ridiculous. Anyway the outcome is he will not be bothering you. *But Pembroke, Ed?*" Tutting, Robert raised the glass Davis had just filled and looked across its rim at Edward. "*He* is not a man to make your enemy. That was a little foolish."

"It was hardly planned," Edward answered, glancing at Ellen, who looked at him. Her eyes showed discomfort and perhaps a desire to be anywhere else but in this room.

"No? Now there is the rub." Robert continued. "I cannot make out how my pragmatic brother, who thinks through everything before he takes a step, is suddenly barrelling off with Gainsborough's—"

Edward's hand curled into a fist and slammed onto the table, visually telling Robert to cease insulting Ellen. She jumped and Davis chose the moment to leave, clicking the door shut behind him. Edward breathed deeply and scowled at his brother while Robert merely skipped the offensive word and carried on with a smirk.

"—in the middle of the night. But then she is pretty. I can see that." He spoke as though Ellen was not there, offering her nothing but disrespect.

"That's enough, Robert," Edward warned and looked at Ellen. "Ellen?" The question asked her if she wished to leave, but Robert progressed before she could answer.

"Very well, then instead tell me what you plan to do?" Edward watched Robert lean back, grip his glass by the bowl and swill his port, smirking all the while.

"I have not decided." Edward answered, wishing he had the power to ignore his brother's taunts, Robert obviously enjoyed prodding. It made Edward feel like a damned puppet the way Robert could pull his strings. And what he had intended to do before his brother returned was ask for a job, but at this particular moment the request stuck in his throat.

"Will you stay then?"

"Do you want me here?"

"What are you asking me to do, beg? I can get along without you if I must."

"I know you can. That was why I left," Edward answered, his eyes fixing on the glinting dark ruby red liquor in his glass as he lifted it to his lips.

"You need not have done so." He glanced up as Robert's voice sobered. Robert had arched one eyebrow, implying, *so why did you?* Edward looked back at his glass and said nothing. He did not wish to have this conversation.

"I'll tell you why you really left," Robert continued. "Because I put your bloody nose out of joint by coming back, that is why. What did you expect me to do, leave you to play Earl until I died? I cannot help it that I was born first."

His brother's statement was unjust. It irritated Edward, and his anger and voice rose in consequence. "I don't care about that."

"No, then what do you care for, Ed? Because you make me feel like a damn leper and I am struggling to understand it."

Ellen coughed, artificially. They both ignored her.

"I did not ask for the responsibility. You left me no choice but to take it on. You were not here."

"Ah, so that is the rub then, that I left the burden on you."

"That is not it at all."

"Then *what is*? I would have to be blind not to see that you have an intense dislike of me."

"How may I dislike you? I hardly know you? We have not seen each other since school."

Keeping his gaze on his glass, immersed in thoughts he did not care to face, Edward heard his brother sit forward in his chair.

"This ends now, Ed."

Edward looked at him. Robert was looking at Ellen, "She is a whore." It was a direct insult and Ellen held his gaze, her chin lifted, defiance glinting in her eyes.

Edward rose. He'd had enough of this. "She is my wife," he clipped out. "Ellen." Lifting his hand, he urged her to come to him.

"And before that Gainsborough's mistress." Robert barked, rising too, his gaze turning to Edward. "For God sake, Ed, you have to divorce her. She is using you. Rupert is right, it is too great a scandal and it affects the whole family. What of our cousin, Rowena? This will affect her too."

Edward's brow furrowed in astonishment. *No.* He lifted his hand higher, calling Ellen to him. *No,* he was not listening to this. He did not care for Robert's opinion. He was not letting his family interfere and he was certainly not letting Ellen go.

She rose and moved to his side.

He gripped her hand in silent reassurance and faced his brother. "No, Robert." Before turning to Ellen and saying, "The air is stale in here, we're leaving."

He walked away then, pulling her after him, without any idea in what direction he led.

"You're a fool," Robert called, as they left the room.

"Where are we going?" Ellen whispered, her fingers clinging on to Edward's as he strode out of the dining room. She was struggling to keep his pace, so he narrowed his stride, but he could not reduce his speed. Striding across the hall he headed towards the family wing opposite

"Somewhere he's unlikely to follow." Edward carried on along the hallway only stopping when they reached the end. There he opened the door of a small sitting-room. It had once been his mother's personal space. It was unlit, dark, bar the bluish-silver moonlight casting shadows from the open curtains. Drawing Ellen in, he left the door ajar and let a little light spill from the distant hall.

Ellen thought the room lifeless and forgotten, as though it had been left untouched for years, lonely. Three single chairs sat in a triangle about the empty fire-grate, and in one corner of the room stood a pianoforte. She freed her hand from Edward's, walked across the room and ran her fingers over the polished mahogany. It was beautiful.

"Do you know how to play that thing?" Edward asked, still standing at the door.

Ellen looked back. His face was in shadow, all she could see was his silhouette against the light from the hall. But even her husband's silhouette was magnificent. The familiar pain of acknowledged love swelled in her chest. What had she done to deserve this man defending her?

"Your brother is right."

"What?" he questioned in an astonished voice.

"My father can make your life hell if he chooses. The ripple of it would run through your whole family. Would you really risk that for me? If you said I lied to you, you could have a divorce."

He'd crossed the room in a second and his hand was at her neck, pulling her close, his thumb beneath her jaw. His brow resting onto hers, his breath brushed her face. He smelt of the richness of port—sweet, warm and intoxicating. She longed to close the distance and kiss him but she had to give him the chance to walk away. He must know exactly what he had agreed to in that small church when he'd married her now—what he'd said I will to.

"I will not give you up," he whispered tipping her face upwards with his thumb so her mouth was just below his own.

"I would not hold it against you. You've done enough for me, Edward."

"I will never do enough for you, Ellen. We are in this together. I am not walking away from you. Get it into your pretty head, sweetheart, *please*."

Her chest tightened so much it was hard to breathe as her fingers reached for the solid rock that was Edward, resting on his midriff. "I don't want to be the reason your family falls apart, Edward."

"Ellen," his thumb brushed the sensitive skin beneath her jaw, "you are my family, you and John. You come before my brother. When we have John back we will make a new life, somewhere else, just the three of us, as we were. We could go to America if you wish? Your father will not find us there."

She didn't speak, just stood before him, breathing in the breath he breathed out.

"Ellen, what do you say?"

"Yes." A breathless whisper left her lips and then his mouth descended to hers. The kiss felt endless, earth shuddering, as though the two of them were lost in time and she knew she would never doubt his commitment again.

"Do you want something to drink?" he asked.

She nodded.

"A glass of good champagne then, to celebrate fetching John back and our future."

She smiled.

"I'll go and find Davis, get him to bring it and a candelabrum along. Perhaps you could play for me, I would like to hear it?" Smiling, he glanced at the pianoforte. Then his lips brushed hers once more before he let her go, stepped back and turned away.

He was humming a hymn they'd sung that morning in church as he walked from the room. Smiling to herself, Ellen turned, and sweeping her dress beneath her she sat on the stool before the pianoforte. She lifted the lid covering the ivory keys carefully and brushed her fingers across them, not playing but revering the beautiful instrument. She had not touched a pianoforte since she'd married Paul. One finger pressed down forming a single note. It was tuned. She played a second and a third, her fingers finding their path from memory, without thought.

The sound of a song her mother had taught her rang throughout the room. Ellen shut her eyes and let it flow through her. She loved music, playing had never been a chore to her. And she was so absorbed in it she only knew someone else was in the room when a hand settled on her shoulder.

She turned, half jumping out of her skin, and then stood. It was not Edward she faced but his brother. "Lord Barrington?" He'd shut the door. "Edward will be back in a moment." Her heart thumped. Fear beating hard inside her.

"He's gone downstairs," The Earl answered. Inoffensive words but his tone set goosebumps tingling across her skin.

"I just wondered, what you—" His gaze held hers, his eyes dark and his hand lifted.

"Don't do this," she urged, cutting over his words as her fingers pressed against his chest. She leaned back as he leaned forward, but he didn't stop.

"*No,*" she forced, her palms pressing harder against his chest, as his hands touched her waist and slid upwards.

"Leave me alone!" She begged and ordered. *Why was he doing this?*

He just smiled. His eyes as hard as flint.

"Get off me!"

Fisting her hands she struck his shoulders and his head, franticly fighting his descent as his weight forced her back, coming down on her. Her bottom pressed onto the pianoforte's keys and they made a sound, a mix of uncoordinated notes as his fingers covered her breast.

"Get off me!"

With a low growl, he taunted, "Wouldn't you rather have the elder brother than the younger? Think how much more you can gain from me?"

Ellen opened her mouth to scream, but the sound was smothered by the sudden pressure of his lips. Pinned beneath him, his hand gripping her breast and pressing her back, she couldn't move. But she wasn't going to let this happen. Her fingers clawed to gain a grip on his hair and pulled and her teeth bit his lip.

Then suddenly, his pressure was gone, lifted from her.

"*Edward.*" She voiced his name on a sob of relief, half cry, half shout.

He'd gripped the Earl's arm, pulled him off and thrust him aside. Edward held out his hand to her. She didn't take it. She hugged him fiercely clinging to his offered safety, embracing his midriff, her cheek pressing against his chest.

"*What the hell were you doing?*" Edward shouted across her head.

"Merely testing—on your behalf, I might add. Don't you want to know if she's loyal?" She looked back, not letting go of Edward. The Earl's fingers touched the blood on his lip as he climbed to his feet.

Edward's body was braced with a violent anger, all his muscles were taut.

The Earl laughed.

Did the man have a death wish?

Edward moved like a striking lion, slipping from her grip. While his brother toppled back against the wall, letting it take his weight. "I don't want a fight with you." He held up his open palms.

"God, I should knock you senseless!" Edward bellowed, chest heaving, and hands curled to fists, while she clung to his coat from behind as though she could hold him back.

His brother laughed again and scathingly concluded, "She's a whore!" As if it meant any man could do anything to her that he wished.

Edward didn't hesitate again, and Ellen let him go. He grasped the lapel of The Earl's coat, yanked him forward and knocked him down with one punch.

"Get up you bastard!" Edward yelled, fists raised and ready to strike again.

"Why, so you can hit me again? I'm trying to help you. She is with you for what she can get, Ed, wake up. Don't be so bloody naïve. And I shan't be your damned punch bag. We both know your anger at me, is about more than *her*."

"Edward, leave him be, please." Ellen whispered. She didn't want this. She didn't want to become the center of their battle.

"Get up!" Edward repeated glowering at his brother, his fists still clenched.

Watching Edward all the time, the Earl stood, showing no intent to fight.

Edward's arms suddenly fell slack and he straightened. "I should kill you, but you are not worth it!"

Ellen gripped his hand, and his fingers wrapped about hers. "Rot in hell Robert, I shan't join you."

Turning away, Edward pulled her with him, speaking as he moved. "We are leaving, Ellen. Jill can pack and send your boxes to Forth's. We'll go on ahead. I'll get Davis to stir up the grooms, I want to ride. I need to burn off his fumes."

❧❧

Bright silver moonlight reflected back from the dew dampened cobbles, when they thundered into Lord Forth's stable-yard less than an hour later. The sound of iron horseshoes clattering and ringing on the cobble, announced their arrival. Ellen patted Pearl's neck, it was damp with sweat. In moments wide-eyed grooms appeared in the empty space, still pulling on boots and buttoning waistcoats as they hailed Edward and came forward to take the horses' bridles.

Edward had ridden like a madman and she'd struggled to keep pace. They'd left everything behind. She'd just had time to change into her riding habit while Edward barked at poor Jill to pack everything else and bring it later.

Beside Ellen, Edward took one foot from the stirrup and swung it across his animal's rump, throwing himself down to the ground. He landed firmly, his strength and agility clearly visible.

As she slipped her knee from the pommel of her side-saddle, he crossed the distance between them and caught her waist as she dropped.

His irritation with his brother had not dissipated despite their hell for leather ride. She could feel it in his tense grip as he caught up her gloved hand. Turning to look at the grooms, he ordered, "Walk the horses before you unsaddle them," then asked, "Is Lord Forth here?"

"Yes, my Lord." Tilting his cap, one groom leaned in a stiff bow. "My Lady."

Edward nodded acknowledgement and tugged her into motion. For each of his long strides she had to take two, the skirts of her habit tangling about her legs. She tried to lift her skirts away from her feet but it distracted her from keeping pace and as her heel struck a damp cobble at the wrong angle, her ankle twisted. Edward's strength took her weight, gripping her hand more firmly and hauling her up, and then she found herself pressed hard against his solid chest and his arm about her. She felt his heart racing, in time now with her own, and the sharp breaths that clawed into his lungs.

"Edward," she met his gaze, "please, forget it."

"Forget? *He is my brother, Ellen.*" There was pain in his voice. His brother's assault had injured Edward more than her. This thing with his brother had brought Edward to London, bitter and angry. It had tormented him then, and now? She felt his next breath swell in his lungs.

Her fingers framing his jaw, she sought to intercede. "I do not think he meant harm, Edward. He did not physically hurt me. He knew where you were. He knew you were coming back. He cannot have planned to do much in the moments he had." She had realized that now, now she could think back and her thoughts were not clouded by fear. "As he said he was testing me and trying to protect you. He did not defend himself or fight you, Edward. I do not think he intended any more than what he did."

The breath he'd taken puffed out in a rush as he caught her hands and pulled them away sharply, his expression twisting in a disgusted sneer. "He insulted you and assaulted you, Ellen! I don't give a damn for his reasons."

"I've experienced far worse, Edward, let it pass,"

She could see his frustration he was clearly itching for a fight. But she knew it was not her he wished to argue with. "I'm sorry, Ellen." He let her hands go. His were shaking. "I am angry because I did not do what I should have done. I should have hit him again, and knocked the hell out of him. But I am too decent to do it, when he has no decency at all. And at this moment, I wish I were more like him, I should have murdered the bastard. He questioned why I don't like him and then attacked you!"

"Edward." she breathed.

"Give me time to get this in perspective, Ellen." His chest rising with a deep breath, one hand lifted to sweep back his hair. "Forth will knock it out of me. Come on." Catching up her hand again, he began walking. But already his pace was slower, the tension in his grip looser.

The butler held the door open when they reached it and as they entered Forth stepped into the hall with Julie behind him, dressed for the evening. "To what do we owe this honour? It's rather late, Ed," Lord Forth challenged.

Ellen had felt anxious about their late intrusion but her fears were misplaced. Despite his words a broad smile split Forth's lips beneath his moustache and Julie rushed forward.

"We're here to take up your offer." Standing tall Edward tilted up his chin.

Ellen understood then—he hated the idea of asking for help, even from his friend. Edward was many wonderful things, but one of them was proud.

Wishing to return the support he always gave her, she moved closer and wrapped both her hands about the one that gripped hers.

"My offer?" Forth questioned, his brow furrowing in confusion.

"Of hospitality, Robert has returned, and if I spend another night beneath his roof I think I'll kill him."

Forth's eyebrows lifted. "Well then you had better stay, I'd rather that than watch you hang." Ellen watched Casper's hand cover his mouth. She could see he'd made the offer but hadn't actually expected Edward to take it up.

"Could we trouble you for coffee?" Edward pressed. "I think Ellen could do with some." The anger had already left his voice.

"Of course," it was Julie who answered, taking Ellen's arm.

Reluctantly Ellen let Edward go.

"What has happened? Where is John?" Julie asked, leading Ellen towards the drawing-room.

Ellen glanced back over her shoulder and saw Edward answer something Casper had said in a low voice she could not hear. When she turned back Julie was looking at her with even greater concern. "You have not left John behind. What has happened?"

Emotion seeped from Ellen's heart, but she steeled herself against it. "There's no need to fuss, Julie, really, I'm fine." But she was not. For the past few hours she'd been strong for Edward, yet suddenly, just hearing John's name, made the weight of it too much. Her emotions toppled. Tears filling her eyes, her words were proved a lie.

"Sit down," Julie quietly commanded leading her to a chair, which Ellen willingly dropped into, her legs now too weak to hold her up.

"Smithers send for the coffee and have a room prepared," Julie ordered of the hovering butler, before turning back to Ellen. "Tell me what has happened?" Concern edged Julie's voice as she sat beside Ellen.

But Julie's kindness only unleashed a torrent of pain. Ellen had known so little kindness in her life. Like a whirlpool pain rose up inside her, and then from the hall she heard Lord Forth say, "I take it he does not like your bride."

And Edward's reply, "Rob likes nothing I do, least of all Ellen."

Everything had gone wrong. Her floodgate broke, tears spilling from her eyes and Ellen covered her face with her hands. Her shoulders shook with soundless sobs and Julie's arm surrounded her.

"Oh, my dear," Julie said, rubbing Ellen's shoulder. "Please, pour Lady Edward a madeira, David." Ellen lowered her hands, her crying easing as she breathed more deeply. The footman across the room moved to do Julie's bidding.

In a moment Julie was pressing a glass into Ellen's shaking fingers, as the echo of male voices in the hall drew nearer. Ellen held her breath and fought for control, her eyes lifting to Julie. "My father took John."

Instantly she was drawn into a tight hug. "Oh, Ellen, why?"

The tears ran anew, and for a moment Ellen just let them run and felt the sorrow she'd hidden deep inside for too many years, and then she heard Edward's footsteps.

Ellen pulled away from Julie and swallowed a mouthful of madeira, wiped at the streaks on her face and sipped the sweet burning liquid again. It eased the knot of emotion in her throat.

As the men entered she set a closed lip smile on her face and looked back at Julie, silently asking her not to tell, but Edward's gaze was already taking in the signs of her distress. Instead of sitting in a chair he moved beside her, perched his hip on the arm of the sofa, reached for her hand and wove his fingers through hers. She knew the remains of his anger had dissolved when he'd seen her upset, he was forever selfless. His anxiety was for her now.

"Tell us what has happened?" Julie queried, watching them both.

"The Duke of Pembroke is my father." With a light sigh Ellen began the explanation. She couldn't not tell them, when they were so generously taking them in. Lifting her gaze to Julie's she waited for the look of sudden understanding that would condemn her. It did not come. She continued, her eyes on Julie's, she wouldn't hide from this—the moment Julie would realize Ellen was unclean and not worthy of her comfort and friendship. "John is his heir. My first husband and I eloped. My father no longer recognises me, but he needs John. We'd taken him from school and my father came to fetch him back. Then Edward's brother returned and now they have fought, because of me." At that she stopped, catching a breath to block the tears which threatened to rise again. Then on another little sigh she concluded. "And now everything is one gigantic muddle."

Contrary to Ellen's expectations, Julie's expression was amazement, not disgust.

"I knew it." Julie exclaimed, turning to Casper. "Did I not tell you?" Then looking back at Ellen, she said. "You have an uncanny resemblance to Penny."

"My sister?" Ellen breathed, feeling a sharp pain grip her heart.

"The Marchioness of Wiltshire is my dear friend." Julie continued, with breathless excitement. "We were presented in the same year. But now I come to think of it Ellen, Eleanor... *Eleanor... Good gracious.*" Julie's fingers pressed to her mouth.

Finally she understood.

"She thinks you dead." Julie said, her hand falling. "They all think you dead. She has spoken of your funeral. Her eldest sister who eloped, it was said you died of a fever on the continent."

Edward lifted their joined hands on to his thigh, covering Ellen's with his other hand and holding it more tightly.

"Yes." Was all Ellen could think to say. What was there to say? It could hardly be a denial. The unbearable silence that followed forced her to say more. "You have answered something for me at least. I'd always wondered if my sisters and my mother knew the truth, or if my father had lied to them too. Now I know."

"But I am sure she would wish to see you." Julie responded, hurriedly. "She speaks of you so often, so fondly. If I write and tell her you are alive, and here, I know she would come."

Ellen shivered. She would love to see her sister, but her father would not agree to it.

"Ah, here is the coffee." Casper stood. "Would you rather have something stronger, Ed? Brandy?"

"Yes." The single word was a solid deep sound, Ellen glanced up at him. He was looking towards Casper, but his thoughts were elsewhere.

"Coffee, Ellen?" Julie asked.

"Yes. Please."

Julie rose and took Ellen's glass of half-drunk Madeira. "I could write to her tomorrow if you wished?" she said, moving to pour the coffee.

Ellen watched Julie. Her heart longed for the opportunity, yet her head warned her it was not possible. Penny was the oldest of her younger sisters. They had been close. It was Ellen's biggest sorrow when she'd eloped with Paul, that she'd been unable to say goodbye. But her father would not let her see Penny. "As much as I would love to see her, Julie, I would not want to involve Penny in this, my father—"

Edward unwound his fingers from hers, interrupting her speech, stood and walked over to Casper to take his drink, then he turned to her, his gaze fixed and intent.

She knew that stubborn look, it meant he would not be shifted from whatever notion he'd set into his head.

"Julie is right," he began, holding Ellen's gaze. "That is the answer—if you want John back. We cannot fight the man with lawyers, but if your family recognize you again your father would look too much the fool to deny you. You should meet your sister and write to the others. They are all married now, none under his control, and all of them to influential men. If together they stood against your father I would like to see him fight against that. He'd look ridiculous if he did.

"We are going to London. That is what we will do, Ellen. Brazen it out and make the man squirm. We shan't go after him. We shall force him to come to us."

Ellen shook her head. "I can't do it, Edward. I could not face them now."

With that Edward set down his glass, walked to where she sat and squatted down onto his haunches. His hands rested on her forearms. "Do you want John back?" When he spoke one eyebrow lifted, visibly adding emphasis to his point.

Ellen didn't hesitate. "You know I do." But this would take more courage than she had.

"Then what choice do you have?" His touch slipped from her arms and he rose. Her eyes followed his movement. "Make them face you. Make your father face what he's done."

"And what if he makes it public?" she whispered.

"Then it is him that is shamed not you," Edward answered.

Ellen took a breath and her eyes turned to the coffee Julie passed her, aware that they all studied her.

She had been the center of attention before. She'd learnt to shut out the scorn, but if it came from people she loved. Could she do it? Could she do it for John? For John the answer could only ever be, yes, she had to try. With Edward, her rock, she could try.

Lord, would he never cease to amaze her, the audacity of this was ridiculous. This was her all powerful father, of whom she had been scared all her life, and yet she could see Edward's vision, he could be right. All she had to do was be brave. Her eyes lifted to Edward, he so very rarely seemed younger than her.

"I will do it."

"And we will come," Julie encouraged, warmth and determination in her voice. "I shall write to Penny and ask her to invite your family to London. We must gather as many people as possible to our side. You will need invitations. We must have a ball to launch her, Casper."

Julie had said 'our side'. She was taking up Ellen's battle then, flying Ellen's colors as it were. Ellen would have Edward's and his friends' support. What Edward had said the night she'd met Julie was true. Julie did not care about her past. It was a freeing thought. Though Edward had said she would not be cut if people knew the truth, she had not believed him. Now she was beginning to.

And if he was right in this, then he could be right about her father. Her eyes lifted to Edward. He'd done so much for her, and in return, their marriage had cast a deathblow to his relationship with his brother. She had to find some way to help him in return.

A while later Ellen stood in one of Lord and Lady Forth's guest bedchambers, dressed in a borrowed nightgown, leaning against the windowsill.

John was somewhere beneath the stars she saw, thinking of her as she thought of him, wondering if she would come for him, waiting. She knew it. Her fingertips touching the window pane, she looked out across the sweeping lawns into the distance as Edward blew out the candle. Darkness absorbed the room, but as it did it made the gardens clearer when her eyes adjusted.

She heard Edward moving behind her, barefoot, the floorboards creaking with his footfalls as he neared her. His fingers slipped about each side of her waist and splayed over her stomach, and his lips brushed her neck.

"Do you think we can really get John back?" she whispered, her breath dewing on the glass. "What if they do not accept me?"

"We can only try, Ellen." His deep voice filled the air, the resonating sound sending a shiver through her body, and his hands swept lower, drawing her back against him stirring her desire. "If they do not accept you then we will simply find an opportunity to take John and leave the country."

Her head tipped back to his shoulder and she sighed into the air, longing to escape thought and heartache.

"I want him back."

"I know sweetheart, I do too. We'll get him back, whichever way. *I promise*."

Chapter Twelve

Unlike their journey north, on their journey south Edward joined Ellen in the carriage. As before they only stopped to eat, sleeping in their borrowed carriage, but this time she slept against him, secure. They traveled faster with the grooms from Park House to ride ahead and set up a change of horses at the next inn.

When they reached London Ellen bowed willingly to Edward's direction. His planning reminded her of the military campaigns she'd heard discussed when she was married to Paul, she knew he was treating this like a war.

His first assault was a visit to his aunt and cousins. An event Ellen did not relish but steeled herself for.

It took all her courage to sit on the long sofa before his aunt and his cousin Rowena, who'd yet to come out. Mentally

Ellen chanted, *I have a right to be here, I am Edward's wife*, pinning on a false smile. She was unbearably self-conscious. Edward led the conversation, painting a picture of her first marriage by elopement and their meeting. In a tearoom of all places. The same white lie she'd weaved barely a month ago to her maid. A story many people would know was false, but Edward insisted few would dare to contradict. While Edward spoke, Ellen nodded when required and contributed to the conversation when she could. Edward explained that her father had disowned her because of her elopement, and that he had taken John because John was heir to the dukedom. That she'd let John go because she'd been forced to work and feared she could not support her son. They'd deliberately left as much truth in the story as they could. Edward only missed one fact, *how* she'd earned her living since Paul's death. Then he told his aunt they wished for her support to re-establish Ellen in society so Ellen may regain access to her son.

Lady Stanforth seemed supportive, if not overly jubilant about her nephew's marriage, and Ellen began relaxing a little.

But then the drawing-room door thrust open and Edward's companion from Madam Marietta's strode into the room. "Ed."

Ellen's heart stopped for a moment before kicking to a wild rhythm.

His cousin, Rupert. Of course. She had not even made the connection when Edward had talked of coming.

Ellen felt instantly unclean and out of place. She supposed Edward must not think it any risk, but this man had seen her in her former life. He'd been there the night Gainsborough had played his lewd games to anger Edward.

She wanted to leave, but she could not. Watching this cousin, she waited to hear his accusations — terrified.

Edward had stood and a smile of genuine pleasure parted his cousin's lips when they shook hands. Then he saw her. Ellen anticipated condemnation, her heart in her mouth. But it did not come. He merely stared.

Immediately Edward launched into a formal introduction, acting as though his cousin had never seen her before. "You must meet my wife, Rupert. I have just been telling your mother how we met." She knew Edward's words were to encourage his cousin to keep their secrets.

Ellen's heart pounded as this Rupert stepped forward and lifted his hand. "Lady Edward, a pleasure." There was no pleasure left in his voice, his smile was now taut and false. She laid her hand in his and he mumbled something supposed to be charming. It did not have the ring of truth at all.

Ellen felt herself blush and he let her fingers fall.

She was silent while Edward explained their cause again. So was Edward's cousin. He did not contradict Edward and tell the truth. His only revealing expression was raised eyebrows at the mention of her father and John. Then it was agreed that the family would accompany them to the theatre four days hence and the interview was concluded.

As the front door shut behind them, Ellen let out a breath and took Edward's arm to descend the few steps to the street. "You did not say your companion from the club would be here. I had forgotten you'd mentioned your cousin."

"He'll say nothing. We've been close since we were boys."

"But did your brother not say it was your cousin Rupert who told him of our association and that he disapproved?" When they reached the pavement, Ellen stopped and turned to face him. "Edward, I have just sat there and lied to your family, while your cousin knows the truth. How do you think it makes me feel?" Clearly Edward did not understand her mortification.

"Wicked," he gave her as answer, laughing, before bending to press a quick kiss on her lips, *in the street, in broad daylight*. Then he turned to lead her to the carriage.

Ellen felt a blush again, but still refused to move. She was angry. She wanted to make him understand. She could not bear this. "Edward, it is not funny. I do not like lying to them."

When he turned back, there was a worn placating smile on his lips. "What would you have me tell them then, Ellen? The truth?" With that he turned away again.

Her fingers still on his arm she pulled him back. "Edward, I cannot do this."

He turned back again and covered her fingers on his arm with his hand in a gesture of reassurance. "Ellen, you can. What is worse, never seeing John again, or telling a few white lies? And Rupert knows we cannot tell the truth, he'll not judge us for it." She didn't need to answer. He knew her answer. Her only reply was beginning to walk.

"And now, we are going shopping."

"Shopping? Edward."

"Shopping, and you are not to argue." The pitch of his voice was light and teasing now, denying their former conversation. He was clearly sweeping it aside.

"You have already bought enough for me in York. There is no need to buy more."

"York, my dear, is not London." Reaching their carriage, he turned to her and tucked his gloved fingers beneath her chin. Beside them the footmen held open the carriage door, looking blankly upwards, and above them the driver looked along the street. Her heart thumping and her breath short Ellen turned her eyes to Edward. All else in the street disappeared as she held his gaze, looking into the deep slate-blue. "You will be mixing with London's elite. I know how much you suffer with self-consciousness. Do you think I would have it any other way than ensuring you feel absolutely equal? And say nothing of the expense, I don't care about it. I do care about you. I promise I shall be cautious. I shall not have us in penury."

Ellen hugged him, her arms about his neck. She loved him, his patience, his kindness—his determination. He deserved far more than her reproach. "Edward, I thank God I have you."

When she let him go, he gave her a benevolent smile. "And I you, you silly woman."

❧ ❧

The second assault of Edward's campaign to return her to her position in society and John to her, took place three days later. Ellen had begun feeling as though she was being swept along by a floodtide. There was no ignoring Edward's resolve once he was set upon a course.

The Forths had arrived in London the day before and they'd immediately sent an invitation to call upon them at three the next afternoon.

Edward was in an exceptionally cheerful mood as they climbed the steps and entered the Forths' townhouse, she saw him smile broadly at the butler. He had been smiling all day. But his hand was beneath her elbow, in a tender gesture of support.

In the hall, Edward let her go, took off his hat and gloves and gave them to a footman, while she untied the lavender ribbons of her new straw bonnet. It was decorated with a seasonal bouquet of white silk crocuses over her left ear. She slipped it off carefully, not disturbing her hair, and passed it to the butler, then undid the buttons of her deeper mauve velvet spencer.

Edward's fingers touched her shoulders, helping her slip it off once the buttons were loose and then he handed that to the butler too. Straightening she smoothed the skirts of her lavender walking dress. It had a pattern of printed cornflowers. Her fingers trembled. She felt ridiculously nervous today. She did not really know why.

With his usual kindness and understanding, Edward smiled more broadly, captured her fingers in his, pressed a kiss on them and then tucked them about the crook of his arm.

Ellen took a breath, trying to calm her nerves, and smiled back at him as the butler opened the drawing-room door.

A hubbub of conversation spilled out into the white marble-lined hall, with more than one female voice.

Ellen's heart thumped harder as the butler announced them formally and she heard the conversation cease. Edward led her in. She doubted she would ever feel comfortable socializing. She felt as though she was always waiting for someone to point her out and name her for the harlot she had once been. Not that she could remember who that person was. Perhaps it was that which made this so hard. With Edward she felt open to being hurt. Before, cold and broken, she had not cared what others thought.

As they stepped into the drawing-room all she saw initially was elegantly clad people. Her gaze quickly circulated about the room and her legs weakened. She saw familiar faces. Faces she had not seen since she'd been young. Edward's arm came about her waist, his other hand taking hers as he led her to a seat.

"Eleanor!" The cry rang from three voices at once, zealous and brimful with joy. Then she was suddenly surrounded and swamped with hugs and kisses as Edward settled her into a chair. It left Ellen bewildered and close to tears. Yet she was still conscious of Edward standing beside her.

Sylvia the youngest of her sisters pulled away first, sniffing while taking out a small embroidered handkerchief from her sleeve, to dry her tears.

"Come forward, James, do." Sylvia beckoned to the man Ellen presumed to be her husband, as Penelope and Rebecca stood back. They stared at Ellen as though she had three heads.

Ellen attempted to rise but her legs were unsteady and then the room undertook a full circle. She gripped Edward's arm.

"You need not rise, Eleanor," Sylvia admonished, sounding concerned as Edward helped Ellen sit again. "My Jamie is not one to stand on show. Do, come here, darling." The man who walked to Sylvia's side was equal in height to Sylvia, fair and lean. On reaching them he touched Sylvia's arm, giving her a tender look and smile. Then he turned to Ellen and bent in a deep bow as he held out his hand.

Ellen laid her fingers in his and he placed a chaste kiss atop her cotton glove.

"I have heard much about you, Lady Eleanor. I know Sylvia looks up to her memory of you. She is deeply relieved to have you returned to us."

Lord James Rush, the Duke of Bradford, Ellen's youngest sister's husband, proved to be charming. Ellen knew they had married nine months ago. Clearly it was a love match.

Ellen smiled as he let her hand go. Then he drew away and wrapped an arm about Sylvia.

Ellen had read about her sisters' lives and matches with trepidation, but from this greeting it seemed all her fears had been for naught, they were happy.

Rebecca stepped forward next, with her husband, Lord David Stewart, the Earl of Preston. His arm about Rebecca, his hand rested on her expanding waist. Ellen knew they already had one child, a girl, who would be three now. "I am honoured to meet you, Lady Eleanor." Lord Stewart bowed and offered his hand as Sylvia's husband had done. "You must come and meet your namesake soon." He lifted Ellen's fingers to his lips and kissed them.

Ellen's heart thumped, this was all so overwhelming.

"When our daughter was born, Rebecca would accept no other name, having spent the years extolling her eldest sister's virtues and mourning your loss. Little Eleanor was named in your memory. She is now overjoyed at the thought she may meet her aunt." With that he let Ellen's hand go and stepped away.

Ellen had said nothing, she was too shocked. But now it was Penny's turn. Ellen stood. Her legs felt like aspic but they held her up.

Penny and her husband the Marquess of Wiltshire stepped forward and Ellen saw tears cloud Penny's eyes. She hugged Ellen and Ellen held her too. Oh, it felt so surreal and wonderful to share an embrace with Penny again, as though the years-in-between had not been. But they had happened.

Penny was the only one of the three who would have known the reasons for Ellen's elopement. Rebecca and Sylvia had been too young. Drawing away from Penny, slipping back into the elder sister role, Ellen brushed a curl she had loosened, behind Penny's ear. "I am glad to see you happy."

"Because of you," Penny whispered. "Mother refused to agree to any of father's plans to arrange a marriage for me. He let me pick whichever man I chose. I think father learned lessons from your disappearance. He was not nearly so hard on us when he returned from France with John."

Nodding Ellen said nothing. She did not wish to speak to her sisters of the truth or of what their father had done. Yet it was hard to lie. Blushing she stepped back and turned on Penny's introduction to the Marquess.

He was the first son of the Duke of Arundel. They had married eight years before, and Ellen knew they had three girls, the youngest of which was just one. Yet even now the admiring look the Marquess sent Penny appeared full of love and understanding. He took Ellen's hand and bowed across it as the other men had done.

"My dear, Eleanor, you must forgive me, I feel as if I know you. You have been a part of my life for a long time. Penny never ceases speaking of you, and I have had the greatest pleasure playing uncle to your son."

A lump stuck in Ellen's throat. She tried to swallow it but could not, then Edward, as ever observant and caring, handed her a glass of orgeat. She sipped it twice before he took it back. Smiling up at him, she felt pride and gratitude swell — she had found love again too.

"Have you met my husband, Lord Wiltshire," she said, turning back to the Marquess. "Lord Edward Marlow?" *Heavens*, it was so good to speak those words of Edward.

The round of introductions repeated and then Edward began explaining how things stood and his plans.

Her sisters took Ellen away to sit across the room, with Julie, and left the men to it. Gathered about Ellen, they then drew out her tale with question after question, asking all about Edward, and how Ellen had met him, about their wedding. Ellen answered what she could, and struggled for words to avoid the answers she could not tell the truth to.

When Sylvia asked where she had been all these years, Ellen sighed and simply answered, "Surviving, Sylvia," in a voice that said, *please do not ask me more.*

But then Penny asked what their father had done when he'd fetched John. She wanted to know why he'd said Ellen was dead. These questions were so hard to answer.

"He is a Duke, Penny," Ellen said at length. "I can understand a little of his unwillingness to acknowledge me. I made the choice to elope with Paul." Then she added, "Paul had no title of his own. He had no inheritance. You have all chosen well. Father cannot condemn you. But Paul was not equal to his status."

"He was the son of an Earl, and I remember him, he was kind and good." A sincere heat sparked in Penny's eyes. Ellen smiled, but internally she baulked in disbelief. She was arguing on her father's behalf.

"He was a sixth son with no allowance and no inheritance." Ellen continued, determined not to widen the rift in her family. "I made my choice, Penny, when I left I knew we would not be wealthy and I knew father would not want me back."

"But there is no excuse for him lying about your death," Penny insisted finally.

Ellen said nothing, what could she say.

Apparently realising her argument had gone too far, Penny ceased railing and gripped Ellen's fingers. "You are here with us now though, and we shall not lose you again. Richard and I called on Mama and Papa on the way to London. Richard has told father plainly, he completely disapproves of his behaviour towards you, and Mama burst into tears when I told her you are alive. She shouted at Papa. I have never seen her do either before. I think she will never speak to him again."

"She will not sway him to receive me," Ellen whispered, unable to think of her mother being so deceived and fighting the surge of emotion which longed for her. Her mother had shown them considerable love to compensate for their father's coldness. Ellen had always missed her, but her mother had little power over their father. He'd never sought their mother's counsel when Ellen was a child, never listened to anyone but himself.

"But Richard will, Eleanor," Penny responded, deep assurance in her voice.

"And James has significant influence in the House of Lords. Father cannot ignore that," Sylvia expanded, glancing across the room at her husband and smiling.

"As does David and his cousins, between us there will be too much pressure for father to ignore you. He will be ridiculed if we recognize you and he does not. It will ruin the reputation he is so proud of."

"When you called to see them did you see John?" Ellen asked of Penny. "Is he well?" Penny squeezed her hand.

"Yes, he is well and was overjoyed when I told him we were coming to see you. At which point his poor little smile cracked, believing he had made a mistake and should pretend not to know of your existence. Then it all spilled out I'm afraid, about how you have written to him for years and that he has a new Papa but Grandpapa took him away. All he wishes for is to see you and Edward again and I have sworn to him we will make it possible just as soon as we can."

Ellen smiled, feeling tears in her eyes.

"I find it wonderful that John loves you despite Papa's influence. It must rile father so." Penny's gaze suddenly focused more sharply and Ellen knew she was about to be asked another awkward question. "Why did you not write to me before this and ask for help?"

Ellen's hands lifted and fell. How could she explain that she had no wish to affect her sisters' reputations without admitting what had happened in the intervening years? When Penny had married, she'd still not dared to write, fearing Penny's husband would react poorly to such news. And then there had been children, and she could not risk destroying her sisters' lives. "Things were not that simple, Penny," was all Ellen said.

Her sister's measured gaze continued to meet Ellen's, and Ellen had a feeling Penny knew exactly what had gone on. Looking up at Edward, Ellen saw him in conversation with the Marquess. Lord Wiltshire's serious expression seemed to indicate the same.

Penny's hand suddenly gripped Ellen's more tightly. "Never mind, it is in the past now, and Richard has sworn to do anything he can to help you."

"Is father coming to town? Will he bring John?"

Penny shook her head. "No, he has not conceded yet, but Richard is certain he will. We are to be as bold and brash as we can be. Julie has already told me of the ball she has planned for next week. We will introduce you as our long lost sister there, make up some nonsense about you being injured in France and losing your memory. We shall make it a tragedy which the *ton* will dine on, and extol Edward as your saviour. You will both be heroes when we are done and then the week after Richard and I will host a ball for you."

"Ah, tea," Julie exclaimed at a knock on the drawing-room door, rising and moving to commence organising and pouring, followed by the other women, leaving Ellen and Penny alone.

Leaning towards her sister, Ellen whispered, "But there are those who will know the truth, Penny. What if your tale is denied?"

"Nonsense." Smiling, Penny waved the comment aside. Ellen knew it expressed Penny's security in her position in society. As children that confidence had been Ellen's too. But Penny neither knew the fickle nature of society, nor its sordid secrets. Ellen did. "They would not dare when Richard, David, James and father are involved, as well as Edward's family."

Ellen was unconvinced, but she said no more and accepted a teacup from Julie. The conversation progressed to less contentious subjects then. Her sisters talked of their plans in town, discussing things they would do together. Ellen merely listened. She was awed by it, feeling as though she was looking down from above on this cosy parlour scene with her family. It was like a dream. She did not feel a part of it. She could not believe her sisters were sat about her, fully grown, wives and mothers, discussing fashions and functions, the years which had passed between their last encounter and today merely swept away — a nothingness — a lie.

Edward came to her, pressing his fingers on her shoulder and she felt his silent offer of reassurance in her heart. Again he'd sensed her moment of need, and as she looked upwards seeking to say thank you in her eyes, he smiled and then mouthed, "You will become used to it."

Used to being part of a family again, to being loved, to being secure — she wanted to, and yet a part of her was afraid of how much further she would have to fall if it all went wrong, and how much more it would hurt.

⤜⥤

The next evening Edward silently watched Ellen preparing for the theatre from the open door of their adjoining rooms. She was looking herself over in the mirror. She wore the green evening dress he'd purchased for her in York, saving her London gowns for the entertainments her sisters had planned. She was, as ever, beautiful, but he doubted she saw it even now.

Having seen her sisters he knew beauty ran in the family. They'd been identical in coloring, and yet to him Ellen would always be the most perfect. He smiled, and she must have glimpsed his movement because she turned.

"What have you there?" she asked, looking at the velvet box he'd forgotten he held in his hand.

"A present," he responded, walking into the room. He had not lied at all when he'd told her he wished her to look equal to the women she would be introduced to, and on the last occasion she'd worn this dress he had noticed his one omission, jewellery. A woman simply could not go abroad in London without some bauble at her throat. He smiled. He could little afford this, but he would worry about that later when they had John back. "Turn back to the mirror," he ordered. "I'll show you."

As she did so he moved behind her, snapping open the box and setting it aside. Then taking the single short string of pearls, he reached across her head, sliding them about her throat, settling them at the base of her neck. They were the perfect accessory for the dress, with its ivory petticoat, just as he'd imaged.

Her fingers touched them and he saw her pale blue eyes crystallize with tears, in the mirror. "They're beautiful, Edward, but you should not have bought them." Her look lifted from studying the pearls in her reflection to meet his gaze.

"I wanted to," he answered. "Do you think I would accompany my wife to the theatre without first dressing her appropriately?"

She turned, reached her arms about his neck, lifted to her toes and pressed a brief kiss on his cheek. "I have no idea how I can thank you for all you are doing."

He held her in return and leaned to whisper to her ear as Jill walked into the room. "I know how—tonight, wear just the pearls to bed."

"Edward!" Slapping his arm Ellen pulled away. He let her go, laughing, as Jill flashed them an intrigued glance.

"Come along then wife, we ought to hurry, my aunt will never forgive us if we are late." Still laughing, he turned to the maid. "Fine work, Jill, as ever, your mistress is perfection without your help but there is no harm in a bit of polish."

Jill smiled in answer as he led Ellen from the room.

He knew Ellen was nervous, meeting her sisters yesterday had done her good and given her more courage, but it was not in her nature to be sure of herself. And she'd talked at length over dinner last night of her past. She'd married Paul before having a season in town. She'd never come to London with her family. All she'd known of the capital was its vulgar side. He'd vowed to give it back to her — that time — the life she'd lost. It was becoming just as important to him as getting John back and he *was* genuinely hopeful now that things would come about. Her brothers-in-law had all joined her cause and their combined influence outweighed her father's tenfold. So Edward had every reason to feel congenial as they descended the stairs, until his eyes were suddenly drawn from Ellen to a movement in the hall.

"Jenkins, is Edward in?"

Robert stood below, handing off his gloves and hat.

Stopping, Edward stared downward with Ellen poised beside him, her fingers clinging to his arm. Instantly Edward's ire rose, but he swallowed it back, feeling Ellen tense.

What the hell did Robert want?

Brazenly acting as though Robert had not recently assaulted Ellen, Edward gritted his teeth and recommenced their decent, determined not to respond to any provocation. He wanted Ellen to be comfortable and confident tonight. He would zap her confidence instantly if he argued with Robert before they left. Still at least they were leaving and he need not stay in and tolerate Robert's company.

Staring at his brother, when Robert noticed their movement and looked up, Edward offered him a mistrustful glare; not making him welcome in his own home. "We are going out," Edward clarified before Robert could speak, while Ellen's grip stiffened on his arm. "And if you have come here to cause trouble, we shall leave your house tomorrow and go to Forth's."

Robert's usual ironic, devil-may-care smile twitching at his lips, Edward could see not an ounce of repentance in Robert's face. "What a lovely tableau," Robert mocked. "I am glad to find you here, actually, but where are you going? May I join you?"

"No," Edward responded.

But beside him Ellen drew a deep breath and launched into speech as they descended from the bottom step. "We are going to the theatre with your aunt and cousins. Edward has purchased a box and there is room for one more if you wish to attend, Lord Barrington."

Edward looked his disapproval, glowering at Ellen. It did not deter her. She did not even glance in his direction as she faced Robert.

Robert rubbed Edward's nose in it. "Your wife is sensible, Ed. Forth wrote and told me what you are about. My absence will raise questions. I have come to support you. Take it, or leave it, as you wish."

Not an apology, no remorse.

Eyeing his brother cynically, Edward could do little but let Robert participate; now he was here. If Robert made his disapproval known it may indeed tip their boat. Then of course there was the old analogy—keep your friends close and your enemies even closer. He did not trust a word his brother said, for good reason—*he had assaulted Ellen, for God's sake.* But if Robert was within sight and earshot, he was less likely to do anything offensive.

"Very well, you may come," Edward tossed the words in his brother's general direction, then turned to the door, but sadly not before he'd noted Robert's instant smile. It only increased Edward's mistrust.

"I'll meet you there," Robert confirmed, his bright tone poking Edward's suspicion further. "Which theatre?"

"Drury Lane, the performance commences in an hour. We are going via your aunt's," Ellen held Edward back to explain.

Why she was inviting Robert after what he'd done, Edward could not understand. By rights Robert deserved for her to cut him dead. It seemed no one could be relied upon to support *him* properly; Rupert had called Robert down to London before and now Forth had done the same, meddling in Edward's disagreement. Edward's life was none of his brother's business. He wished people would stop interfering.

"In an hour then," Robert said, nodding at Ellen, before hastily strolling towards the stairs and ascending at a jog. Edward watched him, he was looking bloody happy with himself for no apparent reason, as usual.

Jenkins opened the front door and Edward led Ellen out and on down the steps, grumbling, "Why on earth are you tolerating him, after what he did?"

Her fingers gently squeezed his arm. "Don't be too hard on him, Edward. I do believe he means good."

"Then you do not know my brother," he answered as a footman held open the door of his brother's secondary carriage.

"Edward, I'm sure he had no intention of really seducing me at Farnborough," Ellen responded, glancing at him as he handed her up.

"No? Then as I said before, you do not know Robert. He never does anything without deliberation, and he never does anything to be nice." He climbed up behind her and slid into the seat next to her. The footman snapped the door shut.

Why on earth she felt the need to defend Robert was beyond him. The carriage drew away. She was silent. Edward looked over at her. Taking her fingers in his, he weaved his in between hers. "Are you all right?" He knew the answer from the tenseness in her body.

She looked at him. "No, I feel awful. I'm terrified someone will know me."

At least now when she set her defenses, she did not shut him out. Letting go her fingers, instead he reached his arm about her shoulders and drew her close. She willingly received his comfort, snuggling up and half turning, one hand sliding behind his back while the other pressed to his chest. "Did you not look at yourself in the mirror this evening?" he said to ease her fears. "You said to me nights ago you don't recognize yourself anymore. You look different because you are more confident, no one will equate this woman with the old one and with my family in our company no one would dare say a thing even if they did."

She sighed, the shadow of her lashes, cast by the lantern inside the carriage, flickering across her cheeks as her eyelids dropped then lifted. "I know you keep telling me this, but I still feel unsure. I suppose I shall not believe it until as usual you are proven right." With another little sigh, she rested her cheek to the lapel of his evening coat, both arms now wrapped about his midriff holding him tightly. Her need of him sent a fresh rush of affection pumping from his heart. The woman had him thoroughly in her thrall. He'd do anything for her, ten times over. She gave him purpose. He'd not even known her three months ago, thank God he'd found her.

"I do try to be positive," she whispered to his cravat pin.

Edward laughed. "Lord woman, you make it sound as though I hound you. Be brave darling, that is all you can be and you are." He kissed her forehead with care not to disturb her hair, Jill's artwork. "You amaze me. You are so tender hearted, Ellen. Lord knows how with the dice life cast you. I know what you have endured and survived, yet you are not bitter. A case in point your kindness to my thrice damned brother. You have no need to be generous to him after what he did." At that she pulled away sitting up and facing him.

"He is your brother, Edward. You've restored my family to me. I will not set yours asunder in return. He made the effort to travel to town. Do you not think that is gesture enough to say he wants to make amends?"

Edward's fingers brushing her cheek, he saw a vehement look form in her gaze. He sighed. She was taking Robert up as her cause. "I know Robert far better than you. It is a sign of his intent to make mischief, and nothing more. I only agreed to the bastard coming to keep an eye on him."

"*Edward*," she chided, ticking him off for his language. As pathetic as he had become, he enjoyed it.

"I cannot see why you are defending him against me in any case." He dug deeper.

In response she looked horrified. "I am not defending him against you. I wouldn't. I am defending your relationship with your brother. All I ask Edward is that you give him a chance."

"A chance?" he laughed, but the sound was hollow. "Do you have a short memory? Did you not hear how he prods my anger for the fun of it? And you say give him a chance. He assaulted you Ellen. I could not care less if he ever speaks to me again."

Saying nothing, she just looked at him, and he could see her reading between the lines of his words and coming to her own conclusions. Conclusions which were a mile south of what he'd said, judging by her expression.

But further discussion on the subject was not possible as the carriage pulled up outside his aunt's.

❧❧

Their theatre box was high up, in line with the upper circle, which was a blessing. It meant few from the dress circle could see her. And despite Edward's aunt urging her to sit in the outer seat Ellen physically claimed the seat by the wall, so she was partially obscured by the sweep of the box's red velvet curtain. She was terrified someone would cry out, 'there's Gainsborough's harlot', pointing up at her, even though Gainsborough had never taken her anywhere other than the gaming hells he favoured.

She was sitting beside Edward's cousin, Rowena, his aunt having finally agreed to take the outer seat. Edward's brother sat behind his aunt, his cousin Rupert in the middle and Edward behind Ellen.

Her heart was thundering by the time the stage curtain swept up. The general chatter immediately subsided. Surreptitiously Ellen let her hand fall from her lap and it hung beside her chair, hopefully. Edward responded. She heard him cough then felt his fingers grip hers. Looking back across her shoulder she gave him a grateful smile. He'd leaned his elbows on to his knees and now sat with his chin resting on one fisted hand while the other held hers. She doubted, like so, he could see anything of the stage, but his touch gave her comfort. When she turned back to the performance, she heard Edward's brother murmur to their cousin. Instinct whispered the subject was her, although she didn't hear the words.

Ignoring it, with her fingers gripped securely in Edward's, she allowed herself to concentrate upon the play, Shakespeare's, Romeo and Juliet.

When the interval came, Edward's brother stood, and Edward's fingers fell away as the Earl spoke. "Refreshments, ladies? Champagne, Aunt? Rowena, that shall be another treat. *Ellen?*" Turning to her, his voice grew deeper, and a smile tugged at his lips, while he awaited her response.

She nodded.

"Edward will accompany me, I'm sure," The Earl concluded, looking from Ellen to Edward.

She looked at Edward too.

Rising, he smiled, a look which seemed to say, *I promise not to hit him, I'll be back soon,* before turning to follow his brother.

When the door closed behind them, Ellen faced Rowena, answering a comment she'd made on the play, thanking heaven the bard's more risqué writing, with its lewd innuendo, had gone over the girl's head as it had gone over hers when she was young. Then Edward's aunt tapped her daughter's arm with her closed fan and nodded towards a family across the theatre Rowena may know, turning the girl's attention away from Ellen.

Lord Rupert slid across into the seat Edward had vacated.

"You have him by a hook." He whispered bluntly.

Ellen swallowed, looking back. What did he mean? But before she could respond he continued.

"I never thought he'd draw you away from Gainsborough, I'd told him so. But I hadn't realized you were angling for marriage. If you think you've found security though you're mistaken, Edward has no income."

Anger heating her skin, Ellen glanced at his sister. Rowena had not heard. She was still speaking with her mother. Ellen twisted in her chair and glared at Lord Rupert. "As

Edward shall tell you," she whispered bitterly. "I was angling for nothing. When Edward made his offer and persuaded me to accept it, he made it very clear he had no income. I do not care. So pray—tell me something I do not know, my Lord. If you are seeking to set me against him you'll not succeed."

"He is a poor love sick fool to even make such an offer. He's infatuated." he scoffed. "Before you, he lived a sheltered life, *all work*. He will tire of you when this adventure—this fight for your son—is over."

"What exists between us is not infatuation," she hissed. "It is love—on both our parts, and no, I do not think he shall ever tire of it, as neither shall I. And if you do not like it, or me, my Lord, then once I have told Edward you will have to accept that my husband will no longer desire your friendship."

Her words were instilled with conviction. But it was a farce. Rupert had just kicked her rock from beneath her feet. Confidence, or rather the lack of it, was her Achilles heel. *What if he was right?*

Looking away, Ellen fought to hide her alarm as the door opened, heralding Edward's and his brother's return, succinctly ending her *tête-à-tête* with his cousin.

A waiter, bearing a bottle of champagne on ice and several glasses, followed Edward and Robert back into the box.

Robert and his cousin had planned this, she realized. It was the purpose of their earlier whispers.

When Robert offered her a glass she declined on principle, seething, incensed by Rupert's cruel attack and Robert's victimisation. She had offered him forgiveness. He had plotted against her again. Yet her vulnerability let Rupert's damning words take hold. Once she had thought Edward's devotion a symptom of his boredom and frustration, but that had been a lifetime ago.

Has he not shown me his true affection dozens of times since? His cousin dislikes me, that is all. He is trying to separate us—just as Edward's brother did at Farnborough. *They are just trying to protect Edward.*

She suddenly felt like crying, shouting and crying. She did not wish to break up Edward's family. They had reasons to dislike her, she knew, but she did not mean ill. She loved Edward. Could they not see that?

Turning her eyes back to the stage as the bell rang to signal the end of the interval, she felt Edward's touch rest on her shoulder. "Is something wrong? You do not want champagne?"

She looked up at him and shook her head. "No, thank you, but I am fine, honestly."

His eyebrows lifted.

She could see he knew she was not, but he said nothing more and a moment later when he returned to his seat she felt his fingers search for hers.

This time she clung to him even harder than before as she watched the tragedy unfold before her on the stage.

Chapter Thirteen

Descending the stairs to the hall the next morning Ellen's thoughts were reeling. Their theatre trip the night before had gone well enough, despite Rupert's malicious taunts. She'd not been recognised. Not one person had batted an eyelid at her presence, but then she'd sought to remain unnoticed.

On the way home she'd considered telling Edward the things Rupert had said, but she had not. And she'd thought of it all night too. But she could not cause more rifts in his family. Yet Rupert's words still niggled.

She walked across the hall to straighten the tulip heads in a vase, rearranging them for no other reason than she had nothing else to do. Edward had gone out early to meet her brothers-in-law, they were discussing an announcement Edward intended publishing to inform society of their marriage and therefore her reappearance. It left her at a loose end, with time on her hands. *A book*, she thought, refusing to let her mind dwell on Rupert's assumptions. Reading would help quell her restlessness and absorb her traitorous thoughts. She knew in her heart Rupert's words were nonsense, but her head, with all its learned insecurity, just seemed to keep chewing on them. Turning back she intended to head for the library but instead found herself facing a wall of muscle as Robert stood before her, hands on hips. Taking a step back, she tilted her gaze from his broad chest to his face, wary despite her bravado the day before when Edward was there.

"Lord Barrington, I'm sorry I didn't realize you were at home." Her heartbeat kicked into a sharp, swift beat, as she waited for him to make the next move, whatever that would be.

"Well, as you see, I am," he answered bluntly, without his usual disrespectful humor. "I wish to speak with you. Will you come into my study?"

His hand reached towards her.

Ellen instinctively stepped back to avoid it and her buttocks hit the edge of the table the flowers stood upon, she gripped its rim.

Robert's eyes rolled upwards, his usual mocking air returning in a flash, clearly ridiculing her concern. Then his brown eyes focusing back on her, he said, "If I promise not to ravish you will you come?" his hand moving, this time he directed her to the room.

Looking from his hand to his eyes Ellen sought some sign of his intention. Nothing in his gaze comforted or threatened. Ellen chose to be valiant and nodded, then turned. Though it was far easier to tell Edward, Robert meant well, than it was to trust him. Leaving a deliberate distance between them, she swept through the open door.

The room was small and filled with bookcases. A large desk with an armchair on either side stood in its center. Bidding her sit, he shut the heavy oak door. It made her jump, but summoning up her courage she took a seat, perching on its edge, her fingers resting together in her lap.

"I wished to speak to you of Edward," he began, walking to the desk, but he didn't go behind it and take a seat, leaving her staring up at him and feeling nervous.

What was he about?

"Yes." Her voice was small.

What new ploy was this?

"I spoke to Rupert last night, after the theatre," he continued, leaning his buttocks back against the lip of his desk, his fingers gripping the rim of it beside his hips as he spoke.

Wary of his every movement she waited, listening.

"We believe your affection for my brother is genuine."

Ellen felt her eyes widen as her gaze struck his. This was not what she'd expected.

"I wish to apologize for my behaviour in Farnborough. I was not certain of your motivation. I thought the best and quickest way to unearth your true colors was to offer you a better deal. I'm sorry." The business-like note was back in his voice. She'd not heard Edward's brother speak with any seriousness before today.

Ellen stood and moved behind her chair, setting a barrier between them as she gripped its back. "I told Edward as much," she answered.

His eyes fixing on her face, his eyebrows lifted.

She dared to press on. "Perhaps it takes one person who carries guilt heavily to recognize another, my Lord. You did not fight back, not then, nor before in the drawing-room. You do care for Edward, I saw that, although he doubts it. But I know you goad him to make yourself feel better. You encourage his anger and hatred to ease your guilt. What I do not understand is why?"

The man folded his arms over his chest but remained leaning back against his desk, watching her. He'd probably had a clear expectation of how this interview was to go and now she had contributed, he was at a loss. After a moment with a shake of his head his lips broke into a broad smile, and then he turned away from her.

"A drink, Ellen?" he offered across his shoulder moving to a decanter.

"No, thank you, my Lord." She watched him pour one and drink it straight down. She understood then there were more anomalies buried inside him, things he kept hidden from Edward. But his secrets were his, not her concern.

Turning back and looking at her, he smiled — his mocking, ironic smile.

"Very observant of you, Ellen. You're right of course. Much was put upon Edward because of me and now I seek to rectify it. And yes, it does satisfy me to spur his anger but that hardly matters, and don't analyze it please, I am not interested in knowing why."

"But I do not understand why you going abroad would cause such a rift between you?" Ellen stepped towards him but stopped as the door opened.

"Shall I answer that?" Edward entered, cutting into their conversation as he eyed his brother accusingly while moving to stand behind her. His possessive, protective hand settled on her hip and drew her back against him and his lips brushed a lock of her hair by her ear when he spoke. "My brother is very good at stirring up hornets' nests and then running away, sweetheart. He left me to face the consequences, while he fled to Europe on the back of debts which caused our father's seizure, and eventually his death. I settled them and picked the estate up from its knees. Is that reason enough, darling?"

Then in a more gentle voice he leaned to her ear and asked, "Has he hurt you, Ellen?"

Before them, Robert smiled, sending Edward a look of acting distress. Ellen gave him a narrow eyed glare. The man was hardly ever serious, but she had seen a glimpse of what lay beneath and she knew how much he really cared despite this urge he had for provocation.

"As you see, Ellen, he thinks badly of me no matter what I do." Robert's words answered her unspoken thought.

Smiling shrewdly, she sought to remind him she knew his game. There was more to the tale he could add, she was sure, but it appeared he refused to tell. She would lay strong odds on the fact that he was not responsible for the situation as Edward saw it. No doubt some foolish notion of honour kept him silent. And on that thought she retorted, "Yet even so you do your best to prod him." Mirroring his mocking tone and expression and allowing a humorous glint to light her eyes, she added, "For instance, as I recall, you did force yourself on me at Farnborough, so you hardly have reason to protest." She turned in Edward's arms then, facing him.

"No, Edward, he has not harmed me. He was actually apologising."

"And as I said, Ellen, *in my apology*, my actions at Farnborough were only to test your intent. Well done by the way, you passed."

Hearing Robert move behind her, Ellen turned back, concerned he was leaving.

As she did so, Edward, having obviously established her lack of concern, left her to cross the room, and walking towards the decanters spoke. "So Ellen said, but you could have just asked."

"That is hardly my style." Robert laughed, his gaze passing from Edward to her and back as he remained hovering at the corner of his desk.

Edward glanced sideways looking askance at his brother before turning to pour himself a drink. "Can you never be serious, Robert? If you are coming to Forth's ball and that of Ellen's sister, you shall have to promise not to stir things up." His voice was at its most commanding. "I have enough to focus on without needing to keep an eye on you too."

"As if I would say anything to offend?" Holding up both hands, palms outward, Robert threw Edward a look, which ironically suggested he was a fool.

"Lord Barrington," Ellen challenged, urging him to be serious, but he stopped her, lifting his hand higher.

"I told you, Edward, I came to help." His voice mimicked his serious tone of before rather than spoke seriously, it was slack and not believable.

Ellen looked at Edward. He was standing on the far side of the room, a glass in one hand, while his other arm lay across his chest. His entire body stated he did not believe a word Robert said.

"Very well, whatever the history of this marriage of yours you have my backing." Obviously seeing Edward's disbelief too, Robert progressed, his tone slipping into a believable pitch. "I approve of your wife, as does Rupert I might add, having observed your wife's ire on your behalf last night. I am not sure our aunt would agree with such open shows of affection though, such as uniting hands through an entire theatre performance, or kissing your wife in the street."

Ellen watched Edward tip his glass and drink the shot of brandy in one swallow. Then his eyes narrowed on his brother.

"What?" Robert responded. "Can I not commend my little brother now?"

"Not when I am uncertain of your intent," Edward answered, setting the empty glass down.

"He's just teasing you," Ellen interceded, smiling at Edward, before this became another row. Then turning back to Robert she moved towards him, reached up onto her toes and kissed his cheek, clearly taking him by surprise. A masculine blush darkened his cheekbones and he shook his head, as she leaned back. "Thank you, my Lord. We shall be very glad of your help."

But he recovered quickly, smiling broadly, and a twinkle entered his eyes. "Robert, Ellen. I can hardly have you addressing me by my title if we are to be close." Then throwing a look at Edward, he added, "Purely platonic of course."

At that Ellen embraced him, setting her arms about his neck and hugging him tightly for a moment, whispering, "Your secret is quite safe with me, Robert."

"What secret?" Edward challenged.

"Nothing important," Ellen answered, and cast Edward a smile over her shoulder, pulling back from Robert. "He will tell you himself when he's ready."

Edward's gaze followed her across the room, as she went to him, assessing her, and clearly wondering what she'd meant, but then he shrugged, apparently casting off the private interaction and changed the subject, looking back at his brother. "Never let it be said I am not man enough to give you the benefit of the doubt. So, if you wish to help, this is how you can. We've heard nothing from Ellen's father, so I've agreed with Richard, the Marquess of Wiltshire, that we will publish the news of my marriage to Ellen in the paper tomorrow. It will make it quite clear who Ellen is." Edward turned to her, "Your father can hardly deny you then." When she did not respond his gaze passed back to his brother. "All the men in Ellen's family intend to circulate the clubs tomorrow afternoon. If there is any gossip it will be quashed instantly. Your involvement would be useful. If you and Rupert help, with the solidarity from both families, we are more likely to silence anyone who would dare to speak of Ellen's past before we flush Pembroke from the country."

"Do you think he will come?" Ellen asked, her eyes widening.

Edward smiled in reassurance. It was Ellen this put on a precipice not him, he was well aware of that. He did not like it, but if they wanted John she had to be brazen. It was the only way. And yes, he did think it would work, it could hardly not, with Pembroke's status the entire *ton* would notice the daughter the man claimed to have brought back home from the continent as a corpse in a coffin turning up again as *his* living and breathing, wife. Pembroke could either choose to never set foot in society, including the House of Lords, again, or come to town and sort it out. Edward's finger lifted to tap his beautiful wife under the chin, and he smiled at her hopeful look.

"Yes, Ellen, I think he'll come. I don't see how he cannot. He's spent years pretending you are dead. He will appear either ridiculous or callous, or both, if he does not come to town to see his daughter, whom, thanks to the story he circulated, has made a miraculous recovery from death. You shall be a veritable Lazarus, my dear. The *ton* will be swarming over you in a week."

"I am not sure I like that idea," Ellen answered her wide beautifully pale blue eyes studying him intently, as though looking for some weakness in his words or in his belief in them.

He gripped her shoulders, gave her a light shake and then kissed her on the bridge of the nose. "I know my little shrinking violet, but you shall suffer it none the less, for John."

"For John, yes," she sighed.

Still looking into her eyes, he smiled as one finger brushed a lock of hair from her brow while his other hand loosely slid to rest at her waist. "I don't think your father will come for Forth's ball. Richard and I think he will wait for home ground and attend theirs."

She nodded.

A deep cough disturbed his concentration, and Edward turned to Robert, bestowing on his errant brother an impatient glare.

"What? I am merely reminding you, you are not alone. Perhaps you should take your wife upstairs?"

"Perhaps you should mind your own damned business," Edward retorted.

"Now, now little brother, is there anything else I may do for you or are you done with me?"

Edward smiled at Robert's undisguised look of amusement. At least now Edward believed this change of attitude. It looked as though Ellen had worked her charm on his brother too, bringing Robert to heel as she had his servants, charming him. How Ellen could be so mindful of others after all she'd been through would never cease to amaze Edward. *Blessed woman.* Hugging her to his chest he looked across at Robert. "Now that you have suggested it, I suppose if I take my wife back up to bed you could go and fill Rupert in on the details and the role he can play."

"Edward!" She pushed him away and he would have received a slap for his forwardness but he caught her hand.

"Sweetheart, it was just a joke." He kissed the palm of her hand then let her go, allowing her to pull away.

"In all seriousness, Robert, please keep an ear out for what is being said and spread our version of the tale as far as you can."

"As you wish," Robert answered, smirking. "I will call on Rupert now and leave you two to—well, whatever." With a wink at Edward, he then nodded to Ellen before walking out, whistling the sharp tune of a ribald country ditty to himself as he left.

"That man," Edward seethed turning back to Ellen.

"But that I think was your fault," she challenged, pouting. "You prompted him."

He stepped forward, settled his hands on her hips and pulled her close again. Her body yielded without any need for coaxing. "Tsk, tsk, such a performance of chastity for my brother, but the minute he is gone," he whispered to her mouth as he lowered his head.

He felt her hand lifting to slap him once more, but caught it playfully as his lips touched hers and again she yielded.

"Shall we do as he proposed and go to bed?"

"*Edward*," she chastened.

"Edward, what? Take me to bed? Make love to me?" he teased, sliding one open palm to the small of her back and the other to cup her breast over her pretty lemon yellow morning gown.

"You're wicked," she said to his mouth, her arms reaching about his neck.

"Forget the bed, I'll lock the door." His hands taking her weight, he deposited her derriere on Robert's desk. And leaving her there, her feet dangling a few inches off the floor, he walked away smiling, shut the door and turned the key, feeling very satisfied with himself as the lock clicked home.

None of Robert's games will ever succeed in stirring my temper in this room again.

Turning back to face his irresistible wife, he saw her leaning on the desk, one palm resting on its surface behind her, one leg crossed over the other, her body swivelled a little towards him, eyeing him with reproach.

"Edward, what if your brother comes back?"

The echo of the front door banging shut resounded from the hall.

"He's gone." Edward laughed, approaching her, knowing desire and hunger must be glowing in his eyes.

"Edward," she whispered, as his fingers brushed her cheek, her tone urging him to be mindful of propriety. Yet despite her verbal protest the onyx circles at the heart of her pale crystalline eyes were widening in anticipation and acceptance of his caress. Her concern was genuine but he knew how easily she could be swayed to forget. All he had to do was touch her.

He kissed her, offering temptation.

And when his fingers began drawing up her dress she uncrossed her legs.

He knew her internal war, the battle of response or denial. Fear of appearance versus her own needs. It had been the same since that first night. The defensive Ellen shutting him out, but the warm hearted one longing to let him in. He loved to kiss her. To feel her anticipation build and know she was incapable of refusing him. She *was* incapable. He appreciated, with an addicted need, every response her body bestowed in sound, or sight, or touch. Most of all he liked to feel the moment when her resistance faded. It had been his addiction since the beginning — the moment he felt her desire leap into life and spill over into the touch of her lips to his.

Like now.

Her arms slid about his neck, pulling him closer and her hot breath spilled into his mouth.

Playing with her, he pulled away slightly to feel her reach for him again.

She gripped his hair and he slipped his fingertips beneath the hem of her skirt.

The woman drove him mad with want, she always did. Her body was arching and her legs were wide as he stood between them, and her hips were braced on the very edge of the desk. This was his heaven, *this*, *her*. Her hands were beneath his morning coat running over his lower back and his found treasure beneath her skirt.

He groaned appreciatively.

He loved every inch of her, every delicate curve of silk soft skin.

When her fingers reached for the buttons of his flap he chuckled into her open mouth. Definitely no more need for persuasion then.

"I want to feel you inside me," her whisper brushed his lips.

"No more than I wish to be in you, you beautiful woman."

Her hands were cold.

"Ellen," he breathed heavily into her mouth, pressing into the heat of her.

Her pale blue eyes shone brightly through the shadow of coal black lashes as he loved her and her calves pressed to the back of his thighs, gripping him. Her cold fingers slipped beneath his shirt on his lower back. *Gorgeous, beautiful, woman. My woman.*

A rasping sigh left her lips and he absorbed it on an inward breath.

He loved her sounds of pleasure — the moment she reached carelessness. Yet now he felt her wilfully fighting it, trying to hold back. He knew she feared the servants hearing.

"Edward." Her bright eyes were shining as she pleaded for him to cease kissing her so she could close her mouth and restrain the sounds.

He didn't care if they heard. If the servants didn't like it they could lose themselves, they didn't have to be in earshot. He was not conceding and an urgency came over him in answer, instead of retreating he assaulted to win all of her attention. His reward was a sharp impassioned cry.

"The servants," she whispered.

"Can go to hell. They are paid not to listen. Forget about them and think of me."

"Think of me."

"Think of me." It was a physical and mental chant.

"Edward," she said again, but this time it was not in battle. This time it was in surrender.

"Darling," he breathed. "I love you."

His fingers slipped into her bodice, popping the tiny buttons which secured it. He felt vigorous and primal like a beast and a roar hovered at the back of his throat which he let out in a low growl. This was what his greedy senses had longed for, for her to yield like this. She was pliant and lush in his hands, and her fingers gripped his forearms as he saw the weakness coming over her.

She lay back on the desk with her eyes shut, her breathing heavy. He watched her face, the flicker of sensual release playing with her lips and eyelids.

He knew when the moment came, even before the sound left her mouth and her fingernails bit into his skin.

His fingers on her thighs he withdrew sharply, he was not ready for this to end, not yet and he dropped to his knees. There was another sense he wished to appease before he finished this — taste.

Her arms slid up in a gorgeous languorous motion above her head across the polished surface of the desk when he leaned over her again, his senses on overload.

Her muscle was trembling.

He gripped her hands and held them above her head, meeting her clouded gaze as her eyes opened and then he simply adored her.

It was only moments later when their joined voices echoed about the small room and his limbs felt numb as his nerves tingled and burned. The sensation flung him mentally to a galaxy a million miles beyond this.

When he returned she'd freed her hands from his and pulled him down, gripping his shoulder and head. He stole a heart-wrenching kiss from her. Robert would not rile him again, not here, not anywhere. Whenever Robert tried it, Edward would think of this, this singular defiance, making love to Ellen, whom Robert had so slandered, on Robert's desk. The salt Robert always rubbed into Edward's wounds had finally lost its sting.

"I ought to be angry, you always spur me to indecency," she whispered as he pulled away.

"You're too sensitive of others' opinions." One of his hands was on the desk, the other brushed her cheek as he held her gaze, "because of your past, I know, but I've told you a dozen times to forget it, sweetheart. We are newly married, Ellen, the world anticipates our insatiable habits, not judges them, or you for them. And if they do judge, they'll blame me not you."

Her lips lifted in a smile, her eyes shining as her arms reached upwards in a satisfied cat like stretch. She was not angry, she was happy, he could see it.

"I am learning," she answered as he withdrew and buttoned his flap. "But you will not persuade me this is not risqué. Could you ever imagine my father and mother thus?"

"Indeed," he laughed, smiled and pulled her up to straighten her clothes, slipping her hem back over her knees.

Still smiling he tucked his shirt back in and reached to secure the buttons of her bodice. "Very well, I admit we may be unusual among the *ton*'s matches." Grinning now, he remembered their week-long affair in London, when they'd laughed and teased one another constantly, and added, "But in my opinion—your husband's—the only opinion you should listen to—*your hunger for me is your finest quality*." But then he sobered his tone. "Do not deny me to please others, Ellen. What do you care for them—*care for me*."

In answer she slid off the desk, lifted onto tiptoe, pressed a kiss to his cheek and whispered, "So are you coming to bed or not?" Before backing away and beckoning with her fingers, tempting him to follow and then disappearing about the door at a run.

Laughing, he set into chase.

Chapter Fourteen

After curtsying to Richard, Penny's husband, Ellen accepted his arm and his escort onto the floor for a country dance, joining the crowd of dancers gathered in the center of the Forths' ballroom. Her other brothers-in-law had already partnered her, as had Rupert, Edward's cousin, who'd apologised for his behaviour at the theatre. Robert had danced with her too. He'd made her laugh through the whole of the Wakefield Hunt, causing her to muddle up her steps, which made her laugh even more, only to receive a questioning, reproachful look from Edward when she was returned to his side.

She knew Edward still did not trust his brother. Edward was closer to Richard than he was Robert. During the week since the theatre excursion Richard and Penny had accompanied

Edward and Ellen to Vauxhall, a musical evening and several other entertainments.

The fortunate consequence of their recent outings was Ellen had become used to the speculating looks and whispers passed behind open fans when she was near.

But so far, despite the constant gossip, she considered Edward's campaign a success. No one had turned her away, cut her, or spoken cruelly to her face, although who knew what they said behind those fans or thought as they stared. People seemed more astounded by her reappearance than outraged, and as Edward predicted, no one had had the will or the courage to challenge the tale they were being told. So with her army of influential family to stand up and escort her, Ellen was forging on, ignoring what others said or did behind their fans or behind her back.

"Are you bearing up, Ellen?" Richard asked as they met in the pattern of the dance.

She smiled as they passed each other, back to back. "I think so, yes." They were parted again, and Ellen took the opportunity to look for Edward. He was where she'd left him, standing against a pillar watching her with deep concentration. As though he half expected a wolf to break through the French-windows leading to the terrace and drag her off, but he smiled as he caught her gaze. To her prejudiced eye, he was the most handsome man in the room.

"Edward is a good man. You are lucky to have found him." Richard spoke as they joined hands to complete a paired formation circle, affording them a moment of more private conversation.

Meeting Richard's searching look Ellen smiled. "I know, I cannot imagine how this would have ended if I had not. I know you are aware of the truth, from things Penny has said."

"I wish I had known before, though. Had I, I would have helped you, Ellen."

The sincerity in his tone moved her. Dropping her gaze to the knot of his cravat to avoid succumbing to tears, she answered. "Thank you."

He meant it, she knew, but the past could not be changed, only the future. As the figures of the dance came to a close, she looked for the man who'd given her the opportunity to change it—Edward.

"I'll take you back," Richard said beside her, his fingers gently touching her arm. "I'm sorry. I upset you. I did not intend to, Ellen. I just wished you to know I would not have left you to suffer by choice."

Glancing up, Ellen forced a smile and then nodded, but words would not come, the lump lodged in her throat prevented them. She turned to look for Edward again and saw him approach.

"Ellen?"

"I upset her I'm afraid, speaking of things I probably should not have mentioned," Richard advised, his hand falling away from her arm, as Edward took her hand and held it firmly.

Edward's solidarity helped Ellen find her voice, and she turned and met Richard's concerned gaze. "Your kindness did not upset me, Richard. It just stirred up emotions I thought I had conquered. Please don't apologize for your consideration. I am grateful for it, truly."

The heir to the Duke of Arundel, a powerful and respected man, gave her an apologetic smile, as he bowed over her hand and kissed her fingers. "I shall seek Penny. I believe she was speaking with Lady Forth. If you need me, Edward, just give me a nod."

"Would you like some air?" Edward bent to whisper to her ear as Richard walked away.

Ellen nodded just as Casper appeared, coming to offer his hand for the next dance.

She watched Edward face his friend with a smile. "I think we've worn her out, Casper, can she cry off?"

"As it gives me opportunity to catch up with my wife I shall not mind at all," Forth answered, smiling broadly at Ellen. "But you will have to promise me a dance later, I refuse to be excluded from the fun."

Smiling too, Ellen touched his arm. "I promise, if I have a dance spare, my sisters have been finding extended family to send in my direction."

"And you will not steal my waltz. I want at least one dance with my wife," Edward insisted.

How bizarre this all seemed from a few months ago when she had not a single friend, now she had acquired so many she could not even keep up with them all. Her eyes lifted to the millions of sparkling prisms of crystal glass, drops of light hanging in the chandeliers, reflecting the glow of hundreds of candles throughout the room. Her sorry story had the lustre of a fairy tale tonight.

"Well then if I miss-out this evening you shall have to accept my hand at Penny's ball is all I can say," Casper answered, already looking for Julie across his shoulder. "So," he turned back, "I'll leave you two to it." With that he bowed briefly and then was gone.

"Come on, Ellen, let's find you some air." Edward gripped her elbow and guided her across the broad room to the bank of closed French-windows, where all the glitter and grandness was reflected upon the glass, with night's black for its backwash. Slipping the latch on one of them Edward opened it, letting in a rush of cooler air as he led her out onto the terrace.

It was empty. As Edward closed the door she walked across it to the balustrade. The light from several small glass lanterns brightened the terrace but she could not see beyond it, the garden was absorbed in the shadow of night. And with clouds obscuring the moon and stars, the blackness was as thick as tar. She shivered. It was still chilly without a cloak. Edward's hands slipped about her waist, resting over her stomach as he pulled her back against him.

"Edward." Elbowing him sharply in the ribs she forced him back.

"What? We are married after all?" he whispered with an earthy masculine chuckle as he lifted his hands away and stepped back. "I was only trying to keep you warm."

"There is enough talk about me, without creating more," she hissed back across her shoulder. No one was here to see, but still she didn't like to take the risk.

Apparently accepting her rebuff he turned to rest his buttocks against the balustrade beside her, folded his arms across his chest and looked back at the windows of the ballroom. "What upset you?"

"Nothing really, Richard just said he would have helped me if he'd known how things stood before." Pressing her palms to the frigid cold stone running along the top of the balustrade, she looked outwards, into the blackness beyond it, facing what had once been her life, before Edward, before her hero had brought this impossible fairy tale to pass.

"He's a good man," Edward answered.

"He said the same about you," she acknowledged, smiling.

A sharp laugh was released from his throat at that, then he pulled up straight and she turned to face him straightening too, sensing a heavier weight to his thoughts. "But I am not good enough for you really. It worries me this is what will hold your father back."

"You are not good enough for me!" She gripped his arm. "Edward! Listen to what you are saying. How can you give credence to such nonsense, when you know what I have really been?" Forgetting her fear of others' opinions, she slipped her hands beneath his black evening coat, over his white silk waistcoat, slotting her fingers together behind his back, locking him securely in her embrace. "You are everything to me." Her eyes met the dark slate blue-gray, almost all black in the darkness. "You had better not consider deserting me."

"I'm hardly likely to do that," he scoffed, tapping her under the chin. The world beyond the narrow terrace faded, forgotten as he bent to kiss her in a soul deep promise of his lifetime commitment. It was not just in his words and touch—it was in every essence of his being.

The first notes of the waltz struck up within the ballroom, the music leaking through the glass and resonating about their solitary space.

Pulling away he laughed lightly, his eyes shining with the intense feelings she felt too. "Shall we dance? I don't fancy being the object of their fascination. I'd rather it was just you and I, here."

"I would like that," Ellen whispered. His strong gentle hand slid to press between her shoulder blades, at her back, and hers slipped from beneath his coat to rest lightly on his shoulder, the other was cradled in his. Then without thought, as though they lived and breathed as one person she followed him into the steps, her gaze holding his. She could feel the masculine power in his broad-framed shoulders as he turned her; the sinuous strength in his thighs brushing hers through the thin fabric of her skirts.

Edward smiled, the press of his hand urging her closer, until she felt her body touching his from pelvis to chest. And now the dance was no longer simply a dance but something else, something unspoken as she laid her head on his shoulder and merely felt his movements. She was so absorbed in him she was caught in shock when she heard a clap ring out.

"Beautiful."

Her heart thumped as she pulled away from Edward and he shoved her behind him.

Gainsborough. It was Lord Gainsborough.

"How the bloody hell did you get in?" Edward yelled.

"Does it matter? I'm here, is all. I saw the pretty piece you ran in the Times. Touching. So I started thinking, what would society say if I printed another that told them where you had been, Ellen, all these intervening years. And then I got to wondering what you would do to keep me silent."

The obnoxious man, stood there, tipping snuff on to his crooked hand as he spoke, then snorted it, eyeing Edward as though Edward was no more than a worm.

Bile rose in Ellen's throat, her hands gripping the waist of Edward's coat, as she struggled to quell her desire to run. She did not want Gainsborough to know the power he still wielded over her. She'd fought so hard to forget her fear and self-disgust, but seeing the man who'd forged and fostered all the emotions of her nightmares—they returned. How could they not, he'd been her puppet master, tormentor and abuser for years.

Swallowing back her need to escape, she forced herself to stand her ground, controlling her fear, not letting it take control of her. She wasn't the Ellen who'd succumbed to his threats anymore.

I will not run from him, or hide from him.

"This is all very cosy, this family reunion, Ellen." Lord Gainsborough directed his words and gaze at her, lecherous and disrespectful, as she stepped out from behind Edward, only a little, her fingers still gripping Edward's coat as if just touching him could protect her. "But I wonder how welcoming your family will be if I go public with the story of our little affair."

"And what's that you bastard?" Edward stormed. "That you held her by force, by threat. Do it Gainsborough, *you* will be disgraced. You sick, evil, bastard, taking advantage of a woman's ill-fate. You may go to the devil, and leave her be! I will pay you nothing, nor will her father bend to your blackmail anymore. No one is interested in what you have to say!"

"No? Are they not?" Gainsborough challenged with a deprecating look, as he glanced towards the ballroom. "Shall we test that theory?"

"No!" Fists clenched, Edward lunged forward, his coat slipping from Ellen's grasp.

"Edward, no!"

"But you don't mind if I do, do you, Ellen?" As Robert stepped from the shadows behind them, Edward stopped dead.

"I thought I'd told you to disappear, Gainsborough." Robert's voice was like steel as he passed Edward and his hand lifted insinuating for Edward to hold back.

"I—I—I—"

Ellen had never heard Gainsborough stutter in all the years she'd been his mistress.

"Afraid of me? If you are not you ought to be! You are pathetic! I warned you, Gainsborough!" Silent and in shock, Ellen watched as Robert pulled the fingers of one glove, taking it off before loosely swiping it across Gainsborough's face, the blow soft and mocking.

Gainsborough's eyes widened, his cheeks quivering as he stuttered again in an attempt to back-out, but Robert towered over him, staring down at her tormentor with a look of disgust. "Tomorrow at seven, on the Heath, by the Black Horse Inn. Find your second." Pressing a hand to Gainsborough's shoulder, Robert shoved him backwards. "Now get out!"

Lord Gainsborough stumbled one step back, apparently stunned for a moment. The man, who had bullied, threatened and assaulted her on numerous occasions, *was afraid*. He mumbled explanations, implying he'd meant no threat; that Robert had misunderstood. Robert did not move. He stood like granite in defense of her.

She was observing a nightmare while awake and Edward said nothing.

The glass between her vision of a fairy tale and reality broke—between past and present—the fantasy cracking, shattering into thousands of shards—sharp twisted little pieces. In answer she leapt into the fray. She would not allow Robert or Edward or anyone else to be injured by this, to be hurt by the fiction of her happy ending. No, she would rather go back to the dark infinity if that was the price. "You are not doing this!" Her voice rang back at her from the stone walls. "I will not be responsible for someone's death!"

Turning to look at her, Robert's expression was fixed and hard. "It is not your doing. It's his. I gave the bastard the option to disappear. He didn't take it. So be it. This is the outcome. Personally, I'll be glad to end his miserable life." A broad smile split Robert's lips. "Besides there's no risk to me, he's all bluster, Ellen." Despite his humor, a dark determined glint shone in his eyes.

"*Robert, no, please,*" Ellen pressed, her voice dropping to a desperate sincerity. He didn't care if he lived or died, she could see it, and perhaps that was why Gainsborough feared him more than he'd feared anyone else. "This is not what I want, Robert."

Edward caught her arm and held her back as she reached for Robert. "Ellen," he whispered, in a harsh commanding tone. "Robert is right, this needs to be resolved. It is not a woman's concern." He'd never distanced her from anything before. It hurt. But she knew Edward, he wouldn't relent, and neither would his brother. There was no point in arguing against them.

Pulling herself free from Edward's grip, glaring at him, her voice broke with a harsh, lost, pain, "I want to go home, Edward. Take me home." Her hopes were hollow. There would never be a happy ending, only more guilt to bear.

"*Bitch.*" Gainsborough yelled viciously behind her and sensing his movement, she spun to see him launch at her. "You'll die for this!"

"No!" Edward cried, his arm painfully grabbing her waist in a brutal grip as he snatched her body back from a blade's tip before it sliced into her throat. She didn't know where the blade had come from. She couldn't think.

Horror chilling and solidifying the blood in her veins, the scene unfolded in an unrealistic, slow, slurred speed. Robert grasped Gainsborough's wrist and in response Gainsborough thrust the blade upwards, slashing at him, cutting the air an inch from Robert's head. Robert twisted, his hand still gripping Gainsborough's wrist, tying the man in a knot as he moved behind Gainsborough, using Gainsborough's body as a shield, while he fought to force Gainsborough into dropping the knife.

The French-windows to the ballroom broke open, several men spilled out, shouting, and she heard the growing chaos through a haze.

Desperate rage and evil in his eyes, Lord Gainsborough flailed, the sharp tipped stabbing blade he wielded striking out in indiscriminate swipes, slashing at the air over his shoulder, trying to pierce Robert's neck.

Robert battled for control, deflecting each blow, while Ellen fought for freedom, screaming. The sound came from a million miles away as Edward restrained her and she dug her fingernails into his arm, which rigidly held her waist.

I have to stop this.

Suddenly time slowed by another degree, flashing in seconds, as Ellen's eyes followed the line of the glinting blade. It was descending now, under Robert's grip on Gainsborough's hand, veering downward. Robert was steering it away from him but in doing so it plunged towards Gainsborough.

When it struck, the blade punctured deep into Lord Gainsborough's chest.

Ellen's scream broke the air as the knife skewered Gainsborough's breadth. She knew the length of the blade must have passed through his ribs, pierced his lungs and thrust into his heart.

Instantly Robert's bloodied hand loosened its grip on Gainsborough's. And Robert stepped back. He looked stunned.

Ellen fell silent and watched, motionless, her fingers still gripping Edward's arm. Everyone standing on the narrow terrace, witnessing the scene, was silent.

Lord Gainsborough's eyes looked at his chest and his fingers, which still gripped the knife. Then he withdrew it.

Blood pulsed from the wound as the blade pulled free and Lord Gainsborough's eyes opened wide, bulging for a moment in shock as the knife fell with a clatter to the stone pavement before he fell too, following the blade that had taken his life, first to his knees and then forward onto his stomach. A gurgling noise escaped his throat, for the length of a single breath, then ebbed rasping into a drowning sound.

His body twitched in a sharp convulsion, once, before falling limp.

Ellen turned in a rush to the balustrade as Edward let her go and cast up her accounts over its edge, her stomach convulsing until there was no more fluid inside her. Only then did she become aware of Edward's hand on her back, and the commotion progressing behind her. She heard Lord Forth giving directions, calling for someone to send for the magistrate, and Richard too, advising someone to ensure the women were kept away. Men confirming to Robert they would bear witness to what had occurred, assuring him it was self-defense.

Shaking uncontrollably, Ellen rose, and Edward instantly gripped her, holding her to his chest, his palm rubbing her back. "Here." She felt a cloak rest over her shoulders, and recognised David's voice, another of her brothers-in-law. She felt sick again, until now David hadn't known the history of her intervening years, what on earth would he think of this. But he said nothing, moving away.

"Come," she heard Edward whisper. "I'll take you home. If the magistrate needs to speak to us it can wait until tomorrow." When her legs would not move, he simply and swiftly picked her up and carried her.

Pressing her face to his shoulder, she gripped the lapel of his evening coat. With her head turned into him, so that she need not look at anyone, she heard Casper guide Edward out through the servants' corridors and Edward muttering about gambling.

Chapter Fifteen

Dressed for the day, Edward bent down to the bed to kiss the forehead of his sleeping wife. She'd cried for hours through the night, despite the dose of laudanum Jenkins has rustled up to calm her jangled nerves. Edward had tried to talk to her but she hadn't been communicative, instead she'd just clung to him until a drug induced sleep had finally claimed her.

Expecting her to lie in this morning, he'd risen early to speak with Robert while she slept, and find out what had occurred once they'd left Forth's. Silently leaving the room, he managed not to disturb her.

Moments later, descending to the hall, he saw Robert hovering in conversation with Jenkins.

"Edward," Robert acknowledged, looking up.

Jogging down the last few steps, Edward asked the butler, "Is breakfast set, I'm starving?"

Jenkins confirmed it with a brisk nod, "My Lord."

Then to his brother, Edward added, "Have you eaten? I wanted to ask you what happened after we left."

"How's Ellen?" Robert asked, while as answer he caught Edward's arm and turned with him, steering him towards the dining room.

"She's sleeping. I don't know how she'll be when she wakes. She never spoke last night."

"She shouldn't have had to witness it," Robert concluded. "I'm sorry she did."

A footman held the door of the dining room open. The table was laid out for breakfast. The sweet smell of freshly baked bread, melting butter, salted meat and smoked fish assailed Edward. His stomach rumbled at the prospect. He hadn't got as far as eating supper last night, and hadn't thought of food at all after the horrific scene with Gainsborough. But now his anxiety over Ellen had made his empty stomach restless, he felt ravenously hungry.

He moved to take the chair beside his brother's at the head of the table. A footman came forward to pour their coffee, while others filled their plates. When they'd finished serving, Robert dismissed them, bidding the last man shut the door.

"So what happened?" Edward asked, tucking into his breakfast and taking a swig of coffee.

Robert took a mouthful, swallowed it and leaned back in his seat, his coffee cup in his hand. "The witnesses were all from Ellen's family or connected, no one else within the ballroom saw anything in any detail. We told the magistrate the story you gave Forth; that Gainsborough had sought to attack you because you'd accused him of cheating at cards and made him look the fool. He bought it, but he wishes to speak with you later and take your statement. I don't think…"

The door clicked open. Edward looked up, as did Robert. It swung wider revealing Ellen. Edward stood, watching her slip quietly into the room. She looked dazed, only half awake, her eyes red rimmed, her hair hastily twisted and pinned in a single loose knot. The crease of her pillow was still imprinted on the skin of her cheek. Her vague shifting gaze met theirs as she leaned back against the door and let it click shut behind her. He held out his hand to her, encouraging her to come to him but she didn't move. Staying at the door her hands pressing to the wood behind her bottom she watched the pair of them with wide eyes.

"Sweetheart," Edward called gently. "I thought you would still be sleeping. Come on, come here and sit beside me." She didn't come, just stood there watching him with an analytical crystalline gaze.

Edward stepped forward, adding. "Ellen, I think you should be resting."

She shook her head, her gaze focusing more directly on him, but with a look that gave him the impression she thought his words bizarre. "Why? I got out of bed each morning after he abused and beat me. Why should I stay abed like some pathetic creature when I have watched his lifeblood ebb away in price of it?"

"I'm sorry, Ellen," Robert said.

Glancing at his brother, Edward saw he'd stood too.

"I'm not," Ellen answered bluntly as Edward turned back and went to her, crossing the room. "He would have killed me if you'd let him have the chance."

She still sounded in shock.

"Perhaps you ought to go back to bed and rest, darling?" Reaching her side Edward touched her arm, but she shrugged him off.

Her eyes looked up, meeting his gaze, sharp determination shone there. "I'm not tired. What happens now?"

Edward sighed. "At least come and sit. I'll pour you a coffee."

She finally moved, walking before him as his fingers, rested to her back guiding her to the chair beside his. There, he withdrew it for her to sit, while Robert poured her a coffee and handed Edward the cup to set before her. When she picked it up her little charade was up as he saw the tremble in her hands. But if she wished to hide her distress he wouldn't make her face it. Instead he ignored it, returning to his seat and his waiting breakfast.

"So what happens now?" Ellen asked again.

Robert answered, while Edward ate, "The magistrate will call on Edward for a statement later. We gave ours last night. Everyone has said Gainsborough attacked Edward, not you, because of an argument over some card game weeks ago."

Edward felt Ellen's gaze rest on him while Robert continued. No doubt she was remembering their first night. He wished he'd had more self-control that night and left her untouched. He'd treated her with the same greed as Gainsborough. He hated himself for it. He didn't dare look up and meet her gaze.

"His body has been returned to his family," Robert progressed. "And for their sake the magistrate has agreed that the cause of death shall not be made public."

Ellen released a heart wrenchingly deep sigh, then whispered, "I had forgotten about his wife and daughters—his grandchildren."

Resting his knife and fork on the plate, Edward leaned back, turning to her. She was looking at Robert, now she looked at *him*.

"I should feel guilty, sorry, but I can't."

"I don't know why anyone would blame you for it, Ellen, if they knew the truth." Robert concluded soundly. "You're right the bastard deserved what he got."

"While that's true, I don't think it's helpful, Robert," Edward said in a low voice as he watched her.

"It is true though isn't it?" she added, looking from one to the other with brightly shining wide eyes. "A part of me hopes he rots in hell for eternity for what he did to me, but another part of me knows I should forgive and forget—being vengeful only hurts. Yet he's dead, because of me, and…" She shrugged; a helpless little gesture. "I don't know what to think. It is still a life lost at my expense and a wife now a widow. His daughters no longer have a father, and his grandchildren—"

"*Not because of you*," Edward urged quietly. "*Because of him*. He chose to do what he did. Last night he attacked *you*. He tried to kill you, Ellen. You are not at fault. Understand it and believe it."

She nodded, but he knew the words had not sunk into either her head or her heart. Still more wounds to be healed.

"You're not at fault, Ellen," Robert echoed Edward's words and Edward looked across at him with gratitude.

She shook her head. "I do know, yet I shall still think of his wife and daughters."

"You're too good, woman," Robert said staring at her. "I'm sorry I ever thought differently." At that, Ellen blushed.

A knock struck the door and Jenkins called from beyond it, "My Lords, my Lady, the Marchioness of Wiltshire is here."

"Penny," Ellen breathed, rising. "Forgive me." She turned back to them. "I'll take her up to my sitting room."

Edward gave her a sharp nod of approval, knowing this was perhaps the best thing for her, to spend some time with her closest sister. "I will come up and see you later."

She nodded too, bobbing a curtsy to Robert and left.

"Ellen." Robert said in parting, standing in recognition of her exit, affording her the respect she deserved as a gently bred woman.

Then seating himself again Robert turned to Edward. "Bloody hell, Ed. How badly did he treat her? God, Rupert and I got it wrong, didn't we?"

"Just a little." Edward let a self-satisfied smile slip across his face as he took a mouthful of his breakfast, washed it down with coffee then looked back at his brother. "In truth, I probably only know half of it myself. Ellen is not the sort of person to share it. But I did see the aftermath of bruises from a beating he had given her, days after it, and they were still vivid beneath the mask of white powder she had tried to hide them with.'

Robert made a disgusted sound. "Now I am even gladder the bastard is dead."

"And as to that I have not yet said thank you," Edward answered, and his words were for so much. He hadn't expected Robert to get involved, let alone to risk his life. Edward hadn't even expected Robert to ever accept Ellen.

"I owed you this, I think, after my misinterpretation of her at Farnborough," Robert said lightly, with a smile, leaning back in his chair, the rare moment of his solemnity gone.

"Perhaps, but this is my fight not yours," Edward answered. "You didn't have to get involved, but I am grateful you did."

"No, I didn't have to, but I chose to, Ed. I know you think ill of me, yet I can be brotherly when I wish. But God forbid I prove not to be the villain you've cast me." At that Robert drained his coffee cup and rose. "I'm done, and now I'm off."

As Robert passed, annoyed with his sudden return to sarcasm, Edward grabbed the cuff of Robert's morning coat, stopping him, and challenged his irritating tone. "Must you make a joke out of everything?"

Robert faced Edward, his expression deadly serious. "I am not joking. I like your wife. I helped you. What more is there to say?"

Edward just looked at him, his grip falling from his brother's sleeve. "I don't think I'll ever understand you." The words, his thoughts, slipped from his lips.

"No," Robert answered with a bitter smile. "Probably not. But perhaps you could try to simply trust me. I didn't leave father knowing he'd die. And in fact when I left I never had a bloody choice." Robert's hands lifted as though he would say more, then fell as he clearly made the decision not to speak. "Still it hardly matters." Shrugging one shoulder, with an air of tired dismissal Robert turned away.

Edward rose facing Robert's departing back, a deep sigh lifting his chest. "But when father died you didn't come back, Rob." Edward had wanted his brother then and Robert had not come back. Leaving Edward to deal with grief, debt and responsibility alone, throwing him into adult life as a child was thrown into water to learn to swim. He'd needed his brother then. He could never forgive Robert for not coming home when he should.

Robert stopped halfway across the room, turned and looked back, his hard brown-eyed stare narrowing. "I couldn't," he answered, before turning away again and shifting back into motion.

"Or rather you wouldn't," Edward continued. "I've heard the stories of your life abroad. You slept and gambled your way through Europe. That's hardly the life of a contrite man who mourned his father. You can't paint it any different now you're back!"

Robert didn't stop.

Yet Edward thought he heard words on his brother's breath as Robert pulled open the door which sounded like, "But perhaps a man who mourned another loss."

A moment after Robert had gone Jenkins's knock resounded on the half open door.

"Come," Edward called, sitting back down to his now cold meal.

"A letter came for you, Lord Edward." Jenkins spoke as he crossed the room holding forth a single letter balanced on a silver tray.

The imprint in the seal was Pembroke's.

Edward lifted it from the tray and dismissed Jenkins with a nod of gratitude, before sliding his thumb beneath the seal to open it.

His eyes scanned the brief letter as Jenkins walked away. A simple statement, not a request, but an order, to attend an appointment. So Ellen's father made his first move.

⋄⋄⋄

Ellen hugged her sister when they reached the privacy of the sitting room attached to her bedchamber and heard Penny sob. The elder sister again, Ellen pulled away and clasped Penny's shoulders, meeting her gaze. "You are crying. I'm sorry, I—"

"It's nothing," Penny answered with a sniff, wiping at the corners of her eyes with a handkerchief. "I'm sorry it's so early but I had to come and see how you are."

"I'm coping," Ellen answered, taking Penny's hand and drawing her to the chintz sofa where they could both sit. Then leaving her sister there, she went to pull the ribbon which rang the servant's bell.

"It's awful," Penny progressed. "Richard told me Lord Gainsborough tried to kill you. I dare not even think how he has treated you in the past." There was now an edge of anger in her voice and her glassy gaze lifted to Ellen's, looking for an answer, but Ellen said nothing. She knew Penny had gleaned something of the past, but they'd never spoken of it. Ellen did not want to.

"Richard and I are distraught to know you have been in London all this time. To think what you have endured. If we had only known, Ellen."

"Do Rebecca and Sylvia know?" Ellen asked, feeling her skin blanch at the prospect.

"No. James and David agreed to tell them the story Edward gave the magistrate. They did not think it would do Rebecca and Sylvia any good to know the truth."

"But James and David know," Ellen breathed, her color rising again as she turned to a knock on the door and called Jill in. "Jill, chocolate please, and bread with honey too, I haven't eaten yet."

"Yes, my Lady." The maid bobbed a curtsy to both of them, smiling at Penny, then left, the door clicking shut behind her.

"Julie was in such a state when we left last night, to think it happened at their home."

"The Forths know too," Ellen whispered, as she crossed the room and dropped onto the seat beside her sister, mortified by the knowledge. "Oh, Penny, I'm sorry. You will tell her so."

"Sorry?" Penny twisted to her side to face Ellen. "What on earth do you have to be sorry for, it's hardly your fault?"

"So Edward said." Ellen's gaze reached across Penny's shoulder to look at the blue sky of the bright spring day through the window, the weather so at odds to the climate in the room.

"I cannot believe you would even think it. The person to blame is Papa. *How he could have done this?*"

"Penny." Ellen, met her sister's gaze. "I don't want to destroy the family."

In answer Penny captured Ellen's fingers in her own. "And *that* you can blame him for too, and do not try to defend him. It is I who attended your funeral, walking, weeping behind an empty coffin to watch it entombed in the mausoleum. I spent a year of my life dressed in black, because of him, for a sister who was alive, who needed my help not my mourning. I cannot, and will not, forgive him, Ellen, and it is through nothing you have done. No one lays any blame or judgement upon you, so please do not place it on yourself. None of us think less of you for how you have been forced to live, Ellen, and that is an end to it."

Ellen blinked at her sister, closer to her now than she had ever been as a child. She reached to hug her and just held her for a moment, until Penny pulled away, dabbing at her eyes again. "I have not told you yet though," she said with another sniff. "Father is in town."

"*In London? Has he brought John?*"

Penny shook her head, squeezing Ellen's hand in consolation. "No, I had a letter from Mama this morning, father refused to bring John. She said *she* would have come without father's permission but she didn't like to leave John alone. He hasn't settled since his return."

"I want to see him so much, Penny," Ellen breathed, accepting the comfort of the hand holding hers.

"I know. Richard told Edward if father does not come about, we will help you take him. We know how we would feel if it were one of our girls." Tears sparkled in her eyes again and she dabbed at them with her handkerchief.

Jill's gentle tap struck the door. "Come in," Ellen called, turning to attend to the pot of chocolate Jill carried, directing the young maid to set it down and leave. Ellen poured the sweet smelling, steaming liquid into two cups, handed one to Penny and then held the other. Thoughts of John forced her memories of last night aside.

"Why do you think father has come? Do you think he intends to speak to me?"

"How can we tell with father? Richard thinks he will not bend so easily. He suspects Papa has some plan afoot, but you are not to worry, because whatever happens, you will have John."

"I'll have John," Ellen whispered, wide eyed as she sipped the sweet liquid and its warmth ran down her throat. "I have you back, and Edward. Don't pinch me Penny, I do not wish to wake from this dream. And yet now I feel guilty for thinking I can be happy again, while Lord Gainsborough's loss is mourned by his family."

Penny set down her cup and pressed her hand on Ellen's shoulder. "It's no dream. You are here, home with us. You will be happy, we will all settle for nothing less. And I positively forbid you from feeling any guilt."

"Home has always been where John is," Ellen sipped from her cup, refusing the threatening tears.

"You will have him back," Penny's touch fell away, "one way or another. But for now, to cheer you up, Sylvia and Rebecca wished us to call. I believe they have a visit to Gunter's planned. They wish to take the girls for ices. You will come?"

Ellen nodded. She loved to see her sisters, but her nieces were an even greater joy. They would chase away the shadows of her past, like a summer breeze sweeping away a morning mist. With a restrained smile Ellen set down her cup, to give Penny another brief hug. "I am so glad I have you all back, but no more talk of the things which have happened in between, Penny. I do not want to discuss them. And let father do what he will, I don't wish to speak of him either."

"Very well," Penny whispered, her voice welling with emotion again. "I shan't, and from now on we shall be above father's games."

⤛⤜

Following in the wake of the Duke of Pembroke's butler, Edward stepped into the grand library. The Duke's town villa was a massive, sprawling monster of a property off Regent Street, set back from the road behind a high wrought iron railing. The stately residence dripped with opulence in every perfectly laid stone, every fixture and fitting, with carved ornate mouldings decorating it within and without and shiny gold gilt adorning every room. Despite his determined self-possession the gravity of the property swayed Edward's confidence. Instantly he was on edge. His own unworthiness of Ellen rubbed at his conviction again as he faced the splendour of the life that had once been, and should still be, hers.

To think I proudly offered her life as the wife of a paid steward. He scoffed at himself, thrusting his trepidation to the back of his mind as the butler moved aside.

The Duke was sitting behind his desk, and made no move to rise.

"You asked to see me, Your Grace." Edward forced civility into his voice. If things worked out as they should this man would be in Ellen's life for the rest of their future, so Edward did not wish to deliberately incite hostility that would hinder her cause or John's.

"Marlow, I'm glad you decided to come." The Duke remained seated, sending the butler away with a nod, offering Edward neither a seat nor refreshment. Edward occupied a chair anyway, and sat back in a deliberately relaxed pose, while his eyes met Pembroke's with an inoffensive but unyielding stare. He was not about to let the bastard bully him the way he had Ellen and John.

"I didn't realize there was a choice," Edward responded, his eyebrows lifting, keeping his voice even, solid. "It was worded as a command, as I recall. Still I am pleased to see you in London. I suppose you have come to attend the Wiltshires' ball on Friday. Have you brought John?"

He received a glare in answer. "I do not intend to reward my daughter's insubordination with my presence, and my grandson is on my estates where he belongs. I will not be manipulated, Marlow, and I shall tell Wiltshire the same."

"No?" Edward challenged, unable to help himself from thrusting a slight stab at the man's oversized ego. "But you are here."

"I am here to put an end to this nonsense." The Duke retorted sharply, deploying the same violent stare he'd threatened them with at Farnborough the day he'd taken John. The look had ripped both John's and Ellen's confidence to shreds. Edward was not so easily disturbed.

Clearly ignoring his inability to intimidate Edward, the Duke picked up a piece of paper then reached across the desk and set it down before Edward, with a self-congratulating yet distrustful expression. "That," Pembroke pointed to the paper, "is my final offer."

Offer? What the hell? Refusing to even look at it, let alone touch the obnoxious article, Edward kept his eyes on Pembroke's face.

"It is a banker's draft, Marlow, for twenty thousand. Take it. I am giving you it to disappear, you understand. Use it to take your wife abroad, New England perhaps, where she will no longer be an embarrassment."

"An embarrassment!" Anger pulsing into his blood, Edward pushed to standing. The man could not even bring himself to use his daughter's name! *God, how can he think I would let him pay me off?* "This is not blackmail. All we want is the boy!"

Pembroke leaned back in his chair, visibly surprised by Edward's anger.

God, Edward felt sick. Pembroke really thought Edward sought money.

Measuring his tone with care, holding back his true ire, Edward spelled out his response bluntly. "Neither myself, nor Ellen, will take it. We will not be bought off. This is not about money, Pembroke." With that he picked up the single slip of paper and tore it in half, lay one sheet across the other then tore it in half again, before letting it flutter down upon Pembroke's desk.

"There is one thing, and one thing only, we shall accept, and that is the return of Ellen's son to her, and," setting his fingers onto Pembroke's desk he leaned across it, "to hear you apologize for what you have done to your daughter, Eleanor. And that, Your Grace, is my final and non-negotiable price."

Saying nothing, Pembroke's rock-hard gaze denied any response, as he reached for a small bell on his desk and rang it once.

Edward's temper finally slipping its tight leash, breaking in a rush, he ground out in an aggressive snarl. "*If*, you had given the blood money Gainsborough blackmailed out of you, to keep her out of the way, to Ellen when she had need of it, and brought her home where she belonged, you would not be in this mess now, would you! How do you sleep at night knowing what you have done to your child, out of stupid bloody-minded arrogance? For-God-sake, she only wed a sixth son instead of a first!"

The door opened. "Your Grace?" The butler entered with three footmen at his rear.

"You have no concerns," Edward spoke. "I am leaving." But before he walked from the door he turned back. "I hope you go to hell, Pembroke. And that Ellen never finds out just how low you have stooped."

Edward shrugged off the footman's hand as the man tried to grasp Edward's arm and then he strode out of the door, straightening his morning coat as he crossed the hall, glad to escape her father's presence. Edward would never be able to forgive Pembroke, even if he did concede to giving them John back.

❦

Ellen gripped her reticule tightly, holding it before her at her waist as though it could act as a shield. Her heartbeat was thundering in a ridiculously fast rhythm. She lifted the lion-head knocker and dropped it, then gripped her reticule with both hands again and waited. Was she a fool to have come?

She'd told no-one about her decision, not even Edward. He'd be cross if he knew she was doing this alone — he'd be cross she was doing it all. But she had spent the morning and luncheon with her sisters and nieces, and constantly she'd thought of Penny's promise to take John. Ellen could not allow her sister to fall foul of her father's fury.

Ellen had signed her son away. She should get him back.

She'd let Robert and Edward take over last night and Gainsborough was gone. The shock of that incident had receded, but last night had persuaded her she must take control. Edward had given her the courage to do so, but she must stand up and fight this battle herself.

Oh but it was easier said than done.

But I want my son.

The door opened. Ellen had never been to her father's townhouse as a child, she had always remained in the country with nursemaids and governesses when her mother and father came to town. But still she felt like a child looking up, awed and bewildered by the opulence.

She lifted her chin and stiffened her spine. She was not a child but John was and he needed her. She was going to make her father face her, and look at her, and say her name and she was going to insist he give her John. John was *her* child.

"Ma'am?"

"Sir…" —*I am the Duke's denounced daughter, tell him I am here* — *I wish to see the Duke, I am Lady Ellen, the daughter he called dead.*

How did she introduce herself? Her heart pounded. "I am Lady Edward. May I speak to the Duke? Is he at home? If he is, please give him this?" Her voice sounded oddly normal. Internally she was in turmoil. Her fingers shook as she passed the man the note she had written when she'd got home from her trip with Penny. It said simply.

Please speak to me, I need you to understand. I wish to explain. Just give me a moment of your time, Papa.

Eleanor.

Edward had been out at White's with her brothers-in-law. She'd snatched the opportunity of his absence and followed through with her decision, coming immediately before she had the chance to let doubt take over. Now doubt flooded in.

She had written the note to try and stir her father's conscience. Somewhere inside him a heart beat. Didn't it? Surely he must feel something for her. He had been more lenient with her sister's after she had left, did that not imply there was some humanity in his soul. But now she was not sure.

Would he speak to her? If he refused, what would she do? Her heartbeat was deafening in her ears and she felt faint as she met the butler's gaze.

He was looking at her with disdain, his nose tipped up as if she smelt bad. Of course she had come without a maid or footman.

No-one knew she was here. She did not want them to know.

Do not look at me like that, not now, that was who I used to be, I do not even know that poisoned, ostracised woman anymore.

Ellen bit her lip and foolishly felt tears flood her eyes.

I just wish this resolved. I just want my son, that is the only reason I am here.

No, no, that was a lie. She was not only here for John. She was here because she needed to break the last barrier between her and acceptance too. She wished to hear her father say he was wrong. If she heard him admit it she could finally believe her own innocence.

She had been jealous of her sisters today—she'd envied them their content, happy lives and she was angry that her father had prevented her from having the same. She did not deserve what he had done to her.

She saw compassion cloud the butler's eyes. Of course he worked for her father. He would know how the Duke could cut people to the quick.

She wiped her tears away. She had done enough crying since Gainsborough's death. Now was the time to end all this. She was strong now.

"His Grace is currently dressing to attend the House of Lords Ma'am, I cannot say how long he shall be…"

"I will wait, if I may? If you will give him that note?"

"Sit then Ma'am." He indicated a gilded red velvet chair by the door.

Nerves making her tremble, still gripping her reticule over-tightly and moving stiffly, Ellen complied and took the seat, an unwelcome guest in what had once been one of the places she could have called home. She felt as though if it were possible she would have been swept beneath the carpet, the family dirt hidden from view. She had not even been invited to wait in a reception room because the butler thought her a woman of ill-morals. She felt sick—she had been a woman of ill-morals.

No, I was never that. It was merely a circumstance I was forced into.

Edward had made her able to say that. Edward was right. The sin had not been hers. It had not been her choice.

I am a wife and a mother and the daughter of a Duke and I am going to make the man who judged me less face the sin he put upon me.

More defiant words trailed through her thoughts as she rehearsed in her head the things she'd say, building her courage and refusing the terror she felt burning in her stomach as a clock ticked on the mantel to one side of the hall. Her heels tapped on the black and white chequered marble floor and the size of the room absorbed her making her feel minuscule as she waited, and waited.

She looked up at the top of the shallow, wide, stone staircase several times. No one came.

Had the butler forgotten her? Would her father not speak to her? How long did she wait? Should she just go upstairs and look for him?

A footman stood across the hall by the stairs, watching her with speculation, no doubt wondering who this lone woman was, and what her connections to the Duke were.

I am his daughter!

She had not said it to the butler because bowing to her father's will was too ingrained and she had known her father would not wish her to state the association.

At last she saw the butler at the head of the stairs.

She stood as he descended.

"His Grace's valet has put your note into His Grace's own hands. He is reading it now Ma'am. I dare say he shall speak with you in a moment."

Ellen's heart was pumping hard again but she sat back down. What else could she do? The butler stood beside the far side of the door observing her as though she was a curiosity. At least she still wore her bonnet and its brim gave her some protection from his view.

She longed for Edward, for his hand to grip. It was probably wrong of her to have kept the visit secret but she could not tell him, he would not understand her need to do this alone. This was her final stance to set her past right. She had to break her father's hold over her and she could only do that if she did it herself. If she hid behind Edward she would not be free and she refused to be imprisoned by fear any longer. That was the old Ellen.

Her jaw firmed and her body stiffened, she had fled Gainsborough, she would fight her father.

The clocked ticked. The butler coughed. The footman shuffled his feet and rocked from side-to-side. Her heart thumped like a fist against her ribs. Her head ached.

Come, Papa.

She was on the verge of rising and storming up the stairs in high dudgeon at the moment she heard his voice.

"Is the person who brought this note still here?"

Oh Lord.

She stood.

His tone was impersonal and judgemental. It had always been so.

"P—Your Grace."

He was on the landing above, out of sight, though the butler was able to see him, he was looking up and he spoke too. "The Lady is here, Your Grace."

"Waiting in the hall? A woman?"

Ellen felt as though her heart would burst from her chest. Was he about to ask them to throw her out?

Then she saw him, he was wearing his formal robes. He looked God like, statuesque and stately. He walked slowly about the corner of the banister and into view. His hand gripping the rail, he looked down, *and he looked at her*, not past her, or beyond her, *but at her*, acknowledging her in a small way, but at least acknowledging she existed.

Relief swept through her as she met his hard unfathomable gaze. It traveled over her face and then absorbed what she wore. She ached to be welcomed by him. He may have treated her with cruelty beyond imagining but he was still her father. She'd grown up with a desire to please him. It had always felt like heaven when she had won a smile from him or earned more than a moment or two of his attention, because those things were so rare.

She felt as if she would faint again but she refused to let herself be weak, Edward had taught her how to be strong and she drew on every ounce of the courage she'd been given by his unswayable love.

No matter what her father thought of her. She had her sisters and Edward, and she was here for John.

"Will you let me speak? Will you listen?" She lifted her chin higher.

He merely looked at her while she waited for his decree. Then finally he spoke. "I thought it was a messenger waiting. I did not realize it was *you* here. Had I known, I would not have left you waiting."

What did that mean?

She felt suspended. She felt like screaming and scratching his face, she felt like weeping, she felt like dropping to her knees and begging him to give her John back. She did none of those things. She did nothing. Yet although her heart still beat steadily, too fast, and her breathing was sharp and shallow and would not catch within her lungs and the palms of her hands felt cold with sweat as she gripped her reticule, she realized she was no longer terrified — she was determined. "I want John back. He is my son."

"Do you?" He stared at her.

"At least let me see him."

"He is not here."

She stepped forward several paces, frustrated by the staircase of steps separating them. "Pa — Your Grace?" There was a plea in her voice she did not like. She was not here to beg. She was here to make him regret what he had done to her. "May I speak with you, please?"

He moved, his long fingers still gripping the banister, progressing along the landing above and then he began descending.

That hand had never held hers as Edward's had John's. This man did not know how to be a father. Her son had been raised by him for the last ten years. She had to set her son free as she was now free and she *was* free, she no longer felt that this man ruled her life — Edward ruled it and Edward loved her.

"Walk this way." Her father left the stairs and walked past her not looking at her now. He had still not used her name.

She wanted him to use her name.

I am Eleanor, Papa!

She longed for him to say it. For him to see his daughter and not a whore. It was who she was. That other woman was the one who was dead.

He entered the library.

The footman had moved to hold the door and when she passed through it too her father nodded and the footman withdrew shutting the door behind him.

They were alone in the room and her father stood with his back to her. Numerous shelves of leather bound books surrounded them and an ornate ceiling towered above them. She could not quite believe she was here, but now was the time to push her case. He had let her stay. "Papa, I did not wish things to end as they did."

He said nothing, and she pressed on, her voice firm and persuasive. "It was not a choice I had made when you found me abroad." She stopped, hoping he might turn and comment. He did not. Her chin lifted and her back stiffened. "I am soiled, I know I am. I was when you came for John. But I had no money to feed us. *What was I to do?* Tell me that, Papa." The pitch of her voice rose. "*Tell me?* You stand in judgement of me, but you had turned your back only because I married Paul. What was so wrong with that? We loved each other, Papa. I know you do not understand love, but I could not have married anyone but him. It broke my heart when he died and I wrote to you and pleaded for your help but you did not come. I was forced into the choice I made *by you*. What else was there? I could hardly have become a governess with a child and I was in the middle of the aftermath of war. Things were in chaos and poverty was rife. Tell me what else I could have done if you must hate me so much for choosing to survive rather than die? Tell me, Papa!"

He had not moved, he still said nothing.

"What could I have done differently!" She could not stop her words, they spilled out of her, anger and regret pouring into the space between her and this man who still turned his back.

"Very well then Judge me if you will. But do not continue to cast my sentence on my son. It was not his fault and I am respectable again now, you have no need to be ashamed of me. I am here, Papa, I am here and alive and you cannot pretend I am not. Edward shall not let you. *I* will not allow it. Face me! Face me and see who I am, Papa! I am your daughter! The mother of your heir! The woman whom you have treated ill. I am sinful. But *you* are guilty. Where is the compassion and forgiveness you preached of to us as children?

"I hope you regret what you did to me. I hope you have suffered. Penny has told me you treated them more leniently when you brought John back—that Mama, persuaded you to. Well you owe me something too, Papa, you owe me an apology. You could have saved me from the life I led after John's birth. If you had accepted Paul, you could have even prevented it. You did neither. You stood back and let me suffer! Well I shall not suffer in silence anymore! Do you hear? Do you hear me, Papa?"

How had she thought herself capable of shifting impervious stone?

She wanted him to at least admit he could hear her. That she was real.

Still gripping her reticule the storm of her outburst taking over she moved to walk about him and make him look at her.

He turned. His eyes were bright and they seemed to burn into her.

She stopped dead, feeling stiff suddenly, as though her body had become lead.

"Papa?" Her voice was quiet now.

"I hear you. I suppose Marlow has told you of the sum I offered him."

Sum? "No." Had he tried to pay Edward to leave her? "What sum?"

"He would not take it."

"What sum, Papa?"

"An amount to take you abroad. If you went away —"

"I am not going away! I am here! I am staying here! I will not let you deny me anymore! You must face me, Papa, you must, please…" her fight died.

Why could he not love her as a father should? Why could he not forgive and let John have his mother.

"Why must you be inhuman? John wishes to be with me. I cannot change what happened, Papa, nor can you, but must you let this go on, can you not simply give in and forgive me."

"No, how may I? Look at what you are…"

"What I am is your daughter."

"You have done appalling things."

Tears flooded her eyes suddenly. "Appalling things have been done to me because you turned your back! You are my father! You should have protected me!"

He merely stared, stiff and still.

"Will you let me have John?"

"I cannot."

"Why?"

"Because—because it is not done."

Her chin lifted once again, her fingers clasping her reticule even tighter if it were possible. "Say my name. Say it. Admit that I am here, admit you are wrong. *You are wrong, Papa.* John needs his mother—*he needs me.*"

"The boy has his grandmother."

"Mama, is not me. He needs his mother. I love him and I want him back. You took him from me when I was beaten by life and too afraid to argue with you. I am not afraid of you now, Papa, I will argue with you. I will go on arguing with you and so will Edward until we have John back do you understand? I am never going to let you keep him willingly, not now."

"And so Marlow said this morning." His eyes shone brighter as if fluid and then he turned away and walked to the decanters which stood on a chest across the room.

He had been silent like this when he'd taken John. Her heart was still racing. *Why would he not listen?* She watched him fill a glass as she wondered what had happened with Edward.

He would have been angry if her father had tried to pay him to take her away. He would have done what she was doing now, refused to go and promised to fight.

She waited. She was not leaving she was not bowing down.

"I did not wish to take your son." He spoke to the wall his fingers gripping the rim of the chest while his other hand held the glass. *What did he mean?*

"I knew then—I knew then things could have been done differently. But I could not change things, could I? You had become what you had become..."

Ellen stared at his back, unbelieving, unemotional. He sounded as if he expected pity. She had no pity for him. He should have pitied her. No, he should have helped her and not taken John.

"I have tried to help you since..."

He had not.

He turned then and faced her and looked straight into her eyes for a moment, but there seemed to be questions in his, doubt. She had never seen her father show any doubt before. He drank some of the brandy in the glass then set it aside.

"I gave them all money to care for you, so you might have some security." He said it to the bureau as he put the glass on it and Ellen felt the world tilt beneath her. She began moving forward to grasp the back of the chair which faced his desk. He continued, looking up and looking at her. "I cannot acknowledge you. I cannot. You have fallen. You are abhorrent to me, how can you raise my heir —"

"My son!" Ellen cried gripping the back of the chair with one hand while her other still held her reticule. "He is my son above anything." She took a breath, still unable to believe what he had just said. "You paid them?"

He nodded. He looked pleased with the notion.

She felt horribly sick. "You paid them to repeatedly rape me. I never gave them conscious consent. Did you know that? Did you know?"

He said nothing but his eyes turned hard and solid as glass. She let go of the chair and pointed her finger at him. "I never chose it. I never chose that. I had to feed myself before John was born and Paul's officer offered to take me in. He did not even mention there would be a cost. He insisted I repay him when John was born. With the money you gave him you could have freed me..."

He opened his mouth but she did not let him speak. She did not wish to hear anything more he might say.

"Did you know Lord Gainsborough is dead? Have you heard that last night he tried to kill me? No you would not have done would you because Edward, his friend and my brothers'-in-law have hushed it up. Let Edward tell you how cruelly Gainsborough beat me. How vilely he treated me, and you paid him to do that!

"Do you understand it now, Papa, do you? And your money was the only reason he would not let me go. If you had not paid him I might have been free years before.

"He told me if I ran from him he would find and kill my son, did you know that? It was the only reason I stayed to endure that evil — *the only reason*. That is why Edward and I rushed to fetch him from school when I finally left."

Her anger flying into a rage which was fuelled by disappointment and disempowerment she strode across the room, her teeth gritted not even knowing what she would do, too angry to think anymore. She picked up the glass beside him and threw the liquid in his face.

His arm lifted to wipe it off, but as he did so, she recoiled. She had been hit too many times to prevent her instinctual reaction to a raised hand. He reached to catch her arm but she backed away. "I am not afraid of you and I shall never forgive you unless you give me back my son." She was no longer shouting. She no longer cared what he thought of her. Let him think what he wished. She just wanted her son. "I want him back. You will give him back to me. You have to. How can you have treated me so poorly? I am your daughter and my name is Eleanor, in case you have forgotten it. *It is Eleanor, Papa.* I am unchanged, I am scarred and I have been bruised, but Edward is helping me heal and I will not let you put me down again. Do you hear?"

He had taken a handkerchief from his pocket and was wiping his face as he watched her warily, questions in his eyes again. But she did not wish to hear anything else he might have to say.

"I am leaving now. We are staying with the Earl of Barrington. Please write and tell me when I may see my son." Her chin tipped up and she glared at him, as he had so often glared at her and then turned and left, striding away from him, as she was certain Edward must have done earlier. "I hope you never sleep again," she said, just before she left the room. "I hope you live my nightmares for the rest of your life. May God be your judge." She did not look back. She did not wish to see him.

As she took the door handle it turned in her hand and footman drew it open, she walked out knowing the servants must have heard. Well, she hoped her father felt shame. Let him burn in it.

Her hands were still shaking as she left the house, though they shook with anger now and not fear.

How could he have done it?

❦

Edward leaned his elbow on the newel post at the bottom of the imposing polished oak staircase in his brother's townhouse, as his gaze transferred from the magnificent five-tier chandelier to the woman who outshone it.

His wife was descending, framed perfectly by the rich dark brown of the oak treads. She had chosen to wear a simple white muslin gown. Its waistline framed her figure, pinching high under her breasts. While the dress's low square neckline bordered on indecent, a slither away from displaying the darkening flesh of each nipple. It presented a delectable décolletage, he might add. As if to highlight the point a thin delicate band of silk, scarlet red, ribbon, threaded through the bright white cloth, at her high waistline, then formed a pert little bow with trailing ends beneath the exquisite curve of her breasts. The vivid contrast of colors highlighted her slight form to perfection, and the color of the red ribbon flashed in clear glass beads sewn in star shapes throughout the dress, which also caught the light, glittering and sparkling about her figure giving her an ethereal air.

She looked unique, incomparable in beauty and in bearing—but then he was biased.

As she descended, his gaze traveled the length of her, and he noted the short puffed sleeves which left the curves of her shapely slender arms displayed from shoulder to elbow above her long red satin evening gloves and the tip of scarlet red satin evening slippers peeping from beneath the long hem too. Lord *but she was beautiful, she would never cease to make him wonder at it.*

Edward turned to the hall table to acquire his present of tonight. He had been saving this gift for when she wore this dress—the only ball gown she'd bought in York. Jill had advised him earlier what her mistress planned to wear. Edward grasped the velvet box and came to greet Ellen as she reached the bottom step.

"Another gift?" she breathed. He'd also given her a gold necklace with a pale sapphire pendent as well as the pearls.

"This is the last, after tonight you will have the full set." Clicking it open so she might see, he watched her face transform, her eyes widening.

"It's magnificent." Her fingers touched the jewels, a cluster of rubies set in silver, which would cascade and cover the expanse of pure white flesh above her bodice perfectly, resting to fall and sit in the cleft of her bosom. He set the box aside, took the clasps in his fingers, lifted its weight from the velvet and bid her turn so he could secure it.

"Thank you," she whispered as he fastened it, her fingertips resting on the jewels. Then she turned again, reaching to kiss his cheek, and Edward felt his heart swell. The necklace had cost him a small fortune but it was worth it to see her smile. He wished he could buy her jewels every day. But he could not, the future from here on was frugal, he needed to find work and he refused to think of Pembroke's damned cheque.

She had told Edward she'd spoken to her father the other day. Edward had been cross that she'd not waited to speak to him about it first. But in the end he'd understood her need to face the man alone. After all there was no physical threat from Pembroke. She'd discussed her conversation and Edward had shared with her the conversation he'd had over the money. They had both been defiant and now Ellen feared her father would not be there tonight. Edward had promised if he was not, tomorrow they would look for him and show him once more neither of them were to be set aside.

"And now I understand," Robert spoke from beside them.

"What?" Edward asked as his hands slipped to Ellen's waist and he embraced her briefly, kissing her temple, before letting her go and stepping away.

When Robert had still not answered, Edward looked at his brother. Robert was smiling at Ellen, knowingly. He winked at her then tapped the edge of his nose twice before letting his hand drop and looking at Edward, "It's a secret."

Edward's gaze turned to Ellen and he saw her blush.

Robert stepped forward, took her hand, bowed over it and pressed a kiss on the back of her satin clad fingers—with a brotherly air, Edward hoped. Then Edward heard Robert say, "There are no odds on who you are taunting."

"May as well be hung for a pound as a penny?" Ellen responded with a brisk laugh and a hesitant smile as she pulled her hand free.

"Want to rub his nose in it more like," Robert answered.

This conversation had Edward at a loss. "Are either of you going to explain?"

"No," Robert answered, a frank note in his voice as he turned to the door.

Edward sighed, caught up Ellen's fingers and set them on his arm. She was his and he was going to make it very clear to everyone tonight. He'd spent too many evenings standing back while her family showed how accepted she was. Tonight was for him. He intended showing the damned pretentious *ton* whose she was. He had no idea if her father would turn-up or not, Edward had heard no more from the man. But if the old goat did not, Edward swore he would not allow Pembroke to continue insulting her. The rest of Edward's life would be spent making Pembroke's hell.

"Are you ready for this?" Edward questioned.

She nodded.

An hour later and he'd had the pleasure of a scandalous four dances with his wife, including one waltz. But there had as yet been no sign of her father, despite the fact that the entire family had rallied to her side.

The Wiltshires' ballroom had wooden parquet flooring and mirrors along three walls reflecting back the sparkle of the three giant chandeliers, each equal to the one specimen in the hall of his brother's town residence. The fourth wall was a bank of windows which dropped to the floor and looked out onto the terrace, where sparkled more than one hundred lanterns to light the way of guests out on to the garden paths, if they cared for a walk. And if they wished to, the night was warmer, although nowhere near balmy.

The room was packed, an absolute crush, and with the season soon to commence many had returned early to town to attend the Wiltshires' ball, probably drawn by Ellen's reappearance from the grave. Fortunately Ellen was accustomed to ignoring their stares and he had successfully made certain that any reports of Gainsborough's death had born no link to her name or his, so their gossip had no further fuel. According to public opinion the man had died of a heart seizure.

Pressing his hand to Ellen's waist Edward shifted their path, guiding her about a large party in their current search for refreshment. In answer, looking back and up at him, she smiled and pressed her gloved fingers over his. Then she took his hand and the lead, letting his fingers loop lightly over hers.

It was ridiculous, but since Gainsborough's death he felt as though they'd become even closer. Just over a week ago he would not have thought that possible. But even more so now, it felt like the two of them against the world.

"There." He pointed over to a door which led to the refreshment room, then suddenly collided into Ellen's back.

Her fingers squeezed his and she was looking up towards the entrance hall.

"What is it?" He bent his head to hear her answer over the general chatter of the ball and the orchestra's current merry country dance.

Ellen turned, rising to her toes to whisper in his ear, "My father," before casting her gaze to the far end of the room again.

"He's here?" Following her gaze, Edward saw the Duke of Pembroke. He was, and from his vantage point, at the top of the stairs which descended into the ballroom, Pembroke had seen them first. His gaze met Edward's across the room, hard and cold.

Lord, Edward hoped the man was not here to make trouble.

Ignoring the silent summons, Edward looked away, scanning the crush of guests for Richard. Both of them over average height he caught his brother-in-law's eye.

Richard was at the edge of the dance floor, in mid-conversation, near the bottom of the stairs. At Edward's nod Richard looked up and saw the Duke, then threw Edward back an answering nod, before visibly giving apologies and then moving to weave a path through the crush to where Pembroke stood.

Edward turned away and back to Ellen. He wouldn't lead her like a lamb to the slaughter. Richard would divine whether it was wise or not to let them speak. "In that case it's even more important to ensure we have a bumper. You'll need a stiff drink to be up to speaking to him *if* he has anything of worth to say. Come on, let's fetch you one."

Again Ellen smiled up at him, and in answer he bent to drop a light kiss on her forehead.

"Lead on then," she whispered, as one hand still gripped in hers he pressed the other to her back.

"Brave girl," he bent to whisper at her ear.

"It's easy to be brave when I have my stalwart defender at my side," she answered, turning her head sideways to plant a kiss on his shaven cheek as they slowly made a path through the crowd.

"Careful, or you shall have people think this is the most despised of articles, a love-match," he whispered as they worked their way past another unknown party. He was rewarded with a nervous laugh, and then at last the refreshment room was in reach and relatively quiet, as the evening was still young.

As they left the crush, before their over indulgent touches became visible, he freed his hand from hers and laid his fingers under her elbow, guiding her towards the table of refreshments. "Champagne I suppose, in the hopes we have something to celebrate." Smiling at her, he collected the tall narrow glass a footman held out and passed it to her. He did not take one for himself. He didn't wish to risk dimming his senses when he was potentially about to face the Duke of Pembroke. For that Edward would need all his wits.

"I don't know that I should. If my father—I don't want him to think me in my cups."

It seemed Ellen was of the same opinion, but he knew she needed a measure of Dutch courage to face her father.

Leaning to her ear he whispered, "You shan't be in your cups after one glass, and it will calm your nerves. Drink it, one will not harm."

Her beautiful smile was his answer. She seemed to trust him in everything these days, as though his word was law since Robert had dispensed with Gainsborough.

He hoped it was where her father was concerned too. He'd hate for her faith in him to be shattered when it was John at stake. He had made her face this, even the other day when she had gone to speak to her father alone, he knew she would not have done it unless he'd encouraged her to fight.

He watched her do as he'd bidden, then cough on the bubbles having drunk too great a mouthful. But his hand caught her wrist before she lifted the glass again. Across her shoulder, he saw Richard approaching with her father. This was more than Edward had hoped already—he'd thought Pembroke would have called them to *his* court.

"Brace up, your father is on his way," Edward whispered through the corner of his mouth.

Ellen glanced backwards, saw her father, and then set down the glass.

Her wide eyes spun back to Edward's face declaring absolute panic, but then almost instantly he watched her overcome it, steeling herself for the meeting, her fear shifting to determination. He took her hand and held it tight, offering what courage he could.

"Eleanor." Ellen jumped inside. He'd used her name. It was a huge leap Edward would not even recognise.

"Your Grace." She curtsied, her heart racing.

"Rise up, girl. I wish to speak with you in private." He turned away then, without even waiting for her agreement.

Her eyes darted to Richard, who sent her a look of reassurance. Then she looked across her shoulder at Edward who stood behind her. A nod encouraged her to go and listen, and touching her elbow Edward guided her on.

"What do you think he will say?" she whispered, as they followed the Duke's statuesque figure back through the ballroom. Even now, even though she refused to fear him anymore and she'd lost all respect for him, she still found his presence imposing. It had been instinct to do everything he said without question when she was a child.

"Hopefully that he is sorry," Edward growled in a low rumble to her ear.

His evident anger set her even more on edge. Her father had never apologised. What if this was to be another rejection? What if Edward lost his temper here, where the story would quickly spread?

Richard led them from the ballroom via a side door, and up a shallow flight of steps. Her eyes were fixed on her father's back as they followed Richard out into the hall and then across to his library. Richard held the door for her father and waited for her and Edward to pass, before following them in and closing it.

Her father stood in the center of the room, his hands clasped behind his back, his angular face fixed in an expression of distaste, his gaze following her. She faced him, with Edward behind her, while Richard stood near the door.

Refusing to shrink back before her father's condescending stare she took two steps closer, unflinching, and felt Edward move too, his fingers gently resting at the curve of her waist.

"You have something to say to me, Father?"

She watched him hesitate and swallow.

"I owe you an apology."

But she noted he could not quite bring himself to give one and say *I am sorry.*

"I accept I have not made the right decisions towards you, and now things are—as they are—you have left me with no choice but to allow you access to your son."

It was as though the weight of years slipped from her shoulders. He was backing down. He had heard her the other day. He was using her name. "I do not want access to my son, I want *my son.*" Her voice was low and measured, brimful with righteous anger. "I want him to live with Edward and I. That is where he wishes to be. It is where he belongs."

Her father's eyes seemed to skim across her face.

"If that is what you wish," he hesitated.

"*It is.*" Ellen held his gaze.

"Then you may collect him in two days' time. Your mother wishes to see you."

"Mama? Is she well?" She heard her voice waver, with a now almost desperate and disorientated note, joy and relief overwhelmed her. *Had he really said she could have John?*

"Yes." Turning away he looked at Richard. "We are done here. You may go back to your frivolity now your plan to force my hand has succeeded."

"You've admitted you were in the wrong," her brother-in-law answered. "I would say you owe Lord Edward a debt of gratitude for this, Your Grace. John shall be in your position one day. I think he will be appalled if he ever learns of the fate you left his mother to live, *your daughter*."

"Look to your own household, my Lord, not mine," her father growled at Richard, before striding from the room.

"*He's said we may have John*." Ellen turned to Edward and wrapped her arms about his neck. "I cannot believe it. I cannot. *We will have John*." Edward picked her up off her feet and twirled her around, clearly jubilant.

"We did it." He set her down and kissed her lips.

"I never thought he would bend," she said in awe, leaning back to meet the glinting light in his eyes and pressing her palms to his cheeks. "It's your doing."

"As I said," Richard spoke from behind them. "I hope your father recognises it. He owes you thanks, Edward, but whether Pembroke can bring himself to admit it is another matter."

"I cannot believe it," Ellen said again, grinning at Richard.

Then looking back at Edward, her hands fell to his shoulders. "I shall not be able to sleep for the next two nights. Oh Edward!" she spoke his name with complete adoration as she reached on to her toes and kissed his lips.

He pulled her into a full embrace.

"I'll leave you two alone then shall I?" Richard laughed, and then the door clicked shut.

"You did it, Edward," she whispered to Edward's mouth, as his lips pulled away from hers. "I thought it was impossible. I had hoped and dreamed, but never believed until I met you." Her lips touched his again.

"Truthfully, I thought it impossible too."

She pulled back from him and her gaze skimmed across his face, from his dark eyes to the perfect lines of his brow, his nose, his jaw, her fingers touching the soft shaven skin of his cheek.

"But you did it, I'll never forget this."

"*We* did it. I am sure your calling on him the other day will have played a part in his choice." He turned his head and kissed her palm. "But now I think we ought to go back."

She nodded. His hand clasped hers.

When they walked from the room, they continued holding hands ignoring any risk of judgement. In the ballroom as the notes of a waltz filled the air, Edward drew her into the dance. It was their fifth, far too many even for a married couple. She did not care. Their bodies moved as one, too close for propriety but she was oblivious to anyone but Edward.

Chapter Sixteen

She was right, she couldn't sleep. Ellen slid from beneath the sheet, careful not to wake Edward, and for a moment she sat at the edge of the bed, looking back at him. Handsome, he lay on his side, hair tussled, one arm curved across her half of the bed over the place where she had lain, the other resting beneath his pillow.

He'd succeeded. He'd brought her father about. It had been Edward not her, without his strength she would not have even found the courage to fight.

She could not believe it—any of it. She was married, walking among the *ton* untainted, as though she had not spent years in the demimonde, the underworld of society. Bright silvery moonlight reached through the slightly parted curtains.

She rose from the bed and crossed the room. A long cheval mirror stood by the window. She stopped before it, her eyes adjusting to the darkness. The silver backed glass glowed in the half-light. Looking at her reflection, even in the dark she could see the tell-tale signs she'd become aware of over the last few days. Her fingers skimmed the curve of her breast.

She remembered the night she'd met Edward, how she had looked at herself in mirrors then, seeing only a wraith — who walked the earth yet did not live in it. She was human again. He'd given her, her soul back — her life back — and now John, and —

"What are you doing?" Edward asked from the bed as she heard him throw the covers aside. Looking back, she smiled.

Still half asleep, his eyes blinking, adjusting to the moonlight, he walked across the room, his glorious naked body magnificent to watch. She turned back to the mirror and felt his tall muscular frame surround her, his hips resting against her buttocks and the skin of his thighs brushing up against the back of hers. His fingers slipped about her body and crossed over her stomach. "Is something wrong?" he whispered into her ear, the breath of his words caressing the sensitive skin of her neck.

"I hope not."

"What do you mean?" he prodded more seriously. "Is something wrong?"

She leaned her head back onto his shoulder and smiled again. His lips touched her neck. It always felt as though they were in another universe when they came to bed, as though nothing of the outer world could touch them here when they were alone, just as it had done in London weeks ago — he was still her island sanctuary. "It depends how you take it."

"Take what?" The words rumbled against her throat, his thoughts clearly progressing to other things. One hand descended and the other closed over her breast.

She looked into the mirror. "It's this." Her hand surrounded his cradling the weight of her breast in his palm. "Can you feel—it's heavier?"

He was watching her in the mirror. He nodded, but he clearly didn't understand.

Gripping his forefinger, she trailed the tip of it about the areola of her breast. "It's darker, do you see?"

He looked bewildered.

"You have no idea what I am saying do you?"

He shook his head.

She laid his palm against her stomach. "We are expecting, Edward. You should know it would not take long the amount of times you try. I'm carrying our child."

His jaw dropped and his eyes lit up with understanding and awe. Then he looked down at their joined hands. "A child?"

Ellen turned in his arms, pressing her naked body to his. "Of course a child, it will hardly be a puppy." She laughed, leaning her head back to see him. "I am undecided whether I hope for a boy or a girl."

"I will be happy with either. I'll leave it up to you." Edward laughed too, then kissed her forehead and hugged her tightly. "It's wonderful, Ellen. John will return to the gift of a brother or sister. How do you think he will take it?"

Setting her palms against his cheeks, Ellen met his gaze. "That first night I knew how much you would mean to me. I tried to tell myself you were not my saviour. I did not believe it possible. But you were. You are—mine *and* John's. You have been my rock for weeks. I've clung to you against the tides. Now you will be our foundation stone. Together we'll build a new life.

To think of John and his feelings first. You amaze me Edward. You do know I love you beyond all reason?"

He smiled. "As I love you. I need you too. You complete me, Ellen. You have done so since that first moment. I had no purpose without you. My life was empty. You saved me from my brother's fate. I would be a bitter cold hearted, pleasure seeker without you—*A child.*" The last was whispered. "A child!" He lifted her and twirled her about.

⤜⤏

Edward threaded and folded his fingers in between Ellen's as they were admitted entry across the threshold of her father's townhouse. Before the door was even closed John flew across the room, jubilant, as though he had been waiting in the hall for hours. Ellen dropped to her knees and hugged the boy.

"Mama, Papa, I saw your carriage from the window upstairs! Grandpapa said I am to live with you!"

"I know, sweetheart." Her hand was on John's hair, and Edward watched her eyes skim every contour of the boy's face soaking him up. "We have come to fetch you."

"Mama!" John hugged her fiercely once more. He needn't speak his feelings his body said it all.

"My child." Another woman's voice echoed back from the white and black marble about the hall.

Edward looked up from the scene of Ellen and John's reunion and saw an older woman. She was framed by the ornately decorated open doors of a state drawing room. A gray swirl of hair was caught up atop her head, her clothing was mauve, a color of half-mourning, but despite her age she still carried a great deal of beauty and a posture that would not have shown her age at all if seen in silhouette. She stepped forward with an air of disbelief and her eyes misted.

Ellen had risen and was watching the woman uncertainly. Yet when her mother opened her arms, he saw the wall of years that stood between them tumble, and it was no different then than how John had come to Ellen. Ellen went to her mother.

"Eleanor—my child. I have missed you." The elder woman's voice rang with heartache as they embraced.

Sensing another presence in the hall Edward turned to see Pembroke standing at the door to the library, the room in which Edward had experienced that appalling interview of only a few days ago. The room in which Ellen had learnt her father's worst betrayal.

"Marlow," the Duke spoke. His expression unreadable as he looked away from the women and his grandson and met Edward's gaze. "I would speak with you if you have a moment?"

Edward nodded, despite the ice cold feeling which settled in his stomach. Whatever this man could have to say it would not be good. But Ellen had John back, and Edward would not jeopardize it now.

A footman held the door open, and after Edward entered the library, it was firmly shut behind him. Edward took a breath, steeling himself for what might come.

"Take a seat."

He did, but remained primed to move if he did not like what was said. The Duke sat behind the broad desk. "I have something for you." He pulled open a drawer and withdrew a piece of paper. *Another bank draft.* Edward did not even wish to touch the thing, but even though he tried not to look at it his eyes took in the sum, fifty thousand, more than before. Rejecting it, he stood.

"I have told you once before, Your Grace, I do not want your money."

"Sit down, Marlow! This is no insult! I want nothing from you for the sum. If you do not wish to take it, so be it, but at least let me explain."

Edward re-took his seat, his eyes threatening an outpouring of disgust if Pembroke dared say anything insulting.

"The sum is equivalent to the dowry I had set for Eleanor. A dower house, which came with her mother, and its surrounding land, was due to be Eleanor's. I sold it off after, well, after she wed Harding. I could no longer bear to think of it. This is the equivalent of the sale plus more I would have settled on her if she had allowed me my choice. John is my heir. He cannot live in the home of a man who must find employment." Edward leaned back uncomfortably, astonished. "Yes, Marlow, I have taken the liberty of looking into your finances."

"But still you do this for John, not Ellen."

"Does it matter?"

Edward took a breath, looking at the note. *Did it matter?* Pembroke was right. With the money Edward could keep them in the status they deserved, but it hurt his pride to accept funds from a man who had treated Ellen so badly.

"I see it does." The Duke sighed and stood, suddenly looking as though he aged a dozen years. He paced across the room, passing Edward's chair. "I know I—what I did to my daughter was wrong, but you have to understand my position. My peers mocked me for not being able to control her. Then I discovered the illicit course her choice had run to. How could I bring a soiled woman home to my wife? I gave in to Gainsborough's blackmail to protect her, not me. I thought her safe at least."

Edward powered to his feet, anger flaring like a torch, facing the Duke as he turned back. "She was not safe! Gainsborough forced and beat her! Have you no idea in what position you had left her? It was not her choice. It was *never* her choice. She felt as though she had no choice! A need to feed and clothe her son was the only reason she took that path and then you took her son and left her there."

The Duke looked upwards.

A man like this would not weep but Edward sensed Pembroke was battling against tears.

Perhaps Edward had misjudged her father—a little. Perhaps Pembroke was more ignorant in his arrogance than callous.

"I know it now. I did not know it then. Eleanor made it all very clear to me the other day." Pembroke said to the ceiling.

His eyes came back to Edward. "Believe me, I am sorry for what I have done yet I cannot change those past decisions. What I can do is see her secure for the rest of her life."

"Will you say this to Ellen?" Edward challenged. "It would do her good to hear it."

"No." The statement was clear. Pembroke could not face what he had done to Ellen now, as previously he been unable to face her. "You may tell her of my feelings. Will you accept the sum?"

Edward held Pembroke's gaze. If Edward did not he would be just like Pembroke, making a decision simply because of pride. But if Edward took the sum he could help restore Ellen's life to what it should be. "Yes, on her behalf."

The Duke's stiff demeanour suddenly disappeared. His shoulders relaxed and he offered his hand. Edward took and shook it. The Duke held on and surrounded Edward's hand with his other. "Wiltshire was right about you, Marlow. I am glad my daughter found you, and grateful for your help. You are stronger than I and you are welcome in my family. You will visit often? I do not want to grow distant from my grandson and I would like to know my daughter again."

A lump rose in Edward's throat, he struggled to swallow it and nodded. Pembroke's hands fell, then he returned to his desk, collected the bank draft and held it out. Edward accepted it, then folded it and slid it into his inside coat pocket.

It was over an hour later before he had a chance to speak to Ellen about the sum once they'd left the house, after taking tea.

Ellen's mother had wept often as they'd taken refreshment. Over how much she'd missed of Ellen's life and Ellen of her son's.

Throughout it the Duke had sat in silence studying Ellen avidly as though mesmerised by what a credit she actually was to him, beautiful, polite, kind, and caring. She'd shown him no enmity.

But as Edward had watched her father and mother he knew the Duke was not unmoved. Edward had seen the brooding weight of guilt in the Duke's eyes.

Now Edward sat with Ellen in the carriage, on their way home. He was facing her. John had curled into her side and fallen asleep, exhausted from the excitement of the day and what Edward guessed were many sleepless nights of fretting. Edward withdrew the bank draft from his pocket and held it out, giving it to Ellen without a word. Her eyebrows lifted in astonishment as she took it.

"A wedding gift from your father. He said I was to take it as your dowry."

She said nothing, simply looking at the sum as though it was something odd.

"You do not mind? If you do, I'll tear it up. But it will give us enough to buy our own home, and it will keep us for life if I invest it wisely."

She still said nothing.

He started to worry. "He told me he is sorry for the decisions he's taken regarding you. He acknowledged they were wrong. He approves of our match, Ellen, and he's asked us to visit them, often. How do you feel about it?"

Her eyes lifted and met his. "If I cannot forgive him, I will be like him. I do forgive him. You may accept his gift."

Edward nodded, understanding. She didn't like it any more than he did, but it was the right thing to do. He looked at John. This was it then, this was their new life begun. As she had said, this was their foundation—their corner stone—what they made of it from here on was up to them.

"The future is ours to build," he stated.

Ellen smiled, recognising his abiding sentiment—the past should lay buried. It could now and the money would give them a broader horizon. Leaning forward, she passed him back the cheque. It still felt like blood money though.

Once he'd slipped it back into his pocket, his eyes fell to John, and she reached to capture his fingers in hers.

"Thank you." She smiled, lifting their joined hands to the carriage's narrow window ledge. "I could not have wanted for a better hero. No one else could have done this for me, Edward."

A soft laugh escaped his throat. "I accept that accolade although I am sure it isn't true. But I prefer the role of husband and father over hero."

"You will be that from now on, I don't need a hero anymore. Just your love and to love you in return."

"You'll have a lifetime of it." He lifted their joined fingers and brushed hers against his lips.

Epilogue

One Year Later

Ellen welcomed Edward's brother, urging him in with a wave of her hand. Robert was the last of their guests to reach the old manor house. They had driven back up from the village church after Mary's christening.

She and Edward had fallen for the manor on first sight, because it was not grand but homely. She never got lost in the same way she had done in her father's palatial properties. There was always the sound of someone's voice in the distance, Edward's, or one of the servants, or John's. She liked the comfort of knowing they were in reach.

The great hall, which she lead Robert into, was the largest of the manor's rooms, its dark oak panelling stretching right up to the giant ornately carved rafters. It was full of people and noise today, conversation and laughter. Robert turned and embraced her, in a brotherly way. Without hesitation she hugged him in return. "You and Edward have much to be proud of."

Robert hadn't liked it when Edward had said they were seeking their own property, but Robert had accepted it in the end. They had not sewn up their rift though, just patched it in places.

Ellen caught up Robert's hand and pulled him towards Edward who stood to one side holding Mary Rose. The infant was gurgling with glee against the lapel of Edward's coat, gripping his cravat. He smiled and gave her their daughter. Ellen passed the baby on to Robert.

"Here, your niece and now your Godchild. She is longing for a cuddle from her favourite uncle."

Robert took her but sneered. He was such a cad. Ellen knew he loved Mary Rose. Whenever he visited he hardly left the nursery. He was either petting Mary or setting John into a riot with a noisy game of war. Proving it, he immediately moved away to show off the child to her aunts. They were gathered in a cluster across the room.

"We are so lucky," Ellen whispered looking up at her husband. He bent and kissed her mouth, as uncaring as ever of what anyone thought.

Ellen swallowed, she had yet to tell him she was pregnant again. Mary was only four months old. Ellen had been waiting until now. She had wanted Mary baptised before their thoughts turned to the next child.

She spoke against his lips. "I have news for you."

"What?" His lips curved into a smile.

"You should expect another christening in a year or so's time."

Edward held her back, grinning now. "You are expecting? I had an inkling but I didn't like to say."

"Yes," Ellen smiled. "You could have told me you knew."

"And steal your thunder," he laughed. "I think not, such news is a woman's prerogative."

One hand slid the length of her arm and captured her fingers, then he turned to the room, picking up a drink from a tray balanced on the hand of a passing footman. "Charge your drinks my friends! We have a double celebration!" There was an instantaneous move to collect glasses, and then they were lifted high. "You are about to again," he turned to face her mother and father, "become grandparents," then he looked about the hall, "and uncles, aunts and cousins" He smiled at the children, and then particularly at John, "*and brother*. In a few months' time. My beautiful wife is expecting another happy arrival! A toast to our children!" It was echoed about the room and then their families moved as one to give their congratulations.

I am truly the luckiest woman, Ellen thought again as John gave her a hug.

"Mama, I would like a brother." She smiled, holding him tight. He now reached above her shoulder and was less like a boy every day and more like a young man.

"I do not think I can control it, John, but we shall see." She kissed his forehead and let him go. He moved to speak to Edward.

Now her sisters, one by one, stepped forward to hug her.

"Ellen. I am very pleased for you." Rebecca held Ellen first then straightened. "You must come and stay with us in the spring. David values Edward's company and his experience in managing estates."

"That's very kind of you, Rebecca. We would love to. I know Edward would enjoy working with David." Rebecca kissed Ellen's cheek and then moved aside.

Sylvia stepped forward.

She was heavy with child and she gave Ellen a superficial cuddle. "Mary Rose is so pretty. I hope my own child is as perfect, But I admit I am nervous of the birth."

Ellen held Sylvia's shoulders. The child was her first. "It is not so bad. As soon as he, or she, is born you will forget the ordeal of birth. But would you like me with you? I will stay when you are due if it will help?"

"I should like that very much, James fusses over me and it makes me more afraid."

"Very well, it is agreed. We shall come and stay. Edward will distract James too." Sylvia nodded and kissed Ellen's cheek before turning to congratulate Edward.

Next Penny stepped forward, her own son of just over a month old cradled in her arms. Ellen's fingers brushed the child's cheek and the infant turned his gaze to her. He was more like Richard than his mother. "He is beautiful," Ellen whispered.

"Richard loves his daughters, but he is thrilled to have a son at last." Penny glanced across her shoulder at Richard. He was standing across the room, and their eldest daughter was tugging his hand, urging him to look at Mary Rose, while he was trying to have a conversation with James.

"He's lovely, I am sure he will grow to be a credit to his father. I am so grateful for all the two of you have done for Edward and I." They'd deliberately moved near to Richard and Penny, and they'd become close friends in the last year. They'd spent hours together.

When Julie and Casper visited they made a six.

"If he is anything like John he will be a son to be proud of," Penny answered. "I hear he is learning the estate work."

"He does not want to go to Eton still and we cannot persuade him. We have hired a tutor to prepare him, but he prefers to spend his time riding out with Edward and learning about the estate. I despair of John sometimes. Perhaps if Richard talked of his school days too John may yet be convinced."

"I will ask Richard to try." Penny smiled. "But do not be too hard on John. He has been through so much. He's been overwhelmed simply getting to know his uncles on his father's side, especially the Earl of Craster. Perhaps it is just too much too soon."

"Perhaps," Ellen acknowledged. They'd known it was important for John to meet his father's family but he was finding it difficult to adjust to his new less restricted life. The only thing he seemed to want was to remain with her.

"Give him more time. He will come about I'm sure."

Ellen nodded, and then kissed Penny's cheek before she turned to Edward.

It had been difficult introducing John into his father's family, but it was right. He'd visited them thrice, staying with the Earl's family for a night or two. It had done John good to know people who spoke of his father. But John had been angry because he could not understand why he'd not been allowed to meet them before.

Ellen looked at her son. He'd taken Mary Rose from Robert and was standing by the hearth talking to him. Ellen's heart filled with pride. One day he would be a Duke.

"Ellen, my dear child." Ellen's thoughts came back to the moment as her mother, with tears in her eyes, drew Ellen into an embrace.

There was a rift in her parents' relationship now. It would never heal. Her mother could not forgive Ellen's father, but Ellen also knew her mother found it hard to forgive herself. She felt guilty for not realising the truth.

"Mama, don't cry, you will have me in tears too and this is a happy occasion."

"I know, darling, I do. I am happy for you." Her mother wiped her eyes. "But however am I to make up for what occurred? If I had only known."

Ellen took her mother's hands. "I have told you a dozen times, I am happy. I have Edward, John and Mary Rose, I do not worry over what happened, nor hold it against you, Mama, so neither should you."

"No, my dear, I know, because you have such a good heart." She squeezed Ellen's hands. "And you have a good man in Edward. I am proud of you both."

"I know, Mama." Ellen kissed her mother's cheek then let her hands go. She turned to Edward.

Ellen's gaze stretched to her father. He would not come close. Their relationship over the last year had been distant and strained. Not by her choice, but because he could not bring himself to face her. His apology, still unspoken, was constantly in his eyes. Yet in his every manner he always held himself back. At the moment he was standing alone to one side of the milling family group looking from the tall window out across the lawn.

Ellen sighed and then closed the distance between them. "Father," she opened as she approached and stopped three feet from his side, her hands clasping behind her back.

His gaze met hers, distant and disengaged. "Eleanor. I am glad for you. I am sure Marlow will want for a son."

"I am sure he does not care. He has no title or entailment to worry over."

"No, of course." Her father's eyes drifted to John.

"John is doing well, but I wish him to come and stay soon, for a while. He should not lose touch with what he will inherit."

"He knows his responsibilities. He will do everything he can to make you proud, Father, but you must not set the bar too high for John to reach. He is a good boy but he can never be perfect."

Her father stepped forward then, as if he would reach for her but stopped himself. "As neither can I, Eleanor, as well you know."

She tore her gaze from his and looked across his shoulder, emotion stirring. She did not wish him to see it. She had forgiven him as best she could and she tried hard not to think of how he had let her down, but at times it was difficult.

"I will not set the bar too high. I have learned my lesson," he added on a whisper.

Her eyes came back to his as she heard rare emotion in his voice.

"I—I—" His voice faltered and he took another step towards her, leaving little more than a foot between them. It forced her to look up into his eyes.

"You need not say it, father, I know how you feel." Her words instantly restored his composure.

"You are too kind to me, Eleanor," he answered, his eyes searching hers.

He'd aged in the last year and he looked tired.

She didn't know what to say.

A hand touched her lower back and slid to rest at her waist. Edward's height and strength settled behind her and his other hand rested on her waist too. She leaned back against him as her father's gaze lifted to her husband's.

"I congratulate you both on your good news and you invested wisely, Marlow, I hear your stocks are doing well."

"Well enough," Edward answered. "As long as I am able to support my wife in the life she deserves I'm happy. I'm not a greedy man."

Ellen pressed an elbow into his ribs. He was antagonising her father—Edward enjoyed the occupation even now. He refused to forgive.

He bent and kissed the crown of her head. It was another gesture intended to infuriate her father.

"Well, I am happy that you are happy," her father dismissed them and walked away.

"Did you have to Edward?" She spun about. "He'd just approached the closest thing I have ever had to an apology from him."

"If he was a man of any worth, he would just out and say it." Edward threw a disparaging look at her father's departing back.

Following her husband's gaze, Ellen whispered, "Sometimes I feel sorry for him. He is so bound by what he perceives to be the requirements of his station in life, he is incapable of being himself, of just doing something because he wants to, or he can."

"He is a pompous ass is what he is," Edward countered.

Ellen slapped at is shoulder in playful rebuttal.

"Do you two never stop canoodling?" Robert's lazy drawl, stretched from beside them as his palm fell on Edward's shoulder. "You are far beyond the honeymoon period now."

"We are in love," Ellen chimed, pulling away from Edward. Then she turned, rose to her toes and pressed a brief kiss on Robert's cheek. "An emotion you, *Robert Marlow*, would not know of, the way you put yourself about. You should stop hell-raising and find yourself a wife, then you would understand."

In answer she was caught to her brother-in-law's chest in a rough hug, and a kiss fell on her forehead. Then he let her go but held her hand.

"I shall have you know, Lady Edward, that I fell in love last night, head-over-heels in fact, and the night before that too if I recall."

She laughed. "But not with the same woman, I do not doubt. You are the worst of rakes, Robert."

"You wound me, sister. I'm merely working damned hard to ensure my reputation remains beyond my brother's. I am supposed to be the black sheep. I cannot have his scandal best mine. Besides I'm simply trying out every woman until I find one like you."

"You rogue." She pulled her hand from his and smacked his shoulder gently then laid her hand on Edward's sleeve instead. "You only say that to stir Edward up. Old habits never die, do they?"

Turning to Edward, she finished, "I will leave you two to talk. Mary is due her feed."

Edward nodded and caught Ellen's fingers before she walked away, then allowed them to slip free.

"She's a beauty inside and out, your wife." Robert spoke as he watched Ellen.

"She is." Edward looked at Robert. "And loyal to a fault," he added seeing the genuine affection in his brother's eyes.

"Rupert apologises for not being able to come, but you know his mother is not well." Robert changed the subject.

"Yes I know. Ellen wishes us to visit them soon. She has a ridiculous need to ensure all family ties are kept."

"Even with your disreputable brother," Robert concluded, his eyes locking with Edward's, saying the words he'd probably read in Edward's gaze. Edward smiled. "You are a fortunate man. John is a son to be proud of, your wife is outstanding, your daughter adorable and now your family grows."

Robert had still never spoken of what had kept him abroad after their father's death, but in the last year they had become closer, largely due to Ellen's persistent pressure. She often invited Robert to stay. What amazed Edward was *their* closeness. She seemed closer to Robert than her sisters sometimes. Edward could not quite fathom it. It did not disturb him though. He knew her heart lay firmly in his own hands. He simply did not understand her affection for Robert and his brother accepted Ellen's advice over anybody else's.

Still, something silent seemed to eat at Robert. He'd not settled into managing his estates and now he left most of it to his steward while he spent more and more time in town—living life to the full and enjoying excess. Rumours of his affairs were constant and a favourite topic of the gossip columns. If anything, his behaviour had worsened since Edward had married Ellen. Yet when Robert came to stay, he changed. He took pleasure in spending time with the children and he relaxed, he lost his façade around Ellen. Robert's amazement at the tiny one-week-old Mary Rose had been almost as great as Edward's. But despite Robert's liking for the children he showed no sign of settling down and away from them he was no different—brash, arrogant and selfish.

"You could have the same," Edward eventually responded, studying the way Robert looked at John with Mary Rose and Ellen.

"Only if I could find the right woman," he answered, and with that he turned away, moving to speak to Edward's brothers-in-law, as though the conversation was too painful.

♦♦

Later, in bed, Edward pulled his wife back against him into an embrace, her back and bottom curled against his stomach and hips, as his palm rested on her stomach. "When do you think the child is due?" he whispered, still in awe of the miracle a woman's body could create.

"June, I think."

"A summer child." His teeth caught her earlobe, and he heard her breathing slow in rhythm in response, a sigh of pleasure escaping her lips as his hand slipped between her legs.

"John wants a brother. I told him I cannot promise."

Laughter escaped his throat as she relaxed against him, her legs parting to his touch.

"Then we will promise that if it is not a boy this time, we will try again."

"I am not your broodmare, Edward," her voice whispered into the dark, in mock severity.

"No, but when there is such joy in making more, how can you deny me, sweetheart?"

Rolling in his arms, turning to face him, she claimed his mouth, her naked body pressed against his.

"See," he whispered to her lips as he moved over her, "you cannot. You have never been able to, if I recall correctly."

"Why would I want to deny you when you give me so much *pleasure*?" she whispered back, mocking.

This woman was everything to him—still. He buried himself in her warmth.

"Ellen," he groaned, threading his fingers between hers and pressing her hands into the mattress, "I dare not think what I would be without you."

The heat intensified to the fire that had always sparked between them and for a while he let it burn, raging though them both in flickering flames. Then he withdrew and knelt upright, resting his buttocks on his heels and smiling down at her.

He'd called her a work of nature's art that first night. She was, only it was more than visual, it was physical too. She could ease his soul, reduce his anger and fear and she made his life something precious.

He gripped her hips and pulled her body back across the bed, sliding her to him in the age old lock and key fit of man and woman.

"Oh, Edward!" Her hands closed over his and her nails pressed into his skin

She made him feel so feral.

Her fingers clinging to his hands she just let him have his way. Sometimes she'd battle as she'd done on their second coupling, sometimes she'd win. Mostly he just took because she gave so beautifully.

She fell quickly and he followed, riding on the surf. He cried out and felt her catch a hold of his shoulders and pull him down on top of her.

"I love you Edward. I always will."

He knew. He kissed her brow and then rolled to his back. Her head lay on his shoulder and her body fell across him, one hand splaying over his pectoral muscle and one leg over his. He kissed her hair and felt her breath on his chest. "I love you too, Ellen." He had loved her ever since she'd gazed at him across the top of a fan, in a smoky gaming-hell, he always would too.

Ellen held him tight. Her life before Edward was now only a dream—a nightmare—which had slipped into murky memory. She kissed his cheek as he drifted into sleep—*he had saved her.*

And it had all come about from the outcome of a single game of cards, perhaps this life with Edward had always been her real throw of fate.

CPSIA information can be obtained at www.ICGtesting.com
Printed in the USA
LVOW05s1802250713

344649LV00006B/723/P